A Stranger is Watching

MARY HIGGINS CLARK

Original English language edition
A Stranger is Watching

Simon & Schuster, New York

Simon & Schuster, Inc.
1230 Avenue of the Americas
New York
New York 10020
U.S.A.

21, rue du Montparnasse
75283 Paris Cedex 06

HARRAP's® est une marque de Larousse SAS
www.harrap.com

ISBN 978 2 81 870323 6

About the author

MARY HIGGINS CLARK is the author of twenty-nine suspense novels; three collections[1] of short stories[2]; a historical novel, *Mount Vernon Love Story*; and a memoir, *Kitchen Privileges*[3]. She is also the author of a children's[4] book, *Ghost Ship*, illustrated by Wendell Minor.

She is also the coauthor with Carol Higgins Clark of five holiday[5] suspense novels: *Deck the Halls*[6], *He Sees You When You're Sleeping*[7], *The Christmas Thief*[8], *Santa Cruise*[9], and *Dashing Through the Snow*[10]. More than one hundred million copies[11] of her books are in print in the United States alone, and her books are worldwide[12] bestsellers.

1. recueils
2. nouvelles
3. [Entre hier et demain]
4. pour enfants
5. dont l'histoire se passe au moment de Noël
6. [Trois jours avant Noël]
7. [Ce soir je veillerai sur toi]
8. [le Voleur de Noël]
9. [la Croisière de Noël]
10. [le Mystère de Noël]
11. d'exemplaires
12. dans le monde entier

Direction de la publication : Carine Girac-Marinier

Direction éditoriale : Claude Nimmo

Notes en marge : Christine Destruhaut

Révision des notes : Marie-Noëlle Tilliette

Informatique éditoriale : Philippe Cazabet, Marie-Noëlle Tilliette

Conception graphique : Uli Meindl

Mise en pages : Cynthia Savage

Fabrication : Rebecca Dubois

Mot de l'Éditeur

Vous aimeriez lire en langue originale, mais le vocabulaire, les expressions figurées ou la syntaxe vous arrêtent parfois ?

Cette collection est faite pour vous !

Vous trouverez en effet, en note dans la marge, une traduction de certains mots et expressions qui vous permettra d'avancer facilement dans votre lecture.

Nous n'avons pas cherché à vous donner une traduction littéraire de l'ouvrage et nous nous sommes parfois écartés du sens littéral pour vous fournir celui qui convient le mieux à l'histoire. Aussi les mots sont-ils traduits dans le contexte du texte original.

Les expressions figées anglaises sont, bien entendu, rendues par une expression équivalente en français.

Les allusions à des réalités culturelles du monde anglo-saxon sont expliquées également dans la marge, pour vous aider à mieux comprendre la trame de l'histoire.

Vous aurez ainsi, en regard du texte original, tout le savoir-faire d'un dictionnaire rien que pour vous et adapté à ce livre !

Notre objectif est de vous mener jusqu'au mot FIN en vous donnant les clés nécessaires à la compréhension du récit.

Laissez-vous gagner par l'angoisse, l'humour et le suspense qui règnent chez les maîtres de la littérature anglo-saxonne.

Lire en VO ? You can indeed!

In joyful memory of Warren[1]
and for
Marilyn, Warren, David, Carol, and Patricia

You are your parents' glass[2] and I in you
Call back[3] the lovely April of our prime[4].

1. À la mémoire de Warren
2. Vous êtes le miroir dans lequel se reflètent vos parents
3. et je retrouve en vous
4. nos plus belles années

Coup de pouce pour vous aider à bien comprendre le début de l'histoire...

Chambre 932 Hôtel Biltmore à New York, en mars.

Un homme est assis devant la télévision et attend que commence un débat dans la matinale « Today » de la chaîne NBC. Le vent froid qui souffle dehors l'a tiré d'un sommeil agité, il s'est douché et rasé, et se remémore son arrivée à l'hôtel la veille au soir. Le jour est enfin arrivé...

Le thème du débat est la peine de mort car dans 52 heures exactement, à 11h30 le 24 mars, un jeune homme de 19 ans, Ronald Thompson, sera exécuté.

Les invités de Tom Brokaw, le présentateur de « Today », sont Sharon Martin, journaliste et écrivaine, et Steven Peterson, rédacteur en chef du magazine Events. Leurs opinions sur le sujet sont diamétralement opposées...

1

He sat perfectly still[1] in front of the television set[2] in room 932 of the Biltmore Hotel. The alarm[3] had gone off[4] at six but he was awake long before that[5]. The wind, cold and forbidding[6], rattled the window-panes[7] and that had been enough to pull him out of the uneasy sleep[8].

The *Today* show[9] came on[10] but he didn't adjust the barely audible sound[11]. He didn't care about the news[12] or the special reports[13]. He just wanted to see the interview.

Shifting[14] in the stiff-backed[15] chair, he crossed and uncrossed[16] his legs. He'd already showered[17] and shaved and put on[18] the green polyester suit[19] he'd worn[20] when he'd checked in[21] the night before. The realization that the day had come at last made his hand tremble and he'd nicked his lip[22] when he shaved. It bled[23] a little and the salty taste[24] of blood in his mouth made him gag[25].

He hated blood.

Last night at the desk in the lobby[26], he'd seen the clerk's eyes sliding over[27] his clothes. He'd carried his coat under his arm because he knew it looked shabby[28]. But the suit was new; he'd

1. immobile
2. devant la télévision
3. réveil
4. avait sonné
5. il s'était réveillé bien avant
6. sinistre
7. faisait trembler les vitres
8. le tirer d'un sommeil agité
9. [matinale de la chaîne de télévision NBC]
10. débuta à l'antenne
11. il ne chercha pas à remonter le son à peine audible
12. nouvelles
13. reportages
14. Changeant de position
15. à dossier raide
16. croisa et décroisa
17. douché
18. avait mis
19. costume
20. qu'il portait
21. il s'était présenté à la réception
22. il s'était coupé la lèvre
23. saignait
24. goût salé
25. lui donnait des haut-le-cœur
26. à la réception de l'hôtel
27. sur
28. avait conscience de son aspect élimé

saved up for it[1]. Still the clerk[2] looked at him like he was dirt[3] and asked if he had a reservation.

He'd never checked into a real hotel before but knew how to do it. "Yes, I have a reservation." He said it very coldly and for a minute[4] the clerk looked uncertain but when he didn't have a credit card and offered to pay cash in advance[5], the sneer was back[6]."I will check out[7] Wednesday morning," he told the clerk.

The room cost one hundred forty dollars for the three nights. That meant he only had thirty dollars left.[8] But that would be plenty for these few days[9] and by Wednesday he'd have eighty-two thousand dollars.

Her face floated across his mind.[10] He blinked to force it away.[11] Because just as always the eyes came after it; the eyes like great lamps that followed him, that were always watching him, that never closed.

He wished he had[12] another cup of coffee. He'd sent for room service[13], reading the instructions how to call for it very carefully. He'd had a large pot of coffee and there'd been a little left[14] but he'd already washed the cup and saucer and orange juice glass and rinsed out the coffeepot before putting the tray[15] on the floor in the hall.

A commercial[16] was just ending. Suddenly interested he leaned forward[17] to get nearer to the set. The interview should be next. It was. He twisted the volume knob to the right.

The familiar face of Tom Brokaw, the *Today* anchorman[18], filled the screen. Unsmiling, his voice subdued, he began to speak. "The restoration of capital punishment[19] has become the most emotional and divisive issue[20] in this country since the Vietnamese War. In just fifty-two hours, at eleven-thirty A.M. on March 24th, the sixth execution this year will

1. il avait économisé pour pouvoir se l'offrir
2. réceptionniste
3. comme un moins que rien
4. l'espace d'un instant
5. payer comptant d'avance
6. le petit rictus de mépris revint
7. Je partirai
8. Il ne lui restait donc plus que trente dollars en poche.
9. cette somme lui suffirait amplement pour ces quelques jours
10. Il repensa à son visage.
11. Il cligna des yeux pour le chasser de son esprit.
12. Il aurait bien voulu
13. appelé le service d'étage
14. il restait un fond
15. plateau
16. spot publicitaire
17. se pencha en avant
18. présentateur
19. rétablissement de la peine de mort
20. le sujet le plus sensible et controversé

take place when nineteen-year-old Ronald Thompson dies in the electric chair. My guests ..."

The camera dollied back[1] to include the two people seated on either side of Tom Brokaw. The man to his right was in his early thirties[2]. His sandy hair was streaked with gray and somewhat disheveled[3]. His hands were together, fingers spread apart[4] and pointing upward. His chin rested on the fingertips[5], giving him a prayerful stance that[6] was accentuated by dark eyebrows arcing[7] over winter-blue eyes.

The young woman on the other side of the interviewer sat stiffly erect[8]. Her hair, the color of warm honey, was pulled back in a soft chignon. Her hands were knotted into fists in her lap.[9] She moistened her lips[10] and pushed back[11] a strand of hair from her forehead.

Tom Brokaw said, "On their previous appearance[12] here, six months ago, our guests made a very strong case supporting their views[13] on capital punishment. Sharon Martin, syndicated columnist[14], is also the author of the best-selling book, The *Crime of Capital Punishment*. Steven Peterson, the editor of Events magazine, is one of the most articulate voices in the media[15] to urge[16] restoration of capital punishment in this country."

His tone became brisk. He turned to Steve. "Let's start with you, Mr. Peterson. After having witnessed the emotional public reaction[17] to the executions that have already taken place, do you still believe that your position is justified?"

Steve leaned forward. When he answered, his voice was calm. "Absolutely," he said quietly.

The interviewer turned to his other guest. "Sharon Martin, what do you think?"

Sharon shifted slightly in her chair to face her interrogator. She was achingly tired[18]. In the last month she'd worked twenty hours a day, contacting

1. fit un travelling arrière
2. avait une petite trentaine d'années
3. étaient striés de gris et quelque peu en bataille
4. écartés
5. Son menton reposait sur le bout de ses doigts
6. donnant l'impression qu'il était en train de prier, ce qui
7. arqués
8. était assise raide comme un piquet
9. Elle gardait les poings serrés sur les genoux.
10. Elle s'humecta les lèvres
11. repoussa
12. passage
13. ont défendu bec et ongles leur opinion
14. journaliste d'agence de presse
15. l'un des porte-parole les plus éloquents des médias
16. qui réclame avec insistance
17. été témoin de la réaction passionnée du public
18. littéralement épuisée

prominent people[1]—senators, congressmen, judges, humanitarians[2], speaking at colleges[3], at women's clubs, urging[4] everyone to write and wire the[5] Connecticut governor and protest Ronald Thompson's execution. The response[6] had been enormous, overwhelming[7]. She had been so sure that Governor Greene would reconsider[8]. She found herself groping for words[9].

"I think," she said, "*I believe* that we, our country, has taken a giant step backwards into the Dark Ages[10]." She held up[11] the newspapers at her side. "Just look at this morning's headlines[12]. Analyze them! They're bloodthirsty[13]." Quickly, she leafed through them[14]. "This one ... listen ... *Connecticut Tests Electric Chair*, and this ... *19-Year-Old Dies Wednesday*, and this, *Doomed Killer Protests Innocence*[15]. They're all like that, sensational, savage!" She bit her lip as her voice broke.

Steve glanced at her swiftly. They'd just been told that the Governor was calling a press conference to announce her absolute refusal to grant Thompson another stay of execution[16]. The news had devastated Sharon. It would be a miracle if she didn't get sick after this. They never should have agreed to come on this show today. The Governor's decision made Sharon's appearance pointless[17], and God knows Steve didn't want to be here. But he had to say something.

"I think every decent human being deplores sensationalism and the need for the death penalty," he said. "But remember it has been applied only after exhaustive consideration of extenuating circumstances[18]. There is no *mandatory*[19] death sentence[20]."

"Do you believe that the circumstances in Ronald Thompson's case, the fact that he committed the murder only days after his seventeenth birth-

1. des personnalités éminentes
2. des membres d'organisations humanitaires
3. des universités
4. elle avait exhorté
5. envoyer des télégrammes au
6. réaction
7. impressionnante
8. reverrait sa position
9. se surprit à chercher ses mots
10. est revenu au Moyen Âge
11. souleva la pile de
12. gros titres
13. assoiffés de sang
14. les feuilleta
15. Le meurtrier condamné clame son innocence
16. d'ajourner une nouvelle fois l'exécution de Thompson
17. inutile
18. avoir pris en compte l'ensemble des circonstances atténuantes
19. obligatoire
20. condamnation à mort

day, making him barely eligible for adult punishment[1], should have been considered?" Brokaw asked quickly.

Steve said, "As you know, I will not comment specifically on[2] the Thompson case. It would be entirely inappropriate."

"I understand your concern[3], Mr. Peterson," the interviewer said, "but you had taken your position on this issue several years before ..." He paused, then continued quietly, "before Ronald Thompson murdered your wife."

Ronald Thompson murdered your wife. The starkness[4] of the words still surprised Steve. After two and a half years, he could still feel the sense of shock and outrage[5] that Nina had died that way, her life snuffed out by the intruder[6] who came into their home, by the hands that had relentlessly[7] twisted[8] her scarf[9] around her throat.

Trying to blot[10] the image from his mind, he looked directly ahead[11]. "At one time[12], I had hoped that the ban[13] on executions in our country might become a permanent one. But as you point out[14], long before the tragedy in my own family, I had come to the conclusion that if we were to preserve the most fundamental right of human beings ... freedom to come and go without fear, freedom to feel sanctuary[15] in our homes, we had to stop the perpetrators of violence[16]. Unfortunately the only way to stop potential murderers seems to be to threaten them[17] with the same harsh judgment they mete out to their victims[18]. And since the first execution was carried out[19] two years ago, the number of murders has dropped dramatically[20] in major cities across the country."

Sharon leaned forward. "You make it sound so reasonable[21]," she cried. "Don't you realize[22] that forty-five percent of murders are committed by peo-

1. le rendant tout juste passible d'une peine pour adultes
2. je ne ferai pas de commentaires particuliers sur
3. préoccupation
4. brutalité
5. d'indignation
6. sa vie soufflée par l'intrus
7. impitoyablement
8. serré
9. écharpe
10. effacer
11. droit devant lui
12. À une certaine époque
13. interdiction
14. comme vous le faites remarquer
15. de se sentir en sécurité
16. auteurs d'actes de violence
17. de les menacer
18. peine impitoyable qu'ils ont appliquée à leurs victimes
19. qui a eu lieu
20. chuté de façon spectaculaire
21. Vous en parlez de façon si rationnelle
22. Avez-vous conscience

1. présentent des antécédents familiaux tragiques
2. téléspectateur
3. détacha son regard de
4. attentivement
5. auquel Steve commençait à s'intéresser sérieusement
6. mince
7. il avait pris sa voiture pour descendre à la plage
8. Il avait entendu dire que
9. cela n'avait pas été très concluant
10. brancher
11. déplacé sa couverture
12. s'était contenté de regarder fixement
13. tumultueux
14. le fait de plaindre
15. ce n'est pas l'un ou l'autre
16. la prison à vie
17. accordez tant de prix à la vie

ple under twenty-five years of age, many of whom have tragic family backgrounds[1] and a history of instability?"

The solitary viewer[2] in Biltmore's room 932 took his eyes from[3] Steve Peterson and studied the girl thoughtfully[4]. This was the writer Steve was getting serious about[5]. She wasn't at all like his wife. She was obviously taller and had the slender[6] body of someone who might be athletic. His wife had been small and doll-like with rounded breasts and jet black hair that curled around her forehead and ears when she turned her head.

Sharon Martin's eyes reminded him of the color of the ocean that day he'd driven down to the beach[7] last summer. He'd heard that[8] Jones Beach was a good place to meet girls but it hadn't worked out[9]. The one he'd started to fool with[10] in the water had called "Bob!" and a minute later this guy had been beside him, asking what his problem was. So he'd moved his blanket[11] and just stared out at[12] the ocean, watching the changing colors. Green. That was it. Green mixed with blue and churning[13]. He liked eyes that color.

What was Steve saying? Oh yes, he'd said something about feeling sorry for[14] the victims, not their murderers, "for people incapable of defending themselves."

"My sympathies are with them too," Sharon cried. But it's not either/or[15]. Don't you see that life imprisonment[16] would be punishment enough for the Ronald Thompsons of this world?" She forgot Tom Brokaw, forgot the television cameras as once again she tried to convince Steve. "How can you … who are so compassionate … who value life so much[17] … want to play God?" she asked. "How can anyone presume to play God?"

It was an argument[1] that began and ended the same way as it had that first time six months ago when they'd met on this program. Finally Tom Brokaw said, "Our time is running out.[2] Can we sum up[3] by saying that notwithstanding the public demonstrations[4], prison riots[5] and student rallys[6] that are regularly occurring[7] all over the country, you still believe, Mr. Peterson, that the sharp drop in random murder[8] justifies execution?"

"I believe in the moral right … the duty[9] … of society to protect itself, and of the government to protect the sacred liberty of its citizens," Steve said.

"Sharon Martin?" Brokaw turned quickly to her.

"I believe that the death penalty is senseless[10] and brutalizing[11]. I believe that we can make the home and streets safe[12] by removing violent offenders[13] and punishing them with swift, sure sentences, by voting for the bond issues[14] that will build the necessary correctional institutions[15] and will pay the people who staff them[16]. I believe that it is our reverence for[17] life, *all* life, that is the final test of us as individuals and as a society."

Tom Brokaw said hurriedly[18], "Sharon Martin, Steven Peterson, thank you for being with us on *Today*. I'll be back after this message …"

The television set in room 932 of the Biltmore was snapped off[19]. For a long time the muscular, thick-chested[20] man in the green-plaid suit[21] sat staring straight ahead at the darkened screen[22]. Once again he reviewed his plan[23], the plan that began with putting the pictures and the suitcase in the secret room in Grand Central Station[24] and would end with bringing Steve Peterson's son Neil there tonight. But now he had to decide. Sharon Martin was going to be at Steve's house this evening. She would be minding[25] Neil until Steve got home.

He'd planned simply to eliminate her there.

1. débat
2. Le temps qui nous est imparti touche à sa fin.
3. résumer.
4. qu'en dépit des manifestations publiques
5. des mutineries dans les prisons
6. des rassemblements étudiants
7. qui ont régulièrement lieu
8. forte baisse des meurtres fortuits
9. devoir
10. dénuée de tout fondement
11. violente
12. garantir la sécurité des foyers et des rues
13. neutralisant les auteurs d'actes de violence
14. émissions d'obligations
15. établissements pénitentiaires
16. qui y travaillent
17. respect de
18. rapidement
19. s'arrêta net
20. robuste
21. costume à carreaux verts
22. fixant l'écran noir droit devant lui
23. passa son plan en revue
24. [grande gare située à Manhattan]
25. garderait

1. devrait-il vraiment le faire ?
2. bienveillants
3. qu'il vienne la chercher
4. de se débarrasser d'elle
5. exploserait
6. pulvérisée

But should he?[1] She was so beautiful.

He thought of those eyes, the color of the ocean, churning, caring[2].

It seemed to him that when she looked directly into the camera she had been looking at *him*.

It seemed as though she wanted him to come for her[3].

Maybe she loved him.

If she didn't it would be easy to get rid of her[4].

He'd just leave her in the room in Grand Central with the child on Wednesday morning.

Then at 11:30 when the bomb went off[5], she, too, would be blown to bits[6].

7. marchant à quelques pas l'un de l'autre
8. pesait lourd sur ses épaules
9. glacés
10. enfila ses gants
11. bague ancienne surmontée d'une pierre de lune
12. laissé une trace sur
13. taux d'acidité de la peau
14. sans avoir une telle réaction
15. passa devant elle et lui tint la porte ouverte
16. avancèrent dans
17. le matin balayé par des rafales de vent
18. des flocons collants
19. glaçaient

2

They left the studio together, walking a few inches apart[7]. Sharon's tweed cape felt heavy on her shoulders[8]. Her hands and feet were icy[9]. She pulled on her gloves[10] and noticed that the antique moonstone ring[11] Steve had given her for Christmas had smudged[12] her finger again. Some people had such a high acid content[13] they couldn't wear real gold without that happening[14].

Steve reached past her and held the door open[15]. They stepped into[16] the windblown morning[17]. It was very cold and just beginning to snow; thick, clinging flakes[18] that chilled[19] their faces.

"I'll get you a cab[1]," he said.

"No ... I'd rather[2] walk."

"That's crazy. You look dead tired[3]."

"It will help clear my head.[4] Oh Steve, how can you be so positive ... so sure ... so relentless[5]?"

"Don't let's start again, dear."

"We have to start again!"

"Not now." Steve looked down at her[6], impatience mingling with concern[7]. Sharon's eyes looked strained, fine, red lines threaded through them[8]; the on-camera makeup[9] she was wearing had not covered the paleness that became accentuated as snow melted[10] on her cheeks and forehead.

"Can you go home and get some rest?" he asked. "You need it."

"I have to turn in my column[11]."

"Well, try to get a few hours' sleep. You'll get up to my place[12] by about quarter of six?"

"Steve, I'm not sure ..."

"I am.[13] We haven't seen each other for three weeks. The Lufts are counting on going out for their anniversary[14] and I want to be in my home tonight with you and Neil."

Ignoring the people scurrying into[15] the Rockefeller Center[16] buildings, Steve put his hands on Sharon's face and lifted it. Her expression was troubled and sad. He said gravely, "I love you, Sharon. You know that. I've missed you terribly[17] these past weeks. We've got to talk about us."

"Steve, we don't think alike[18]. We ..."

Bending down he kissed her.[19] Her lips were unyielding. He felt her body tense[20]. Stepping back[21] he raised his hand to signal a passing cab[22]. When it pulled over to the curb[23], he held the door for her and gave the driver the address of the *News Dispatch* building. Before he shut the door, he asked, "Can I count on you for tonight?"

1. Je t'appelle un taxi
2. Je préfère
3. morte de fatigue
4. Ça m'aidera à y voir plus clair.
5. impitoyable
6. baissa les yeux vers elle
7. son regard empli d'une impatience mêlée d'inquiétude
8. affichaient une grande lassitude et étaient striés de rouge
9. maquillage de plateau
10. fondait
11. rendre mon article
12. Tu viendras chez moi
13. Moi, si.
14. anniversaire de mariage
15. qui se ruaient
16. [complexe commercial et culturel de Manhattan]
17. Tu m'as horriblement manqué
18. nous n'avons pas la même façon de voir les choses
19. Il se pencha pour l'embrasser.
20. se raidir
21. Tout en reculant
22. héler un taxi qui passait par là
23. se gara le long du trottoir

She nodded[1] silently. Steve watched the cab turn down[2] Fifth Avenue, then quickly walked west. He had stayed overnight[3] at the Gotham Hotel because he had to be at the studio at 6:30, and was anxious[4] to call Neil before he left for school. Everytime he was away from home, he worried[5]. Neil still had nightmares[6], still woke up with suffocating attacks of asthma[7]. Mrs. Lufts always called the doctor quickly but even so …

The winter had been so damp[8] and cold. Maybe in the spring[9] when Neil could get out[10] more, he'd build up a little[11]. He looked so pale all the time.

Spring! My God, it was spring. Sometime during the night the vernal equinox[12] had taken place and winter had officially ended. You'd never guess it from the weather prediction[13].

Steve reached the corner[14] and turned north, reflecting that[15] he and Sharon had been seeing each other exactly six months now. When he picked her up[16] at her apartment that first evening, she'd suggested walking through[17] Central Park[18] to the Tavern on the Green. He warned her[19] that it had become much cooler in the last few hours and reminded her[20] it was the first day of fall[21].

"Wonderful," she said. "I was just getting bored with summer." For the first few blocks[22] they'd been almost silent. He studied the way she walked, easily in stride with him[23], her slender frame[24] accentuated by the belted tawny gold suit[25] that exactly matched[26] the color of her hair. He remembered that the sharp breeze was pulling the first dead leaves from the trees and the setting sun[27] accentuated the deep blue of the autumn sky.

"On a night like this, I always think of that song from *Camelot*," she told him. "You know the one, *If Ever I Would Leave You*[28]." She sang softly, "How I'd leave in autumn, I never would know. I've seen

1. hocha la tête
2. tourner dans
3. passé la nuit
4. impatient
5. s'inquiétait
6. faisait encore des cauchemars
7. crises d'asthme
8. humide
9. au printemps
10. sortir
11. il reprendrait quelques forces
12. l'équinoxe de printemps
13. au vu des prévisions météorologiques
14. arriva au coin de la rue
15. se faisant la réflexion que
16. était venu la chercher
17. de traverser à pied
18. [immense espace vert à Manhattan]
19. l'avait prévenue
20. lui avait rappelé
21. l'automne
22. pâtés de maisons
23. au même rythme que lui
24. silhouette
25. tailleur couleur fauve
26. était assorti à
27. soleil couchant
28. Si jamais je te quittais

how you sparkle when fall nips the air[1]. I know you in autumn and I must be there ..." She had a lovely contralto voice.

If ever I would leave you ...

Was that the minute he fell in love with her?

That evening had been so good. They'd lingered over dinner[2] talking while the people at other tables left, and new people came.

What had they talked about? Everything. Her father was an engineer for an oil company[3]. She and her two sisters were born abroad[4]. Both sisters were married now.

"How have you escaped?[5]" It was a question that he had to ask. They both knew what he was really asking, "Is there anyone important in your life?"

But there wasn't[6]. She'd traveled almost constantly for her last newspaper before she started writing the column. It was interesting and lots of fun[7] and she didn't know where the seven years since college had vanished[8].

They walked back[9] to the apartment and by the second block[10] they were holding hands[11]. She invited him up for a nightcap[12]. There was the slightest emphasis on *nightcap*.

While he made[13] drinks, she touched a match to the kindling[14] in the fireplace[15] and they sat side by side[16] watching the flames.

Steven could still remember vividly the feeling of that night[17], the way the fire brought out[18] the gold in her hair, threw shadows[19] on her classic profile, highlighted[20] her sudden beautiful smile. He'd ached[21] to put his arms around her then but simply kissed her lightly[22] when he left. "Saturday, if you're not busy ..." He waited.

"I'm not busy."

"I'll call you in the morning."

1. la fraîcheur automnale se fait sentir
2. Ils s'étaient attardés après le dîner
3. travaillait comme ingénieur dans une compagnie pétrolière
4. à l'étranger
5. Comment y avez-vous échappé ?
6. ce n'était pas le cas
7. très amusant
8. étaient passées
9. étaient rentrés à pied
10. dès le second pâté de maisons
11. ils se tenaient la main
12. à monter boire un dernier verre
13. préparait
14. avait allumé le petit bois
15. cheminée
16. côte à côte
17. gardait un souvenir vivace de ce qu'il avait ressenti ce soir-là
18. faisait ressortir
19. des ombres
20. soulignait
21. Il avait eu très envie
22. il lui avait simplement donné un léger baiser

And on the drive home[1], he'd known that the restless, ceaseless heart hunger[2] of the last two years might be ending. If ever I would leave you ... Don't leave me, Sharon.

It was quarter of eight when he turned into the building[3] at 1347 Avenue of the Americas. *Events* magazine staffers[4] were not noted for their early arrivals[5]. The corridors were deserted. Nodding to[6] the security guard at the elevator[7], Steve went up to his thirty-sixth-floor office and dialed his home[8].

Mrs. Lufts answered. "Oh, Neil's fine. He's just eating his breakfast, or picking at it[9], I should say. Neil, it's your dad."

Neil got on[10]. "Hi, Dad, when are you coming home?"

"By eight-thirty sure. I have a five o'clock meeting. The Lufts still want to go to the movies[11], don't they?"

"I guess so.[12]"

"Sharon will be up[13] before six so they can leave."

"I know. You told me." Neil's voice was noncommittal[14].

"Well have a good day, son. And dress warmly. It's getting pretty[15] cold down here. Is it snowing up there yet[16]?"

"No, it's just sort of cloudy[17]."

"All right. See you tonight."

"Bye, Dad."

Steve frowned[18]. It was hard to remember that at one time Neil had been such a vibrant, happy-go-lucky kid[19]. Nina's death had changed that. He wished that Neil and Sharon would get closer. Sharon was trying, really trying, to break through Neil's reserve[20], but he just wouldn't give an inch[21], at least not so far[22].

1. sur le chemin du retour
2. l'interminable désert sentimental
3. tourna pour pénétrer dans le bâtiment
4. le personnel du magazine
5. n'avait pas pour habitude d'être matinal
6. Tout en saluant d'un signe de tête
7. ascenseur
8. composa le numéro de son domicile
9. de le manger du bout des dents
10. prit le téléphone
11. aller au cinéma
12. Je crois que oui.
13. sera là
14. était inexpressive
15. plutôt
16. déjà là-haut
17. c'est juste un peu couvert
18. fronça les sourcils
19. gosse insouciant et plein de vie
20. faire sortir Neil de sa réserve
21. ne cédait pas d'un pouce
22. pas jusqu'ici

Time. Everything took time. Sighing[1], Steve turned to the table behind his desk and reached for the editorial he had been working on the night before.

1. En soupirant

3

The occupant of room 932 left the Biltmore at 9:30 A.M. He exited by the Forty-fourth Street door[2] and headed east toward[3] Second Avenue. The sharp[4], snow-filled wind was hurrying pedestrians along[5], making them shrink within themselves[6], tuck their necks into upturned collars[7].

It was good weather for him, the kind of weather when people didn't bother to notice[8] what other people were doing.

His first stop was a thrift shop[9] on Second Avenue below Thirty-fourth Street. Ignoring the buses that passed every few minutes, he walked the fourteen blocks. Walking was good exercise and it was important to keep in shape[10].

The thrift shop was empty except for the elderly salesclerk[11] who sat listlessly[12] reading the morning paper. "Anything particular you want?" she asked.

"No. I'll just look around." He spotted the rack[13] with the women's coats and went over to it. Pushing through[14] the shabby garments[15], he selected a dark gray tent-shaped wool coat that looked long enough. Sharon Martin was fairly tall, he reflec-

2. sortit par la porte qui donnait dans la 42e Rue
3. marcha en direction de l'est vers
4. vif
5. poussait les piétons à presser le pas
6. se recroqueviller sur eux-mêmes
7. le cou rentré dans les cols remontés
8. on ne prête pas attention à
9. friperie
10. rester en forme
11. vendeuse âgée
12. d'un air morne
13. repéra le portant
14. Fouillant parmi
15. vêtements élimés

ted. There was a tray of folded kerchiefs[1] near the rack. He reached for[2] the largest one, a faded bluish[3] rectangle.

The woman stuffed his purchases[4] in a shopping bag.

The Army-Navy store[5] was next. That was easy. In the camping-gear section[6] he bought a large canvas duffel bag[7]. He selected it carefully, making sure it was long enough to hold the boy, thick enough that you couldn't tell from the shape what he'd be carrying, wide enough to let sufficient air in when the drawstring was loose[8].

In a First Avenue Woolworth's[9], he bought six rolls of wide bandage and two large spools of thick twine[10]. He brought his purchases back to the Biltmore. The bed in his room was made and there were clean towels in the bathroom.

His eyes darted around[11] for signs that the maid[12] had gone through the closet[13]. But his other pair of shoes was right there, exactly as he had left them, one a hairsbreadth behind the other[14], neither quite touching the old black double-locked suitcase[15] that was standing in the corner.

Slipping the deadlock on the room door[16], he placed the bags with his purchases on the bed. With infinite care, he lifted the suitcase from the closet and laid it the foot of the bed. Reaching into[17] a compartment in his wallet[18], he extracted a key and opened the suitcase.

He made a thorough check of[19] the contents, the pictures, the powder, the clock, the wires[20], the fuses[21], the hunting[22] knife and the gun. Satisfied, he closed the bag again.

Carrying the suitcase and the shopping bag, he left the room. This time he went into the lower lobby of the Biltmore to the underground arcade[23] which led to the upper level of Grand Central Station. The

1. foulards
2. tendit la main pour prendre
3. d'un bleu délavé
4. fourra ses emplettes
5. [magasin de surplus de l'Armée et de la Marine]
6. rayon matériel de camping
7. sac de marin en toile
8. le cordon n'était pas serré
9. [chaîne de magasins à bas prix]
10. ficelle
11. Il parcourut rapidement la chambre du regard
12. pour voir si la femme de chambre
13. fouillé dans le placard
14. l'une légèrement en retrait par rapport à l'autre
15. valise
16. Après avoir verrouillé la porte de la chambre
17. Glissant la main dans
18. portefeuille
19. vérifia minutieusement
20. fils métalliques
21. fusibles
22. de chasse
23. galerie marchande souterraine

early morning commuter rush[1] was over but the terminal[2] was still filled with people scurrying to and from trains[3], people using the station as a shortcut[4] to Forty-second Street or Park Avenue, people on their way to arcade shops, to the off-track betting center[5], the quick-service restaurants, the newsstands[6].

Moving quickly, he went down the stairs to the lower level and drifted over toward platform 112 from which Mount Vernon trains arrived and departed. There was no train due[7] for eighteen minutes and the area was deserted. Glancing around swiftly, he made sure no guard was looking in his direction and disappeared down the stairs to the platform.

The platform extended in a U shape[8] around the end of the tracks. From the other side a sloping ramp led into the depths of the terminal. Hurrying around the tracks[9], he made his way[10] to that ramp. Now his movements became quicker, furtive. The sounds became different in this other world of the terminal. Overhead[11] the station was bustling with the comings and goings[12] of thousands of travelers. Here a pneumatic pump was throbbing, ventilating fans were rumbling, water was trickling across[13] the damp floor. The silent, starved[14] forms of beggar cats slithered in and out of the nearby tunnel[15] under Park Avenue. A continuing dull[16] railroad sound came from the loop[17] where all the trains, beginning their outgoing journey, turned and chugged in gathering momentum[18] away from[19] the terminal.

He continued his gradual descent until he was at the foot of a steep iron staircase. He hurried up[20] the metal steps, carefully placing one foot silently on the rung[21] above. An occasional guard wandered through[22] this area. The light was poor but even so …

At the head of the small landing[23] there was a heavy metal door. Carefully depositing the suitcase

1. flot des banlieusards matinaux
2. gare
3. qui se hâtaient au départ et à l'arrivée des trains
4. raccourci
5. l'établissement de paris mutuels
6. kiosques à journaux
7. attendu
8. se prolongeait en forme de U
9. Contournant rapidement les voies
10. se fraya un chemin
11. Au-dessus
12. grouillait au rythme des allées et venues
13. un mince filet d'eau traversait
14. faméliques
15. entraient et sortaient subrepticement du tunnel situé non loin de là
16. sourd
17. boucle d'évitement
18. soufflaient alors qu'ils prenaient de la vitesse
19. en s'éloignant de
20. monta quatre à quatre
21. marche
22. faisait une ronde dans
23. Au bout du petit palier

and the shopping bag on the landing, he fished for[1] and found the key in his wallet. Quickly, nervously, he inserted it in the lock[2]. Reluctantly[3], the lock yielded its authority[4] and the door swung open[5].

Inside it was pitch black[6]. He fumbled for the light switch[7], found it, and keeping one hand firmly on it, reached down and lifted the suitcase and shopping bag into the room. He let the door close noiselessly.

The dark now was absolute. He could see the outlines[8] of the room. The musty smell[9] was overwhelming[10]. Letting out a protracted sigh[11], the intruder consciously tried to relax. Deliberately he listened for the station sounds but they were far off, discernible only when a distinct effort was made to hear them.

It was all right.

He flicked the switch and the room became gloomy-bright. The dusty fluorescent lamps glared on[12] the peeling[13] ceiling and walls, casting deep shadows[14] in the corners. The room was L-shaped, a cement room with cement walls from which thick layers[15] of gray, moisture-repellent paint[16] were hanging in jagged flaps[17]. An ancient outsize pair of laundry tubs[18] were to the left of the door. Dripping water from the faucets[19] had streaked their insides with canals of rust[20] through thick layers of caked[21] dirt. In the middle of the room, uneven, tightly nailed boards[22] entombed a chimney-like object, a dumbwaiter[23]. A narrow door off the far right[24] of the L-shaped room was ajar[25], revealing a grimy toilet[26].

He knew the toilet worked. He'd come into this room last week for the first time in over twenty years and checked the lights and plumbing[27]. Something had made him come here, had reminded him of this room when he was making his plan.

A rickety canvas army cot[28] leaned lopsided[29] against the far wall, an overturned orange crate[30]

1. fouilla
2. serrure
3. Avec réticence
4. céda sous sa pression
5. s'ouvrit
6. il faisait noir comme dans un four
7. chercha l'interrupteur à tâtons
8. contours
9. odeur de renfermé
10. suffocante
11. long soupir
12. éclairaient d'une lumière vive
13. lépreux
14. projetant de larges ombres
15. couches
16. peinture anti-moisissures
17. pendaient en lambeaux
18. Deux énormes bacs à lessive antédiluviens
19. L'eau qui gouttait des robinets
20. rouille
21. incrustée
22. planches
23. monte-plats
24. tout à droite
25. entrouverte
26. W-C crasseux
27. la plomberie
28. lit de camp bancal
29. était appuyé de guingois
30. caisse à oranges retournée

next to it. The cot and crate worried him. Someone else, sometime, had stumbled onto[1] this room and stayed in it. But the dust on the cot and the stale dampness could only mean the room had been unopened for months at least, maybe years.

He hadn't been here since he was sixteen, more than half a lifetime ago[2]. That was when this room was used by the Oyster Bar. Located directly below the Oyster Bar kitchen, the old boarded-up[3] dumbwaiter used to bring mounds[4] of greasy dishes to be washed in the deep sinks[5] and dried and sent back upstairs.

Years ago the Oyster Bar kitchen had been renovated and dishwashing machines installed. And this room sealed off[6]. Just as well. No one would work in this smelly hole[7].

But it could still serve a purpose[8].

When he'd pondered where[9] he could keep Peterson's son until the ransom[10] was paid, he'd remembered this room. He'd investigated it and then realized how well it fit into his plan[11]. When he'd been working here, with his hands all swollen[12] from irritating detergents and scalding[13] water and heavy wet towels[14], all through the terminal well-dressed[15] people had been rushing home[16] to their expensive houses and cars, or sitting in the restaurant eating the shrimp[17] and clams[18] and oysters[19] and bass[20] and snapper[21] he'd had to scrape off their plates[22], never caring about him at all.

He'd make everyone[23] in Grand Central, in New York, *in the world* notice him. After Wednesday they'd never forget him.

It had been simple to get into this room. A wax impression[24] in the door of the rusty[25] old lock. Then he'd made a key. Now he could come and go as he pleased.

1. trouvé
2. il y avait pratiquement une éternité
3. condamné
4. des piles
5. éviers
6. l'accès à cette pièce interdit
7. trou puant
8. encore servir à quelque chose
9. réfléchi au lieu où
10. rançon
11. qu'elle cadrait à la perfection avec son plan
12. enflées
13. bouillante
14. serviettes
15. bien habillés
16. se hâtaient de rentrer chez eux
17. crevettes
18. palourdes
19. huîtres
20. bars
21. vivaneaux
22. récurer leurs assiettes
23. Il ferait en sorte que tout le monde
24. empreinte à la cire
25. rouillée

Tonight Sharon Martin and the boy would be here with him. Grand Central Station. The world's busiest railroad terminal.[1] The best place in the world to hide people.

He laughed aloud. Now that he was here, he could begin to laugh. He felt clear[2] and brilliant and stimulated. The peeling walls and sagging[3] cot and leaking[4] water and splintered[5] boards excited him.

Here he was the master, the planner[6]. He'd arrange[7] to get his money. He'd close the eyes forever. He couldn't stand dreaming about the eyes anymore.[8] He couldn't stand it. And now they had become a real danger.

Wednesday. Eleven-thirty Wednesday morning was exactly forty-eight hours away[9]. He'd be on a plane leaving for[10] Arizona where no one knew him. It wasn't safe for him in[11] Carley. There were too many questions being asked.

But out there[12], with the money ... and the eyes gone[13] ... and if Sharon Martin was in love with him, he'd bring her with him.

He carried the suitcase past the army cot and carefully laid it flat[14] on the floor. Opening it, he removed[15] the tiny[16] cassette recorder[17] and camera[18] and put them in the lefthand pocket of his shapeless brown overcoat[19]. The hunting knife and gun went into the righthand pocket. No bulges showed through the deep, thick pockets.[20]

He picked up the shopping bag and methodically spread its contents[21] on the cot. The coat and scarf and twine and tape[22] and bandage rolls, he stuffed into the duffel bag. Finally he reached for the packet of neatly rolled posters. He opened them, smoothing them down[23], bending them to reduce the curling. His eyes lingered[24] on them. A smile, reminiscent, thoughtful, extended[25] his narrow lips.

1. Le plus important terminal ferroviaire au monde.
2. lucide
3. défoncé
4. suintante
5. fendues
6. maître d'œuvre
7. Il ferait en sorte
8. Il ne pouvait plus supporter de rêver aux yeux.
9. dans 48 heures
10. à destination de l'
11. Il n'était plus en sécurité à
12. là-bas
13. disparus
14. la posa avec précaution à plat
15. en sortit
16. minuscules
17. magnétophone à cassettes
18. appareil photo
19. manteau marron informe
20. Les poches épaisses et profondes ne laissaient rien deviner.
21. étala son contenu
22. ruban adhésif
23. les lissa
24. s'attarda
25. vint étirer

The first three pictures he hung on the wall[1], over the cot securing them[2] carefully with surgical tape[3]. The fourth he studied, and slowly rolled up again.

Not yet, he decided.

Time was passing. Carefully he turned out the light[4] before opening the door a few inches[5]. He listened intently[6], but there were no footsteps[7] in the area.

Slipping[8] outside, he noiselessly descended the metal steps and hurried past[9] the throbbing generator, the rumbling fans, the yawning tunnel, up[10] the ramp, around[11] the Mt. Vernon tracks, up the steps to the lower level of Grand Central Station. There he became part of the flow of people[12], a barrel-chested[13] man in his late thirties[14] with a muscular frame, a stiff, straight carriage, a chapped, puffy, high-cheekboned[15] face with narrow lips that he pressed together and heavy lids that only partially concealed[16] the pale eyes that darted from side to side[17].

A ticket in his hand, he hurried to the gate on the upper level where the train was leaving for Carley, Connecticut.

1. accrocha au mur
2. les fixant
3. du sparadrap
4. éteignit la lumière
5. avant d'entrebâiller la porte de quelques centimètres
6. tendit l'oreille
7. bruit de pas
8. Se glissant
9. passa en hâte devant
10. monta
11. contourna
12. se fondit dans la foule
13. au torse puissant
14. pas loin de la quarantaine
15. aux pommettes saillantes
16. dissimulaient
17. au regard fureteur

4

Neil stood on the corner[18] waiting for the school bus[19]. He knew Mrs. Lufts was watching him[20] from

18. se tenait au coin de la rue
19. car de ramassage scolaire
20. le surveillait

the window. He hated that. None of his friends' mothers watched them like Mrs. Lufts did. You'd think he was a kindergarten[1] baby instead of a first-grader[2].

Whenever it was raining[3], he had to wait in the house until the bus came. He hated that too. It made him look like a big sissy[4]. He tried to explain that[5] to his father but Dad hadn't understood. He'd just said that Neil had to take some special care[6] because of his asthma attacks.

Sandy Parker was in the fourth grade[7]. He lived on the next street but got on the bus[8] at this stop[9]. He always wanted to sit next to[10] Neil. Neil wished that he wouldn't[11]. Sandy always talked about things Neil didn't want to talk about.

Just as the bus turned the corner, Sandy came puffing up[12], his books sliding around[13] in his arms. Neil tried to head for an empty seat near the back[14] but Sandy said, "Here, Neil, here are two seats together[15]." The bus was noisy[16]. All the kids talked at the tops of their voices[17]. Sandy didn't talk loud[18] but you couldn't miss a single word he said.

Sandy was bursting with excitement[19]. They'd barely sat down[20] when he said, "We saw your father on the *Today* show when we were having breakfast."

"My father?" Neil shook his head. "You're kidding.[21]"

"No, I'm not. That lady I met at your house was on it too, Sharon Martin. They were arguing[22]."

"Why?" Neil didn't want to ask. He was never sure if he should believe Sandy.

"Because she doesn't believe in killing bad people[23] and your father does. My dad said that your dad's right. He said that the guy[24] who killed your mother should fry[25]." Sandy repeated the word with emphasis, "*Fry!*"

Neil turned to the window. He leaned his forehead[26] against the cool glass. Outside it looked so

1. de la maternelle
2. élève du CP
3. Chaque fois qu'il pleuvait
4. poule mouillée
5. Il avait bien essayé d'expliquer cela
6. faire très attention
7. [équivalent du CM1]
8. prenait le car
9. arrêt
10. à côté de
11. souhaitait tout le contraire
12. à bout de souffle
13. glissant
14. trouver un siège libre à l'arrière
15. côte à côte
16. bruyant
17. parlaient à tue-tête
18. ne parlait pas fort
19. tout excité
20. Ils venaient à peine de s'asseoir
21. Tu rigoles.
22. se disputaient
23. les méchants
24. type
25. griller
26. appuya son front

gray and it was just starting to snow. He wished it were tonight.[1] He wished his dad had been home last night. He didn't like being just with the Lufts. They were both nice to him[2] but they argued a lot and Mr. Lufts went out to the bar and Mrs. Lufts was mad[3] even though she tried not to show it in front of him.

"Aren't you glad they're going to kill Ronald Thompson Wednesday?" Sandy persisted.

"No ... I mean ... I don't think about it," Neil said in a low voice.

That wasn't true. He did think about it a lot.[4] He dreamt about it all the time too, always the same dream about that night. He was playing with his trains up[5] in his room. Mommy was in the kitchen putting away the shopping[6]. It was just getting dark out.[7] One of his trains went off the track[8] and he switched off the power[9].

That was when he heard the funny sound[10], like a scream[11] but not a loud scream[12]. He'd run downstairs[13]. The living room was almost dark but he'd seen her. Mommy. Her arms were trying to push someone back[14]. She was making awful choking sounds[15]. The man was twisting something around her neck[16].

Neil had stood on the landing. He wanted to help her but he couldn't move. He wanted to shout for help[17] but he couldn't make his voice work[18]. He started to breathe[19] like Mommy, funny, gurgly sounds[20], then his knees went all crumbly[21]. The man turned when he heard him and let Mommy fall.

Neil was falling too. He could feel himself falling. Then the room got brighter. Mommy was lying on the floor[22]. Her tongue was sticking out[23], her face was blue, her eyes were staring[24]. The man was kneeling[25] beside her now; his hands were all over her throat. He looked up at[26] Neil and started to run

1. Il avait envie d'être à ce soir.
2. gentils avec lui
3. furieuse
4. Il y pensait effectivement beaucoup.
5. en haut
6. en train de ranger les courses
7. La nuit commençait à tomber.
8. avait déraillé
9. avait coupé le courant
10. bruit bizarre
11. cri
12. hurlement
13. Il avait dévalé les escaliers.
14. repousser quelqu'un
15. d'horribles bruits étouffés
16. serrait quelque chose autour de son cou
17. appeler à l'aide
18. proférer un seul mot
19. respirer
20. bruits de gargouillis
21. étaient devenus tout mous
22. était étendue sur le sol
23. Sa langue sortait
24. fixes
25. était agenouillé
26. avait levé les yeux vers

but Neil could see his face clearly. It was all sweaty[1] and scared[2].

Neil had had to tell all about that to the policemen and point out[3] the man at the trial[4]. Then Daddy said, try to forget it, Neil. Just think of[5] all the happy times with Mommy. But he couldn't forget. He kept dreaming about it all the time and he'd wake up with asthma.

Now maybe Daddy was going to marry Sharon. Sandy had told him that everybody said his dad would probably get married again[6]. Sandy said that nobody wants other women's kids, especially kids who are sick a lot[7].

Mr. and Mrs. Lufts kept talking about wanting to move to[8] Florida. Neil wondered[9] if Daddy would give him to the Lufts if he married Sharon. He hoped not. Miserably[10], he stared out the window[11], so deep in thought[12] that Sandy had to poke him[13] when the bus pulled up[14] in front of their school.

1. couvert de sueur
2. effrayé
3. désigner
4. au procès
5. Ne retiens que
6. se remarierait probablement
7. souvent malades
8. ne cessaient de dire qu'ils aimeraient aller habiter en
9. se demandait
10. L'air triste
11. regardait fixement par la vitre
12. plongé dans ses pensées
13. lui donner un coup de coude
14. s'arrêta

5

The cab screeched to a stop[15] at the *News Dispatch* building on East Forty-second Street. Sharon rummaged[16] in her handbag, pulled out[17] two dollars and paid the driver.

15. Le taxi s'arrêta dans un crissement de pneus
16. fouilla
17. en sortit

The snow flurry[1] had stopped for the moment but the temperature was still dropping[2] and the sidewalk felt slick underfoot[3].

She went directly to the newsroom[4] that was already bustling with preparations for[5] the afternoon edition. There was a note in her box to see the City Editor[6] immediately.

Disturbed by the implied urgency[7], she hurried across the noisy room. He was alone in his small, cluttered[8] office. "Come in and close the door." He waved her to a seat[9]. "Got your column for today?"

"Yes."

"Any reference to telegraphing or phoning Governor Greene to commute[10] Thompson's sentence?"

"Certainly. I've been thinking about it. I'll change the lead[11]. The fact that the Governor said she won't stop the execution might be a break[12]. It might jog a lot more people into action[13]. We've still got forty-eight hours."

"Forget it.[14]"

Sharon stared. "What do you mean, 'forget it'? You've been right with me all through this.[15]"

"I said, forget it. After the Governor made her decision, she personally called the old man and blasted him[16]. Said that we were deliberately creating sensationalism to sell papers. She said that she doesn't believe in capital punishment either but she has no right to interfere with the sentence[17] of the court without new evidence[18]. She said if we wanted to campaign to amend[19] the Constitution, it was our right and she'd help us every step of the way[20], but to pressure her[21] to interfere in one particular case had the effect of trying to apply justice capriciously[22]. The old man ended up agreeing with her[23]."

Sharon felt her stomach twist[24] as though she'd been kicked[25]. For an instant she was afraid she was going to get sick[26]. Pressing her lips together, she

1. averse
2. continuait de baisser
3. le trottoir était glissant
4. salle de rédaction
5. affairée à préparer
6. rédacteur en chef adjoint
7. Troublée par l'urgence du message
8. encombré
9. lui fit signe de s'asseoir
10. commuer
11. la une
12. pourrait nous aider
13. inciter davantage de monde à agir
14. Laissez tomber.
15. Vous m'avez toujours soutenue dans cette affaire.
16. l'a violemment critiqué.
17. de s'ingérer dans la décision
18. preuves
19. faire campagne pour modifier
20. qu'elle soutiendrait notre démarche
21. faire pression sur elle
22. de manière fantasque
23. a fini par lui donner raison
24. se nouer
25. elle avait reçu un coup de pied
26. se sentir mal

1. essaya d'avaler
2. malgré la boule qu'elle avait soudain dans la gorge
3. refouler l'arrière-goût acide
4. Vous feriez mieux de prendre quelques jours de congé.
5. Assemblée législative
6. l'abolition de
7. Faites comme vous voulez.
8. Remettez votre article
9. compatissante
10. être adopté
11. contesté
12. à fermeture Éclair
13. sac à bandoulière
14. tapées à la machine et pliées
15. déchira
16. les regarda virevolter avant d'atterrir dans la corbeille à papier cabossée
17. nouvelle
18. recouvrée

tried to swallow[1] over the sudden constriction in her throat[2]. The editor looked at her closely. "You all right, Sharon? You look pretty pale."

She managed to force back the brackish taste[3]. "I'm all right."

"I can get someone to cover that meeting tomorrow. You better take a few days off.[4]"

"No." The Massachusetts legislature[5] was debating outlawing[6] capital punishment in that state. She intended to be there.

"Have it your way.[7] File your column[8] and go home." His voice became sympathetic[9]. "I'm sorry, Sharon. A constitutional amendment could take years to get passed[10] and I thought if we got Governor Greene to be the first one to commute a death sentence, the same approach could be used case by case across the country. But I can understand her position."

Sharon said, "I understand that legalized murder is not to be protested[11] anymore except in the abstract." Without waiting for his reaction, she abruptly got up and left the room. Going to her desk, she reached into the zipper[12] compartment of her oversized shoulderbag[13] and pulled out the folded typewritten[14] pages that contained the article she had worked on most of the night. She carefully tore[15] the pages in half, then in quarters, finally in eighths. She watched as they fluttered into the battered wastebasket[16] next to her desk.

Putting a fresh[17] sheet of paper in the typewriter, she began to write. "Society is again about to exercise its recently regained[18] prerogative, the right to kill. Almost four hundred years ago, the French philosopher Montaigne wrote, 'The horror of one man killing another makes me fear the horror of killing him.'

"If you agree that capital punishment should be outlawed by the constitution ..."

She wrote steadily for[1] two hours, slashing[2] whole paragraphs, inserting phrases, rewriting. When she had completed the column, she retyped it[3] quickly, turned it in[4], left the building and hailed a cab[5]. "Ninety-fifth Street just off[6] Central Park West, please," she said.

The cab turned north at the Avenue of the Americas, entered the park at Central Park South. Sharon watched somberly as new snow flurries settled over the grass. If this kept up, by tomorrow, children would be sleigh-riding[7] here.

Just last month Steve had brought his ice skates[8] down and they'd gone skating[9] at Wollman Rink. Neil was supposed to have come with him[10]. Sharon had planned that after skating, they'd go to the zoo and then have dinner at the Tavern on the Green. But at the last minute, Neil claimed[11] he didn't feel well and stayed home. He didn't like her, that was obvious[12].

"Okay, Miss."

"What? Oh, I'm sorry." They were turning onto Ninety-fifth Street. "The third house on the left." She lived in the ground-level-with-garden apartment[13] of a renovated brownstone[14].

The cab pulled in front of it. The driver, a slight, graying man[15], looked over his shoulder at her quizzically[16]. "It can't be all that bad[17], lady," he said. "You sure look down.[18]"

She attempted a smile[19]. "It's that kind of day, I guess." Glancing at the meter[20], she fished in her pocket for money, making the tip generous[21].

The driver reached back[22] and opened the door for her. "Boy[23], this weather is going to have a lot of people in the dumps[24] by rush hour[25]. Supposed to

1. sans s'arrêter pendant
2. biffant
3. le retapa
4. le remit
5. héla un taxi
6. non loin de
7. feraient des balades en traîneau
8. patins à glace
9. ils étaient allés faire du patin
10. devait l'accompagner
11. avait prétexté
12. clair
13. l'appartement en rez-de-jardin
14. bâtiment de grès brun
15. un homme mince aux cheveux grisonnants
16. d'un air interrogateur
17. Ça ne peut pas être aussi grave
18. Vous avez vraiment l'air à plat.
19. esquissa un sourire
20. compteur
21. laissant un pourboire généreux
22. se tourna vers l'arrière
23. Dites donc !
24. va en déprimer plus d'un
25. à l'heure de pointe

really start snowing.[1] If you're smart[2], you'll stay inside from now on."

"I'm driving up to Connecticut later."

"Better you than me[3], lady. Thanks."

Angie, her two-mornings-a-week[4] cleaning woman, had obviously just left. There was a faint smell of lemon polish[5]; the fireplace had been swept[6]; the plants trimmed and watered[7]. As always the apartment offered a restful welcome to Sharon. The old oriental rug[8] that had been her grandmother's had mellowed into soft shades of blue and red. She'd reupholstered[9] in blue the couch[10] and chair she bought secondhand[11], a labor of love[12] that had taken the better part of four weekends but turned out well[13]. The pictures and prints[14] on the walls and over the fireplace she'd selected one by one, in small antique shops[15], at auctions[16], on trips abroad.

Steve loved this room. He always noticed even the smallest change in it. "You have a way with a home[17]," he told her.

Mechanically, she walked into the bedroom and began to undress. She'd shower and change and make tea and try to sleep for a while. She couldn't even think coherently now.

It was nearly noon when she got into bed and she set the alarm for[18] three-thirty. For a long time sleep didn't come. Ronald Thompson. She'd been so *sure* the Governor would commute his sentence. There was no question that he was guilty[19], and lying about it[20] had certainly hurt him. But except for that one other serious episode[21] when he was fifteen, his record was good[22]. And he was so *young*.

Steve. It was people like Steve who were molding[23] public opinion. It was Steve's reputation for integrity, for fair play that made people listen to him.

Did she love Steve?

Yes.

1. Paraît qu'il va sérieusement commencer à neiger.
2. Si vous voulez mon avis
3. Je n'aimerais pas être à votre place
4. qui venait deux matinées par semaine
5. cire parfumée au citron
6. la cheminée avait été nettoyée
7. taillées et arrosées
8. tapis
9. recouvert
10. canapé
11. d'occasion
12. une occupation qu'elle avait adorée
13. dont elle s'était plutôt bien sortie
14. gravures
15. boutiques d'antiquités
16. dans des ventes aux enchères
17. Tu es douée pour aménager un intérieur
18. régla le réveil sur
19. Sa culpabilité ne faisait aucun doute
20. le nier
21. affaire sérieuse
22. son casier judiciaire était vierge
23. façonnaient

How much?

Very, very much.

Did she want to marry him? They were going to have to talk about that tonight. She knew that was why Steve wanted her to stay at his place. And he wanted so much for Neil to begin to accept her. But it wouldn't work; you can't force a relationship. Neil was so standoffish[1] with her, so rejecting[2]. Was it that he didn't like her or would he react the same way to any woman who took his father's attention from him[3]? She wasn't sure.

Did she want to live in Carley? She loved New York so much, loved it seven days a week. But Steve would never agree to move Neil to the city.

She was just beginning to make it as a writer[4]. Her book was in its sixth printing[5]. It had been published as a paperback[6]; no hardcover house[7] had been interested, but the reviews[8] and sales had been unexpectedly[9] good.

Was this the time to get involved in marriage[10]—marriage to a man whose child resented her[11]?

Steve. Unconsciously she touched her face, remembering the feeling of those big, gentle hands warming it as he said goodbye to her this morning. They were so desperately attracted to each other[12] ...

But how could she accept the uncompromising stubborn side of him[13] when he made up his mind on an issue[14]?

Finally she dozed off[15]. Almost immediately she began to dream. She was writing a column. She had to finish it. It was important to finish it. But no matter[16] how frantically[17] she pressed the typewriter keys[18] no impressions were being made on the paper. Then Steve was in the room. He was pulling a young man by the arm. She was still trying to make the words come out on the paper[19]. Steve made the boy sit down. "I am so sorry," he kept saying to him,

1. distant
2. prompt à la rejeter
3. détournait son père de lui
4. réussir comme écrivaine
5. avait été réédité pour la sixième fois
6. en livre de poche
7. maison d'édition spécialisée dans les livres reliés
8. critiques
9. exceptionnellement
10. de s'engager dans le mariage
11. la rejetait
12. terriblement attirés l'un par l'autre
13. son côté intransigeant et obstiné
14. s'était forgé une opinion sur une question
15. s'assoupit
16. peu importe
17. la vigueur avec laquelle
18. appuyait sur les touches de la machine à écrire
19. faire apparaître les mots sur le papier

"but it is necessary. You must understand this is necessary." Then while Sharon tried to scream, Steve fastened the boy's arms and legs in shackles[1] and reached for a switch[2].

Sharon was awakened[3] by the sound of a hoarse[4] voice, her own, shrieking, "No ... No ... No ..."

6

At five minutes of six[5] the few[6] people in the streets of Carley, Connecticut, were hurrying from cars to stores, heedless of anything except[7] the bitter[8], snowy night.

The man standing in the shadows[9] near the edge of the[10] Cabin Restaurant parking lot was completely unobserved[11]. His eyes constantly roved the area[12] as pelting snow blew in his face[13]. He'd been there nearly twenty minutes and his feet were freezing[14].

Impatiently, he shifted[15] and his toe[16] touched the duffel bag at his feet. He felt for the weapons in the pocket of his coat.[17] They were at his fingertips[18] and he nodded[19], satisfied.

The Lufts should be along any minute[20]. He'd phoned the restaurant and confirmed the six o'clock reservation. They were planning to have dinner and then go to see Selznick's *Gone With the Wind*[21]. It was playing in the[22] Carley Square Theater diagonal-

1. entrava les bras et les jambes du garçon
2. tendit le bras pour atteindre l'interrupteur
3. fut réveillée
4. rauque
5. six heures moins cinq
6. les rares
7. insensibles à tout sauf à
8. glaciale
9. debout dans l'obscurité
10. aux abords du
11. passait totalement inaperçu
12. Son regard balayait sans cesse l'endroit
13. alors que la neige lui tombait à gros flocons sur le visage
14. gelés
15. changea de position
16. orteil
17. Il tâta la poche de son manteau à la recherche des armes.
18. à portée de main
19. hocha la tête
20. arriver d'un instant à l'autre
21. Autant en emporte le vent
22. Il passait au

ly across the street. The 4:00 P.M. performance was on now.[1] They were going to the 7:30 showing[2].

He stiffened[3]. A car was coming down the block, was turning into the parking lot. He shrank behind[4] the spruce trees edging the area[5]. It was their station wagon[6]. He watched as they parked near the restaurant entrance. The driver got out and went around to help his wife who was clumsily stepping onto the slick tarpin[7]. Their bodies bent against the wind[8], their gait awkward[9], his hand under her elbow, the Lufts moved with cautious haste toward the door of the restaurant.

He waited till they were safely inside before bending down and picking up[10] the duffel bag. Moving swiftly, he circled[11] the parking lot, keeping well behind the shrubbery[12]. He cut across[13] the street and hurried behind the movie house[14].

There were about fifty cars parked in the lot. He headed toward an eight-year-old dark-brown Chevrolet sedan[15] parked unobtrusively[16] in the far right corner.

In an instant he had the door unlocked. He slipped into the seat, put the key in the ignition[17] and turned it. The engine purred[18] with quiet pep. With a slight smile and a last overall glance at the deserted surroundings[19], he started the car. He did not turn the lights on[20] as he drove past the theater into the quiet street. Four minutes later the shabby[21] brown sedan pulled into[22] the circular driveway[23] of the Peterson home on Driftwood Lane and parked behind a small red Vega.

1. La séance de 16 heures était en cours.
2. projection
3. se raidit
4. recula derrière
5. épicéas qui bordaient l'endroit
6. break
7. avait du mal à descendre de voiture sur la chaussée glissante
8. Penchés en avant pour lutter contre le vent
9. le pas mal assuré
10. avant de se pencher pour prendre
11. contourna
12. massif d'arbustes
13. traversa
14. se rendit en toute hâte derrière le cinéma
15. berline
16. discrètement
17. mit la clé de contact
18. ronronna
19. un dernier regard aux alentours déserts
20. n'alluma pas les phares
21. vieille
22. s'engagea dans
23. allée

7

The drive[1] from Manhattan to Carley usually took less than an hour but the ominous weather forecast[2] had sent commuters scurrying to their cars early[3]. The traffic buildup[4] combined with icy spots[5] on the parkways[6] made Sharon's trip to Steve's house last nearly an hour and twenty minutes. But she was almost unaware of the maddening delays[7]. All the way up[8], she rehearsed[9] what she would say to Steve, "It won't work for us. … We don't think alike. … Neil will never accept me … it will be easier if we don't see each other anymore. …"

Steve's house, a white clapboard colonial with black shutters, vaguely depressed Sharon. The porchlight was too bright. The foundation shrubs were too high. Sharon knew that Steve and Nina had lived in this house only a few weeks before her death and that he hadn't done any of the renovating they'd planned when they bought it.

She parked just past the porch steps and unconsciously braced herself[10] for Mrs. Lufts' rapid-fire greeting[11] and Neil's coolness. But this would be the last time. That thought deepened her depression.

Mrs. Lufts had obviously been watching for her[12]. The front door was yanked open[13] as she got out

1. trajet en voiture
2. prévisions météo alarmantes
3. avaient précipité les banlieusards dans leurs voitures plus tôt que d'habitude
4. bouchons
5. conjugués au verglas
6. [aux États-Unis, route à plusieurs voies bordées d'espaces verts]
7. se souciait peu des retards exaspérants
8. Pendant tout le trajet
9. avait répété
10. s'arma de courage
11. salutations en rafale
12. la guettait de toute évidence
13. s'ouvrit brusquement

of the car. "Miss Martin, my, it's nice to see you." Mrs. Lufts' stocky frame filled the doorway. Her small-featured[1] face was squirrel-like[2] with bright, inquisitive eyes. She was wearing a heavy red-plaid coat and galoshes[3].

"How are you, Mrs. Lufts?" Sharon stepped past her into the house. Mrs. Lufts had a habit of always standing close to[4] the person she was with so that contact with her invariably had a smothering effect[5]. Now she moved back barely enough to let Sharon squeeze past[6].

"It's awfully nice of you[7] to come," Mrs. Lufts said. "Here, let me take your cape. I love capes. Make you look sweet and feminine, don't you think?"

Sharon set her pocketbook[8] and overnight bag[9] down in the foyer[10]. She pulled off[11] her gloves. "I guess so.[12] I've never really thought about it ..." She glanced into the living room. "Oh ..."

Neil was sitting, cross-legged[13], on the carpet, magazines scattered[14] around him, a pair of blunt scissors in his hand. His sandy hair, exactly the shade of Steve's, fell over his forehead, leaving his bent neck thin and vulnerable. His bony shoulders stuck out[15] under a brown-and-white flannel shirt. His face looked thin and pale except for the red streaks[16] around the enormous dark brown eyes that were welling with tears[17].

"Neil, say hello to Sharon," Mrs. Lufts commanded[18].

He looked up[19], listlessly[20]. "Hello, Sharon." His voice was low and quivering[21].

He looked so little and scrawny[22] and woebegone[23]. Sharon ached[24] to put her arms around him but knew that if she did, he'd only pull away from her[25].

Mrs. Lufts made a clicking sound with her tongue[26]. "I'll be blessed if I know what the trouble is.[27] Just started crying[28] a few minutes ago. Won't tell me

1. aux traits miniatures
2. la faisait ressembler à un écureuil
3. [caoutchoucs enfilés par-dessus les chaussures]
4. se tenir tout près de
5. créait une sensation d'étouffement
6. passer
7. extrêmement gentil de votre part
8. sac à main
9. sac de voyage
10. vestibule
11. enleva
12. Je pense que oui.
13. en tailleur
14. éparpillés
15. épaules osseuses saillaient
16. traces rouges
17. embués de larmes
18. ordonna
19. leva les yeux
20. avec indifférence
21. tremblante
22. efflanqué
23. abattu
24. avait très envie
25. il se détournerait d'elle
26. fit claquer sa langue
27. Mon Dieu, si je pouvais comprendre ce qui ne va pas.
28. Vient tout juste de se mettre à pleurer

why. You never can figure[1] what goes on in that little head. Well, maybe you or his dad can get it out of him[2]." Her voice rose an octave, "Billllllll …"

Sharon jumped, her eardrums ringing[3]. Hastily she went into the living room and stood in front of Neil. "What are you supposed to cut out[4]?" she asked.

"Just some dumb[5] pictures with animals." Neil did not look at her again. She knew he was embarrassed[6] to be seen crying.

"Why don't I get myself a sherry and then give you a hand[7]. Want a Coke or something?"

"No." Neil hesitated, then reluctantly added, "Thank you."

"Just help yourself[8]," Mrs. Lufts said. "Make yourself at home.[9] You know where everything is. I got everything on the list Mr. Peterson left, steak and salad makings[10] and asparagus[11] and ice cream. It's all in the refrigerator. I'm sorry to be rushing[12] but we do want to have dinner before the movie. Bill …"

"I'm coming, Dora." There was annoyance[13] in the voice. Bill Lufts came up the stairway from the basement[14]. "Just wanted to check on[15] the windows," he said, "make sure they're locked. Hello, Miss Martin."

"How are you, Mr. Lufts?" He was a short, thick-necked man in his mid-sixties[16] with watery blue eyes[17]. Tiny broken capillaries formed telltale patches on his cheeks and nostrils, reminding[18] Sharon that Steve was worried about Bill Lufts' heavy drinking[19].

"Bill, get a move on[20], will you[21]?" His wife's voice was edged with impatience[22]. "You know how I hate to gulp my food[23], and we're running late now[24]. The only time you take me out is our anniversary, seems to me, and I do think you could hurry …"

"All right. All right." Bill sighed heavily and nodded to Sharon. "See you later, Miss Martin."

1. deviner
2. le lui faire dire
3. elle en avait les oreilles qui bourdonnaient
4. découper
5. stupides
6. qu'il était gêné
7. je viens ensuite te donner un coup de main
8. Servez-vous
9. Faites comme chez vous.
10. tout ce qu'il faut pour préparer une salade
11. des asperges
12. expéditive
13. une certaine irritation
14. sous-sol
15. vérifier
16. petit sexagénaire au cou épais
17. aux yeux d'un bleu délavé
18. De la couperose sur ses joues et ses narines était un signe révélateur qui rappela à
19. s'inquiétait de la consommation excessive d'alcool de Bill Lufts
20. bouge-toi
21. s'il te plaît
22. teintée d'impatience
23. avaler mon repas en vitesse
24. nous sommes maintenant en retard

"Have a good time." Sharon followed him into the foyer. "And, oh yes, happy anniversary."

"Wear a hat, Bill. You'll catch your death[1] … What? Oh, thank you, thank you, Miss Martin. Soon as I sit down and get a rest and something to eat, I'll start feeling like an anniversary. Right now with all this rushing[2] …"

"Dora, you're the one who wants to see this movie …"

"All right. I've got everything. Have a nice time, together, you two. Neil, show your report card[3] to Sharon. He's a real bright boy[4], no trouble either[5], are you, Neil? I gave him a snack[6] to hold him over[7] till dinner but he hardly touched it[8]. Don't eat enough to keep a bird alive.[9] All right, Bill, all right!"

They were finally off[10]. Sharon shivered[11] as a chilly blast of air rushed into[12] the foyer before she could close the door after them. She went back into the kitchen, opened the refrigerator and reached for the bottle of Bristol cream sherry. She hesitated, then took out a carton[13] of milk. Neil might have said he didn't want anything but she was going to make him some hot cocoa[14].

While she waited for the milk to heat, she sipped[15] the sherry and glanced around. Mrs. Lufts did her best[16] but she wasn't a good housekeeper[17] and the kitchen had a vaguely untidy look[18]. There were crumbs spilling around the[19] toaster on the counter[20]. The top of the stove[21] needed a good scrubbing[22]. Really the whole house needed a face lifting[23].

Steve's property backed onto[24] Long Island Sound[25]. "I'd cut all those trees that block the view," Sharon thought, "and enclose[26] the back porch and make it part of the living room with floor-to-ceiling windows[27], and knock out[28] most of the walls and put in a breakfast bar …" Sharply she

1. Tu vas attraper la mort
2. précipitation
3. bulletin scolaire
4. C'est un garçon très intelligent
5. et en plus il est facile
6. goûter
7. pour qu'il puisse tenir
8. y a à peine touché
9. Il a un appétit d'oiseau.
10. partirent enfin
11. frissonna
12. courant d'air glacé s'engouffra dans
13. brique
14. du chocolat chaud
15. sirota
16. faisait de son mieux
17. maîtresse de maison
18. n'était pas nette
19. Il y avait des miettes autour du
20. plan de travail
21. cuisinière
22. bon nettoyage
23. d'être retapée
24. donnait sur
25. le détroit de Long Island
26. fermerais
27. des baies vitrées
28. j'abattrais

checked herself.[1] It was none of her business.[2] It was just that the house and Neil and even Steve had such a neglected look.

But it was not for her to change. The thought of not seeing Steve again, not expecting his call, not feeling those strong, gentle arms around her, not watching that suddenly carefree look[3] light up[4] his face when she said something that amused him, filled her with bleak loneliness[5]. This is how it feels to know you have to give up someone[6], she thought. How does Mrs. Thompson feel, knowing that her only child will die day after tomorrow?

She knew Mrs. Thompson's number. She'd interviewed her after deciding to get involved in Ron's case[7]. A number of times during this last trip, she'd tried to phone Mrs. Thompson to share the news that so many important people had promised to contact Governor Greene and urge clemency[8]. But she'd never caught her home[9]. Probably because Mrs. Thompson had been working on a petition for clemency[10] from the people in Fairfield County.

That poor woman. She'd been so hopeful[11] when Sharon visited her, then seemed so upset[12] when she realized[13] that Sharon didn't think Ron was innocent.

But what mother could believe her son was capable of murder? Maybe Mrs. Thompson was home now. Maybe it would help just to talk with someone who had worked to save[14] Ronald.

Sharon lowered the flame[15] under the saucepan[16], went over to the wall-phone[17] and dialed the number[18]. The phone was answered on the first ring.[19] Mrs. Thompson's voice was surprisingly steady[20]. "Hello."

"Mrs. Thompson, this is Sharon Martin. I had to call to tell you how sorry I am, to ask if there's anything I can do ..."

1. Elle se retint brusquement.
2. Ce n'était pas ses affaires.
3. regard insouciant
4. illuminer
5. solitude
6. renoncer à quelqu'un
7. s'impliquer dans l'affaire de Ron
8. pour l'exhorter à la clémence
9. elle n'avait jamais pu la joindre chez elle
10. demande de grâce
11. Elle avait fondé tant d'espoirs
12. peinée
13. s'était rendu compte que
14. sauver
15. baissa le feu
16. casserole
17. téléphone mural
18. composa le numéro
19. On décrocha à la première sonnerie.
20. assurée

"You've done enough[1], Miss Martin." The bitterness[2] in the woman's voice stunned[3] Sharon. "If my boy dies Wednesday, I want you to know that I hold you responsible[4]. I begged you to keep out of this.[5]"

"Mrs. Thompson ... I don't know what you mean ..."

"I mean, that in all your columns you have over and over again[6] written that there was no question of Ronald's guilt[7] but that wasn't the issue. It *is* the issue[8], Miss Martin!" The woman's voice became high-pitched[9]. "It *is* the issue. There were many people who know my boy, who know that he's incapable of hurting anyone, who were working to get him clemency. But you ... you've forced the Governor not to examine his case just on its own merits[10] ... We're still trying, and I don't believe God will do this to me, but if my son dies, I don't think I'll be responsible for[11] what I might do to you."

The connection was broken.[12] Bewildered[13], Sharon stared at the receiver[14] in her hand. Could Mrs. Thompson really believe ...? Numbly[15] she replaced the receiver on the hook.

The milk was almost boiling in the saucepan on the stove. Mechanically[16], she reached for the box of Quik in the cabinet[17] and scooped a heaping teaspoon of it[18] into a mug[19]. She poured the milk in, stirred[20] it, and put the pot[21] in the sink to soak[22].

Stunned by the implication of Mrs. Thompson's attack, she started for[23] the living room.

The bell rang.

Neil scrambled for the door[24] before she could stop him. "Maybe it's my dad." He sounded relieved[25].

He doesn't want to be alone with me at all, Sharon thought. She heard him click the double lock[26] and a sense of alarm jangled through her[27]. "Neil, wait a minute," she called. "Ask who it is. Your dad would have his key[28]."

1. Vous en avez assez fait
2. amertume
3. stupéfia
4. sachez que je vous tiens pour responsable
5. Je vous avais priée de ne pas vous en mêler.
6. à maintes reprises
7. la culpabilité de Ron ne faisait aucun doute
8. Mais le problème est pourtant bien là
9. stridente
10. à ne pas évaluer sa demande sans préjugé
11. être tenue responsable de
12. La communication fut coupée.
13. Éberluée
14. combiné
15. Hébétée
16. Machinalement
17. placard
18. en versa une bonne cuillère
19. tasse
20. remua
21. casserole
22. la faire tremper
23. se dirigea vers
24. se rua vers la porte
25. semblait soulagé
26. déverrouiller la porte
27. un sentiment d'inquiétude l'envahit
28. clé

Hastily[1] she set down[2] the cocoa mug and sherry glass on a table near the fireplace and ran into the hall.

Neil obeyed her. He had one hand on the knob[3] but hesitated and called, "Who is it?"

"Is Bill Lufts there?" a voice called. "I have the generator he ordered[4] for Mr. Peterson's boat."

"Oh, that's all right," Neil told Sharon. "Mr. Lufts is waiting for that."

He turned the handle[5] of the door and was starting to pull it open[6] when it was pushed in with violent force[7], slamming Neil back against the wall[8]. Stunned, Sharon watched as a man stepped into[9] the foyer and with a lightning-quick movement closed the door behind him[10]. Gasping[11], Neil fell to the floor[12]. Instinctively, Sharon ran over to[13] him. She helped him to his feet[14], and keeping one arm around him, turned to face the intruder[15].

Two distinctively separate impressions burned into her consciousness[16]. One was the glittering stare in the stranger's eyes[17]. The other was the thin, long-barreled pistol[18] he was pointing at her head.

1. À la hâte
2. posa
3. poignée
4. a commandé
5. poignée
6. l'entrouvrait
7. lorsqu'elle fut violemment ouverte
8. plaquant Neil contre le mur
9. vit un homme entrer dans
10. refermer la porte derrière lui à la vitesse de l'éclair
11. Suffoquant
12. tomba par terre
13. se précipita vers
14. à se relever
15. intrus
16. se gravèrent au fer rouge dans sa conscience
17. regard fixe étincelant de l'inconnu
18. pistolet à canon long

8

The meeting in the conference room of *Events* magazine lasted[19] until 7:10 P.M[20]. The main topic[21] of conversation was the just-released Nielson report[22] that

19. dura
20. 19 heures 10
21. principal sujet
22. le rapport Nielson qui venait d'être publié

had been highly[1] favorable. Two out of three of the surveyed college graduates[2] in the twenty-five to forty age bracket[3] preferred *Events* to *Time* or *Newsweek*. Besides that, the paid circulation[4] was up fifteen percent over the previous year[5] and the new regional advertising[6] was working well.

At the end of the meeting, Bradley Robertson, the publisher[7], stood up. "I think we can all take a great deal of pride in[8] these statistics," he said. "We've been working hard for nearly three years but we've done it[9]. It's not easy to launch[10] a new magazine these days[11] and I, for one, want to say[12], that in my mind[13], the creative direction of Steve Peterson has been the decisive factor in our success."

After the meeting, Steve went down in the elevator with the publisher. "Thanks, again, Brad," he said, "that was very generous of you."

The older man shrugged[14]. "It was honest of me.[15] We've made it, Steve. We'll all be able to start taking some decent money[16] soon. It's about time, too.[17] I know it hasn't been easy for you."

Steve smiled grimly[18]. "No, it hasn't."

The elevator door opened in the main lobby.

"Goodnight, Brad. I'm going to run. I want to catch the seven-thirty …"

"Wait a minute. Steve, I saw you on the *Today* show this morning."

"Yes."

"I thought you were excellent, but so was Sharon. And, personally, I confess I go along with her thinking[19]."

"A lot of people do."

"I like her, Steve. She's as bright as they come[20] … damn good-looking[21] too. And a real lady."

"I agree."

"Steve, I know how much you've been through[22] the last couple of years[23]. I don't want to butt in[24],

1. et qui leur était très
2. diplômés universitaires interrogés
3. tranche d'âge 25-40 ans
4. tirage des journaux payants
5. avait augmenté de 15% l'année précédente
6. publicité
7. directeur de la publication
8. être très fiers de
9. nous avons réussi
10. lancer
11. de nos jours
12. pour ma part, je voudrais dire
13. qu'à mes yeux
14. haussa les épaules
15. J'étais sincère.
16. commencer à gagner decemment notre vie
17. Il est grand temps.
18. d'un air grave
19. partage son opinion
20. Elle est on ne peut plus intelligente
21. sacrément belle
22. toutes les épreuves que vous avez traversées
23. ces deux dernières années
24. m'immiscer dans vos affaires

1. Ne laissez pas des questions, aussi fondamentales soient-elles, vous séparer.
2. Je prie pour que ça n'arrive pas
3. type en proie à d'énormes difficultés financières
4. famille toute prête
5. Elle aurait une sacrée chance
6. Je vais vous déposer
7. chez moi
8. se faufiler à travers
9. embouteillages du centre-ville
10. fatigué
11. doit être particulièrement éprouvante
12. ressasse
13. terriblement navré
14. jusqu'à ce que tout ceci soit terminé
15. réfléchit
16. s'arrêta devant
17. dans les années trente
18. plaque tournante du transport
19. Il y avait même autrefois
20. carrefour
21. message publicitaire

but Sharon would be good for you … and for Neil. Don't let issues, no matter how compelling, come between you.[1]"

"I pray they don't[2]," Steve answered quietly.

"And at least now I'll be able to offer Sharon something more than a financially strapped guy[3] with a ready-made family[4]."

"She'd be darn lucky[5] to get both you and Neil! Come on, my car's outside. I'll drop you off[6] at Grand Central."

"Great. Sharon is up at my place[7] and I don't want to miss the train."

Bradley's limousine was at the door. The driver quickly began to thread through[8] the snarled midtown traffic[9]. Steve leaned back and unconsciously sighed.

"You look tired[10], Steve. This Thompson execution has got to be getting to you[11]."

Steve shrugged. "It is. Naturally it brings everything back. Every paper in Connecticut is rehashing[12] the … Nina's death. I know that the kids have to be talking about it in school. I worry about how much Neil is hearing. I'm desperately sorry[13] for Thompson's mother … and for him too."

"Why don't you take Neil and get away for a few days until this is over[14]?"

Steve considered[15]. "I might do that. It probably would be a good idea."

The limousine pulled up to[16] the Vanderbilt Avenue entrance to Grand Central. Bradley Robertson shook his head. "You're too young to remember, Steve, but during the thirties[17], Grand Central was the hub of transportation[18] in this country. There even used to be[19] a radio series …" He closed his eyes. " 'Grand Central Station, crossroads[20] of a million private lives,' that was the blurb[21] for it."

Steve laughed. "And then along came the jet age[1]." He opened the door. "Thanks for the lift.[2]"

Pulling out his commuter book[3], he walked quickly down into the terminal. He had five minutes till train time and decided to phone home to tell Sharon he was definitely making[4] the 7:30 train.

He shrugged. Don't kid yourself[5], he thought. You just want to talk to her, to make sure she didn't change her mind about coming. He stepped into a phonebooth[6]. He didn't have much change[7] and made the call collect[8].

The phone rang once … twice … three times.

The operator came in.[9] "I am rrringing your number[10] but there is no answer."

"There has to be someone there. Keep trying[11], operator, please."

"Certainly, sir."

The jabbing sound continued.[12] After the fifth time, the operator came back on[13]. "There is no answer, sir. Will you place your call later[14], please?"

"Operator, would you mind checking[15] the number? Are you sure we're ringing 203-565-1313?"

"I'll dial it again, sir."

Steve stared at the receiver in his hand. Where could they be? If Sharon hadn't come up, would the Lufts have perhaps asked the Perrys if Neil could stay with them?

No. Sharon would have phoned him if she decided not to go to his house. Suppose Neil had had an asthma attack … suppose he'd had to be rushed to the hospital again[16]?

An attack wouldn't be surprising if he'd heard any talk[17] in school about the Thompson execution.

Neil had been having more frequent nightmares lately[18].

It was 7:29. The train was leaving in one minute. If he tried to phone the doctor or the hospital or the

1. vint l'ère des avions à réaction
2. Merci de m'avoir déposé.
3. carte de transport
4. prenait
5. Ne te raconte pas d'histoires
6. entra dans une cabine téléphonique
7. monnaie
8. appela en PCV
9. Il entendit la voix de la standardiste.
10. Je n'arrête pas d'appeler votre numéro
11. Insistez
12. Il l'entendit à nouveau composer le numéro.
13. s'adressa à nouveau à lui
14. Pourriez-vous rappeler plus tard
15. auriez-vous l'amabilité de vérifier
16. et s'il avait fallu à nouveau le conduire à l'hôpital en urgence
17. s'il avait entendu parler
18. récemment

Perrys, he'd miss the train and have to wait forty-five minutes for the next one.

Perhaps there was trouble with the phone lines[1] because of the storm. That didn't always show up at once.[2]

Steve started to dial the Perrys, then changed his mind[3]. He replaced the phone on the hook[4], then raced across the station in long, sprinting strides[5]. Taking the stairs down to the platform two at a time[6], he barely reached the train[7] as the doors were closing.

At that same instant, a man and woman passed in front of the phonebooth he had just abandoned. The woman was wearing a long, shabby gray coat. Her head was covered with a soiled[8], bluish kerchief. The man's arm was through hers[9]. Under his other arm, he clutched[10] a heavy khaki duffel bag.

1. les lignes de téléphone étaient-elles en dérangement
2. On ne s'en apercevait pas toujours immédiatement.
3. changea d'avis
4. raccrocha
5. traversa la gare au pas de course
6. Il descendit quatre à quatre l'escalier qui menait au quai
7. et attrapa de justesse le train
8. défraîchi
9. L'homme la tenait par le bras
10. serrait fortement

9

Sharon stared at the powerful[11] hands that held the gun, at the eyes that slithered from side to side[12], into the living room, up the staircase, over her body[13].

"What do you want?" she whispered[14]. Within the crook of her arm[15], she could feel the violent trembling of Neil's body. She tightened her grip[16], pressed him to her[17].

11. puissantes
12. fureteurs
13. qui passaient du salon à l'escalier et glissaient sur son corps
14. murmura-t-elle
15. Dans le creux de son bras
16. resserra son étreinte
17. contre elle

"You're Sharon Martin." It was a statement[1]. The voice was a monotone, without inflection. Sharon felt a pulse pounding in her throat, closing it[2]. She tried to swallow[3]. "What do you want?" she asked again. The persistent soft whistle[4] in Neil's breathing … suppose he was frightened into one[5] of his asthma attacks? She would offer cooperation. "I have about ninety dollars in my purse …"

"Shut up!"[6]

The evenly spoken words[7] chilled her[8]. The stranger dropped the bag he was carrying. It was a large khaki duffel bag, the kind military personnel used. He reached into[9] his pocket and pulled out a ball of thick twine[10] and a roll of wide bandages[11]. He dropped them next to her. "Blindfold the boy[12] and tie him up[13]," he ordered[14].

"No! I won't."

"You'd better![15]"

Sharon looked down at Neil. He was staring at the man. His eyes were cloudy[16]; the pupils enormous. She remembered that after his mother's death he'd been in deep shock[17].

"Neil, I …" How could she help him, reassure him?

"Sit down." The intruder's voice was a sharp order[18] to Neil. The child looked up beseechingly at[19] Sharon, then obediently[20] sat on the bottom step of the staircase[21].

Sharon knelt beside him. "Neil, don't be afraid. I'm with you." Her hands fumbled[22] as she reached for one of the bandages and wound it[23] around his eyes, tying it[24] at the back of his head.

She looked up. The intruder was staring at Neil. The gun was pointed at him. She heard a click. She pulled Neil against her, shielding him[25]. "No … no … don't[26]."

1. affirmation
2. sentit sa gorge se nouer au point de ne pouvoir proférer le moindre mot
3. d'avaler
4. constant sifflement ténu
5. et si la peur déclenchait l'une
6. La ferme !
7. mots énoncés d'une voix monocorde
8. la glacèrent
9. fouilla dans
10. pelote de ficelle épaisse
11. rouleau de larges bandes
12. Bandez les yeux du garçon
13. attachez-le
14. ordonna-t-il
15. Vous avez intérêt !
16. Ses yeux étaient vitreux
17. en état de choc extrême
18. ordre cinglant
19. leva les yeux d'un air implorant vers
20. docilement
21. première marche de l'escalier
22. tremblaient
23. l'enroula
24. la nouant
25. lui faisant un bouclier de son corps
26. ne faites pas ça

The intruder looked at her; slowly he lowered the gun letting it dangle from his hand[1]. He would have killed Neil, she thought. He was ready to kill him …

"Tie up the boy, Sharon." There was an intimacy[2] about the command.

With hands that fumbled at the ropes, she obeyed. She tied Neil's wrists together[3], trying to leave the bindings loose[4] enough to allow for circulation. After she fastened his wrists, she pressed her hands on his.

The stranger reached past her, cut the end of the twine with a knife. "Hurry up … tie his feet!"

She heard the edginess[5] in the tone. Quickly she obeyed. Neil's knees were trembling so, making his legs jerk apart[6]. She wound the twine around his ankles and knotted it[7].

"Gag him[8]!"

"He'll choke[9]; he has asthma …" The protest died on her lips. The man's face was different somehow, whiter, strained[10]. His high cheekbones were throbbing under stretched skin[11]. He was near panic[12]. Desperately, she bound Neil's mouth[13], leaving the gag as loose as she dared[14]. If only Neil didn't struggle[15]…

A hand shoved her away from[16] the child. She toppled to the floor[17]. The man was leaning over her. His knee dug into her back[18]. He pulled her arms behind her. She felt the twine biting her wrists[19]. She opened her mouth to protest, felt a wad of cloth stuffed into it[20]. He yanked a strip of gauze[21] over her mouth and cheeks, knotted it at the back of her head.

She couldn't breathe. Please … No … Hands slid over her thighs[22], lingered. Her legs were pulled together[23]; twine cut through the soft leather boots[24].

She felt herself being lifted. Her head fell backward. What was he going to do to her?

1. pendre au bout de sa main
2. familiarité
3. joignit les poignets de Neil pour les attacher
4. ne pas trop serrer les liens
5. nervosité
6. qu'il avait du mal à garder les jambes jointes
7. la noua
8. Bâillonnez-le
9. Il va s'étouffer
10. tendu
11. palpitaient sous la peau tendue
12. près de céder à la panique
13. bâillonna Neil
14. bâillon aussi lâche que possible
15. ne se débattait pas
16. l'envoya valser loin de
17. tomba à la renverse sur le sol
18. s'enfonça dans son dos
19. lui scier les poignets
20. qu'on y fourrait une boule de tissu
21. D'un coup sec, il mit une bande de gaze
22. glissèrent sur ses cuisses
23. Il lui joignit les jambes
24. bottes en cuir souple

The front door was opened. Cold, wet air stung her face[1]. She weighed 120 pounds[2] but the abductor[3] was rushing down the slippery porch steps as though she were weightless[4]. It was so dark. He must have turned off the outside lights. She felt her shoulders hit against something cold, metallic. A car. She tried to inhale deeply through her nostrils; to adjust her eyes to the darkness. She must clear her head[5]; stop panicking, think.

The grating sound[6] of a door being opened[7]. Sharon felt herself falling. Her head glanced against[8] an open ashtray[9]. Her elbows and ankles took the force of the jolt[10] as she hit[11] the musty smelling floor. She was in the back of a car.

She heard crunching footsteps retreating[12]. The man was going back into the house. Neil! What would he do to Neil? Frantically[13] Sharon tried to wrench her hands free[14]. Pain shot through her arms.[15] The rough twine bit deeply into her wrists. She thought of the way the intruder had stared at Neil, had released the safety catch[16] on the gun.

Minutes passed. Please, dear God, please … The sound of a door opening. Crunching footsteps coming toward the car. The front right door swung open[17]. Her eyes were adjusted to the darkness[18]. Through the shadows, she could see his outline[19]. He was carrying something … the canvas bag. Oh, God, Neil was in that bag! She knew it.

He was leaning into the car, dropping the bag onto the seat, pushing it down on the floor. Sharon heard the dull thud[20]. He'll hurt Neil. He'll hurt him. A door closed. Footsteps scurried around[21] the car. The driver's door opened, clicked shut[22]. The shadows moved. She heard harsh breathing[23]. He was leaning down[24], looking at her.

Sharon felt something fall on her, something that scratched her cheek[25] … a blanket or a coat. She

1. lui piqua le visage
2. une soixantaine de kilos
3. ravisseur
4. légère comme une plume
5. rester lucide
6. grincement
7. qu'on ouvrait
8. rebondit contre
9. cendrier
10. amortirent le choc
11. atterrit sur
12. des pas s'éloigner en crissant
13. Désespérément
14. se libérer les mains
15. La douleur irradia dans ses bras.
16. relâché le cran de sûreté
17. s'ouvrit
18. s'étaient habitués à l'obscurité
19. silhouette
20. bruit sourd
21. Des pas contournèrent précipitamment
22. se referma avec un bruit sec
23. une respiration heurtée
24. se penchait sur elle
25. lui grattait la joue

1. l'odeur âcre et suffocante de transpiration

2. le tremblement incontrôlé resserra les liens

3. s'enfoncer plus profondément

4. membres

5. protestèrent violemment

6. traces

7. pendant un certain temps

8. neige fondue

9. bâillon

10. Il l'étouffait.

11. accéléra

moved her head trying to free her face from the choking, acrid smell of stale perspiration[1].

The engine started. The car began to move.

Concentrate on directions. Remember every detail. Later the police would want to know. The car was turning left onto the street. It was cold, so cold. Sharon shivered and the tremulous movement tightened the knots[2], causing the cords to dig tighter[3] into her legs and arms and wrists. Her limbs[4] shrieked a protest[5]. Stop moving! Calm. Be calm. Don't panic.

Snow. If it was still snowing, there might be tracks[6] for a while.[7] But no. There was too much sleet[8] mixed in with the snow. She could hear it on the windows. Where were they going?

The gag[9]. It was choking her.[10] Breathe slowly through the nostrils. Neil. How could he breathe inside that sack? He would suffocate.

The car picked up speed[11]. Where was he taking them?

10

12. regardait distraitement par la fenêtre

13. Il faisait un temps de chien cette nuit-là

Roger Perry stared unseeingly out the window[12] of his living room on Driftwood Lane. It was a rotten night[13] and it was good to be home. He became aware of how much faster the snow was falling even in the fifteen minutes since he'd been in.

Funny[1], all day a sense[2] of apprehension had been making him edgy[3]. Glenda hadn't looked well these past couple of weeks[4]. That was it.[5] He always teased[6] her that she was one of those lucky women who grew better looking[7] with every birthday. Her hair, now pure silver[8], strikingly accentuated[9] her cornflower-blue[10] eyes and lovely complexion[11]. She'd been a size 14[12] when the boys were growing up but ten years ago had slimmed down to a size 8[13]. Just want to look good[14] in my declining years[15], she'd joked[16]. But this morning when he'd brought coffee to her in bed, he noticed how deadly pale she was[17], how thin her face looked. He'd phoned the doctor from the office and they'd agreed that it was the execution Wednesday that was weighing on her mind[18]. Her testimony[19] had helped convict[20] the Thompson boy.

Roger shook his head. It was a dreadful[21] business. Dreadful for that unfortunate boy, for everyone connected with it[22]. Steve ... little Neil ... the Thompson boy's mother ... Glenda. Glenda couldn't take this kind of strain[23]. She'd had a coronary[24] right after she testified at the trial[25]. Roger pushed back the fear that another attack might kill her. Glenda was only fifty-eight. Now that their boys were raised[26], he wanted these years with her. He couldn't do without her [27]

He was glad that she'd finally agreed to hiring a daily housekeeper[28]. Mrs. Vogler was to start in the morning and work weekdays[29] from nine till one. That way Glenda could rest more without worrying about the house.

He turned when he heard Glenda come into the room: She was carrying a small tray.

"I was just about to do that," he protested.

1. Bizarre
2. sentiment
3. à cran
4. n'était pas bien depuis deux semaines
5. C'était ça.
6. taquinait
7. embellissaient
8. d'un pur gris argenté
9. mettaient en valeur de façon saisissante
10. d'un bleu vif
11. son teint lumineux
12. taille 44
13. avait minci et faisait dorénavant du 38
14. paraître à mon avantage
15. au soir de ma vie
16. disait-elle en plaisantant
17. combien elle était pâle
18. l'accablait
19. témoignage
20. avait contribué à faire condamner
21. épouvantable
22. lié à cet événement
23. supporter une telle pression
24. infarctus
25. juste après avoir témoigné au procès
26. étaient grands
27. ne pouvait se passer d'elle
28. prendre une femme de ménage
29. du lundi au vendredi

"Never mind, you look as though you can use this." She handed him[1] a bourbon old-fashioned[2] and stood companionably[3] beside him at the window.

"I do need it. Thank you, dear." He noticed that she was sipping a Coke. If Glenda didn't have a predinner cocktail with him, it meant only one thing. "Chest pains[4] today?" But it was not a question.

"Just a few[5] …"

"How many nitros[6] did you take?"

"Only a couple[7]. Don't worry, I'm fine. Oh look! That's funny."

"What is?" Don't change the subject, Roger thought.

"Steve's house. The outside lights are off[8]."

"That's why it just seemed so dark to me," Roger said. He paused[9]. "I'm positive[10]. Steve's lights were on[11] when I came home."

"I wonder why anyone would turn them off[12]." Glenda's voice was troubled.[13] "Dora Lufts is so nervous[14]. Maybe you should take a walk over[15] …"

"Oh, I don't want to do that, dear. I'm sure there's a simple explanation."

She sighed. "I suppose. It's just that … well, what happened … has been on my mind so much[16] these days."

"I know it has." He put a comforting arm around her shoulders[17], felt the tension in her body. "Now, let's sit down and relax …"

"Wait, Roger, look!" She leaned forward. "There's a car pulling out of[18] Steve's driveway. The headlights aren't on. I wonder who …"

"Now you just stop wondering and sit down." Roger's tone was firm. "I'll get some cheese."

"The Brie is out on the table." Ignoring the gentle tug of his arm[19] on her elbow, Glenda reached into the pocket of her long quilted skirt[20] and pulled out her glasses[21]. Slipping them on[22], she bent forward again and stared at the dark, quiet outline of the

1. lui tendit
2. [cocktail à base de bourbon]
3. se tint affectueusement
4. Des douleurs à la poitrine
5. Quelques-unes seulement
6. comprimés de trinitrine
7. deux
8. éteintes
9. marqua un temps d'arrêt
10. catégorique
11. étaient allumées
12. les éteindrait
13. La voix de Glenda trahissait son inquiétude.
14. anxieuse
15. aller faire un saut
16. me préoccupe tellement
17. Il passa son bras autour de ses épaules pour la réconforter
18. qui sort de
19. légère pression de la main de Roger
20. longue jupe matelassée
21. sortit ses lunettes
22. Alors qu'elle les mettait

house diagonally across the road[1]. But the car she'd noticed coming from the Peterson driveway had already passed[2] her window and was disappearing down the block[3] into the swirling[4] snow.

11

"After all, tomorrow is another day." Crouched on the staircase[5], a lilt of hope[6] in her voice, Scarlett O'Hara murmured the final words and the music rose to a crescendo as the picture on the screen dissolved into a long view of[7] Tara.

Marian Vogler sighed as the music faded out[8] and the lights in the theater went up[9]. They don't make pictures[10] like that any more, she thought. She absolutely didn't want to see the sequel to[11] *Gone With the Wind*. It would just have to be a letdown[12].

She got to her feet[13] reluctantly. Time to come to earth.[14] Her pleasant, freckle-spattered[15] face slipped back into worried lines[16] as she walked up the carpeted, sloping floor to[17] the back of the theater.

Every one of the kids needed new clothes. Oh well, at least Jim had agreed that she could take the housekeeping job[18].

He'd arranged[19] to get a ride to the plant[20] so she could use the car. She'd have the kids off to school[21] and time to tidy up[22] before driving to the Perrys'. Tomorrow would be her first day on the job. She was a lit-

1. de l'autre côté de la rue
2. dépassé
3. au coin de la rue
4. tourbillonnante
5. Accroupie dans l'escalier
6. note d'espoir
7. se fondait en un long travelling sur
8. faiblissait
9. se rallumaient
10. de films
11. suite de
12. déception
13. se leva
14. Il était temps de redescendre sur terre.
15. parsemé de taches de rousseur
16. reprenait peu à peu son expression soucieuse
17. l'allée en pente, recouverte de moquette qui menait à
18. cette place de femme de ménage
19. pris toutes les dispositions
20. pour qu'on le conduise à l'usine
21. déposerait les enfants à l'école
22. aurait le temps de ranger la maison

tle nervous about it. She hadn't worked in twelve years … since young Jim was born. But if there was one thing she knew, it was how to keep a house shining[1].

She emerged from the warmth of the theater into the biting cold of the raw[2] March evening. Shivering, she turned right and began walking briskly[3]. Tiny pellets of sleet[4] mixed with snow bit at her face and she huddled[5] into the worn fur collar[6] of her coat.

The car was in the parking lot behind the theater. Thank God they'd decided to spend the money and have it fixed[7]. It was eight years old but the body[8] still looked all right, and as Jim said, better to spend the four hundred dollars to get it shipshape[9] than use the same money to buy another man's troubles[10].

Marian had walked so fast she was ahead of[11] most of the movie crowd. Expectantly[12], she hurried into the parking area. Jim had promised to have supper ready and she was hungry.

But it had done her good[13] to get out. He'd sensed her depression[14] and said, "Three bucks won't make or break us[15] and I'll take care of the kids[16]. Enjoy yourself, Babe[17], and forget the bills[18]."

His words echoed[19] in Marian's ears as she slowed and frowned[20]. She was sure that she'd parked the car over here to the right. She remembered that she'd been able to see the ad[21] in the bank window[22], the one about "we want to say *yes* to your loan[23]." Big deal[24], she thought. *Yes* if you don't need it, *no* if your guts are hanging out for it[25].

She had parked the car over here. She *had.* She could see the bank window, lighted up now, the ad prominent[26] even through the snow.

Ten minutes later, Marian called Jim from the police station[27]. Choking back[28] the angry, despairing tears that crowded her throat[29], she sobbed[30], "Jim … Jim … no … I'm all right … but Jim, some … some *bastard* stole[31] our car."

1. astiquer une maison
2. froid
3. d'un bon pas
4. Le grésil
5. s'emmitoufla
6. col en fourrure usé
7. réviser
8. carrosserie
9. la remettre en parfait état
10. un tacot susceptible de tomber en panne à la moindre occasion
11. était devant
12. Impatiente
13. cela lui avait fait du bien
14. qu'elle était déprimée
15. Trois dollars ne nous rendront pas plus riches ou plus pauvres
16. je m'occuperai des gosses
17. Amuse-toi bien, mon chou
18. factures
19. résonnaient
20. en fronçant les sourcils
21. publicité
22. vitrine
23. emprunt
24. La belle affaire
25. on en a désespérément besoin
26. bien visible
27. poste de police
28. Ravalant
29. lui nouaient la gorge
30. sanglota
31. un salaud a volé

12

As he drove through the thickening[1] snow, he reviewed his timetable[2]. Just about now this car should be missed[3]. The woman would probably walk around a bit to be sure she hadn't made a mistake about where she'd left it. Then she'd start screaming for the police or call home. By the time[4] the dispatcher put out a radio bulletin to squad cars[5], he'd be far away from the nosy[6] Connecticut cops[7].

Not that anybody would look very hard for this heap[8]. The cops would just roll their eyes when they heard an APB[9] for a stolen car worth[10] a couple of hundred bucks.

To have Sharon Martin in his possession! Excitement made his skin glisten[11]. He remembered the rush of warmth he felt when he tied her up. Her body was so slender[12] but her thighs and hips[13] were curved[14] and soft. He could feel that even through her heavy wool skirt. She had acted hostile and scared[15] when he carried her to the car, but he was sure that she deliberately nuzzled[16] her head against his side.

He had taken the Connecticut Turnpike[17] to the Hutchinson River Parkway south to the Cross County to the Henry Hudson Parkway. He felt safe[18] on

1. de plus en plus épaisse
2. passait en revue son plan de bataille
3. on avait dû constater la disparition de la voiture
4. Le temps que
5. l'information soit transmise par radio aux voitures de patrouille
6. fouineurs
7. flics
8. rechercherait activement ce tas de ferraille
9. alerte à toutes les patrouilles
10. valant
11. luire sa peau
12. svelte
13. ses cuisses et ses hanches
14. galbées
15. s'était montrée hostile et effrayée
16. avait blotti
17. [autoroute autrefois à péage]
18. en sécurité

the heavily traveled[1] roads. But by the time he was approaching the West Side Highway into downtown Manhattan[2], he was behind schedule[3]. Suppose, just suppose they *were* already watching for this car!

The other drivers were crawling along[4]. Fools.[5] Afraid of slippery[6] roads, afraid to take a chance[7], delaying him[8], making problems. The pulse in his cheekbone started to throb.[9] He felt the quickening, pressed one finger on it. He'd expected to go through the terminal by[10] seven at the latest before the commuter rush was over. They'd be less noticeable then.

It was ten past seven when he exited from the West Side Highway at Forty-sixth Street. He drove a half block east[11], then made a quick right turn into a driveway that wound behind a warehouse[12]. There were no guards here … and he only needed a minute.

Stopping the car, he turned off the lights[13]. Fine, powdery snow stung his eyes[14] and face when he opened the door. Cold. It was so damn cold[15].

With intense concentration, his eyes darted around the darkened parking area. Satisfied, he reached into the back of the car and lifted the coat he'd thrown over Sharon. He felt her eyes blazing up at him[16]. Laughing softly, he pulled out a tiny camera and snapped her picture[17]. The sudden flash made her blink. Now he extracted a pencil-thin flashlight[18] from his inside pocket. He waited until his hand was deep in the car to flip it on[19].

Deliberately he shone the narrow beam[20] of light in Sharon's eyes, moving it back and forth[21] slowly, an inch from her face[22], until she squeezed her eyes shut[23] and tried to turn her head.

It felt good to tease her. With a short, soundless laugh, he grabbed her shoulders[24] and forced her to lie on her stomach. Quick strokes of

1. très fréquentées
2. [sud de Manhattan]
3. avait pris du retard
4. avançaient à une allure d'escargot
5. Les imbéciles.
6. glissantes
7. des risques
8. le retardant
9. La veine sous sa pommette se mit à palpiter.
10. d'ici
11. parcourut un demi-pâté de maisons vers l'est
12. menait à l'arrière d'un entrepôt
13. éteignit les phares
14. lui piqua les yeux
15. sacrément froid
16. qu'elle le foudroyait du regard
17. la prit en photo
18. lampe de poche
19. l'allumer
20. faisceau
21. d'avant en arrière
22. à environ deux centimètres de son visage
23. finisse par fermer les yeux
24. l'agrippa par les épaules

the knife[1] sliced the cords on[2] her ankles and wrists. A faint sigh, muffled[3] by the gag, a shuddering movement[4] of her body …

"Feels pretty good, don't it[5], Sharon?" he whispered. "Now I'm going to take that gag off. If one scream comes out of you, the boy dies. Understand?"

He did not wait for the affirmative nod[6] before he cut the knotted cloth[7] at the back of her head. Sharon spat out[8] the wad of gauze in her mouth. Desperately she tried not to moan[9]. "Neil … please …" Her whisper was almost inaudible. "He'll suffocate …"

"That's up to you[10]." The stranger pulled her up[11], stood her on her feet next to the car. Vaguely, Sharon felt the snow on her face. She was so dizzy[12]. The muscles in her arms and legs were frantic with cramps[13]. She staggered[14], was roughly grabbed[15].

"Put this on." The voice was different now … urgent

She reached out[16], felt greasy, rough material… the coat that he'd thrown over her. She raised her arm. The man pulled the coat around her. Her other arm was thrust into it.[17]

"Put this scarf[18] on."

It felt so dirty. She tried to fold it. It was so big, woolly. Somehow[19] her fingers managed to knot it under her chin[20].

"Get back in the car. The faster we move, the faster the boy has that gag off[21]." Roughly, he pushed her into the front seat. The khaki bag was on the floor. She stumbled[22], trying to keep her boots from hitting it[23]. Leaning down, she ran her hands over the bag, felt the outline[24] of Neil's head. She realized that the drawstring wasn't tied[25]. At least Neil was getting air—"Neil, Neil, I'm here. We'll be all right, Neil …"

1. D'un rapide coup de couteau
2. il coupa les liens autour de
3. étouffé
4. frémissement
5. Ça fait plutôt du bien, n'est-ce pas
6. hochement de tête affirmatif
7. bout de tissu noué
8. recracha
9. gémir
10. La balle est dans votre camp.
11. la releva
12. étourdie
13. tétanisés
14. chancela
15. il la retint sans ménagement
16. tendit la main
17. Il lui fourra l'autre bras à l'intérieur.
18. foulard
19. Tant bien que mal,
20. menton
21. se verra retirer le bâillon
22. trébucha
23. d'éviter d'y donner un coup de pied
24. contour
25. le cordon n'était pas noué

Did she feel him moving? Oh God, don't let him strangle[1].

The stranger darted around the car, was in the driver's seat, turned the key in the engine[2]. The car moved cautiously forward.

We're in midtown[3]*!* The realization shocked Sharon, helped her to focus[4]. She had to be calm. She had to do whatever this man ordered. The car approached Broadway. She saw the Times Square billboard clock[5]: 7:20 ... it was only 7:20.

At this time last night, she'd just gotten home from Washington. She'd showered and put chops on[6] and sipped Chablis while they broiled[7]. She'd been tired and uptight[8] and trying to unwind[9] before writing her column.

And she'd thought about Steve, how missing him[10] had become a steady ache[11] over the three weeks they'd been apart[12].

He'd phoned. The sound of his voice brought a peculiar combination of pleasure and anxiety. But he'd kept the conversation brief, almost impersonal. "Hi[13] ... just wanted to be sure you got in all right. Understand[14] Washington has lousy weather[15] and it's heading our way[16]. I'll see you at the studio." Then he'd paused and added, "I've missed you. Don't forget you're staying with us tomorrow night."

She'd hung up[17], her need to see him intensified by talking with him and yet she'd somehow felt letdown[18] and worried. What did she want, anyhow? What would he think when he got home and found them missing[19]? Oh, Steve!

They stopped for a red light[20] on Sixth Avenue. A patrol car[21] drew up beside them[22]. Sharon watched as the young driver pushed his peaked uniform hat[23] back on his forehead. He glanced out the window[24] and their eyes locked[25]. Sharon felt the car begin to move. She kept her eyes directly on the policeman,

1. s'étouffer
2. tourna la clé de contact
3. dans le centre
4. fixer son attention
5. [horloge affichée sur un écran numérique diffusant des publicités]
6. mit des côtelettes à cuire
7. pendant qu'elle les faisait griller
8. très tendue
9. se détendre
10. à quel point le vide créé par son absence
11. douleur permanente
12. séparés
13. Salut
14. Je crois savoir
15. qu'il fait un temps pourri à Washington
16. se dirige vers nous
17. avait raccroché
18. déçue
19. constaterait leur absence
20. à un feu rouge
21. voiture de police
22. s'avança à leur hauteur
23. casquette
24. jeta un coup d'œil par la vitre
25. leurs yeux se croisèrent

willing him to keep looking at her[1], to sense something wrong[2].

She felt a sharp prodding against her side[3] and looked down. The stranger had the knife in his hand. "If we get followed now, you get it first[4]," he said. "I'll still have plenty of time for the boy."

There was icy matter-of-factness in his tone.[5] The patrol car was directly behind them. Its dome light[6] began flashing. Its siren began blasting[7]. "No! Please ..." In a burst of speed[8] the police car sped around them[9] and disappeared down the block.

They were turning south on Fifth Avenue. Pedestrian traffic was almost non-existent. It was too stormy, too icy to walk around New York.

The car made a quick left[10] onto Forty-fourth Street. Where was he taking them? Forty-fourth wasn't a through street[11]. It was blocked by Grand Central Station. Didn't he know that?[12]

The stranger drove the two blocks to Vanderbilt Avenue and turned right. He parked near the entrance to the Biltmore Hotel, directly opposite[13] the terminal.

"We're getting out," he said, his voice low. "We're going into[14] the terminal. Walk next to me[15]. Don't try anything. I'll be carrying the bag and if anybody pays any attention to us, the boy gets the knife." He looked down at Sharon. His eyes were glittering[16] again. A pulse throbbed in his cheek. "Understand?[17]"

She nodded. Could Neil hear him?

"Wait a minute." He was staring at her. Reaching past her into the glove compartment[18], he pulled out dark glasses[19]. "Put these on."

He pushed the door open[20], looked around, and stepped out[21] quickly. The street was deserted. Only a few cabs were lined up[22] in the enclosed drive-

1. souhaitant ardemment qu'il continue à la regarder
2. et qu'il comprenne que quelque chose clochait
3. un objet pointu lui rentrer dans les côtes
4. le premier coup sera pour vous
5. Le ton de sa voix était neutre et glacial.
6. gyrophare
7. à hurler
8. Accélérant brusquement
9. les dépassa à vive allure
10. tourna rapidement à gauche
11. était une voie sans issue
12. L'ignorait-il ?
13. juste en face de
14. allons entrer dans
15. à côté de moi
16. étincelaient
17. Compris ?
18. boîte à gants
19. des lunettes noires
20. poussa la porte pour l'ouvrir
21. sortit
22. faisaient la queue

1. la file qui leur était réservée devant
2. à des kilomètres
3. sentit soudain une vive douleur à la main gauche
4. avait tourné
5. monture en or
6. lui avait fait une entaille
7. enleva la bague
8. l'enfoncer partiellement
9. D'un pas chancelant
10. trottoir
11. lui saisit le poignet
12. quand il l'avait détachée
13. retint son souffle
14. se pencha
15. serra le cordon
16. fit un nœud
17. lame
18. presque entièrement dissimulée dans
19. la manche ample de son manteau
20. directement
21. son compte est bon
22. Allez !
23. De son autre main, il la tenait par le coude
24. à son pas
25. quelconques à tous égards
26. dans le hall qui donnait sur
27. à quelques pas, sur

way at[1] the terminal. There was no one to see them or care …

He's taking us on a train, Sharon thought. We'll be miles away[2] before anyone even begins to look for us!

She became aware of a stinging in her left hand[3]. The ring! The antique moonstone ring Steve had given her for Christmas … it had turned sideways[4] when her hands were tied. The raised gold setting[5] had been cutting her[6]. Almost without thinking, Sharon slipped the ring off[7]. She just had time to force it partly down[8] into the seat cushion before the car door opened.

Unsteadily[9], she got out and onto the slippery sidewalk[10]. The man gripped her wrist with his hand[11] and looked carefully around inside the car. He quickly leaned down and picked up the gag that had been on her mouth, the cords he had cut when releasing her[12]. Sharon held her breath[13]. But he didn't notice the ring.

He bent down[14] and picked up the duffel bag, pulled the drawstring tight[15] and knotted the ends[16]. Neil could suffocate with that bag closed.

"Look." She stared at the blade[17] in his hand that was nearly concealed by[18] his loose overcoat sleeve[19]. "This is pointed right[20] at the kid's heart. You try anything and he gets it[21]."

"Come on[22]!" His other hand was at her elbow.[23] He was forcing her to walk in step with him[24] across the street. They were a man and woman hurrying out of the cold into the terminal, nondescript in every way[25], anonymous in their cheap clothes with duffel bag instead of suitcase.

Even behind the dark glasses, the brightly lit terminal made Sharon blink. They stood on the concourse overlooking[26] the main terminal. There was a newsstand a few feet to[27] their left. The vendor looked at them indifferently. They started down the steps to the first landing[1]. The huge Kodak display[2] caught Sharon's eye. It read[3], "Capture beauty where you find it ..."

An hysterical laugh threatened[4] to escape her lips. *Capture? Capture?* The clock. The famous clock over the center of the Information Booth[5] in the middle of the terminal. It was harder to see now that the investment office counter[6] had been built in front of it. Sharon had read somewhere that when the six red lights around the clock's base were flashing[7], it signaled an emergency to Grand Central's private police force. What would they think if they knew what was happening now?

It was 7:29. Steve. *Steve was catching the 7:30.* He was here right now[8] ... in a train in this terminal, a train that in a minute would be taking him away. Steve, she wanted to shriek[9] ... Steve ...

Steely[10] fingers bit into her arm[11]. "Down here.[12]" He was forcing her to go down the stairs to the lower terminal. The rush hour was over. There weren't many people in the main terminal ... there were even fewer going down the stairs. Should she try to fall ... draw attention to them[13]? No ... she couldn't take the chance[14], not with that burly[15] arm encircling the duffel bag, that knife ready to plunge into Neil ...

They were on the lower level. Over to the right[16] she could see the entrance to the Oyster Bar. She and Steve had met[17] there for a quick lunch last month. They'd sat at the counter and had steaming[18] bowls of oyster stew[19] ... Steve, find us, help us ...

She was being pushed toward[20] the left. "We're going down there ... not so fast ..." Track[21] 112. The sign said[22] "Mount Vernon—8:10." A train must have just left. Why would he go there?

1. étage
2. panneau publicitaire
3. On pouvait y lire
4. faillit
5. Point Information
6. guichet du bureau de placements
7. clignotaient
8. à cet instant même
9. hurler
10. d'acier
11. s'enfoncèrent comme une morsure dans son bras
12. Par ici.
13. d'attirer l'attention sur eux
14. courir le risque
15. costaud
16. Sur la droite
17. s'étaient retrouvés
18. fumants
19. ragoût
20. On la poussait vers
21. Voie
22. panneau indiquait

To the left of the ramp leading down to the tracks Sharon saw a shabby[1] old woman carrying a shopping bag. She was bundled[2] in a man's jacket over a ragged woolen skirt[3]. Thick cotton stockings[4] drooped on[5] her legs. The woman was staring at her. Did she realize something was wrong?

"Keep moving[6] ..."

They were going down the ramp on the 112 platform. Their footsteps echoed, a pinging sound[7] on metal steps[8]. The murmur of voices receded[9], the warmth of the terminal was vanquished by a clammy cold draft[10].

The platform was deserted.

"Around here.[11]" He was forcing her to move faster now, around the end of the platform[12] where the track terminated, down another ramp. Water was trickling[13] nearby[14]. Where were they going? The dark glasses made it hard to see here. A rhythmic, throbbing sound[15] ... a pump ... a pneumatic pump ... they were going down into the depths of the terminal ... far underground[16]. What was he going to do to them? She could hear the rumbling sounds[17] of trains ... there must be a tunnel nearby ...

The concrete[18] floor was still sloping down[19]. The passage widened[20]. They were in an area half the size of a football field; an area of thick pipes[21] and shafts[22] and rumbling motors. To the left, about twenty feet[23], there was a narrow staircase.

"Over there[24]... hurry up!" Now his breath was coming in harsh gasps[25]. She could hear him puffing[26] as he followed her. She scrambled up[27] the staircase, unconsciously counting the steps ... ten ... eleven ... twelve. She was on a narrow landing[28], facing a thick metal door.

"Move over[29]." She felt the heaviness of his body against her and shrank away[30]. He set down the duffel bag, glanced at her quickly. In the dim[31] light she

1. misérable
2. emmitouflée
3. jupe de laine en loques
4. bas
5. pendouillaient sur
6. Avancez
7. faisant un bruit métallique
8. marches
9. s'estompait
10. laissait place à un courant d'air froid et humide
11. Par ici.
12. en suivant l'extrémité du quai
13. s'écoulait en un mince filet
14. à proximité
15. vrombissement
16. dans les profondeurs de la terre
17. grondements
18. en béton
19. continuait à descendre en pente
20. s'élargit
21. canalisations
22. conduits
23. à environ six mètres
24. Par là
25. était entrecoupée de halètements rauques
26. souffler
27. grimpa avec difficulté
28. palier étroit
29. Poussez-vous
30. eut un mouvement de recul
31. faible

saw shiny beads of perspiration glistening on[1] his forehead. He pulled out a key, put it in the lock. A grating sound[2] and the handle turned. He pushed the door open, thrust her in[3] before him. She heard him grunt[4] as he picked up the duffel bag again. The door closed behind them. Through the clammy[5] darkness she heard the snap of a switch[6].

A half-second delay and the dusty overhead fluorescent lights blinked on[7].

Sharon looked around at the filthy[8], damp room, at rusty sinks, a boarded-up shaft, a sagging cot, an overturned crate, an old black suitcase on the floor.

"Where are we? What do you want with us?" Her voice was a near-whisper[9] but took on an echo sound in this dungeon-like[10] room.

Her abductor didn't answer. Pushing her forward, he hurried toward the cot. He laid the duffel bag on it, then flexed[11] his arms. Dropping to her knees, Sharon fumbled with the drawstring on the bag.

At last she had it untied, was pulling it apart, pulling the bag down, reaching for the small, crumbled figure[12]. She freed Neil's head. Frantically, she tugged at[13] the gag, pulling it down[14] over his chin.

Neil gasped[15], clawing for air[16], his breath harsh and sobbing. She heard the wheeze in his breath[17], felt the jerking[18] of his chest. Supporting[19] his head with her arm, she began to tug at the blindfold[20].

"Let that alone![21]" The order was sharp, violent.

"Please," she cried, "he's sick … he's having an asthma attack. Help him."

She looked up, then bit her lips to force back[22] a scream.

Over the army cot, three enormous pictures were taped[23] to the wall.

A young woman running, hands outstretched[24], looking back over her shoulder, terror stamped on her face[25] … her mouth a twisted, screaming arc[26].

1. vit briller les gouttes de sueur qui perlaient sur
2. grincement
3. la poussa violemment à l'intérieur
4. grogner
5. moite
6. l'entendit appuyer sur un interrupteur
7. les néons poussiéreux au plafond clignotèrent
8. crasseuse
9. n'était qu'un murmure
10. aux allures de cachot
11. fléchit
12. silhouette recroquevillée
13. tira sur
14. l'abaissant
15. haleta
16. cherchant l'air désespérément
17. sa respiration sifflante
18. mouvements saccadés
19. Soutenant
20. bandeau qui couvrait ses yeux
21. N'y touchez pas !
22. pour réprimer
23. scotchées
24. tendues devant elle
25. le visage empreint de terreur
26. la bouche arrondie et déformée par un hurlement

A blond woman lying by a car, her legs jack-knifed[1] under her.

A dark-haired teenager with one hand raised to her throat, a look of puzzled detachment[2] settling into her staring eyes[3].

1. repliées
2. air détaché empreint de perplexité
3. s'installant dans ses yeux fixes

13

Long ago Lally had been a schoolteacher in Nebraska. Finally retired[4], alone, she had come to New York for a visit. She never went back home.

The night she'd arrived in Grand Central Station was the turning point[5]. Bewildered and awed[6], she'd carried her one suitcase across the enormous Concourse, looked up, and stopped. She was one of the few[7] to realize immediately that the sky on the great vaulted ceiling[8] had been painted on backward[9]. The eastern stars were in the west.

She'd laughed aloud. Her lips parted[10], revealing two enormous front teeth. People glanced her way, then hurried along[11]. Their reaction had delighted her[12]. At home if Lally were seen looking up and laughing by herself[13], it would be all over town[14] the next day.

She checked her suitcase in a locker[15], and washed up[16] in the main-floor ladies' room[17], smoothing[18] her shapeless brown wool skirt, buttoning the thick cardigan sweater. Finally she combed[19] the short

4. à la retraite
5. tournant
6. Déroutée et impressionnée
7. était l'une des rares personnes
8. voûte
9. à l'envers
10. étaient entrouvertes
11. sans s'arrêter
12. l'avait réjouie
13. et de rire toute seule
14. toute la ville l'aurait su
15. déposa sa valise à la consigne
16. fit un brin de toilette
17. toilettes pour dames au rez-de-chaussée
18. défroissant
19. donna un coup de peigne à

gray hair, plastering it damply around[1] her broad, chinless face[2].

For the next six hours Lally had toured[3] the terminal, taking a childish delight in the bustling, rushing crowds. She ate at a counter in one of the small, cheap lunch-stands[4], window-shopped[5] in the corridors[6] leading to the hotels, and finally returned to settle down[7] in the main waiting room[8].

Fascinated, she watched a young mother breastfeed[9] a screaming baby, stared at a young couple passionately embracing, followed the progress of a card game four men were playing.

The crowd thinned, swelled[10], thinned out again under the signs of the zodiac. It was nearly midnight when she noticed that one group had stayed a long time, six men and a tiny[11], birdlike woman who were clustered together[12], talking with the easy camaraderie of[13] old friends.

The woman seemed to notice her watching them and came over to her[14]. "You new here?" Her voice was raspy[15] but kind. Earlier Lally had seen this woman take a newspaper from a disposal bin[16].

"Yes," she said.

"Got any place to go?"

Lally had a reservation at the Y[17] but some instinct made her lie. "No."

"Just arrived here?"

"Yes."

"Got any money?"

"Not much." Another lie[18].

"Well, don't worry. We'll show you around[19]. We're the regulars[20]." Her arm jerked backward toward the group.[21]

"You live near here then?" Lally asked.

A smile quirked the woman's eyes, revealed decaying[22] teeth. "No, we live *here*. I'm Rosie Bidwell."

1. les aplatissant en les mouillant autour
2. visage large, au menton fuyant
3. visité
4. buffets
5. fit du lèche-vitrines
6. galeries marchandes
7. s'installer
8. salle d'attente
9. donner le sein
10. diminuait, grossissait
11. minuscule
12. s'étaient rassemblés
13. ce ton de franche camaraderie qui caractérise
14. s'avança vers elle
15. rauque
16. poubelle
17. [YMCA, sorte d'auberge de jeunesse]
18. mensonge
19. allons te faire visiter
20. habitués
21. D'un geste, elle désigna le groupe derrière elle.
22. cariées

In all her cheerless sixty-two years[1], Lally had never had a close friend. Rosie Bidwell changed that. Soon Lally was accepted as one of the regulars. She got rid of[2] the suitcase and like Rosie, kept all her possessions in shopping bags. She learned the routine … dawdling over cheap meals[3] in the Automat[4], occasional showers in the public bath house[5] in the Village[6], sleeping in flop houses[7], dollar a night hotels[8], or at the Salvation Army center.

Or … in her own room in Grand Central.

That was the one secret Lally kept from[9] Rosie. A tireless explorer, she'd become familiar with every inch[10] of her terminal. She climbed the stairs behind the orange doors on the platforms and wandered around[11] the gloomy cavernous area between the floor of the upper level and the ceiling of the lower level. She found the hidden[12] staircase that connected the two ladies' rooms and when the downstairs one was closed for repairs, she often slipped down that staircase[13] and spent the night there with no one the wiser[14].

She even walked along the tracks of the tunnel that yawned[15] under Park Avenue, flattening herself against the concrete wall when a train thundered by[16] and sharing scraps of food[17] with the hungry cats that prowled[18] the tunnel.

But she was especially fascinated by the area right in the depths of the station that the guards called Sing-Sing[19]. With its pumps and vents[20] and airshafts and generators throbbing and creaking and groaning[21] it was like being part of the very heartbeat[22] of her station. The unmarked door at the head of[23] a narrow staircase in Sing-Sing intrigued her. Cautiously, she'd mentioned it to one of the security guards who became a good friend. Rusty said that was only the miserable hole where they used to wash dishes for the Oyster Bar and she had no busi-

1. Au cours des 62 années de sa morne existence
2. se débarrassa de
3. traînant en quête de repas bon marché
4. cafétéria dotée de distributeurs automatiques
5. bains publics
6. [Greenwich Village]
7. des asiles de nuit
8. des hôtels à 1 dollar la nuit
9. ne confia pas à
10. s'était familiarisée avec le moindre recoin
11. flânait dans
12. caché
13. se faufilait souvent dans cet escalier
14. à l'insu de tous
15. s'étirait
16. passait dans un grondement de tonnerre
17. des restes de nourriture
18. rôdaient dans
19. [prison de l'État de New York, peut-être un jeu de mots par rapport au bruit ambiant]
20. conduits
21. qui vibraient, grinçaient et gémissaient
22. comme se trouver au cœur même
23. en haut d'

ness in that area[1]. But she'd worn him down[2] until he took her to see the room.

She'd been delighted with it. The musty[3], peeling walls and ceilings didn't bother her[4] at all. The room was large. The lights and sinks worked. There was even the tiny cubbyhole[5] with the toilet. She'd known immediately that this place would fill her one remaining need, for occasional absolute privacy[6].

"Room and bath[7]," she said. "Rusty, let me sleep here."

He'd looked shocked[8]. "No way![9] It'd cost me my job." But she'd worn him down on that, too, and every once in a while[10] he'd let her spend a night there. Then one day she managed to borrow his key for a few hours and secretly had another one made from it. When Rusty retired she made the room her own[11].

Little by little, Lally carried objects up the steps, a dilapidated[12] canvas army cot, a lumpy mattress[13], an orange crate.

She began to stay there regularly. That was what she liked best of all, to sleep in the womblike darkness[14], tucked[15] in the very depth of her station, to hear the faint roar and rumble[16] of trains that became less and less frequent as the night grew late[17], then accelerated again into the morning frenzy[18].

Sometimes lying there, she thought about teaching *Phantom of the Opera*[19] to her classes. "And under that beautiful, gilded[20] opera house, there was another world," she'd told them, "a world dark and mysterious, a world of alleys[21] and sewers[22] and dampness where a man could hide away from everyone[23]."

The only cloud on her horizon was the awful, gnawing fear[24] that someday they'd tear her station down[25]. When the Committee to Save Grand Central held the rally[26], she'd been there, unobtrusively[27] in

1. n'avait rien à y faire
2. était revenue à la charge
3. moisis
4. ne la gênaient pas
5. cagibi
6. intimité
7. Chambre avec salle de bains
8. avait eu l'air scandalisé
9. Pas question !
10. de temps à autre,
11. transforma cette pièce en un lieu bien à elle
12. délabré
13. matelas défoncé
14. cocon obscur
15. bien à l'abri
16. faible grondement
17. avançait
18. agitation matinale
19. [Le Fantôme de l'Opera, roman inspiré de faits survenus à l'Opéra Garnier]
20. plein de dorures
21. de couloirs
22. d'égouts
23. se cacher de tous
24. cette peur horrible qui la rongeait
25. on rase sa gare
26. avait organisé un rassemblement
27. se tenant discrètement

a corner, but applauding loudly[1] when all the celebrities like Jackie Onassis said that Grand Central Terminal was a part of the tradition of New York and should never be destroyed.

But even though they had managed to get it designated as an historical landmark[2], Lally knew there were still plenty of people trying to get it pulled down[3]. No, God, please, not my station!

She never used her room during the winter. It was too cold and damp. But from May till September she stayed there about twice a week, just infrequently enough[4] so the cops didn't catch her, so Rosie didn't get curious.

Six years passed, the best six years of Lally's life. She came to know all the guards, the paper vendors[5], the countermen[6]. She recognized the faces of commuters, knew which ones took which trains, at what time. She even grew to know[7] the faces of the drinkers who usually caught the late trains home[8], hurrying unsteadily[9] to their platforms.

That Monday evening, Lally was meeting Rosie in the main waiting room. She'd had severe arthritis over the winter. That was the only thing that had kept her from going[10] to her room. But it had been six months now and suddenly she felt she couldn't wait any longer to use it again. "I'll just go down and see how it looks[11]," she thought. Maybe if it wasn't too cold, she'd even sleep there tonight. But probably not[12].

She walked heavily down the stairs[13] to the lower terminal. There weren't many people there. Carefully, she moseyed around[14], watching for the[15] policemen. She couldn't take a chance of being spotted[16] going to the room. They'd never let her stay there, not even the nice guys[17].

She noticed a family with three young children. Nice-looking[18], all of them. She liked children and

1. elle avait applaudi à tout rompre
2. monument historique
3. la faire démolir
4. assez rarement
5. vendeurs de journaux
6. serveurs
7. finit même par connaître
8. regagnaient leur domicile par le dernier train
9. d'un pas chancelant
10. l'avait empêchée de se rendre
11. si tout est en ordre
12. c'était improbable
13. descendit d'un pas lourd les escaliers
14. déambula d'un pas tranquille
15. faisant attention aux
16. qu'on la remarque
17. braves gars
18. Ils étaient beaux

she'd been a good teacher, too. After the class finished making fun of her homeliness[1], she usually got along well with her pupils[2]. Not that she'd want those days back, not for anything[3].

She was about to drift down[4] the ramp to track 112 when her attention was caught by a tattered, scarlet lining[5] drooping[6] below an old gray coat.

Lally recognized the coat. She'd tried it on in a Second Avenue thrift shop the week before. There couldn't be two like that, not with that lining. Her curiosity piqued[7], she studied the face of the woman wearing the coat and was surprised to see how young and pretty she was behind the scarf and dark glasses.

The man she was with ... he was someone Lally had seen around the station lately. Lally noticed the expensive leather boots the girl was wearing; the kind the people wore who traveled the Connecticut line[8].

Funny combination[9], she thought. A thrift coat[10] and those boots. Now fully interested, she watched the couple cross the terminal. The bag the man was carrying seemed pretty[11] heavy. She frowned when she saw them go down to track 112. There wouldn't be a train for another forty minutes. Crazy[12], she thought. Why wait on the platform? It's cold and damp.

She shrugged. That settled that.[13] She couldn't go to her room with them on the platform to see her. She'd have to wait until tomorrow.

Philosophically dismissing her disappointment[14], Lally headed for the main waiting room in search of Rosie.

1. Une fois que ses élèves avaient fini de se moquer de sa laideur
2. s'entendait bien avec eux
3. pour rien au monde
4. descendre tranquillement
5. doublure écarlate en lambeaux
6. pendouillant
7. Cela éveilla sa curiosité et
8. empruntait la ligne du Connecticut pour leurs déplacements
9. Étrange association
10. manteau acheté dans une friperie
11. assez
12. C'est dingue
13. La question était réglée.
14. Ravalant sa déception avec philosophie

14

1. bon sang
2. avocat
3. appuya sur la touche « enregistrement »
4. magnétophone
5. couchette
6. arpenta nerveusement
7. cellule
8. barreaux de la fenêtre
9. se détourna
10. À quoi bon ?
11. La lèvre du jeune homme de 19 ans se mit à trembler.
12. L'expression de son visage
13. se passa la main sur les yeux
14. accorder sa grâce
15. sursis
16. n'a pas réussi

"Talk, Ron, talk, damn you[1]!" The dark-haired attorney[2] depressed the "record" button[3]. The cassette player[4] was on the bunk[5] between the two seated young men.

"No!" Ron Thompson got up, walked restlessly across[6] the narrow cell[7] and stared out through the barred window[8]. Quickly he turned away[9]. "Even snow looks dirty here," he said, "dirty and gray and cold. Do you want to record that?"

"No, I don't." Bob Kurner stood up and put his arms on the boy's shoulders. "Ron, please ..."

"What good?[10] What good?" The nineteen-year-old's lip quivered.[11] His expression[12] changed, became young and defenseless. Quickly he bit his lip, brushed a hand across his eyes[13]. "Bob, you did your best ... I know you did. But there's nothing anyone can do now."

"Nothing except give the Governor a reason why she should grant executive clemency[14] ... even a stay[15] ... even a stay, Ron."

"But you've tried ... that writer Sharon Martin ... if she couldn't[16] with all the important signatures she got ..."

"Damn that stinking Sharon Martin to hell![1]" Bob Kurner clenched his hands into fists[2]. "Damn all these do-gooders[3] who don't know their way out of a paper bag[4]. She loused you up[5], Ron. We had a petition going[6], a *real* one from people who know you, people who know you're incapable of hurting anyone, and she goes screaming all over the country that of course you're guilty[7] but you shouldn't die. She made it impossible[8] for the Governor to commute your sentence—*impossible.*"

"Then why waste your time[9]? If it's no use[10], if it's hopeless[11], I don't want to talk about it anymore!"

"You've got to![12]" Bob Kurner's voice softened as he looked into the younger man's eyes. There was a compelling directness[13] and honesty in them. Bob thought of himself at[14] nineteen. Ten years ago he'd been a sophomore[15] at Villanova[16]. Ron had been planning to go to college... instead he was going to die in the electric chair. Even the two years in prison hadn't made his muscular body flabby[17]. Ron exercised regularly in his cell, he was such a disciplined kid. But he'd lost twenty pounds[18] and his face was chalk white[19].

"Look," Bob said, "there's got to be something somewhere that I missed[20] ..."

"You didn't miss anything."

"Ron, I defended you but you *didn't* kill Nina Peterson and you *were* convicted[21]. If we can just find one piece of evidence[22] to take to the Governor ... one valid reason[23] to make it possible for her to grant you a stay[24]. We've got forty-two hours ... only forty-two hours."

"You just said she won't commute any sentence."

Bob Kurner bent down and snapped off[25] the cassette player. "Ron, maybe I shouldn't tell you this. God knows it's a long shot[26]. But listen to me. When you were convicted of Nina Peterson's murder, a lot

1. Que cette Sharon Martin de malheur aille au diable !
2. serra les poings
3. bonnes âmes
4. sont de véritables empotés
5. a foutu en l'air toutes tes chances
6. pétition qui circulait
7. coupable
8. a agi de telle sorte qu'il était impossible
9. perdre votre temps
10. Si tout cela est inutile
11. sans espoir
12. Il le faut !
13. droiture incontestable
14. lorsqu'il avait
15. étudiant de deuxième année
16. [université privée dans la banlieue de Philadelphie]
17. ramolli son corps musclé
18. environ 10 kilos
19. d'un blanc crayeux
20. qui m'a échappé
21. reconnu coupable
22. élément de preuve
23. motif valable
24. t'accorder un sursis
25. arrêta
26. que les chances sont très minces

1. meurtres non résolus
2. Ils n'ont pas cessé de me cuisiner à ce sujet
3. déblayé
4. C'était dans l'ordre des choses que l'on t'interroge
5. jusqu'à présent
6. comté
7. présenter un élément
8. avancer un argument
9. lien
10. pénible
11. les épreuves que tu traverses actuellement
12. le nombre de fois où
13. t'es repassé dans la tête le déroulement de cette journée
14. s'écarta
15. enregistrée avec netteté
16. Fronçant les sourcils sous l'effet de la concentration
17. hésitante
18. faisait ses courses
19. me mettre à la porte
20. temps libre dont j'avais besoin pour m'entraîner au baseball
21. à mettre ses provisions dans la voiture

of people felt that you were guilty of committing those two other unsolved murders[1]. You know that."

"They asked me enough about them[2] ..."

"You went to school with the Carfolli girl. You'd shoveled[3] snow for Mrs. Weiss. It made sense to ask[4]. That's just normal procedure. Then after you were arrested there weren't any more murders—*till now*[5]. Ron, there have been two more murders of young women in Fairfield County[6] in the last month. If we can just introduce something[7], some doubt, come up with something[8] that might suggest a link[9] between Nina Peterson's death and the others."

He put his arms around the boy. "Ron, I know how lousy[10] this is for you. I can only guess what you're going through[11]. But you've told me how often[12] you go over that day in your mind[13]. Maybe there's something ... something that didn't seem important, some detail. If you'd just *talk*."

Ron pulled himself away[14], walked over to the bunk and sat down. He depressed the "record" button on the cassette player and turned his head so that his voice would be picked up clearly[15]. Frowning in concentration[16], his voice halting[17], he began to speak.

"I was working that afternoon after school in Timberly's Market. Mrs. Peterson was in shopping[18]. Mr. Timberly had just told me that he was going to fire me[19] because of the time I needed off for baseball practice[20]. She heard him. When I helped her to the car with the groceries[21], she said ..."

15

The train pulled into the Carley station[1] at nine o'clock. By then[2] Steve's frantic impatience had settled into[3] deep, gnawing worry. He should have phoned the doctor. If Neil were sick Sharon might have taken him for an injection[4]. Maybe that was why there was no answer.

Sharon had come. He was sure of that. She simply wouldn't have changed her mind[5] without calling him.

Maybe it was just that the phones were going fluky[6]. And if he'd missed this train, God knows when the next one would get in[7]. The conductor said something about the tracks freezing.

Something was wrong. He felt it. He knew it.

But maybe it was the execution coming up[8] that had him so rattled, so apprehensive[9]. God, the paper tonight had rehashed the whole mess[10]. Nina's picture on the front page[11]. The caption[12] "Youth[13] to die for brutal murder of young Connecticut mother."

Thompson's picture next to hers. A nice-looking kid. Hard to believe he'd been capable of cold-blooded murder[14].

Nina's picture. Over and over[15] on the long train ride[16], Steve found himself staring down at it. The

1. entra en gare de Carley
2. À ce moment-là
3. laissé place à
4. piqûre
5. changé d'avis
6. lignes téléphoniques étaient capricieuses
7. serait arrivé
8. l'approche de l'exécution
9. le secouait ainsi, le rendait si inquiet
10. remis sur le tapis tout cet imbroglio
11. à la une
12. légende
13. Un jeune
14. de commettre un meurtre de sang-froid
15. À maintes reprises
16. trajet

reporters had all clamored for[1] a photograph at the time of the murder, but he cursed himself[2] for letting them make copies of this one. It had been his favorite; a snapshot[3] he'd taken of her with the breeze blowing the dark curls[4] around her face, and the small straight nose wrinkled a little the way it always had when[5] she laughed. And the scarf tied loosely around her neck. It was only afterward that he'd realized that was the scarf Thompson had used to strangle her.

Oh Christ!

Steve was the first one waiting to rush out[6] when the train finally arrived at Carley forty minutes late[7]. Racing down[8] the slippery platform stairs, he hurried into the parking lot and attempted to brush the snow from the windshield[9] of his car. A thin, ice-crusted layer[10] resisted his efforts. Impatiently, he opened the trunk[11] and reached for the de-icer[12] and scraper[13].

The last time he'd seen Nina alive[14] she'd driven him to the train. He'd noticed that the balding spare tire[15] was on her right front wheel. Then she'd admitted that she had a flat[16] the night before and was riding around without a spare[17].

He'd been ticked off[18] and exploded at her[19]. "You shouldn't be riding on that lousy tire. Damn it, honey[20], your carelessness will get you killed."

Will get you killed!

She'd promised to pick up the other tire right away[21]. At the station, he'd started to get out of the car without kissing her goodbye[22]. But she'd leaned over and her kiss had brushed[23] his cheek, and with that familiar ripple of laughter[24] in her voice, she'd said, "Have a good day, Grouchy[25]. I love you."

He hadn't answered her, or looked back at her[26], just run for his train. He'd debated about[27] calling her from the office but told himself that he wanted

1. réclamé
2. se maudissait
3. photo
4. le vent balayant ses boucles noires
5. un peu plissé, comme à chaque fois qu'
6. descendre précipitamment
7. avec quarante minutes de retard
8. Dévalant
9. pare-brise
10. couche fine et givrée
11. coffre
12. dégivreur
13. la raclette
14. en vie
15. pneu de rechange lisse
16. crevaison
17. roue de secours
18. pété les plombs
19. s'était emporté contre elle
20. chérie
21. aussitôt
22. l'embrasser avant de partir
23. effleuré
24. rire discret
25. Grincheux
26. ne s'était pas retourné pour la regarder
27. s'était demandé s'il devait

her to think he was really upset with her[1]. He worried about her. She was careless in ways that mattered[2]. A couple of nights, when he'd worked late, he'd come home to find her and Neil asleep and the door unlocked[3].

And so he hadn't called, hadn't made up with her[4]. And when he got off the 5:30 train that night, Roger Perry was waiting for him at the station, waiting to ride home with him[5] and tell him that Nina was dead.

And then nearly two years of bleak pain[6] until that morning six months ago when he'd been introduced to the other guest on the *Today* show, Sharon Martin.

The windshield was clear enough. Steve got in the car, turned the key, and barely giving the engine time to catch[7], put his foot on the gas[8]. He wanted to get home and find Neil all right He wanted to make Neil happy again. He wanted to put his arms around Sharon and hold her. Tonight he wanted to hear her moving around in the guest room[9], know that she was near. They'd have to work it out[10]. Nothing could be allowed to spoil it between them[11]

The five-minute drive took fifteen minutes. The roads were a sheet of ice[12]. At one "stop" sign he put his foot on the brake[13] and the car just slid onto the intersection[14]. Thank God there was no one coming.

At last he turned onto Driftwood Lane. It seemed uncommonly[15] dark to him. It was *his* place[16]—the lights were off! A shock of fear tensed his body. Ignoring the slippery road, he floored the accelerator[17] and the car shot forward[18], careened down the block[19]. He turned into his driveway and jammed to a halt[20] behind Sharon's car. Racing up the stairs, he thrust[21] his key in the lock and pushed the front door open. "Sharon ... Neil," he called. "Sharon ... Neil ..."

1. fâché contre elle
2. insouciante à bien des égards
3. n'était pas fermée à clé
4. ne s'était pas réconcilié avec elle
5. pour le ramener à la maison
6. douleur infinie
7. au moteur le temps de démarrer
8. appuya sur l'accélérateur
9. chambre d'amis
10. trouver une solution
11. venir gâcher leur relation
12. vraie patinoire
13. freina
14. jusqu'au milieu du carrefour
15. anormalement
16. sa maison
17. écrasa l'accélérateur au plancher
18. fit un bond en avant
19. passa à tout allure devant le pâté de maisons
20. stoppa net
21. introduisit

Chilling[1] silence offset[2] the warmth of the foyer[3], made his hands clammy. "Sharon … Neil," he called again.

He looked into the living room. Papers were scattered on the floor. Neil must have been doing cut-outs[4]; there were scissors and scraps on one open page. An untouched cup of cocoa and a glass of sherry were on the small end table[5] near the fireplace. Hurrying over, Steve felt the cup. The cocoa was cold. He rushed into the kitchen, noticed the saucepan in the sink, then ran down the hall to the den[6]. The sense of danger was overwhelming, stifling[7]. The den was empty too. A fire was flickering in the hearth[8]. He'd asked Bill to make one before he left.

Not knowing what he was looking for, Steve raced from the[9] den back to the foyer and noticed Sharon's overnight bag and purse[10]. He opened the door of the guest. Her cape was there! What would make her rush out without it? Neil! Neil must have had one of those violent attacks, the kind that come on so suddenly, that almost suffocated him.

Steve raced to the phone on the kitchen wall. The emergency numbers[11]—hospital, police, fire[12], their own doctor—were clearly listed. He called the doctor's office[13] first. The nurse[14] was still there. "No, Mr. Peterson, we didn't get a call about Neil. Is there anything …"

He hung up without explaining.

He called the emergency room[15] at the hospital. "We have no record[16] …"

Where were they? What happened to them? His breath was coming in hard gasps.[17] He looked at the wall clock. Nine-twenty. Nearly two hours since he'd tried to phone home. They'd been gone at least that long[18]. The Perrys! Maybe they'd gone across[19] the

1. glaçant
2. contrastait avec
3. entrée
4. des découpages
5. table basse
6. emprunta au pas de course le couloir jusqu'au bureau
7. le submergeait, l'étouffait
8. était allumé dans la cheminée
9. revint à toute allure du
10. son sac à main
11. numéros d'urgence
12. les pompiers
13. cabinet du médecin
14. infirmière
15. urgences
16. n'avons aucune trace d'un appel
17. Il respirait avec difficulté.
18. tout ce temps-là
19. traversé

street to the Perrys[1]. Sharon might have rushed over there with Neil if he started to get sick[2].

Steve reached for the phone again. Please God, please let them be at the Perrys'. Let them be all right.

And then he saw it. The message on the memo board. Printed in chalk[3]. Thick, uneven lettering[4].

"If you want your kid and girlfriend alive, wait for instructions." The next three words were heavily underlined[5]. "*Don't call police.*" The message was signed "Foxy[6]."

1. pour se rendre chez les Perry
2. s'était senti mal
3. à la craie
4. en lettres irrégulières
5. soulignés à gros traits
6. Renard [l'adjectif «foxy» signifie également rusé]

16

In the midtown Manhattan office of the FBI, Hugh Taylor sighed as he closed the top drawer[7] of his desk. God, it would be good to get home, he thought. Nearly 9:30, so traffic should be okay. But the storm would botch up[8] the West Side Highway and the bridge was probably a mess[9] by now.

He stood up and stretched[10]. His shoulders and neck were tense and stiff. Pushing fifty[11] and feel like I'm eighty, he thought. It had been a rotten day[12]. Another attempted bank robbery[13], this time the Chase Bank at Forty-eighth and Madison. A teller[14] had managed to sound the alarm and they'd rounded up the perpetrators[15], but not until the

7. tiroir supérieur
8. ficherait le bazar sur
9. un chaos indescriptible
10. s'étira
11. J'approche de la cinquantaine
12. sale journée
13. tentative de braquage de banque
14. caissier
15. arrêté les auteurs du délit

guard had been shot. Poor guy was in critical condition[1] and probably wouldn't make it[2].

Hugh's face hardened[3]. Criminals who could do that should be locked up for good[4].

But not executed. Hugh reached for his coat. That was one of the reasons he'd been so depressed today. That Thompson kid. He couldn't get him out of his mind[5]: the Peterson case two years ago. Hugh had been in charge of the investigation[6]. With his squad[7], he'd traced[8] Thompson to the motel in Virginia where they'd nabbed him[9].

The kid had so persistently denied[10] he'd murdered Nina Peterson. Even when he knew the only chance to save his skin was by throwing himself at the mercy of the court[11], he'd still denied the murder.

Hugh shrugged. It was out of his hands.[12] That was for sure[13]. And day after tomorrow Ronald Thompson would be electrocuted.

Hugh walked down the hall, pushed the button for the elevator[14].

Bone-tired.[15] He really was bone-tired.

Half a minute later a car[16] stopped at his floor. The door slid open[17]. He stepped in[18], pushed the "M" button.

He heard his name being shouted. Automatically he reached out and held the door, keeping it from closing. Running feet raced to[19] the elevator. His arm was grabbed by Hank Lamont, one of the younger agents.

"Hugh," he was out of breath[20]. "Steve Peterson is on the phone … you know … Nina Peterson's husband … the Thompson kid …"

"I know who he is," Hugh snapped[21]. "What does he want?"

"It's his son, he says his son and that writer, Sharon Martin, have been kidnapped."

1. dans un état critique
2. ne s'en sortirait pas
3. se durcit
4. enfermés une bonne fois pour toutes
5. se le sortir de la tête
6. enquête
7. brigade
8. filé
9. l'avaient pincé
10. nié si obstinément
11. s'en remettre à la clémence du tribunal
12. Ce n'était plus de son ressort.
13. Pour sûr.
14. appela l'ascenseur
15. Épuisé.
16. cabine
17. s'ouvrit en coulissant
18. entra
19. Quelqu'un courait à toute allure vers
20. hors d'haleine
21. rétorqua Hugh sèchement

17

"Who took those pictures?" Sharon heard the shrill fear[1] in her voice, knew it was a mistake. She met his eye[2] and saw that her tone had startled him[3]. His lips narrowed, the pulse in his cheek quickened. Intuitively she said, "I mean[4], they're so realistic."

Something of the rigidity eased.[5] "Maybe I found them."

She remembered the flash that had blinded her in the car.

"Or maybe you took them." There was a hint of[6] a compliment.

"Maybe."

She felt his hand touch her hair, linger on[7] her cheek. Don't act afraid[8], she thought frantically. She was still supporting[9] Neil's head against her arm. He began to tremble. Sobs broke[10] under the harsh asthmatic wheezing[11].

"Neil, don't cry," she implored. "You'll choke yourself[12]." She looked up at their captor[13]. "He's so frightened. Cut him loose.[14]"

"Will you like me if I do?" His leg was pressing against her side as she knelt by the cot.

1. peur qui perçait
2. croisa son regard
3. l'avait fait sursauter
4. Je veux dire
5. La sensation de tension se relâcha quelque peu.
6. Son ton laissait entendre qu'll s'agissait d'
7. s'attarder sur
8. Ne montre pas que tu as peur
9. soutenait
10. Des sanglots éclatèrent
11. respiration rude et sifflante due à l'asthme
12. t'étouffer
13. ravisseur
14. Détachez-le.

1. par pitié
2. lissaient les boucles blondes trempées de sueur
3. Avec une poigne d'acier, il écarta brutalement sa main du
4. Je n'en ferai rien.
5. apaisante
6. Un petit moment.
7. allongez-vous
8. Lâchez
9. sinon obéir
10. se penchait
11. écarta les mains
12. s'agitèrent violemment
13. saccadés
14. sa respiration sifflante devenant toujours plus stridente
15. sur ses genoux
16. l'enveloppa
17. se débattit
18. se dégager de son étreinte
19. Calme-toi !
20. Ne bouge pas
21. son ombre, sombre et floue
22. peinture écaillée
23. robinet qui gouttait
24. cracha quelques gouttes dans un gargouillement
25. échapper à

"Of course I'll like you, but *please*[1]." Her fingers smoothed damp sandy ringlets[2] from the small forehead.

"Don't touch that blindfold!" His hand, steely on hers, pulling it away from[3] Neil's face.

"I won't.[4]" Her voice was placating[5].

"All right. For a little while.[6] But just his hands. First, you lay down[7]."

She stiffened. "Why?"

"I can't let both of you untied. Let go of[8] the boy."

There was nothing to do except obey[9]. This time he tied her legs together from knees to ankles, then pulled her to a sitting position on the cot. "I won't tie your hands until I'm ready to go, Sharon." It was a concession. His voice lingered over her name.

Ready to go? Was he going to leave them here alone? He was bending[10] over Neil, cutting the cords on his wrists. Neil pulled his hands apart[11]. They flailed the air[12]. His gasps were staccato-paced[13]; the wheeze a constant, rising pitch[14].

Sharon pulled him on her lap[15]. She was still wearing the gray coat. She wrapped him[16] inside it with her. The shaking body struggled[17], trying to pull away[18].

"Neil, stop that! Calm down![19]" Her voice was firm. "Remember what your dad told you to do when you get asthma. Be very still[20] and breathe very slowly." She looked up. "Please, will you get him a drink of water?"

In the uneven, dusty lighting, his shadow, dark and blotchy[21] against the concrete wall, seemed fragmented by the peeling paint[22]. He nodded and went over to the rusty sink. The dripping faucet[23] sputtered in an uneven gurgling[24]. While his back was turned, Sharon looked up at the posters. Two of those women were dead or dying; the other was trying to run from[25] something or someone. Had he done that to them? What kind of madman[1] was he? Why had he kidnapped her and Neil? It had taken daring[2] to walk through the terminal with them. This man has planned this carefully. Why?

Neil's breath caught[3], choked. He began to cough a harsh, racking sound[4].

The abductor turned from the sink, a paper cup[5] in his hand. The choking sound seemed to agitate[6] him. When he handed Sharon the cup, his hand trembled. "Make him stop that," he said.

Sharon held the cup to Neil's lips. "Neil, sip this." He gulped[7] the water. "No, slowly, Neil. Now lean back[8]." The boy finished the water, sighed. She felt a faint relaxing of the slight body[9]. "That's it.[10]"

The captor was leaning over her. "You're a very kind person, Sharon," he said. "That's why I fell in love with you. Because you're not frightened of me, are you?"

"No, of course not. I know you don't want to hurt us[11]." Her tone was easy[12], conversational[13]. "But why did you bring us here?"

Without answering, he walked over to[14] the black suitcase, lifted it carefully and set it on the ground a few feet from[15] the door. Crouching over the bag, he opened it.

"What is in there?" Sharon asked.

"Just something I have to make before I go."

"Where are you going to go?"

"Don't ask me so many questions, Sharon."

"I was just interested in your plans." She watched as his fingers moved among the contents of the suitcase[16]. The fingers had a life of their own now, an existence in which they expertly handled[17] wires[18] and powder.

"I can't talk when I'm working like this. You have to be careful with nitroglycerin, even I do[19]."

1. aliéné
2. Il fallait être audacieux
3. Neil ne parvenait pas à reprendre son souffle
4. fut pris d'une toux rauque et atroce
5. gobelet en carton
6. troubler
7. avala d'un trait
8. installe-toi confortablement
9. sentit que son corps menu se détendait légèrement
10. C'est bien.
11. nous faire du mal
12. Elle prenait un ton dégagé
13. comme lors d'une conversation
14. se dirigea vers
15. à quelque pas de
16. farfouillaient dans la valise
17. maniaient avec habileté
18. des fils
19. même moi

Sharon's arms tightened around Neil. This insane man[1] was handling[2] explosives a few feet away from them. If he made a mistake, if he jarred[3] something … She remembered the story of the brownstone[4] in Greenwich Village that had exploded. She'd been in New York on a school break[5] that day and shopping a few blocks away[6] when the deafening sound[7] came. She thought of the mass of rubble[8], of the piles of broken stone and splintered wood[9]. Those people thought they knew how to handle explosives too.

Prayerfully[10], she watched as he worked with painstaking care[11], watched as the circulation in her legs stopped, as the dampness penetrated her skin, as her ear became attuned to the[12] faint rumbling sound of trains. The wheezing in Neil's chest developed a rhythm; fast, gasping, but not quite so frantic.

Finally the man straightened up[13]. "It's all right." He sounded satisfied[14].

"What are you going to do with that?"

"It's your babysitter."

"What do you mean?"

"I have to leave you until morning. I can't take any chance[15] of losing you, can I[16]?"

"How can you lose us[17], if we're tied up alone here?"

"One in a million[18], one in ten million, someone tries to get in this room while I'm out …"

"How long[19] are you going to keep us here?"

"Until Wednesday. Sharon, don't ask me questions. I'll tell you what I want you to know."

"I'm sorry. It's just that I don't understand."

"I can't let anyone find you. But I have to be away[20]. So if the door is wired[21] and someone tries to come in …"

1. fou
2. manipulait
3. heurtait
4. [explosion qui eut lieu en 1970, lors de la préparation d'une bombe par un groupe radical]
5. en congé scolaire
6. à quelques pâtés de maison de là
7. bruit assourdissant
8. gravats
9. éclats de bois
10. Tout en priant
11. avec un soin méticuleux
12. s'habituait au
13. se redressa
14. parut satisfait
15. prendre le risque
16. n'est-ce pas ?
17. nous perdre
18. Une chance sur un million
19. Combien de temps
20. m'absenter
21. reliée à la bombe

She was not here. She was not hearing this. This could not be.[1]

"Don't worry, Sharon. Tomorrow night Steve Peterson is going to give me eighty-two thousand dollars, and this will be all over[2]."

"Eighty-two thousand dollars?"

"Yes. And then Wednesday morning you and I will go away and I'll leave word[3] where they can find the boy." Somewhere far off[4] there was a faint echo of a roar, a silence, another roar.

He came across[5] the room. "I'm sorry, Sharon." In a sudden movement, he yanked Neil from her arms[6], dropped him[7] on the cot. Before she could move, he pulled her hands behind her[8]. He let the coat slide off[9] before he tied her wrists together.

He reached for Neil. "Don't gag Neil, please," she begged. "If he chokes … you may not be able to get the money … you may have to prove[10] he's alive. Please … I … I like you. Because you're so smart[11]."

He was watching her, considering[12].

"You … you know my name but you haven't even told me your name. I'd like to be thinking about you."

His hands turned her face to him. They were callused[13], rough[14]. Impossible to think they were so dexterous[15] with delicate wires. He bent down over her[16]. His breath was stale[17], hot. She suffered[18] his kiss, harsh on her lips, moist, lingering on her cheek and ear. "My name is Foxy," he said huskily[19]. "Say my name, Sharon."

"Foxy."

He tied Neil's wrists and pulled him beside her. There was barely room[20] for both of them lying sideways[21] on the narrow cot. Sharon's hands were squeezed[22] against the rough concrete wall. He covered them with the soiled gray coat, then stood

1. C'était impossible.
2. tout sera fini
3. laisserai un mot indiquant
4. Quelque part au loin,
5. traversa
6. arracha Neil de ses bras
7. le laissa tomber
8. ramena ses mains derrière son dos
9. glisser
10. prouver
11. intelligent
12. réfléchissant
13. calleuses
14. rêches
15. adroites
16. se pencha vers elle
17. fétide
18. subit
19. d'une voix rauque
20. à peine la place
21. pour qu'ils puissent tous les deux être allongés sur le côté
22. coincées

1. avait l'air mécontent
2. n'osa pas
3. l'envahissait à nouveau
4. en connut la raison
5. avec d'alarmantes précautions
6. attachait
7. le tirait
8. d'aventure entrait ici
9. se déclencherait
10. couvertes de poussières
11. vacillèrent puis finirent par s'éteindre
12. sa silhouette se découpa sur l'obscurité qui régnait à l'extérieur de la pièce
13. respiration difficile
14. assourdi

over them. He looked from them to the boarded-up dumbwaiter.

"No." He looked dissatisfied[1], uncertain. "I can't take the chance that someone might hear you."

The gags were around their mouths again, but not quite so tight this time. She dared not[2] protest any more. The nervousness was building up in him again[3].

And then she knew why[4]. Because slowly, with agonizing care[5], he was fastening[6] a slender wire to something in the suitcase and trailing it[7] from the suitcase to the door. He was going to attach that wire to the door. Then if anyone happened to come in here[8], the bomb would be triggered[9]!

She heard the snap of the switch, and the dust-shrouded[10] lights flickered away[11]. The door opened and closed noiselessly. For an instant he was silhouetted against the outside gloom[12], and then he was gone.

The room was desperately dark now and the cavernous silence was broken only by Neil's labored breathing[13] and the occasional muted[14] rumble of a train entering the tunnel.

18

Roger and Glenda Perry decided to watch the eleven o'clock news in bed. She had already bathed and offered to make a hot toddy[1] for him while he showered.

"Sounds good[2], but don't start puttering around[3]." He checked the lock on the kitchen door[4] and went upstairs. The shower was hot, needle sharp[5], infinitely satisfying. Quickly he got into[6] blue-striped pyjamas, folded back[7] the heavy spread[8] from the king-sized bed[9], and turned on the reading lights[10] that beamed on[11] both pillows[12].

Just before getting into bed, he walked over to the front[13] window. Even in weather like this, he and Glenda enjoyed the feel of fresh night air in the room. Automatically he glanced over at the Peterson house. It was lighted now, outside and in. Through the granular snow[14] he could see cars parked in the driveway.

Glenda came into the bedroom carrying a steaming[15] cup. "Roger, whatever are you looking at?"

He turned, sheepishly[16]. "Nothing. But you don't have to worry about Steve's lights being off. His place is bright as a Christmas tree[17] now."

"He must have company[18]. Well, thank heaven[19] we're not out tonight." She put the cup down[20] on his night table, slipped off her robe[21] and got into bed. "Oh, I am tired." Her expression changed, became thoughtful. Her body stilled.

"A pain?"

"Yes."

"Lie still.[22] I'll get you a pill[23]." With fingers that tried not to fumble, he reached for the ever-present bottle of nitroglycerin tablets[24]. He watched as she slipped one under her tongue[25] and closed her eyes. A minute later, she sighed, "Oh, that was a pretty bad one[26]. But it's all right now."

The phone rang. Roger reached for it, angrily. "If it's for you, I'll say you're asleep," he muttered[27].

1. grog
2. Bonne idée
3. à trop t'affairer dans la maison
4. vérifia que la porte de la cuisine était fermée à clef
5. revigorante
6. enfila
7. replia
8. couvre-lit
9. très grand lit
10. lampes de chevet
11. éclairèrent
12. oreillers
13. de devant
14. les flocons de neige
15. fumante
16. tout penaud
17. brille comme un sapin de Noël
18. avoir de la visite
19. Dieu merci
20. posa la tasse
21. enleva son peignoir
22. Reste tranquille.
23. cachet
24. flacon contenant les comprimés de trinitrine, qui était toujours à portée de main
25. langue
26. celle-ci a eu du mal à passer
27. grommela-t-il

1. Franchement
2. décrocha le combiné
3. Il dit « oui » sèchement.
4. préoccupé
5. quelque chose ne va pas
6. Mon Dieu !
7. J'arrive tout de suite.
8. avec précaution
9. ont... disparu
10. Par amour pour moi
11. un pantalon
12. fourra
13. venait de
14. sortit en courant
15. tourbillonnante
16. coupa à travers sa pelouse
17. traversa
18. et remonta
19. nues
20. haletait bruyamment
21. battant à tout rompre
22. homme à l'allure svelte
23. à l'air déterminé
24. grisonnants
25. renversée
26. s'enfuyait de
27. les mains jointes
28. se tenait, voûté,
29. l'air impuissant

"Some people[1] ..." He picked up the receiver[2]. His "yes" was curt.[3]

Immediately his tone changed, became concerned[4]. "Steve ... is something wrong[5]? No. No. Nothing. Of course. Oh, dear God![6] I'll be right over.[7]"

As Glenda stared, he replaced the receiver and reached for her hands. "Something's wrong at Steve's," he said carefully[8]. "Neil and Sharon Martin are ... missing[9]. I'm going over there, but I'll be back as fast as I possibly can."

"Roger ..."

"Please, Glenda. For my sake[10], stay calm. You know how you've been feeling lately. Please!"

He pulled a heavy sweater and slacks[11] over his pyjamas and stuffed[12] his feet into moccasins.

He was just[13] closing the front door when he heard the telephone ring again. Knowing Glenda would pick it up, Roger ran out[14] into the swirling[15] snow. He cut diagonally across his lawn[16], down[17] the street, up[18] the Peterson driveway. He was barely aware of the cold that chilled his bare[19] ankles, that made his breath come harsh and uneven.

He was panting heavily[20], his heart racing[21] when he hurried up the steps. The door was opened by a trim-looking man[22] with bold features[23] and graying[24] hair. "Mr. Perry. I'm Hugh Taylor, FBI. We met two years ago ..."

Roger thought of that day when Glenda had been knocked down[25] by Ronald Thompson as he ran from[26] this house, when she'd rushed in to find Nina's body.

"I remember." Shaking his head, he went into the living room. Steve was standing by the fireplace, his hands gripped together[27]. Red-eyed and sobbing, Dora Lufts was seated on the couch. Beside her, Bill Lufts hunched forward[28] helplessly[29].

Roger went directly to Steve and gripped his shoulders. "Steve, my God, I don't know what to say."

"Roger, thanks for coming so fast."

"How long have they been gone?"

"We're not sure. It happened sometime between six and seven-thirty."

"Sharon and Neil were alone here?"

"Yes. They ..." Steve's voice broke[1]. Quickly he recovered[2]. "They were alone."

"Mr. Perry," Hugh Taylor interrupted. "Is there anything you can tell us? Did you notice any strangers in the neighborhood[3], strange cars[4] or vans[5] or trucks[6]—anything[7]? Can you think of anything unusual?"

Roger sat down heavily. Think. There *was*[8] something. What was it? Yes. "Your outside lights!"

Steve turned to him, his expression intense. "Bill is positive[9] they were on when he and Dora went out. They were off when I got home. What did you notice about them?"

Roger's analytical mind offered a precise timetable[10] of his evening activities. He'd left the office at ten past five, driven into his garage at twenty of six[11]. "Your lights must have been on when I got home at about twenty of six," he told Steve. "Otherwise[12] I'd have noticed. Glenda made a cocktail. It wasn't more than fifteen minutes later that[13] we were looking out our front window and she remarked that your place was dark."

He frowned. "As a matter of fact[14], the clock was chiming shortly before that[15] so it must have been about five past six[16]." He paused. "Glenda said something about a car coming from your driveway."

"A car! What kind of car?" Hugh Taylor snapped[17].

"I don't know. Glenda mentioned it to me. I had turned my back to the window."

"You're sure of the time?"

1. se brisa
2. se ressaisit
3. voisinage
4. une voiture suspecte
5. une camionnette
6. un camion
7. quoi que ce soit
8. Il y avait bien
9. affirme
10. emploi du temps
11. 17h40
12. Sinon
13. Il ne s'était pas écoulé plus de quinze minutes lorsque
14. En fait
15. avait sonné peu de temps auparavant
16. 18h05
17. dit Hugh Taylor d'un ton brusque

Roger looked directly at the FBI agent. "I'm positive.[1]" He realized that he was having difficulty[2] making sense out of[3] what he was hearing. Had Glenda actually[4] watched a car drive away[5] with Neil and Sharon in it? Neil and Sharon being abducted[6]! Shouldn't some instinct have warned them that something was wrong[7]? But it had.[8] He remembered the feeling of alarm Glenda had at the window, how she'd wanted him to walk over here. And he'd cautioned her about overreacting[9].

Glenda!

How much could he tell her.[10] He looked at Hugh Taylor. "My wife will be terribly upset[11]."

Hugh nodded. "I understand. And Mr. Peterson feels she can be trusted to[12] know the truth. But it is absolutely vital that there be no publicity[13] about this. We don't want to scare the abductor or abductors off"[14].

"I understand."

"Two lives depend on all of you acting as normally as possible."

"Two lives …" Dora Lufts broke into dry, racking sobs[15]. "My little Neil … and that pretty girl. I can't believe this, not after Mrs. Peterson …"

"Dora, keep quiet[16]." Bill Lufts' voice was a whiny plea[17].

Roger watched as Steve's face contorted into a spasm of pain[18].

"Mr. Perry, do you know Miss Martin?" Hugh Taylor asked.

"Yes. I've met Sharon several times both here and at my home. Now may I please go over for[19] my wife?"

"Certainly. We want to speak with her about the car she saw. I have another agent with me. I can send him[20]."

1. Absolument.
2. avait du mal à
3. comprendre exactement
4. véritablement
5. s'éloigner
6. qui se faisaient enlever
7. n'allait pas
8. À vrai dire, cela avait été le cas.
9. l'avait mise en garde contre sa tendance à tout dramatiser
10. À quel point pouvait-il se confier à elle ?
11. bouleversée
12. est suffisamment digne de confiance pour
13. de rester très discret
14. faire fuir le ou les ravisseurs
15. fut secouée de violents sanglots
16. tais-toi
17. Bill Lufts l'implora d'une voix geignarde
18. se crispa sous l'effet de la douleur
19. rejoindre
20. l'envoyer chez vous

"No. I'd prefer to go myself. She's not well and Neil means a great deal to her[1]."

Roger thought, I am making conversation. I don't believe this. I don't. Steve. How can Steve stand[2] this? He looked at the younger man compassionately. Steve was outwardly calm[3] but the bleak look of suffering that had been etched in his face, that had only begun to lighten[4] in these last months, was there again in the gray pallor[5], in the suddenly deepened creases in his forehead[6], the taut lines[7] around his mouth. "Why don't you have a drink or some coffee[8], Steve," he suggested. "You look pretty shaken[9]."

"Maybe coffee ..."

Dora looked up eagerly[10]. "I'll make it, and some sandwiches. Oh my God, when I think ... Neil ... Why did I have to go to the movies tonight? If anything has happened to that boy, I can't take it[11]. I can't take it!"

Bill Lufts put his hand over his wife's mouth. "For once in your life, shut up![12]" he barked[13]. "Shut up!" There was ferocity, bitterness[14] in his voice. Roger realized that Hugh Taylor was studying the couple intensely.

The Lufts? Could he suspect them? No. Never. Impossible.

He was in the foyer when the chimes began to peal[15] frantically. They all jumped[16] as an agent, who'd been in the kitchen, covered the length of the foyer in seconds[17], raced past Roger and pulled the door open.

Glenda stood in the doorway[18]. Her hair and face were wet[19] with snow. Her feet were in open satin slippers[20]. Her pink wool dressing gown[21] was her only protection against the sharp, wet wind. Her face was marble-white[22]. The pupils of her eyes were

1. compte beaucoup à ses yeux
2. supporter
3. en apparence calme
4. s'était installé sur son visage et avait commencé à s'effacer seulement
5. son teint pâle et gris
6. dans les rides soudain plus profondes de son front
7. et dans les sillons
8. Pourquoi ne pas prendre un verre ou un café
9. avez l'air assez secoué
10. leva des yeux pleins d'empressement
11. je ne pourrai pas le supporter
12. Pour une fois dans ta vie, ferme-la !
13. aboya
14. de l'amertume
15. on sonna à la porte
16. sursautèrent
17. en quelques secondes
18. devant la porte
19. mouillés
20. pantoufles
21. robe de chambre
22. livide

dilated and staring. In her hand she was clutching[1] a sheet[2] of notepaper. She was trembling violently.

Roger ran to her[3], caught her[4] just before she collapsed[5]. He held her against him.

"Roger, the call, the phone call …" She was sobbing now. "He made me write it down. He made me read it back to him. He said, get it right[6] or … or … Neil …"

Hugh snatched[7] the paper from her hand and read it aloud[8]. "Tell Steven Peterson if he wants his son and girlfriend back[9] to be in the telephone booth of the Exxon station at exit[10] 22 of the Merritt Parkway tomorrow morning at eight o'clock. He'll get instructions for the ransom[11]."

Hugh frowned. The last word was indistinguishable. "What is this word, Mrs. Perry?" he demanded.

"He made me read it back[12] … I could hardly[13] write … he was so impatient … it's 'Foxy.' That's it. He repeated it." Glenda's voice rose in pitch[14]. Her face twisted in pain[15]. She pulled away from[16] Roger, clutching[17] her chest. "He … he was trying to disguise his voice … but when he repeated that name … Roger, *I've heard*[18] *that voice.* That man is someone I know."

1. serrait fort
2. feuille
3. se précipita vers elle
4. la rattrapa
5. qu'elle ne s'écroule
6. faites bien les choses
7. arracha
8. le lut à haute voix
9. revoir son fils et sa petite amie
10. la sortie
11. rançon
12. de le relire
13. à peine
14. devint stridente
15. se tordit de douleur
16. s'écarta de
17. étreignant
18. j'ai déjà entendu

19

Before he left Somers State Prison, Bob Kurner phoned Kathy Moore and asked her to meet him in her office.

Kathy was an assistant prosecutor[1] in Bridgeport assigned to Juvenile Court[2], and they'd met when he was serving as Public Defender[3] there. They'd been going together[4] for three months and Kathy had become deeply involved in his fight[5] to save Ron Thompson.

She was waiting for him in the reception area with the typist[6] he'd requested. "Marge said she'll stay all night if necessary. How much have you got?[7]"

"A lot," Bob said. "I made him go over the story[8] four times. There's a good two hours' worth.[9]"

Marge Evans stretched out her hand. "Just give it to me." Her tone was businesslike[10]. She set the recorder on her desk, squeezed her massive body onto the swivel[11] chair, inserted the cassette labeled "1" in the machine and ran it back to the beginning[12]. Ron Thompson's voice, halting and low, began to speak: "I was working that afternoon after school in Timberly's Market ..."

1. assistante du procureur
2. affectée au tribunal pour enfants
3. exerçait les fonctions d'avocat de l'assistance judiciaire
4. sortaient ensemble
5. s'était peu à peu engagée pleinement dans son combat
6. dactylo
7. Qu'est-ce qu'on a ?
8. répéter l'histoire
9. Il y en a pour deux bonnes heures.
10. net et précis
11. pivotante
12. la rembobina jusqu'au début

Marge snapped the "off" button and said, "Okay, you two get to something else[1]. I'll take care of this.[2]"

"Thanks, Marge." Bob turned to Kathy. "Did you get those files[3]?"

"Yes, they're inside." He followed her into her small crammed cubbyhole of an office[4]. The desk was bare[5] except for four manila folders[6] labeled "Carfolli," "Weiss," "Ambrose," "Callahan."

"The police reports are right on top[7]. Les Brooks wouldn't appreciate this, Bob. In fact, he'll probably fire me if he finds out about it[8]."

Les Brooks was the prosecutor. Bob sat down at the desk and reached for the first file. Before he opened it he looked up at Kathy. She was wearing dungarees[9] and a heavy sweater. Her dark hair was held back by a rubberband[10] at the nape of her neck[11]. She looked more like an eighteen-year-old co-ed[12] than a twenty-five-year-old lawyer[13]. But after the first time he'd been pitted against her in court[14] Bob never made the mistake of underestimating Kathy. She was a good lawyer with a keen[15], analytical mind and a passion for justice.

"I know the chance you're taking, Kath. But if we can only find some thread[16] between these murders and Nina Peterson's ... Our one hope for Ron now is new evidence[17]."

Kathy pulled a chair to the other side of the desk and reached for two of the files. "Well, God knows, if we can find any connection[18] between these cases, Les will forget the irregularity in your seeing our files. The newspapers are really on his back. As of this morning[19] they're calling these last two the 'Citizen Band[20] Murders.' "

"How come?[21]"

"Both the Callahan girl and Mrs. Ambrose had C.B. radios and had called for assistance[22]. Mrs. Am-

1. faites autre chose
2. Je m'occupe de ça.
3. dossiers
4. cagibi encombré lui servant de bureau
5. Il n'y avait rien sur le bureau
6. dossiers en papier kraft
7. sur le haut de la pile
8. s'il l'apprenait
9. une salopette
10. élastique
11. sur sa nuque
12. [aux États-Unis, étudiante dans un établissement mixte]
13. avocate
14. opposé à elle au tribunal
15. vif
16. fil conducteur
17. est d'obtenir de nouvelles preuves
18. un lien quel qu'il soit
19. Depuis ce matin,
20. [fréquence de radio réservée au public pour des radiocommunications effectuées à titre privé]
21. Comment ça se fait ?
22. pour demander de l'aide

brose was lost and almost out of gas[1] and Barbara Callahan had had a blowout[2].

"And two years ago Mrs. Weiss and Jean Carfolli were killed while driving alone at night on lonely roads."

"But that doesn't prove any connection. When Jean and Mrs. Weiss were killed the papers had started to write about the 'Highwayman[3] Murders.' It's all catch phrases[4] to make headlines[5]."

"What do you think?"

"I don't know what I think. After Ron Thompson was arrested for the Peterson murder, we didn't have another woman killed in Fairfield County until last month. Now we have two unsolved deaths. But there have been other C.B.-related[6] murders around the country. Those radios are great to have but it's insanity[7] for a woman to get on the air[8] and say she's alone on a deserted road and her car has broken down[9]. It's an open invitation to every kook[10] in the area who's listening to head straight to her[11]. My God, they had a case in Long Island last year of a fifteen-year-old kid who used to listen to the police channel[12] and head for trouble spots[13]. They finally got him when he knifed a woman who'd called for assistance."

"I still say[14] there's a connection between these four cases and that somehow Nina Peterson's case is linked with them," Bob said. "Call it a hunch[15]. Call it grasping at straws[16]. Call it anything. But help me."

"I want to.[17] How do we go about it?[18]"

"We'll start with a list: place, time, cause of death, weapon used, weather condition[19], kind of car, family background[20], witnesses' testimony[21], where victims were going, where they'd been that evening. In the last two cases, we'll measure the time elapsed[22] between the message they sent out on the C.B.

1. n'avait presque plus d'essence
2. crevaison
3. du bandit de grand chemin
4. des accroches
5. faire les gros titres
6. liés à la CB
7. c'est de la folie
8. d'aller parler à la radio
9. est tombée en panne
10. dingue
11. lui tomber dessus
12. fréquence de la police
13. lieux chauds
14. persiste à dire
15. intuition
16. se raccrocher aux branches
17. C'est bien mon intention.
18. Comment va-t-on s'y prendre ?
19. conditions météorologiques
20. milieu familial
21. témoignages
22. écoulé

and the finding of the body. When we're finished, we'll compare everything with the circumstances of Mrs. Peterson's death. If there's nothing there, we'll start from another angle."

They began at ten past eight. At midnight, Marge came in with four sets of papers[1]. "All finished," she said. "I typed them triple-spaced[2] to make it easier to pick up discrepancies[3] in any of the versions. You know, listening to that boy is enough to break your heart[4]. I've been a legal stenographer[5] for twenty years and I've heard an awful lot of stuff[6] but I know the ring of truth[7] when I hear it and that kid's telling the truth."

Bob smiled wearily[8]. "I wish to God[9] you were the Governor, Marge," he said. "Thanks so much."

"How're you two doing?[10]"

Kathy shook her head. "Nothing. Absolutely nothing."

"Well, maybe these will show something. Why don't I get you some coffee. Bet neither one of you had dinner.[11]"

When she came back ten minutes later, Bob and Kathy were sitting with two sets of papers in front of each of them. Bob was reading aloud. They were making line by line comparisons of the transcripts.

Marge set the coffee down and left silently. A security guard let her out of the building. As she huddled into the warmth of her heavy storm coat, bracing herself[12] for the long walk across the snow-blown parking lot, she realized she was praying. "Please God, if there's anything there to find that will help that boy, let those kids find it."

Bob and Kathy worked until dawn[13]. Then she said, "We've got to quit[14]. I have to go home and shower and dress. I'm due in court[15] at eight o'clock. And anyhow, I don't want anyone to see you here."

1. jeux de documents
2. avec un triple interligne
3. relever les contradictions
4. c'est à vous briser le cœur
5. sténographe juridique
6. un tas de choses horribles
7. accent de la vérité
8. sourit avec lassitude
9. Si seulement
10. Comment ça avance de votre côté ?
11. Je parie qu'aucun de vous n'a dîné.
12. s'armant de courage
13. l'aube
14. arrêter
15. Je suis attendue au tribunal

Bob nodded. The words he was reading were blurring[1] in his mind now. Over and over they'd compared the four versions of Ron's account[2] of his activities the day of the murder. They'd concentrated on the time Nina Peterson talked to him in Timberly's Market until he ran panic-stricken from her home[3]. There wasn't a single meaningful[4] discrepancy they could pick up. "There's got to be something here[5]," Bob said stubbornly[6]. "I'll take these home with me, and let me have the lists we made on the other four cases."

"I can't let you take the files[7]."

"I know that. But maybe we missed[8] some factor[9] in comparing the cases."

"We didn't, Bob." Kathy's voice was gentle[10].

He stood up. "I'll go right to my office[11] and start again. I'll compare these with the trial transcript[12] now."

Kathy helped him to put the material in his briefcase[13]. "Don't forget the recorder and the cassettes," she said.

"I won't." He reached his arm out and encircled her[14]. For an instant she leaned against him. "Love you, Kath."

"Love you."

"If we only had more time," he cried. "It's this damn capital punishment. How the hell[15] can twelve people have come in and said[16] that kid has to die. When, and if, they get the real killer it will be too late for Ron."

Kathy rubbed her forehead[17]. "At first, I was glad when capital punishment was reinstated. I'm sorry for victims, a lot sorrier for them than for perpetrators. But yesterday we had a kid in Juvenile. He's fourteen and looks about eleven; a skinny, small kid. Both parents are hopeless alcoholics[18]. They signed a complaint[19] against him as an incorrigible

1. se brouillaient
2. récit
3. pris de panique, il s'enfuit de son domicile
4. significative
5. Il doit forcément y avoir quelque chose
6. s'entêtait à dire Bob
7. emporter les dossiers
8. avons laissé passer
9. un élément
10. douce
11. fonce à mon bureau
12. procès-verbal d'audience
13. serviette
14. l'entoura de son bras
15. Bon sang, comment
16. en sont-elles arrivées à dire
17. se frotta le front
18. des alcooliques invétérés
19. ont déposé plainte

when he was seven years old, *seven years old*. He's been in and out of children's homes[1] since then. He keeps running away[2]. This time the mother signed the complaint and the father is fighting it[3]. They're separated and he wants the kid with him."

"What happened?"

"I won, if you can call it that. I insisted that he be sent back to a juvenile home[4] and the judge agreed. The father's so disoriented from booze[5] that he's not much more than a vegetable[6]. The boy tried to run out of the courtroom[7]; the sheriff's officer[8] had to tackle[9] him to catch him. He got hysterical and kept screaming, 'I hate everybody. Why can't I have a home like other kids?' Psychologically, he's so damaged[10] that it's probably already too late to save him. If in five or six years he kills someone, will we burn him[11]? Should we?[12]" Weary tears glistened in her eyes.

"I know, Kath. Why'd we get into law[13], anyhow? Maybe we should have been smarter. This tears your guts out[14]." He bent down and kissed her forehead. "Talk to you later."

In his office, Bob put the kettle[15], brimming with[16] water, on the hotplate[17]. Four cups of Nescafé, strong and black, cleared the sensation of fogginess[18]. He splashed cold water on his face and sat down at the long table in his office. Neatly[19], he laid out the rows of papers. He glanced at the clock over his desk. It was 7:30. He had just twenty-eight hours till[20] the execution. That was why his heart was pounding[21], why his throat felt so constricted[22].

No. It was more than the frantic sense of urgency. Something was hammering at his consciousness[23]. *There is something we have missed*, he thought.

This time it was not a hunch. It was certainty.

1. Il a fait plusieurs séjours dans des foyers pour enfants
2. n'arrête pas de s'enfuir
3. la conteste
4. structure d'accueil pour mineurs
5. ses beuveries
6. n'est guère plus qu'un légume
7. s'échapper de la salle d'audience
8. [équivalent du grade de capitaine de gendarmerie]
9. saisir à bras-le-corps
10. abîmé
11. fera passer sur la chaise électrique
12. Est-ce la solution ?
13. choisi le droit comme carrière
14. vous arrache les tripes
15. bouilloire
16. remplie à ras bord d'
17. plaque chauffante
18. dissipèrent la sensation de brouillard
19. Avec soin
20. jusqu'à
21. battait la chamade
22. il avait la gorge si serrée
23. le taraudait

20

Long after the Perrys went home and the Lufts retired[1], Steve and Hugh Taylor sat at the dining-room table.

Quietly and efficiently, other agents had dusted the house for fingerprints[2] and searched[3] house and grounds for signs of the[4] abductor. But the scrawled[5] message was the only evidence to be found.

"The prints[6] on the glass and cup will probably match[7] the ones on Sharon Martin's purse," Hugh told Steve.

Steve nodded. His mouth felt dry and brackish[8]. Four cups of coffee. Endless cigarettes.[9] He'd given up smoking when he turned thirty[10]. Then when Nina died he'd started again. It was Hugh Taylor who gave him the first one. Something like a smile, grim[11] and humorless, tugged at the corners of his mouth[12]. "You're the one who got me back on these weeds[13]," he said as he lit another one.

Hugh nodded. If ever a guy needed a cigarette that last time[14], it was Steve Peterson. And now his child! Hugh remembered how he was sitting with Steve at this table when some crackpot[15] mystic phoned to say Nina had a message for him. The message was,

1. étaient allés se coucher
2. relevé les empreintes dans la maison
3. perquisitionné
4. les alentours à la recherche d'indices pouvant les mener au
5. griffonné
6. empreintes
7. correspondront probablement à
8. Il avait la bouche sèche et l'haleine chargée
9. Il avait fumé cigarette sur cigarette.
10. arrêté de fumer à trente ans
11. sombre
12. s'étirait à la commissure de ses lèvres
13. m'avez fait reprendre la cigarette
14. cette fois-là
15. tordu

"Tell my husband to beware[1]. My son is in danger." That was the morning of Nina's funeral[2].

Remembering the incident, Hugh flinched[3]. He hoped Steve wasn't thinking about that. He studied the methodical notes he had made. "There's a pay telephone[4] in an outside booth[5] at that Exxon station," he told Steve. "We're putting a tap[6] on it as well as on this house and the Perrys' line. The thing to remember when you talk to Foxy is to try to keep him on the phone. That'll give us a chance to run a trace[7] and record his voice. Our big break may be that[8] Mrs. Perry will be able to remember who he is if she hears him again."

"Do you really think it's possible that she isn't just imagining she recognized the voice? You saw how upset she was."

"Anything's possible. But she seems like a level-headed[9] woman to me and she's so *positive*. Anyhow, cooperate[10]. Tell Foxy you want proof[11] that Sharon and Neil are alive and unharmed[12], that you must have a message from them on a cassette or tape[13]. Whatever money[14] he asks for, promise to get it, but insist that you'll pay it only when you receive the proof."

"That won't antagonize him[15]?" Steve wondered that he could sound[16] so detached.

"No. But it will help insure that he won't panic and ..." Abruptly Hugh clamped his lips together[17]. But he knew Steve had gotten his meaning[18]. He picked up his notebook[19].

"Let's start all over again.[20] How many people knew the schedule[21] of this house tonight, that the Lufts were planning to go out, that Sharon was coming up?"

"I don't know."

"The Perrys?"

1. de faire attention
2. des obsèques
3. tressaillit
4. téléphone public
5. cabine extérieure
6. mouchard
7. de le localiser
8. Une chance formidable serait que
9. équilibrée
10. soyez coopératif
11. une preuve
12. indemnes
13. sur une bande magnétique
14. Quel que soit le montant
15. ne va pas le contrarier
16. s'étonna de pouvoir s'exprimer de manière
17. serra les lèvres
18. avait compris ce qu'il voulait dire
19. calepin
20. Reprenons depuis le début.
21. l'emploi du temps des occupants

"No. I hadn't seen them over the last week except to wave hello[1]."

"Then it was just the Lufts and Sharon Martin and yourself?"

"And Neil."

"That's right. Is there any chance that Neil would have talked about Sharon's coming to other people, to his friends or his teachers at school?"

"It's possible."

"How serious is your friendship[2] with Sharon? Sorry, but I have to ask."

"Very serious. I'm planning[3] to ask her to marry me."

"I understand that you and Miss Martin were on the *Today* show this morning and that you disagreed strongly[4] about the capital punishment issue and specifically that she was terribly upset about the Thompson execution."

"You work fast."

"We have to, Mr. Peterson. How much did that disagreement affect your personal relationship?"

"What's that supposed to mean?[5]"

"Only this. As you know, Sharon Martin has been desperately trying to save Ronald Thompson's life. She's been in the Perry home and could have made a note of[6] the phone number. Don't forget it's unlisted[7]. Do you think there's a possibility that this kidnapping is a hoax[8], that she's hoping somehow to delay the execution?"

"No … no … no! Hugh, I understand you have to look at that angle[9], but please, for God's sake[10], don't waste your time on it. Whoever[11] wrote that message could have copied the Perrys' number. It's right on the blackboard[12] with the doctor's. Sharon would be incapable of doing this to me, incapable."

Hugh looked unconvinced[13]. "Mr. Peterson, we've had some mighty[14] unusual people breaking

1. si ce n'est pour un rapide bonjour
2. Quels sont vos relations
3. J'envisage
4. aviez de fortes divergences d'opinion
5. Que voulez-vous dire ?
6. pu noter
7. sur liste rouge
8. qu'il s'agisse d'un faux enlèvement
9. examiner l'affaire sous cet angle
10. pour l'amour du ciel
11. Celui qui
12. tableau
13. n'avait pas l'air convaincu
14. rudement

the law[1] in the name of causes these last ten years. I only offer this thought[2], if Sharon Martin engineered[3] this, your child is safe."

A tiny flicker of hope[4] flared in[5] Steve. This morning Sharon saying to him, "How can you be so positive, so sure, so relentless?" If that was the way she thought of him, could she … ? The hope died. "No," he said flatly[6]. "That's impossible."

"Very well. We'll leave it at that for the moment. What about your mail[7]—any threats[8], hate letters[9], anything at all?"

"Quite a few[10] hate letters because of my editorial stand[11] on capital punishment, especially with the Thompson execution so near. But that isn't surprising."

"You've received no direct threats?"

"No." Steve frowned.

"What are you thinking?" Hugh asked quickly.

"Just that Ronald Thompson's mother stopped me[12] last week. I take Neil for antihistimine shots[13] every Saturday morning. She was in the parking lot of the medical building when we came out. She asked me to beg the Governor to spare[14] Thompson."

"What did you tell her?"

"I said I couldn't do anything. I was anxious[15] to get Neil away. Naturally I didn't want him to be aware about[16] Wednesday. I wanted to get him inside the car as quickly as possible so he wouldn't hear us talking and so I turned my back to her. But she seemed to think I was ignoring her. She said something like[17], 'How would you feel if it was your only son[18], how would you feel?' And then she walked away[19]."

Hugh made a note in his book[20]. "We'll check her out[21]." Standing up, he flexed his shoulders[22], vaguely aware that hours ago he'd been looking forward[23] to going to bed. "Mr. Peterson," he said, "try to hang

1. qui ont enfreint la loi
2. vous fais juste part de cette réflexion
3. a manigancé
4. lueur d'espoir
5. traversa
6. d'une voix éteinte
7. courrier
8. des menaces
9. des lettres d'insultes
10. Quelques
11. ligne éditoriale
12. m'a arrêté dans la rue
13. piqûres d'antihistaminique
14. supplier la gouverneure d'épargner la vie de
15. pressé
16. qu'il sache pour
17. du genre
18. s'il s'agissait de votre fils unique
19. s'est éloignée
20. carnet
21. allons l'interroger
22. s'étira
23. s'était réjoui à l'idée

on to the thought[1] that our record of recovering kidnapping victims is a very good one[2] and everything possible will be done. Now, I'd suggest that you try to get a few hours' sleep[3]."

"Sleep?" Steve looked at him incredulously.

"Then rest.[4] Go up to your room and lie down. We'll be right here and we'll call you if there's any reason. If the phone rings, you pick it up. We've got a tap on it now. But I don't think you'll get any further word[5] from the abductor tonight."

"All right." Wearily, Steve walked out of the dining room. He stopped in the kitchen to get a glass of water and was sorry he had. The mug of cocoa and glass of sherry, smeared now with sooty powder[6], were on the kitchen table.

Sharon. Only a few hours ago she had been here in this house with Neil. He hadn't realized just how much he wanted Neil to trust and like Sharon until these last three weeks when she'd been away and he'd missed her so terribly[7].

Silently he left the kitchen, went into the foyer, up the stairs, down the hallway[8] past Neil's room and the guest room to the master bedroom[9]. Overhead, he could hear footsteps. The Lufts were walking around their third-floor room. Obviously they couldn't sleep either.

He switched on the light and stood near the door, studying the room. After Nina died, he'd refurnished it[10]. He hadn't wanted to be around the antique white furniture[11] she'd loved so much. He'd replaced the double bed with a twin-size brass four-poster[12], selected a color scheme of brown-and-white tweed[13]. A man's room, the decorating shop had assured him.

He'd never cared for it[14]. It was lonely and barren[15] and impersonal, like a motel room. The whole house was like that. They'd bought it because they

1. vous raccrocher à la pensée

2. nous avons de très bons résultats dans les affaires d'enlèvement

3. de dormir quelques heures

4. Au moins vous reposer.

5. aurez d'autres nouvelles

6. dorénavant recouverts d'une poudre charbonneuse

7. elle lui avait terriblement manqué

8. couloir

9. chambre principale

10. l'avait remeublée

11. conserver les meubles anciens blancs

12. lit à colonnes en cuivre

13. une combinaison de couleurs dans les tons bruns et blancs

14. n'y avait jamais vraiment fait attention

15. nue

1. une résidence en front de mer

2. rêvé

3. reposante et engageante

4. style épuré

5. Retirant

6. couvre-lit plié

7. s'en couvrit

8. plafonnier

9. faisait taper les branches des cornouillers

10. bruit ouaté

11. s'assoupit, mais d'un sommeil léger et agité

12. courant le long d'

13. ouvrit toute grande la porte

14. craie

15. délimitant le contour de

wanted waterfront property[1]. Nina had said, "The house has real possibilities. Just wait and see. Give me six months with it." She'd had two weeks ...

The last time he'd been in Sharon's apartment, he'd daydreamed[2] about redoing this room, this house with her. She knew how to make a home charming and restful and inviting[3], too. It was the colors she used and the uncluttered look[4]. And it was her presence.

Pulling off[5] his shoes, he lay heavily across the bed. The room felt cool and he reached for the folded coverlet[6] and drew it up[7]. He touched the switch that turned off the overhead light[8].

The room was completely dark. Outside the wind was slapping branches of the dogwood trees[9] against the house. The snow made a furry pelting sound[10] against the windows.

Steve dozed off into a light, uneasy sleep[11]. He began to dream. Sharon, Neil. They wanted him to help them. He was running through a thick fog ... running down[12] a long hallway. There was a room at the end of it. He was trying to get into the room. He *had* to get into the room. He reached it and threw the door open[13]. And the fog cleared. The fog was gone. And Neil and Sharon were lying on the floor, scarves knotted around their throats and iridescent chalk[14] marks outlining[15] their bodies.

21

It was much too dangerous to be seen coming up from the Mount Vernon tracks alone late in the evening[1]. The guards in the lower terminal had eyes for[2] details like that. That was why he left Sharon and the boy at two minutes of eleven. Because at exactly eleven a train chugged into the station[3] and he was able to go up the ramp and stairs with the eight or ten people who got off it[4].

He drifted near[5] three of them who went to the Vanderbilt Avenue exit. He knew that to anyone watching he was one of a group of four people. He slipped away[6] from the others when they turned left on Vanderbilt Avenue. He turned right, glanced across the street and stopped short[7]. A police tow truck[8] was there. Clanging chains were being attached to a shabby brown Chevrolet. They were just about[9] to tow the car away[10]!

Hugely amused, he started uptown[11]. He was planning to make the phone call[12] from a booth in front of Bloomingdale's[13]. The fifteen-block walk up Lexington Avenue chilled him[14] and reduced some of the pulsing desire[15] he'd experienced when he kissed Sharon. And she wanted him just as much[16]. He could feel it.

1. en fin de soirée
2. repéraient
3. entrait en gare
4. en descendaient
5. s'approcha de
6. s'éloigna
7. s'arrêta net
8. dépanneuse de la police
9. sur le point
10. d'emmener la voiture à la fourrière
11. [quartier riche, bordé par Central Park]
12. téléphoner
13. [chaîne de grands magasins]
14. le calma
15. élan de désir
16. tout autant que lui

He might have made love to Sharon then except for the boy. Even with the blindfold the eyes were there. Maybe the boy could see through the blindfold. The thought made him shiver[1].

The snow had tapered off some[2] but the sky was still dark and heavy. He frowned, remembering how important it would be for the roads to be clear[3] when he picked up the money.

He was planning to phone the Perrys and if they weren't home he'd call the Peterson house directly. But that could be risky.

He was lucky. Mrs. Perry picked up the phone on the first ring[4]. He could tell by her voice[5] that she was extremely nervous. Probably Peterson had called over there[6] when he found the boy and Sharon missing[7]. He gave Mrs. Perry the message in the low, gruff[8] voice he'd practiced. It was only when she couldn't get the name[9] that he exploded and raised his tone[10]. Careless of him![11] Stupid! But she probably was too upset to notice.

Gently replacing the phone, he smiled. If the FBI had been called they'd tap the phone[12] in the Exxon station. That was why in the morning when he called Peterson on that phone, he'd tell him to go right to[13] the booth in the next service station. They wouldn't have time to put a tracer[14] on it.

He left the phonebooth feeling exhilarated[15], brilliant. A girl was standing in the doorway[16] of a small dress shop. In spite of the cold she was wearing a miniskirt. White boots and a white fur jacket completed an outfit[17] he thought very attractive. She smiled at him. Her hair was thick and curly around her face. She was young, not more than eighteen or nineteen and she liked him. He could tell. Her eyes were smiling at him and he started walking toward her.

1. frémir
2. La neige tombait avec moins d'intensité
3. dégagées
4. décrocha à la première sonnerie
5. sentit au son de sa voix
6. les avaient appelés
7. n'étaient pas là
8. rauque
9. ne comprit pas le nom
10. avait haussé le ton
11. Quelle imprudence de sa part !
12. mettraient le téléphone sur écoute
13. se rendre directement à
14. mouchard
15. euphorique
16. se tenait dans l'embrasure de la porte
17. tenue

But then he stopped. She was undoubtedly[1] a prostitute and even though she was sincere about liking him, just suppose[2] the police were watching and arrested them both? He looked around fearfully[3]. He'd read about great plans being ruined by a small mistake.

Stoically passing the girl, he permitted her a brief, skeletal[4] smile before he put his head down into the frigid wind[5] and hurried to the Biltmore.

The same sneering night clerk gave him his key. He hadn't had dinner and was very hungry. And he'd order two or three bottles of beer from room service too. Around this time[6] he always got thirsty for beer[7]. Habit[8], maybe.

While he waited for the two hamburgers and French fries[9] and apple pie[10], he soaked in the tub[11]. It had felt so musty and cold and dirty in the room. After drying himself[12], he put on the pyjamas he'd bought for this trip and examined his suit carefully. But it wasn't soiled[13].

He tipped the room service waiter generously[14]. They always did that in the movies[15]. The first bottle of beer he gulped down. The second he had with the hamburgers. The third he sipped[16] listening to the midnight news. There was more about that Thompson kid. "The last possibility of a reprieve from death[17] for Ronald Thompson was ended yesterday. Plans are being made to carry out the execution at 11:30 A.M. tomorrow as scheduled[18] ..." But not a whisper about[19] Neil or Sharon. Publicity was the one thing that he feared. Because someone might start putting two and two together[20].

The girls last month had been a mistake. It was just that he couldn't help it.[21] He never went cruising around anymore[22]. Too dangerous. But when he heard them on the C.B., something made him go to them.

1. sans aucun doute
2. supposons un seul instant
3. jeta des regards inquiets autour de lui
4. maigre
5. avant de foncer, tête baissée, dans le vent glacial
6. Vers cette heure-ci,
7. avait toujours envie d'une bière
8. La force de l'habitude
9. les frites
10. la tarte aux pommes
11. prit un bain
12. s'être séché
13. taché
14. gratifia le garçon d'étage d'un pourboire généreux
15. au cinéma
16. la sirota
17. grâce
18. comme prévu
19. pas un mot sur
20. à faire des recoupements
21. Il n'avait pas pu se retenir, tout simplement.
22. n'allait plus jamais draguer en voiture désormais

The thought of the girls made him churn up inside[1]. Restlessly, he switched off the radio. He really shouldn't ... it might excite him.

He *had* to[2].

From his coat pocket he took out the expensive miniature recorder and the cassettes he always carried with him. Selecting one, he slipped it in the recorder, got into bed and turned out the light. He snuggled[3] under the covers, appreciating the clean, crisp sheets, the warm blanket and coverlet. He and Sharon would stay in many hotels together.

Putting the earplug[4] in his right ear, he cautiously deflected the "play" button[5] of the machine. For several minutes there was only the sound of a car engine, then the faint squeal of brakes[6], a door opening and his own voice friendly and helpful as he got out of the Volks.

He let the cassette run[7] until he got to the best part. That[8] he kept replaying over and over again[9]. Finally he had heard enough. He turned off the recorder, pulled out the earplug, and fell into deep sleep[10], the sound of Jean Carfolli's sobbing scream, "Don't[11] ... please don't[12] ... ringing in his ears[13].

1. le remua profondément
2. le fallait
3. se pelotonna
4. écouteur
5. appuya sur la touche « marche »
6. crissement léger des freins
7. défiler
8. Cette partie-là,
9. la repassa en boucle
10. sombra dans un profond sommeil
11. Ne faites pas ça
12. par pitié, non
13. résonnant à ses oreilles

22

Marian and Jim Vogler talked far into the night[1]. Despite Jim's efforts to console her, something like[2] despair had seeped into[3] Marian's soul.

"I wouldn't mind so much[4] if we hadn't just spent all that money! *Four hundred dollars!* If someone had to steal the car why didn't they take it last week before we fixed it[5]? And it was running[6] so well. Arty did such a good job on it[7]. And now how can I get to the Perrys? I'll lose that job!"

"Babe, you won't have to give up the[8] job. I'll get somebody to lend[9] me a couple of hundred bucks and I'll look around for another jalopy[10] tomorrow."

"Oh, Jim, would you[11]?" Marian knew how Jim hated borrowing[12] from friends, but if he would do it just this once[13] ...

It was too dark for Jim to see her face but he felt the faint relaxing of her body. "Babe" he reassured her, "someday we'll laugh about these lousy bills[14]. Before you know it[15], we'll get caught up[16]."

"I guess so," Marian agreed. Suddenly she felt desperately tired. Her eyes began to close.

They were just drifting off to sleep[17] when the phone rang. Its jangle[18] startled them. Marian pulled

1. jusqu'à une heure avancée de la nuit
2. une sensation s'apparentant au
3. avait envahi
4. Ça ne me dérangerait pas autant
5. avant qu'on la fasse réparer
6. marchait
7. a fait de l'excellent travail
8. à renoncer au
9. prêter
10. chercherai un autre tacot
11. tu veux bien
12. emprunter
13. si, juste pour cette fois, il le faisait
14. on rira de ces saletés de factures
15. En moins de deux
16. on se rattrapera
17. venaient de sombrer dans le sommeil
18. sonnerie

herself up on one elbow[1] as Jim fumbled for[2] the lamp on the night table and reached for the phone.

"Hello. Yeah[3], this is Jim—James Vogler. Tonight. That's right. Oh, that's good! Where? When can I get it? You're kidding. *You're kidding.*[4] If that don't beat![5] All right ... Thirty-sixth Street and Twelfth Avenue. I know. Right. Thanks." He hung up the phone.

"The car," Marian cried. "They found our car!"

"Yeah, in New York City. It was parked illegally[6] in midtown and the cops towed it away. We can get it[7] in the morning. The cop said it was probably heisted[8] by some fool kids joyriding[9]."

"Oh, Jim, that's wonderful!"

"There's a hitch[10]."

"What is it?"

Jim Vogler's eyes crinkled[11]. His lips twitched[12]. "Babe, can you believe ... we're stuck with[13] the fifteen-buck parking ticket and the sixty-buck tow charge[14]?"

Marian gasped. "That's my first week's pay!" She began to laugh helplessly[15] with him.

In the morning Jim took the 6:15 train to New York and was back with the car at five of nine. Marian was ready to leave. Promptly at nine o'clock[16] she turned into Driftwood Lane. The car was none the worse[17] for its unauthorized trip into New York and she was grateful for[18] the new snow tires. You sure needed them in this weather.

A Mercury was parked in the Perrys' driveway. It looked like the one she'd noticed in front of the house across the street when she'd come for the interview[19] last week. The Perrys must have company.

Somewhat uncertainly[20] she pulled up beside the Mercury taking care that[21] her car didn't block access to the garage. Then she lingered a moment before opening the door. She was a little nervous ...

1. se redressa sur un coude
2. cherchait à tâtons
3. Ouais
4. Vous vous fichez vraiment de moi.
5. C'est le bouquet !
6. en stationnement interdit
7. la récupérer
8. piquée
9. qui voulaient faire une virée dans une voiture volée
10. Il y a un hic
11. se plissèrent
12. se contractèrent
13. on doit régler
14. frais de fourrière s'élevant à soixante billets
15. nerveusement
16. À 9 heures pile,
17. ne se ressentait pas
18. se félicitait d'avoir
19. entretien d'embauche
20. Un peu hésitante,
21. en faisant attention à ce que

all that excitement with the car just when she was starting a job. Well, just get yourself together[1], she thought. Count your blessings[2]. The car was back. Affectionately, she patted the seat beside her with her gloved[3] hand.

Her hand stopped moving. One of the fingers had touched something hard. She looked down, and with two fingers tugged a shiny object from where it was wedged[4] between the cushion and the backrest[5].

Why[6], it was a ring. She inspected it closely. How pretty—a pale, pink moonstone in a lovely raised antique gold setting. Whoever stole the car must have lost it.

Well, it was a cinch[7] they wouldn't come around to claim it[8]. As far as she was concerned the ring was hers. It made up for[9] the seventy-five dollars Jim laid out[10] for the ticket and towing fee[11]. She pulled off her glove and slipped the ring on her finger. It fit perfectly.

It was a good omen[12]. Wait until Jim found out about this[13]. Suddenly confident[14], Marian opened the door of the car, stepped out into the snow, and walked briskly around to the kitchen door of the Perry home.

1. ressaisis-toi
2. Estime-toi heureuse
3. gantée
4. coincé
5. dossier
6. Ça alors
7. c'était clair qu'
8. la réclamer
9. compensait
10. avait déboursés
11. frais d'enlèvement
12. présage
13. l'apprenne
14. confiante

23

The phone in the outside booth of the Exxon station rang promptly at eight o'clock. Swallowing over the convulsion of his throat muscles, the sudden, absolute dryness in his mouth, Steve picked up the receiver[1]. "Hello."

"Peterson?" A voice so muffled, so low, he had to strain[2] to hear it.

"Yes."

"In ten minutes I'll call you at the payphone of the service station just past exit twenty-one."

The connection was broken.[3]

"Wait … wait …" A buzzing sound assaulted his ear.[4]

Desperately he looked over to the service island[5]. Hugh had driven into the station a few minutes before him. The hood[6] of his car was up and he was standing outside with the attendant[7], pointing at one of the tires. Steve knew he was watching him. Shaking his head, he got back in his own car and careened onto the parkway[8]. Before he turned, he caught a glimpse of Hugh, jumping into his car.

The traffic was creeping cautiously down[9] the slippery road. Steve clenched the wheel[10]. He'd never make it to[11] the next station in ten minutes.

1. décrocha le combiné
2. tendre l'oreille
3. La communication fut coupée.
4. Seule la tonalité résonna à son oreille.
5. aire de service
6. capot
7. pompiste
8. fonça sur la route express
9. progressait très lentement et avec prudence sur
10. agrippait le volant
11. n'arriverait jamais à

Twisting[1] the wheel, he rode down the right-hand shoulder[2] of the parkway.

The voice. He could hardly hear it. The FBI wouldn't have a prayer[3] of tracing the call.

This time he'd try to keep Foxy on the phone longer. Maybe it was a voice he'd recognize too. He felt for the pad[4] and paper in his pocket. He had to write down everything Foxy said. In the rearview mirror[5], he could see a green car behind him, Hugh's car.

It was eleven minutes past eight when Steve pulled into the next service station. The public phone was ringing insistently. He raced into the booth, grabbed the receiver.

"Peterson?"

This time the caller spoke so softly that he had to cover his other ear to block out[6] the highway sounds. "Yes."

"I want eighty-two thousand dollars in tens, twenties and fifties[7]. *No new bills.*[8] At two o'clock tomorrow morning be at the payphone on the southwest corner of Fifty-fifth and Lexington in Manhattan. Drive in your own car. Be alone. You'll be told where[9] to leave the money."

"Eighty-two thousand dollars ..." Steve began to repeat the instructions. The voice, he thought frantically. Listen to the intonation, try to memorize it, be able to mimic it[10].

"Hurry up, Peterson."

"I'm writing this down. I'll get the money. I'll be there. But how do I know my son and Sharon are still alive? How do I know that you have them? I need proof."

"Proof? What kind of proof?" The whisper was angry now.

"A tape ... or a cassette ... something with them talking[11]."

"A *cassette*!"

1. Tournant
2. bas-côté droit
3. n'aurait pas la moindre chance
4. bloc-notes
5. rétroviseur
6. masquer
7. en coupures de dix, vingt et cinquante dollars
8. Aucun billet neuf.
9. On vous indiquera le lieu où
10. il faut que tu puisses l'imiter
11. où on les entend parler

Was that muffled sound a laugh? Was the caller[1] *laughing*? "I must have it," Steve insisted. Oh God, he prayed, don't let this be a mistake[2].

"You'll get your cassette, Peterson." The receiver on the other end was slammed down.[3]

"Wait!" Steve shouted. "Wait!"

Silence. The dial tone[4]. He hung up slowly.

As they'd arranged[5], he drove directly to the Perrys' and waited for Hugh. Too restless to stay in the car, he got out and stood in the driveway. The icy, moisture-filled wind made him shiver. Oh God, was this happening? Was this nightmare real?

Hugh drove down the block, parked. "What'd he say?"

Steve pulled out the pad, read the instructions. The sense of unreality deepened[6].

"How about[7] the voice?" Hugh asked.

"Disguised I think, very low. I don't think anybody could possibly identify it even if you had been able to tap that second phone." He stared unseeingly across the street, groped for comfort[8], found a slender thread[9].

"He promised the cassette. That means they're probably still alive."

"I'm sure of it.[10]" Hugh did not voice the gnawing worry[11] that it would be virtually[12] impossible for a cassette to reach Steve before he paid the ransom. There wasn't time to mail it[13] even special delivery[14]. A messenger service[15] would be too easy to trace. The abductor didn't want the kidnapping publicized[16] so he'd hardly leave a cassette at a newspaper or radio station. "How about the ransom?" he asked Steve. "Can you raise[17] eighty-two thousand dollars today?"

"I couldn't raise five cents myself," Steve said. "I've invested so much in the magazine that I'm absolutely strapped[18]. Second mortgage[19], you name it[20].

1. auteur de l'appel téléphonique
2. pourvu que cela ne soit pas une erreur
3. On raccrocha brutalement à l'autre bout de la ligne.
4. tonalité
5. Comme convenu
6. s'intensifiait
7. Qu'en est-il de
8. chercha tant bien que mal du réconfort
9. se raccrocha à ce qu'il pouvait
10. J'en suis certain.
11. n'exprima pas à haute voix l'inquiétude qui le tenaillait,
12. à savoir qu'il serait pratiquement
13. la poster
14. en exprès
15. coursier
16. rendre public le kidnapping
17. réunir
18. complètement fauché
19. hypothèque
20. et j'en passe

But thanks to Neil's mother, I can get that much money[1]."

"Neil's mother?"

"She inherited[2] seventy-five thousand dollars from her grandmother just before she died. I put it in a trust fund[3] for Neil for college[4]. It's in a bank in New York. With the interest it comes to just over[5] eighty-two thousand."

"*Just over eighty-two thousand.* Mr. Peterson, how many people are aware of[6] that trust?"

"I don't know. Nobody except my lawyer and accountant[7]. You don't go around talking about that.[8]"

"What about Sharon Martin?"

"I don't remember mentioning it to her."

"But it is possible you told her?"

"I don't think I did."

Hugh started to go up the porch steps. "Mr. Peterson," he said carefully, "you have got to go over in your own mind everyone who[9] knows about that money. That and the possibility that Mrs. Perry can identify the kidnapper's voice are our only leads[10]."

When they rang the front doorbell, Roger answered quickly. He put a finger to his lips as they came in. His face was pale and strained, his shoulders sagging[11]. "The doctor just left. He's given Glenda a sedative. She refuses to go to the hospital but he thinks she's on the verge of another coronary[12]."

"Mr. Perry, I'm sorry. But we have to ask her to listen to a recording of the first call the kidnapper made this morning."

"She can't! Not now! This is killing her. It's killing her!" Clenching his fists[13], he swallowed[14], "Steve, I'm sorry ... what happened?"

Mechanically, Steve explained. He still had the feeling of unreality, of being an observer, watching a tragedy being acted out[15] without power to interfere[16].

1. réunir une pareille somme
2. avait hérité
3. les ai investis dans un fonds de placement
4. financer ses études supérieures
5. on arrive précisément à un peu plus de
6. sont au courant de
7. mon comptable
8. On ne passe pas son temps à parler de telles choses.
9. il est important que vous essayiez de vous rappeler qui
10. pistes
11. il se tenait voûté
12. risque un autre infarctus
13. Serrant les poings
14. avala sa salive
15. en train de se jouer
16. sans qu'il puisse s'interposer

There was a long pause, then Roger said slowly, "Glenda refused to go to the hospital because she knew you'd need her to hear that tape. The doctor gave her a strong tranquilizer. If she just slept for a little while ... Can you bring it over later?[1] She absolutely can't get out of bed[2]."

"Of course," Hugh said.

Chimes were an intrusion.[3] "That's the back door," Roger said. "Who on earth[4] ... ? Oh my God, the new housekeeper. I forgot all about her.[5]"

"How long will she be here?" Hugh asked quickly.

"Four hours."

"No good.[6] She might overhear[7] something. Introduce me as the doctor. When we leave, send her home[8]. Say you'll call her in a day or two. Where is she from anyhow?"

"Carley."

The chimes sounded again.

"She been in this house before?"

"Last week."

"We may want to check her out[9]."

"All right." Roger hurried to the back door and returned with Marian. Hugh studied the pleasant-looking woman carefully.

"I've explained to Mrs. Vogler that my wife is ill," Roger said. "Mrs. Vogler, my neighbor, Mr. Peterson, and err[10] ... Doctor Taylor."

"How do you do?[11]" Her voice was warm, a little shy[12]. "Oh, Mr. Peterson, is that Mercury your car?"

"Yes."

"Then that must be your little boy. He's the dearest thing.[13] He was out front when I came here last week and he pointed out this house to me[14]. He was so polite. You must be very proud[15] of him." Marian was peeling off[16] her glove, reaching out her hand to[17] Steve.

1. Pouvez-vous la rapporter un peu plus tard ?
2. se lever
3. Ils furent interrompus par un coup de sonnette.
4. Qui diable
5. Je l'avais complètement oubliée.
6. Ça ne va pas.
7. surprendre
8. renvoyez-la chez elle
9. nous renseigner sur elle
10. euh
11. Enchantée.
12. timide
13. C'est un véritable amour.
14. m'a indiqué la maison
15. fier
16. enlevait
17. tendant la main à

"I ... am proud of Neil." Abruptly Steve turned his back to her and reached for the knob of the front door. Blinding tears stung his eyes.[1] "Oh, God, please ..."

Hugh jumped into the breach[2], shaking Marian's hand, careful not to squeeze[3] the unusual ring she was wearing. Pretty fancy[4] to do housework in[5], he thought. His expression had changed subtly[6]. "I think it's a very good idea Mrs. Vogler is here, Mr. Perry," he said. "You know how concerned your wife gets about[7] the house. I'd have her start today just as you originally planned."

"Oh ... I see ... very well." Roger stared at Hugh, understanding the implication[8]. Did Hugh think this woman might be tied to[9] Neil's disappearance?

Bewildered, Marian looked past Hugh and Roger and watched Steve open the front door. Maybe he thought she was too forward[10] offering to shake hands. Maybe she should apologize[11]. She'd better remember she was the housekeeper here. She started to[12] touch his shoulder, thought better of it[13], and silently held the door open for Hugh. Embarrassed, she closed it quietly behind them and as she did the moonstone ring made a faint clinking sound[14] on the knob.

1. Des larmes l'aveuglaient et lui piquaient les yeux.

2. intervint rapidement

3. appuyer sur

4. Un peu chic

5. pour faire le ménage avec

6. imperceptiblement

7. à quel point votre femme s'inquiète pour

8. sous-entendu

9. pouvait avoir un lien avec

10. cavalière

11. s'excuser

12. était sur le point de

13. se ravisa

14. tinta faiblement

24

He didn't want to be a crybaby[1]. He tried so hard not to cry but it was like when the asthma came[2]. He couldn't stop it. He'd get that gulpy feeling in his throat[3] and his nose would start running[4] and big baby tears would get his face all wet. He cried a lot in school. He knew the other kids thought he was a baby and the teacher did, too[5], even though she wasn't mean about it[6].

It was just that there was something inside him that kept bothering him all the time[7], some scared, worried feeling. It all began that day when Mommy got hurt[8] and went to heaven[9]. He'd been playing with his trains. He never played with them anymore.

The thought of that day made Neil's breath come faster. He couldn't breathe through his mouth because of the rag[10] over it. His chest began to heave[11]. He gulped[12] and a piece of the rag went into his mouth. It tasted thick and raspy on his tongue.[13] He tried to say, "I can't breathe." The rag went back further[14] in his mouth. He was gagging[15]. He was going to start crying …

"Neil, stop that." Sharon's voice sounded funny[16] and low and hoarse like she was talking from somewhere down in her throat[17]. But her face was right

1. un pleurnicheur
2. quand il avait une crise d'asthme
3. cette sensation d'avoir la gorge serrée
4. à couler
5. tout comme la maîtresse
6. ne le lui reprochait pas
7. ne cessait de le tracasser
8. on avait fait du mal à maman
9. au ciel
10. chiffon
11. se soulever
12. déglutit
13. C'était épais et ça lui râpait la langue.
14. s'enfonça encore plus profondément
15. étouffait
16. était bizarre
17. elle provenait du tréfonds de sa gorge

next to his[1] and through some kind of cloth he could feel her face move when she talked. She must have something around her mouth too.

Where were they? It was so cold and so smelly here. There was something over him, a smelly[2] blanket, he guessed[3]. His eyes were so squeezed together and it was so dark.

The man had opened the door and knocked him down[4]. He had tied them up and he'd taken Sharon away. Then he'd come back and Neil had felt himself being picked up and squished into some kind of bag[5]. Once[6], over at Sandy's[7], they'd played hide-and-seek[8] and he'd hidden in a big leaf bag[9] that he found in the garage. It had felt like that.[10] He didn't remember anything after the man put him in the bag, not until Sharon was pulling him out of it[11]. He wondered why he didn't remember. It was like when Mommy fell.

He didn't want to think about that. Sharon was saying, "Breathe slowly, Neil. Don't cry, Neil, you're brave[12]."

She probably thought he was a crybaby too. Tonight he'd been crying when she came. It was just that when he didn't eat the toast and tea Mrs. Lufts made for him she said, "Looks like[13] we'll have to take you to Florida when we go, Neil. Got to fatten you up somehow.[14]"

See[15]. That proved it.[16] If Daddy married Sharon it was like[17] Sandy said. Nobody wanted sick kids and they'd make him go with the Lufts.

And he'd started to cry.

But Sharon didn't seem to be mad[18] that he was sick now. In that funny voice she was saying, "in ... out[19] ... slowly breathe through your nose ..." He tried to obey, in ... out ... "You're brave, Neil, think about when you tell all this to your friends."

1. tout près du sien
2. qui sentait mauvais
3. pensa-t-il
4. l'avait fait tomber
5. qu'on l'attrapait et le tassait dans une espèce de sac
6. Une fois
7. chez Sandy
8. joué à cache-cache
9. sac pour les feuilles mortes
10. C'était la même sensation.
11. l'en fasse sortir
12. courageux
13. Il semblerait que
14. Il faut qu'on trouve un moyen de t'engraisser.
15. Voilà.
16. C'était bien la preuve.
17. ça se passerait comme
18. être furieuse
19. inspire... expire

Sometimes Sandy asked him about the day Mommy got hurt. Sandy said, "If anybody started to hurt my mother, I'd make them stop."

Maybe he should have been able to make the man stop. He wanted to ask Daddy about that but he never had[1]. Daddy always told him not to think about that day anymore.

But sometimes he couldn't help it[2].

In … out … Sharon's hair was on his cheek. She didn't seem to mind that he was all squished[3] against her. Why had that man brought them here? He knew who he was. He'd seen him a couple of weeks ago when Mr. Lufts took him to where the man worked[4].

He'd been getting a lot of bad dreams[5] since that day. He'd started to tell Daddy about them but Mrs. Lufts came in and he felt stupid and didn't say anymore. Mrs. Lufts always asked so many dumb[6] questions: "Did you brush your teeth?[7] Did you keep your scarf on at lunch[8]? Do you feel all right? Did you sleep well? Did you eat all your lunch? Did you get your feet wet? Did you hang up your clothes?[9]" And she never let him answer really. She'd just rummage through his lunchbox[10] to see if he'd eaten or make him open his mouth so she could look down his throat[11].

It was different when Mommy was there. Mrs. Lufts came in just one day every week to clean. It was after Mommy went to heaven that she and Mr. Lufts moved in upstairs[12] and that was when everything changed.

Thinking about all that, listening to Sharon, had made the tears go away by themselves[13]. He was scared now but it wasn't like that day when Mommy fell and he'd been alone. It wasn't like that …

The man …

His breathing got fast again[14], chokey[15]. "Neil." Now Sharon was rubbing her face against his. "Try

1. ne l'avait jamais fait
2. ne pouvait pas s'en empêcher
3. être ennuyée par le fait qu'il soit tout pelotonné
4. sur le lieu de travail de cet homme
5. faisait beaucoup de cauchemars
6. bêtes
7. Tu t'es brossé les dents ?
8. pendant le déjeuner
9. Tu as mis tes vêtements dans la penderie ?
10. se contentait de fouiller dans sa boîte-repas
11. regarder au fond de sa gorge
12. avaient emménagé à l'étage
13. les larmes séchèrent d'elles-mêmes
14. s'accéléra de nouveau
15. étranglée

to think about when we get out of here. Your dad will be so glad to see us. I bet he'll take us out[1]. You know, I'd like to go ice-skating[2] with you. You didn't come with us that time your dad came down to New York. And afterwards we were going to take you to the zoo next to the rink[3] …"

He listened. Sharon sounded as though[4] she really meant it[5]. He'd been planning to go down that day, but when he told Sandy he was going, Sandy said that Sharon probably didn't want him but was just trying to make his father feel good[6] by asking him along[7] too.

"Your dad tells me that he wants to start taking you to football games at Princeton next fall[8]," she said. "I used to go to Dartmouth games all the time when I was in college[9]. Every year they played Princeton[10], but your dad had graduated by then[11]. I went to a girls'[12] college, Mount Holyoke. It was just two hours from Dartmouth and a whole bunch of us[13] used to go up[14] some weekends, especially in football season …"

Her voice sounded so funny, like a growly whisper[15], Neil decided.

"Lots of men bring their families to the games[16]. Your dad's so proud of you. He says you're so brave when you get the asthma shots. He said most kids would be carrying on about having to have a shot every single week, but you never complain or cry. That's pretty brave."

It was so hard to talk. She tried to swallow.

"Neil, plan now[17]. That's what I do when I'm scared or sick. I plan something nice that I know will be fun. Last year when I was in Lebanon[18]—that's a country about five thousand miles from here[19]—I was writing a story about the war they'd had, and I was staying in this ratty[20] place, and one night I was so sick. I had flu[21] and a fever and I was

1. qu'on fera une sortie avec lui
2. faire du patin à glace
3. patinoire
4. donnait l'impression
5. de vraiment penser ce qu'elle disait
6. de faire plaisir à son père
7. lui demandant de venir
8. l'automne prochain
9. à l'université
10. jouait contre Princeton
11. avait obtenu son diplôme à cette époque-là
12. pour filles
13. on était toute une bande
14. qui avait l'habitude d'y aller
15. un peu comme si elle grommelait doucement
16. assister aux matchs
17. imagine un peu
18. Liban
19. à environ huit mille kilomètres d'ici
20. miteux
21. la grippe

by myself[1] and everything ached[2], my arms and legs, just the way they hurt now all tied up[3], and I made myself think of something nice[4] that I'd do when I got home. And I remembered a painting that I wanted to buy. It was of a harbor[5] with sailboats. And I promised myself that as soon as I got home, I'd treat myself to that picture[6]. And I did.[7]"

Her voice was getting lower[8]. He had to listen hard to catch every word[9].

"And I think we should plan a treat for you[10], a real treat[11]. You know your dad says that the Lufts are really anxious to move to[12] Florida now."

Neil felt a giant fist[13] squeeze his chest.

"Easy[14], Neil! Remember, in… out … breathe slowly. Well, when your dad showed me your house and I saw the Lufts' room and looked out the window, it was just like my painting. Because you can see all over[15] the harbor and the boats and the Sound and the island. And if I were you, when the Lufts move to Florida, I'd take that room for myself. I'd put bookcases[16] in it and shelves[17] for your games and a desk. The alcove is so big you could really put tracks[18] all over it for your trains. Your dad said you loved your trains. I had them when I was little too. In fact, I've got some great Lionel[19] trains that used to be *my* dad's. That's how old they are.[20] I'd like you to have them."

When the Lufts move to Florida … when the Lufts move to Florida … Sharon didn't expect him to go with them. Sharon thought he should have their room.

"And I'm scared now and I'm uncomfortable[21] and I wish I was out of here but I'm glad you're with me and I'm going to tell your dad how brave you were and how careful you were to breathe slowly and not get all chokey."

1. j'étais toute seule
2. j'avais mal partout
3. maintenant qu'ils sont attachés
4. me suis obligée à penser à des choses agréables
5. port
6. m'offrirais ce tableau
7. Et c'est ce que j'ai fait.
8. faiblissait
9. tendre l'oreille pour saisir chaque mot
10. songer à te faire plaisir
11. vraiment plaisir
12. très impatients d'aller habiter en
13. poing
14. Doucement
15. embrasser d'un seul regard
16. une bibliothèque
17. des étagères
18. des rails
19. [marque américaine de jouets et de trains miniatures qui a disparu en 1993]
20. C'est dire leur ancienneté.
21. je ne suis pas bien

The heavy, black stone that always seemed to be lying on Neil's chest moved a little. Just the way he could wiggle a baby tooth[1] when it got loose[2], Sharon's voice was moving the stone back and forth[3]. Suddenly Neil felt desperately sleepy[4]. His hands were tied but he could move his fingers and slide them along[5] Sharon's arm until he found what he wanted, a piece of her sleeve that he could hold. Wrapping his fingers around[6] the soft wool, he drifted into sleep[7].

The harsh, raspy breathing assumed an even pattern[8]. Apprehensively, Sharon listened to the thick wheeze, felt the labored[9] movement of Neil's chest. This room was so freezing, so damp, and Neil already had a cold[10]. But at least lying this close together meant[11] their shared body heat gave some warmth[12].

What time was it? They'd gotten to this place just past seven-thirty. The man … Foxy … had stayed at least a few hours with them. How long had he been gone? It must be past midnight. It was Tuesday now. Foxy had said that they'd be here till Wednesday. Where would Steve get eighty-two thousand dollars ransom money in one day? And why that crazy figure[13]? Would he try to get in touch with[14] her parents? It would be hard[15], with them living in Iran now. When Neil woke up[16], she'd tell him about that and about how her father was an engineer.

"Wednesday morning you and I are going away and I'll leave word where to find the boy." She explored[17] the promise. She would have to act as though she wanted to go with him. As soon as[18] Neil was safe and only she and the kidnapper were in the terminal, she'd start screaming. No matter what he might do to her, she'd have to take the chance.

Why in God's name[19] had he kidnapped them? There was something about the way he looked at

1. faire bouger une dent de lait
2. commençait à branler
3. d'avant en arrière
4. ressentit une envie irrésistible de dormir
5. glisser le long du
6. Enroulant entre ses doigts
7. s'endormit
8. se fit régulière
9. laborieux
10. rhume
11. à être étendus si près l'un de l'autre,
12. ils se réchauffaient mutuellement
13. chiffre insensé
14. joindre
15. difficile
16. se réveillerait
17. étudia sous tous ses angles
18. Dès que
19. au nom du ciel

Neil. As though he hated him and was … frightened of him. But that was impossible.

Had he kept the blindfold on Neil because he was afraid Neil might recognize him? Maybe he was someone from around[1] Carley. If that were true, how could he let Neil live? Neil had seen him when he pushed his way[2] into the house. Neil had *stared* at him. Neil would recognize this man if he saw him again. She was sure of it. He must realize that too. Was he planning to kill Neil as soon as he had the money?

Yes he was.[3]

Even if he brought her out of this place[4], it might be too late for Neil.

A passion of[5] fear and anger made her press closer to[6] Neil, bend her legs[7] against his, attempt to enfold him[8] in the woman's arc of her body.

Tomorrow. Wednesday.

This must be the way Mrs. Thompson was feeling now, this minute[9]. This sense of rage and fear and helplessness[10], this primal need[11] to protect one's young[12]. Neil was Steve's son and Steve had suffered so much already. Steve must be frantic[13]. He and Mrs. Thompson were going through identical agony[14].

She didn't blame Mrs. Thompson for lashing out at her[15]. She didn't mean[16] what she said; she couldn't[17]. Ron was guilty; there was no hope of anyone believing anything else. That was what Mrs. Thompson didn't understand; that the only possible hope of saving him was to have a massive outcry[18] against the execution.

At least she, Sharon, had tried to help him. Steve, oh Steve, she cried silently, now do you understand? Now do you see?

She tried to rub her wrists against the wall. The cinderblocks[19] were rough and jagged[20] but the way

1. originaire de
2. s'était introduit de force
3. Oui, c'était certain.
4. la faisait sortir de cet endroit
5. Une vague de
6. la poussa à se plaquer davantage contre
7. à replier ses jambes
8. dans un effort pour l'envelopper
9. à cet instant même
10. d'impuissance
11. besoin primitif
12. son petit
13. affolé
14. enduraient le même supplice
15. de s'être répandue en invectives à son encontre
16. ne pensait pas
17. c'était impossible
18. tollé général
19. parpaings
20. rugueux et granuleux

the cords were tied, the knuckles[1] and sides of her hand were taking the brunt of the contact[2].

When Foxy came back, she'd tell him she had to use the bathroom[3]. He'd have to untie her[4]. Maybe then, somehow ...

Those pictures. He had killed those women. Only a madman would take pictures as he murdered and blow them up to that size[5].

He had taken *her* picture.

That bomb. Suppose someone did come near this room? If that bomb went off[6], she and Neil and how many others[7]? How powerful was it?[8]

She tried to pray, could only say over and over again[9], "Please, let[10] Steve find us in time, please don't take his son from him."

That must be Mrs. Thompson's prayer. "Spare[11] my son."

I blame you, Miss Martin ...

Time moved agonizingly past[12]. Her arms and legs subsided from pain into sudden numbness[13]. Miraculously, Neil slept. Sometimes he'd moan[14] and his breath would catch and he'd gasp, but then he'd sink back into fitful sleep[15].

It must be getting toward morning.[16] The train sounds were becoming more frequent. What time did the station open? Five o'clock? It must be that now.[17]

By eight[18] this terminal would be swarming with people[19]. Suppose that bomb went off?

Neil stirred restlessly[20]. He muttered something. She couldn't make it out[21]. He was waking up.

Neil tried to open his eyes and could not. He had to go to the bathroom. His arms and legs hurt. It was hard to breathe. Then he remembered what had happened. He'd run to the door and said, "Oh, that's all right," and opened it. Why had he said that?

He remembered.

1. de la façon dont les liens étaient noués, c'était la jointure de ses doigts
2. qu'elle écorchait contre le mur
3. devait aller aux toilettes
4. qu'il la détache
5. les agrandirait dans de telles proportions
6. explosait
7. combien d'autres
8. Quelle était sa puissance ?
9. mais ne put que répéter à l'infini
10. Je vous en supplie, faites que
11. Épargnez
12. s'écoulait, inexorable
13. s'engourdirent soudain au point de faire envoler toute douleur
14. gémissait
15. replongeait dans un sommeil agité
16. Le matin ne devait plus être loin.
17. Il devait être 5 heures maintenant.
18. À 8 heures
19. grouillerait de monde
20. s'agita nerveusement
21. ne comprit pas ce qu'il disait

1. la pierre dans sa poitrine bouger d'avant en arrière
2. au lointain
3. était penché sur
4. s'était tenu au-dessus de lui
5. s'était avancé vers lui
6. tendu les mains
7. s'était penché pour le regarder droit dans les yeux
8. s'était enfui
9. s'était baissé pour l'attraper
10. s'évertuait à parler
11. en dépit de sa respiration bruyante et voilée

He felt the rock moving back and forth in his chest[1]. He felt Sharon's breath on his face. There was a far-off[2] train sound.

A train sound.

And Mommy. He'd run downstairs.

And the man let Mommy drop and turned to him.

And then the man was bending over[3] Mommy, looking all sweaty and scared.

No.

The man who pushed the door in last night, who stood over him[4] and looked down at him; he'd done that before.

He'd come at him[5]. He'd let Mommy drop and come at him. He'd put his hands out[6] and looked right down at him[7].

And something happened.

The chimes. The chimes from the front door.

The man had run away[8]. Neil had watched him run away.

That was why he couldn't stop dreaming about that day. Because of the part he forgot … the scary part when the man came to him and had his hands out and reached down to him[9].

The man …

The man who'd been talking to Mr. Lufts.

And last night had come pushing into the house and stood over him.

"Sharon." Neil's voice was muffled and hoarse as he struggled to speak[10] through the thick wheeze[11] …

"Yes, Neil. I'm here."

"Sharon, that man, the bad man who tied us up …"

"Yes, dear, don't be afraid, I'll take care of you."

"Sharon, that's the man who killed my Mommy."

25

The room. Lally *had* to go to her room. It didn't matter how cold it was.[1] Newspapers between her two blankets[2] would keep her warm enough[3]. She missed it so much.[4] The Tenth Avenue flop she and Rosie and some of the others[5] had slept in most of the winter was too crowded[6]. She needed her alone time[7]. She needed her place to dream.

Years ago when she was young, after she read the Louella Parsons and Hedda Hopper[8] columns, Lally would lull herself to sleep[9] pretending that instead of being a homely spinster[10] schoolteacher, she was a movie star coming into Grand Central Station with all the reporters and photographers waiting.

Sometimes she'd be in white fox when she stepped off the[11] *Twentieth Century Limited*[12]; or she'd be wearing a tailored silk suit[13], holding sable skins[14], and her secretary would be carrying the dressing case[15] with her jewels.

Once she fantasized[16] that she was already in an evening gown[17] because she was going directly to the premiere of her movie on Broadway, wearing that ball gown Ginger Rogers wore in *Top Hat*[18].

After a while the dreams faded[19] and she became used to life as it was[20]; dreary[21], monotonous, lone-

1. Peu importe le froid qui y régnait.
2. couvertures
3. lui tiendraient suffisamment chaud
4. Cela lui manquait tant.
5. L'asile de nuit de la 10ᵉ avenue dans lequel elle, Rosie et quelques autres
6. bondé
7. avait besoin de passer du temps seule
8. [célèbres chroniqueuses mondaines]
9. s'assoupissait
10. célibataire et peu séduisante
11. descendait du
12. [train express qui fonctionna de 1902 à 1967 entre New York et Chicago]
13. tailleur en soie
14. une fourrure en zibeline
15. mallette de voyage
16. rêva
17. robe de soirée
18. [film musical mettant en scène F. Astaire et G. Rogers]
19. s'évanouirent
20. telle qu'elle était vraiment
21. morne

ly. But when she arrived in New York and began to spend all her time in Grand Central, it was as though she really was remembering her heyday[1] as a star; not pretending at all[2].

Then when Rusty gave her the key to the room and she could sleep nestled[3] in her station, listening to the faint sound of her trains coming and going, it made everything perfect[4].

At 8:30 Tuesday morning, armed with[5] her shopping bags, she was heading toward the lower terminal to the Mount Vernon track. Her plan was to mosey down[6] the ramp with the people who were taking the 8:50 and then slip around[7] to her room. On the way she stopped at the Nedicks in the corridor leading from the Biltmore and ordered coffee and donuts[8]. She had already finished the *Times* and *News*, which she had gotten out of a receptacle[9].

The man ahead of her[10] at the takeout counter[11] looked vaguely familiar. Why[12], he was the one who spoiled her plans[13] last night by going down to the Mount Vernon platform with the girl in the gray coat! Resentfully[14], she heard him order two coffees and rolls[15] and milk. With hostile eyes she watched him pay his bill and pick up his package. She wondered if he worked around here. Somehow she didn't think so.

After leaving Nedicks, she deliberately dawdled through[16] the terminal so the cops who knew her wouldn't think she was doing anything out of the ordinary[17]. But at last she was at the ramp to the 132 Mount Vernon track. The train was loading[18]. People were hurrying now. Delighted, Lally fell into step with them[19], moving down the platform. As the others rushed into the train, she slipped around[20] the last car and turned right. In an instant she'd be out of sight[21].

1. se souvenait réellement du temps de sa splendeur
2. sans aucun faux-semblant
3. blottie
4. tout lui sembla parfait
5. munie de
6. de descendre d'un pas nonchalant
7. de filer
8. [beignets sucrés de forme annulaire, aux diverses saveurs]
9. avait sortis d'une poubelle
10. devant elle
11. point de vente à emporter
12. Mais oui
13. avait gâché ses plans
14. Pleine de ressentiment
15. des petits pains
16. traînassa dans tous les recoins de
17. qu'elle se conduisait étrangement
18. se remplissait
19. leur emboîta le pas
20. contourna
21. serait hors de vue

And then she saw him. The man who'd just bought the coffee and milk and rolls. The man who'd come down here last night. His back was to her.[1] He was hurrying now, disappearing into the gloom of the throbbing depths[2] of the terminal.

There was only one place where he could be going. *Her room.*

He had found it! That was why he went down on the platform last night. He wasn't waiting for the train. He had gone to her room with the girl.

And he had two coffees and milk and four rolls. So the girl must be there now.

Bitter, disappointed tears[3] welled up in Lally's eyes[4]. They had taken over[5] her room! Then her lifelong ability to cope[6] rescued her[7]. She could handle this[8]. She'd get rid of them[9]! She'd watch and when she was sure he was out, she'd go into the room and warn[10] the girl that the cops knew they were there and were coming to arrest them. That'd scare her off[11] fast enough. He was a mean-looking one[12], but the girl wasn't the kind to be hanging around[13] stations. Probably thought it was some kind of game being there. She'd probably clear out fast[14] and take him with her.

Grimly satisfied at the prospect of[15] tricking the interlopers[16], Lally turned around[17] and headed for the upstairs waiting room. Her imagination leaped to[18] the girl who was probably right now lying on *her* cot waiting for her boyfriend to bring in breakfast. "Don't get too comfortable in there[19], missy[20]," she thought, "you're going to have company real soon[21]."

1. Il lui tournait le dos.
2. les profondeurs obscures et vibrantes
3. Des larmes d'amertume et de déception
4. montèrent aux yeux de Lally
5. investi
6. cette capacité à faire face, qu'elle avait acquise au cours de son existence,
7. la sauva
8. faire face à cette situation
9. se débarrasserait d'eux
10. préviendrait
11. la ferait fuir
12. avait un air méchant
13. à traîner dans
14. décamperait probablement vite fait
15. à la perspective de
16. piéger les intrus
17. fit volte-face
18. la ramena d'un coup à
19. Ne prends pas trop tes aises
20. ma petite demoiselle
21. très bientôt

26

1. venait d'apporter
2. tout droit sortis du four
3. [petits pains ronds et plats au maïs]
4. appuyé sur
5. de ne pas mettre mes coudes
6. Clignant des yeux, il chassa cette pensée.
7. Ça ne servait à rien.
8. en picolant dans la nuit
9. injectés de sang
10. de dire si la voix était familière
11. la repassa
12. l'arrêta d'un coup sec
13. nous mettions certaines choses au point
14. vingt-quatre heures sur vingt-quatre
15. réglé
16. intelligent

Steve, Hugh, the Lufts and agent Hank Lamont sat at the dining-room table. Dora Lufts had just brought[1] a pot of coffee and freshly baked[2] corn muffins[3] to the table. Steve looked at them without interest. His chin was resting on[4] his hand. Just the other night Neil had said to him, "You're always telling me not to put my elbows[5] on the table and you always sit like that, Daddy."

He blinked away the thought.[6] No use.[7] No use. Keep concentrating on what could be done. Carefully, he studied Bill Lufts. Undoubtedly Bill had consoled himself with booze during the night[8]. His eyes were bloodshot[9] and his hands were shaking.

They had just heard the nineteen-word tape of the first phonecall. Muffled, indistinct, it was impossible to recognize the voice as familiar[10]. Hugh played it[11] three times, then snapped it off[12]. "All right. We'll take it over to Mrs. Perry, as soon as Mr. Perry calls us, and see what she says about it. Now it's very, very important that we get a few things straight[13]."

He consulted the list in front of him. "First, there'll be an agent here 'round the clock[14] till this is settled[15]. I think the man who calls himself Foxy is too clever[16] to call this phone or the Perrys'. He'll guess[1] that we have taps[2] on them. But there's always the chance[3] …

"Mr. Peterson has to go down[4] to New York, so if the phone rings, Mrs. Lufts, you must answer it immediately. Agent Lamont will be on the extension[5] and we'll be recording it as well. But if the abductor does call, you must not get rattled[6]. You must try to keep him on the phone as long as possible. Can you do that?"

"I'll try," Dora quavered[7].

"What about Neil's school? Did you phone and report him ill[8]?"

"Yes. Right at eight-thirty[9], just as you told me."

"Fine." Hugh turned to Steve. "Did you reach[10] your office, Mr. Peterson?"

"Yes. The publisher had suggested I take Neil away[11] for a few days until after the Thompson execution tomorrow. I left word[12] I was doing that."

Hugh turned to Bill Lufts. "Mr. Lufts, I'd like you to stay right here in the house for today at least. Would anyone find that unusual?"

His wife laughed mirthlessly[13]. "Only the regulars[14] at the Mill Tavern," she said.

"All right, thank you both." Hugh's tone dismissed the Lufts[15]. They got up and went into the kitchen, partially closing the door behind them.

Hugh leaned over and closed it with a decided thud[16]. He raised one eyebrow to Steve[17]. "I don't think the Lufts miss very much[18] of what's said in this house, Mr. Peterson," he commented[19].

Steve shrugged. "I know. But ever since Bill retired the first of the year[20], they've really been staying on as a favor to me[21]. They're very anxious to get to Florida."

"You said they've been here two years?"

"A little longer than that. Dora was our cleaning woman. She came in one day a week since before

1. aura deviné
2. avons installé des écoutes téléphoniques
3. Mais sait-on jamais
4. se rendre
5. l'autre poste
6. vous laisser déstabiliser
7. répondit d'une voix tremblotante
8. pour signaler qu'il était malade
9. À huit heures trente précises
10. joint
11. m'avait suggéré d'éloigner Neil
12. J'ai laissé un message disant que
13. émit un rire sans joie
14. les habitués
15. invitait les Lufts à prendre congé
16. claqua la porte
17. regarda Steve, le sourcil levé
18. Je pense que les Lufts ne perdent pas une miette
19. fit-il remarquer
20. a pris sa retraite le 1er janvier
21. pour me rendre service

Neil was born[1]. Our other house was only six blocks from here, you know. They were saving money for their retirement[2]. When Nina was killed we'd just moved in[3] here and I had to have someone to take care of Neil. I suggested that they take that large third-floor room. That way they could save the overhead[4] they'd been paying, and I paid Dora as much as she was getting for all her cleaning jobs."

"How has it worked out?"

"Reasonably well. They're both very fond of[5] Neil and she looks after him very carefully, too carefully maybe. She's always fussing over him[6]. But since Bill's been hanging around with nothing to do, he's been into a lot of drinking[7]. Frankly, I'll be glad when they do make the move[8]."

"What's been holding them back[9]?" Hugh asked sharply[10]. "Money?"

"No. I don't think so. Dora would love to see me remarried so that Neil would have a mother again. Dora's really an awfully good soul[11]."

"And you've been getting close to that with[12] Sharon Martin?"

Steve's smile was wintry[13]. "I hope so.[14]" Restlessly, he stood up and walked to the window. The snow was falling again, effortlessly, noiselessly. It seemed to him that he had as much control over his life[15] as one of those snowflakes[16] had over its ultimate destination ... to fall, land on shrub[17] or grass or street, to melt[18] or freeze on contact, to be swept away[19], driven over, crunched down by[20] boots.

He was getting fanciful, lightheaded.[21] Deliberately he pulled his mind back to the present.[22] He could not be helpless[23], waiting here immobilized. He had to *do*[24] something.

"I'll get the bankbook[25] and start down to New York," he told Hugh.

1. même avant la naissance de Neil
2. économisaient pour leur retraite
3. on venait d'emménager
4. le loyer
5. aiment tous les deux beaucoup
6. est constamment aux petits soins pour lui
7. s'est mis à boire énormément
8. partiront
9. les a retenus
10. sèchement
11. est vraiment un ange
12. c'est ce que vous vous apprêtez à faire avec
13. glacial
14. Je l'espère.
15. autant de prise sur sa vie
16. flocons de neige
17. atterrir sur un buisson
18. fondre
19. être balayé
20. écrasé sous
21. Il perdait pied, et la tête lui tournait.
22. Il fit un effort pour revenir au présent.
23. impuissant
24. impérativement faire
25. livret d'épargne

"Just a minute[1], Mr. Peterson. There are a few things we need to discuss."

Steve waited.

"What happens if you don't get a tape of your son and Sharon?"

"He *promised* ..."

"He may not be able to deliver[2]. How would he get it to you, assuming he makes it[3]? The point is[4], are you prepared to pay the money without the proof?"

Steve considered. "Yes. I won't take the chance of antagonizing him. Maybe he'll leave a tape or cassette somewhere expecting it to be found[5], and then if I don't follow through[6] ..."

"All right. We'll face that later. If it hasn't come by two A.M. when he calls you at the Fifty-ninth Street payphone, you can consider stalling[7]. Tell him you didn't get it. If he claims[8] he left it somewhere, it's easy enough to pick it up.

"Now the next consideration[9]. Do you want to give him real cash[10]? We could get counterfeit money[11] that would be easy to trace."

"I simply won't take that chance. The money in the trust is for Neil's education[12]. If anything hap pens to him ..."

"All right. So you'll get the money from your account[13] and take it down[14] to the Federal Reserve Bank[15]. Get a cashier's check[16]. Our men will be there photographing the ransom bills[17]. That way at least we'll have some record[18]."

Steve interrupted. "I don't want the money marked."

"I'm not talking about *marking* it. There's no way the abductor can possibly know if we've *photographed* it. But that will take time. Eighty-two thousand dollars in tens, twenties and fifties is a lot of bills to handle[19]."

"I know."

1. Un petit instant
2. vous la faire parvenir
3. à supposer qu'il l'enregistre
4. La question est
5. dans un endroit où il s'attend à ce qu'on la trouve
6. je ne vais pas jusqu'au bout
7. chercher à gagner du temps
8. prétend
9. passons à autre chose
10. vrais billets
11. faux billets
12. études
13. retirerez l'argent de votre compte
14. le déposerez
15. Banque fédérale de réserve
16. chèque de banque
17. billets de la rançon
18. une trace
19. à manipuler

"Mr. Peterson, there are several precautions I'm going to urge you[1] to take. One, let us rig cameras[2] into your car. That way we may have some kind of lead to follow[3] after you make contact[4] with the abductor. We may be able to get a picture of him or pick up the license number[5] of the car he's driving. We'd also like to install a beeper device[6] in your car so that we can follow you from a distance. I promise you they'll be impossible to detect. Last, and this is entirely up to you[7], we'd like to conceal an electronic tracer[8] in the suitcase with the money."

"Suppose it's found. The abductor will know I brought you in[9]."

"Suppose you *don't* put it in and you don't hear another word[10]. You've paid the money and you don't have your child or Sharon. Believe me, Mr. Peterson, our first concern is to get them back safely[11]. After that we'll pull out all the stops[12] to find the perpetrators[13]. But it's up to you[14]."

"What would you do if it were your son and your ... wife?"

"Mr. Peterson, we're not dealing with[15] honorable people. It's not as simple as pay the money and you get them back. Maybe they'll release them[16]. *Maybe.* But maybe they'll just abandon them somewhere unable to free themselves. That has to be considered.[17] At least the area may be narrowed down[18] if we can follow the kidnapper's trail electronically."

Steve shrugged helplessly. "Do what you have to. I'll take Bill's car to New York."

"No. I'd like to suggest that you take your own car and park it in the lot near the station as usual. It's very possible your movements are being watched. We'll have a loose tail on you[19], an agent following you from a distance. Leave your keys on the floor. We'll pick the car up and get the equipment installed

1. vous conseiller vivement
2. laissez-nous installer des caméras
3. pourrons avoir une piste à suivre
4. serez entré en contact
5. relever le numéro d'immatriculation
6. émetteur
7. Enfin, et la décision vous appartient totalement
8. dissimuler un autre émetteur
9. vous ai prévenus
10. que vous n'entendiez plus parler de lui
11. de les ramener sains et saufs
12. mettrons tout en œuvre
13. les auteurs de l'enlèvement
14. c'est votre décision
15. n'avons pas affaire à
16. les relâcheront
17. Il faut prendre cet aspect en compte.
18. on pourra réduire le champ des recherches
19. On vous filera discrètement

and have it there when you come back. Now here's where you go with the money ..."

Steve caught the 10:40 train to Grand Central Station. It was ten minutes behind schedule[1] and he arrived at the terminal at 11:50. Electing[2] to walk up Park Avenue, he carried a large, empty suitcase in his hand.

His sense of futility and misery[3] deepened as he trudged the blocks[4] between the terminal and Fifty-first Street. On this, the second day of the snowstorm, New Yorkers, exhibiting their customary resiliency[5], were out on the streets as usual. There was even a buoyancy[6] about the way they stepped over icy curbs, maneuvered around drifts[7]. Yesterday morning he and Sharon had stood in the falling snow a few blocks from here and he'd held her face in his hands and kissed her goodbye. Her lips had been unresponsive[8] just as he'd been unresponsive when Nina kissed him goodbye that last day.

He arrived at the bank. The news that he wanted to withdraw all but[9] two hundred dollars from Neil's account was greeted with a lifted eyebrow. The teller[10] left her cage[11] and consulted with a senior vice-president[12], who hurried over[13] to Steve.

"Mr. Peterson," he asked, "is there any problem?"

"No, Mr. Strauss. I simply wish to make a withdrawal."

"I'll have to ask you to fill out state and federal forms[14]. It's required for any withdrawal that large[15]. I hope there has been no dissatisfaction with our handling[16] of your son's account."

Steve struggled to keep his tone and expression even[17]. "None at all."

"Very well." The vice-president's tone became coolly[18] professional. "You can fill out the necessary forms at my desk. Follow me, please."

1. Il avait dix minutes de retard
2. Choisissant
3. de détresse
4. avançait péniblement d'une rue à l'autre
5. faisant montre de leur vitalité coutumière
6. entrain
7. évitaient les congères
8. Elle ne lui avait pas rendu son baiser
9. retirer la totalité de l'argent à l'exception de
10. caissière
11. guichet
12. directeur général adjoint
13. se précipita
14. remplir les formulaires de l'État du Connecticut et ceux du gouvernement fédéral
15. retrait de cette importance
16. gestion
17. calmes
18. froidement

Mechanically, Steve scrawled[1] the required information. By the time[2] he was finished, the teller had brought the cashier's check to the desk.

Mr. Strauss quickly signed it, handed it to him and stood up. The man's face had become thoughtful. "I don't mean to intrude[3], but there isn't any trouble, is there[4], Mr. Peterson? Perhaps something we can help with[5]?"

Steve stood up. "No, no, thank you, Mr. Strauss." To his own ears, he sounded strained[6], unconvincing.

"I hope not. We value you very much, as a client of this bank and, I hope, as a friend. If there *is*[7] a problem and if we can help, please give us the chance." He held out his hand.

Steve grasped it. "You're very kind but it's quite all right[8], I assure you."

Carrying the suitcase, he went out, hailed[9] a cab and directed it to the Federal Reserve Bank. There he was taken to a room where grim-faced FBI agents were busily counting and photographing the money he would exchange for the check he was carrying. Bleakly he watched them.

"The king was in the counting house[10], counting up his money[11]." The nursery rhyme[12] ran through his head[13]. Nina used to singsong it to[14] Neil when she was getting him ready for bed[15].

He returned to Grand Central just in time to miss[16] the 3:05 train. The next train wouldn't leave for an hour. He called home. Dora answered and agent Lamont spoke from the extension. No further[17] news. No sign of a cassette. Hugh Taylor would be back by the time he arrived.

The prospect of the hour to kill[18] appalled[19] Steve. His head was aching[20]; a slow, burning ache that began in the center of his forehead and traveled back on each side[21] like an ever tightening vise[22]. He realized he'd eaten nothing since yesterday's lunch.

1. griffonna
2. Le temps qu'
3. Je ne veux pas être indiscret
4. n'est-ce pas ?
5. pouvons-nous vous aider d'une façon ou d'une autre
6. tendu
7. il y a vraiment
8. tout va bien
9. héla
10. salle du trésor
11. à compter ses sous
12. comptine
13. lui passa par la tête
14. la chantait souvent à
15. s'apprêtait à le mettre au lit
16. et rata de peu
17. d'autres
18. perspective d'avoir une heure à tuer
19. épouvantait
20. Il avait mal à la tête
21. remontait sur les tempes
22. comme un étau toujours plus serré

The Oyster Bar. He'd go down there and order a plate of oyster stew and a drink. He passed the phone[1] he'd used last night when he tried to call Sharon. That had been the beginning of this nightmare. When he didn't get an answer, he'd known that something was wrong. That was only twenty hours ago. It seemed a lifetime.[2]

Twenty hours. Where were Sharon and Neil? Had they been given anything to eat? It was so cold out. Were they in a place with heat[3]? If there was any way possible[4], Sharon would take care of Neil, he knew that. Suppose Sharon had answered the phone when he'd called last night. Suppose the three of them had spent the evening together as they'd planned. After Neil went to bed, he was going to say, "You won't be getting much[5], Sharon. You probably could do a lot better[6] if you waited, but don't wait. Marry me. We're good together.[7]"

She probably would have turned him down[8]. She despised[9] his position on capital punishment. Well, he'd been sure enough of it, relentless about it, positive he was right.

Was this the way Ronald Thompson's mother was feeling right this minute[10]? Even when it was over[11] for that boy, she'd go on suffering the rest of her life.

As he would[12], if anything happened to Sharon and Neil.

The pace of this terminal[13] was beginning to quicken. Executives[14] leaving early to avoid the commuter rush[15] walked briskly to the New Haven trains that would take them to Westchester and Connecticut. Women in[16] for a day of shopping crossed the terminal, consulting timetables[17], anxious to be home in time to start dinner.

Steve descended the stairs to the lower level and went into the Oyster Bar. It was nearly empty. The lunch rush[18] was long since over[19]. It was too early

1. passa devant le téléphone
2. Cela lui sembla une éternité.
3. dans un lieu chauffé
4. Quoi qu'il en soit
5. Je n'ai pas grand-chose à t'offrir
6. pourrais sans doute trouver bien mieux
7. On est bien ensemble.
8. aurait probablement rejeté sa proposition
9. méprisait
10. en ce moment même
11. tout serait fini
12. Tout comme lui
13. Le rythme à l'intérieur de la gare
14. Des cadres
15. l'heure de pointe
16. venues en ville
17. horaires
18. L'heure d'affluence du déjeuner
19. passée depuis longtemps

1. euphorique
2. nombre impressionnant de réactions
3. On va y arriver
4. ça lui tenait tellement à cœur.
5. prochain déplacement
6. pour rallier davantage de partisans
7. Tu vas me manquer
8. avala d'un trait
9. barman
10. sans toucher à son ragoût fumant et bouillonnant
11. se rendait dans le wagon fumeurs
12. à l'arrière
13. cachait son visage
14. des yeux brillants le regardèrent avancer
15. descendit
16. se soit éloigné au volant de la voiture
17. phares

for the cocktail and dinner crowd. He sat at the bar and ordered, carefully keeping the suitcase right under his foot.

Last month he and Sharon had met here for lunch. She'd been exhilarated[1] because of the overwhelming response[2] to her campaign to have Thompson's sentence commuted to life imprisonment. "We're going to make it[3], Steve," she said confidently. She'd been so happy; she cared so much.[4] She'd talked about her forthcoming trip[5] to raise more support[6].

"I'll miss you[7]," he'd said.

"I'll miss you, too."

I love you, Sharon. I love you, Sharon. I love you, Sharon. Had he said it then?

He gulped[8] the martini the bartender[9] put in front of him.

He sat in the Oyster Bar, the steaming, bubbling stew untouched[10], until at five minutes of four he paid his bill and went to the upper terminal and the Carley train. He didn't notice that as he made his way to the smoking car[11], a man seated in the rear[12] of the car he entered, buried his face[13] behind a newspaper. It was only after he had passed that the newspaper was lowered slightly and glittering eyes followed his progress[14] through the coach with the heavy suitcase.

That same passenger got off[15] at Carley, but carefully waited on the platform until Steve had entered the parking lot and driven away in the car[16] which now had powerful cameras hidden in the headlights[17] and behind the rearview mirror.

27

Glenda Perry slept until one o'clock. It was the sound of Marian's car pulling out of the driveway that brought her to full wakefulness[1]. Before she opened her eyes she lay perfectly still[2], waiting. But the pain that often accompanied that first stirring[3] did not come. It had been so bad during the night, worse than she had let on to[4] Roger. Except he probably guessed, and she knew the doctor was concerned about the cardiogram.

She was *not* going[5] to the hospital. They'd sedate her so much[6] there that she'd be useless[7]. She wouldn't let it happen[8]. She knew why the pains had been so frequent lately. It was the Thompson boy. He was so young and her testimony had helped[9] condemn him.

"He knocked you down, Mrs. Perry ..."

"Yes, he was running from the house."

"It was dark, Mrs. Perry. Can you be sure it wasn't somebody else running away?"

"Positive.[10] He hesitated in the doorway before he collided into me[11]. The kitchen light was on[12]."

And now Neil and Sharon. Oh God, let me remember. She bit her lip ... a flicker of pain[13] ... no, don't get upset[14]. That won't do any good.[15] For God sake,

1. la réveilla complètement
2. resta parfaitement immobile
3. qu'elle ressentait souvent dès le réveil
4. ne l'avait avoué à
5. n'irait pour rien au monde
6. On lui donnerait tant de tranquillisants
7. bonne à rien
8. ferait tout pour que ça n'arrive pas
9. contribué à
10. Absolument certaine.
11. avant de me percuter
12. allumée
13. une pointe de douleur
14. ne te tourmente pas
15. Ça ne servira à rien.

1. réfléchis
2. préviendrait la douleur
3. intense
4. Qu'est-ce que ça lui rappelait ?
5. Il n'y avait pas si longtemps, en plus.
6. s'entrouvrit
7. Pas mal
8. escabeau
9. à retirer des choses des étagères du haut
10. Dieu merci.
11. tendre le bras jusque là-haut
12. n'ont enregistré que quelques mots
13. Je sens-tu prête
14. adossée à des oreillers
15. C'est gentil de votre part
16. gros effort
17. balaya son inquiétude d'un revers de la main
18. Je suis tout simplement confuse
19. mettez-le en marche
20. La tension liée à l'espoir disparut du
21. pour établir une empreinte vocale
22. une preuve recevable

think[1]. She slipped a nitro under her tongue. That would ward off the pain[2] before it became acute[3]. Foxy. The way he said it. What was the association?[4] It wasn't that long ago, either[5].

The door opened a crack[6] and she saw Roger looking in at her. "It's all right, dear, I'm awake."

"How do you feel?" He hurried over to the bed, touched her hand.

"Not bad[7]. How long have I been asleep?"

"Over four hours."

"Whose car just left?"

"That was Mrs. Vogler."

"Oh, I forgot. What did she do?"

"She seemed to keep herself pretty busy in the kitchen. Was on the stepladder[8] taking things from the top shelves[9]."

"Thank heaven.[10] I've been afraid to stretch up there[11] and they're so dusty. Roger, what happened? Did Steve talk to … Foxy?"

Roger explained—"… so they only have a few words[12]. Are you up[13] to listening to them?"

"Yes."

Fifteen minutes later, propped up on pillows[14], a cup of tea in her hand, Glenda watched Hugh Taylor enter her bedroom.

"This is good of you[15], Mrs. Perry. I understand that it's a strain[16] for you."

She waved away his concern[17]. "Mr. Taylor, I'm just ashamed[18] I've wasted the whole morning. Please turn that on[19]."

She listened intently as Hugh ran the cassette.

"Oh, it's so low. It's impossible …"

The tense expectancy slid from[20] Hugh's face. His tone was emotionless as he said, "Well, thank you very much for listening, Mrs. Perry. We're going to analyze this for voice pattern[21]. It isn't admissible evidence[22], but when we get the abductor it may help to confirm the identification." He picked up the recorder.

"No ... wait!" Glenda put her hand on the machine.

"Is this your only record of the call?"

"No. We ran both a tape and cassette during the wiretap[1]."

"Will you leave this with me?"

"Why?"

"Because I *know* the person I spoke to last night. I know him. I'm going to try now to retrace every single thing I've done[2] in the last few weeks. Maybe something will come to me[3]. And I'd like to be able to hear that tape again."

"Mrs. Perry, if you could only remember ..." Hugh bit his lip as Roger Perry shot a warning glance at him[4]. Quickly he left the room, followed by Roger.

When they were downstairs, Roger asked, "Why did you have me keep Mrs. Vogler here today? Surely you don't suspect ... ?"

"We can't let any possibility pass[5]. But she seems all right[6]. Good character[7], good family situation, well-liked[8]. It's just coincidence that she talked about Neil this morning. And anyhow, she's got the best alibi of anyone[9] last night and so does her husband."

"Why is that?"

"She was seen by the cashier both entering and leaving the movie[10]. Her husband was seen by his neighbors at home with their kids. And shortly after seven o'clock they were in the police station reporting a stolen car[11]."

"Oh yes. She did mention that. Lucky she got it back."

"Yeah. She gets a lousy eight-year-old car back and we haven't got a trace of two kidnap victims. Mr. Perry, what *is* your impression of[12] Sharon Martin? Do you think she's capable of planning this?"

Roger considered. "Every instinct says no.[13]"

1. écoute téléphonique
2. reconstituer mes moindres faits et gestes
3. que quelque chose me reviendra
4. lui jeta un regard pour lui demander de se taire
5. écarter aucune possibilité
6. semble très bien
7. Bonne moralité
8. appréciée de tous
9. un très bon alibi s'il en est
10. cinéma
11. pour déclarer un vol de voiture
12. quelle impression vous fait vraiment
13. D'instinct, je dirai non, pas du tout.

1. Quelle est votre opinion sur
2. étaient passés chez eux
3. chercher des glaçons
4. ne m'accepte pas du tout
5. lui avait ébouriffé les cheveux
6. perturbée que Neil la rejette
7. a été très juste financièrement
8. a mis
9. cela s'avèrera payant
10. cela a été une source de souci
11. En tout cas, c'est ce qu'il m'a dit.
12. réussirait à
13. a la mort dans l'âme à la pensée de
14. affaire
15. intervienne auprès
16. ne pouvait être que contrariée par
17. recours
18. durement
19. puissent être mêlés à tout ça
20. Aucun risque.
21. qu'elle lui a bien rendu la monnaie exacte
22. pour la faire réviser

"How do you size up[1] her relationship with Mr. Peterson?"

Roger thought of the last time Sharon and Steve had been over[2]. She'd seemed a little depressed and Glenda asked her if anything was wrong. Steve had gone into the kitchen for ice[3] and she'd said, "Oh, it's just that Neil shuts me out so[4]." Then when Steve came back, he'd ruffled her hair[5] as he passed her. Roger remembered the expression on both their faces. "I think they were ... are ... very much in love, more than either one of them realizes. I think Sharon has been troubled by Neil's rejection[6], and of course Steve is worried about it too. Then he's been pretty strapped financially[7]. He sank[8] everything he had into *Events*. I'm sure it will pay off[9], but that's had him concerned[10]. He's said as much to me.[11]"

"And there was the Thompson execution."

"Yes. Glenda and I both hoped that Sharon would succeed in[12] saving him. Glenda is heartsick over[13] her role in that case[14]."

"Did Sharon want Mr. Peterson to intercede with[15] the Governor?"

"I think she realized that he wouldn't do it and that the Governor would only resent[16] a purely emotional appeal[17]. Don't forget, she's been bitterly[18] criticized for the two stays she's already granted Thompson."

"Mr. Perry, what do you think of the Lufts? Is it possible that they might be part of this[19]? They're trying to save money; they've had access to your private number. They could have known about the trust fund."

Roger shook his head. "Not a chance.[20] If Dora ever picks up anything for Glenda at the store, she spends twenty minutes making sure she's given her the exact change[21]. He's like that too. Sometimes he takes my car to be serviced[22] and always brags about how much he saves me[1]. Neither one of them has the capacity to be anything except[2] painfully honest[3]."

"Okay. I know you'll call us at the Petersons' immediately if Mrs. Perry has anything to tell us."

Hank Lamont was waiting for Hugh. Something in his manner telegraphed the fact[4] that he had news. Hugh didn't waste time on preliminaries. "What have you got?"

"Mrs. Thompson ..."

"What about her?"

"Last night. She talked to Sharon Martin!"

"She *what*?"

"The Thompson kid told us. Don and Stan interviewed him[5] in his cell[6]. Said[7] there'd been some threats against the Peterson boy and warned him that if his friends were pulling something[8], we'd better get their names[9] before they got into deep trouble[10]."

"They didn't admit[11] Neil and Sharon were kidnapped?"

"Of course not."

"What did he say?"

"He's clean.[12] The only visitors he's had in the last year are his mother, his lawyer and the parish priest[13]. His closest friends from high school[14] are in college now. He gave us their names. Everyone of them is away[15]. But he did tell us that Sharon called his mother."

"Did they talk to the mother?"

"Yes. She's staying at a motel near the prison. They found her."

"In the motel?"

"No, in church. God help her[16], Hugh, she's just kneeling there praying. Won't believe[17] the kid's going to be executed tomorrow. Won't believe it. She says Sharon called her a few minutes before six.

1. se vante toujours des économies qu'il m'a fait faire
2. n'est capable de faire preuve d'autre chose que
3. d'une honnêteté sans faille
4. indiquait
5. l'ont interrogé
6. cellule
7. Ils lui ont dit
8. tramaient quelque chose
9. il vaudrait mieux nous donner leurs noms
10. se mettent dans un drôle de pétrin
11. révélé
12. Il n'y est pour rien.
13. prêtre de sa paroisse
14. lycée
15. absent
16. Que Dieu lui vienne en aide
17. Elle ne peut croire

Wanted to know if she could do anything. Admitted she blew up at her[1], blamed her for running around[2] the country saying the boy is guilty. Threatened that she wouldn't know what she'd do to Sharon if the boy dies. What do you make of it?[3]"

"Let's try this[4]," Hugh said. "Sharon Martin is upset by the phone call, maybe even thinks there's some validity in what the mother said[5]. She's desperate and calls someone to come for her and the boy[6]. She's planning a grandstand stunt[7], make it look like a bona fide[8] kidnapping and then make Neil a hostage for Thompson's life[9]."

"It's a possibility," Hank said.

Hugh's face hardened. "I think it's more than a possibility. I think that poor guy, Peterson, is having his guts torn out[10] and Mrs. Perry is verging on[11] a coronary because Sharon Martin thinks she can manipulate justice."

"What do we do now?"

"Continue to treat this[12] as a real snatch[13]. And dig up everything we can[14] about Sharon Martin's associates[15], particularly anyone she knows in this area. If only Mrs. Perry can remember where she heard that voice, we'll crack this wide open[16]."

In her room, Glenda was playing the cassette over and over[17]. ("Peterson? In ten minutes I'll call you at the payphone of the service station just past exit twenty-one.") Helplessly, she shook her head and turned off the machine. That wasn't the way to do it. Start retracing this last couple of weeks. *But what was it about*[18] *that cassette?*

Yesterday she hadn't gone out at all. She'd talked on the phone to the drugstore, and to Agnes and then to Julie about the hospital benefit[19]. Chip and Maria had called from California and put

1. lui a passé un savon
2. d'avoir sillonné
3. Que déduire de tout cela ?
4. Avançons cette hypothèse
5. un fond de vérité dans les propos de la mère
6. demande à quelqu'un de les emmener, elle et le garçon
7. coup monté de haut vol
8. véritable
9. se sert de Neil comme otage en échange de la vie de Thompson
10. est sens dessus dessous
11. est au bord de
12. considérer cette affaire
13. kidnapping
14. à déterrer toutes les informations possibles
15. connaissances
16. pourrions résoudre l'affaire
17. se repassait inlassablement la cassette
18. qu'est-ce qui la perturbait sur
19. prestations hospitalières

the baby on[1]. That was the last time she was on the phone yesterday until Foxy called.

Sunday she and Roger drove to New York right after church and had brunch in the Pierre and went to Carnegie Hall to hear Serkin. She hadn't spoken to anyone on the phone at all.

Saturday, she'd been at the decorator's about the slipcovers[2]. And she'd had her hair done[3], or was that Friday? She shook her head impatiently. This wasn't the way to go about it at all[4]. Getting out of bed, she walked slowly over to her desk and reached for her appointment book[5]. She'd ask Roger to bring up the calendar[6] from the kitchen wall too. Sometimes she jotted notes[7] on it. And her charge slips[8]. She kept them together. They were all dated. They'd help her to remember where she'd stopped. And her checkbook[9]. She pulled the checkbook out of a compartment, the charge slips out of a drawer.

Carrying the items, she got back into bed, sighing as a constriction began in her chest[10] and mounted into sharp pain[11]. As she reached for a nitroglycerin pill she pushed the button of the recorder and began running the cassette. Once again, the muffled, throaty[12] whisper filled her ears. "Peterson? In ten minutes I'll call you at the payphone of the service station just past exit twenty-one."

1. lui avaient passé le bébé
2. housses
3. était allée chez le coiffeur
4. n'était pas du tout la bonne façon de procéder
5. carnet de rendez-vous
6. calendrier
7. griffonnait des notes
8. reçus de carte bleue
9. carnet de chèques
10. alors qu'elle ressentait une contraction dans la poitrine
11. qui se transforma en douleur aiguë
12. guttural

28

1. Revenant de
2. Il valait mieux les rejoindre
3. voyageurs de banlieue
4. qui n'avaient rien à faire dans
5. ne donnait pas à manger au garçon
6. les pupilles si dilatées
7. tout serait terminé
8. inventer

Walking back from[1] the phonebooth, he thought about the cassette. After he recorded Sharon and the boy, should he do it?

Why not?

He went directly to Grand Central. Better to go to them[2] while there was still some commuter activity[3]. Those guards had a sixth sense about people who didn't belong in[4] the terminal.

Sharon and the kid probably hadn't had any dinner last night. They'd be hungry. He didn't want her to be hungry. But she probably wouldn't eat if he didn't feed the boy[5] too. Thinking of the boy always made him nervous. A couple of weeks ago, he'd almost panicked when he'd looked out and seen the boy staring at him from the car. Just the way he did in the dream, those round brown eyes, pupils so wide[6] they looked black, accusing, always accusing.

Tomorrow it would be all over[7]. He'd have to buy Sharon a ticket on the plane. He didn't have enough money now but after tonight he would. He could make a reservation. But what name would he use? He'd have to make up[8] a name for her.

Yesterday on the *Today* show, she'd been introduced as the author and columnist. She was very well known and very popular. That's why it was so wonderful that she was so much in love with him.

She was very well known.

She'd been on the *Today* show.

Lots of people would recognize her.

Frowning, he stopped short[1], was jostled[2] by the woman hurrying along behind him. He glowered at her[3] and she said, "Oh, excuse me," and hurried past him down the street. He softened. She hadn't meant to be rude[4]. In fact, she had smiled at him, really smiled at him. Lots of women would smile at him when they knew how wealthy he was[5].

Slowly he resumed the walk[6] along Lexington Avenue. Buses had ground the fallen snow into filthy slush[7]. Even that was freezing except what was directly in the path[8] of buses and cars. He wished he were going to the[9] Biltmore. That room was so comfortable. He'd never been in a place quite like that.

He'd stay with Sharon and the child until this afternoon. Then he'd take the train up to Carley. He'd go over to his place[10] and see if there were any messages. No point in having people wondering[11] why he wasn't around[12]. He struggled to think of where[13] he could leave the cassette. Maybe Peterson wouldn't pay if he didn't get it.

He had to have[14] the money. It was too dangerous for him to stay in Fairfield County now. And he had a good reason to leave. Everyone expected him to leave.

"Any unexpected departures[15] in this area?" the cops might start asking.

"Him? No. He's been complaining about losing the place; begged[16] the old man to renew his lease[17]."

But that was before the last two girls. "The C.B. Murderer," the papers were calling him. If they only knew …

1. s'arrêta net
2. bousculé
3. lui lança un regard noir
4. n'avait pas eu l'intention d'être grossière
5. à quel point il était riche
6. se remit à marcher
7. réduit la neige qui était tombée en une gadoue sale
8. traces
9. aurait aimé se rendre au
10. se rendrait chez lui
11. Autant éviter que des gens se demandent
12. dans les parages
13. s'efforça de penser au lieu où
14. Il lui fallait
15. Des départs imprévus
16. il a supplié
17. renouveler son bail

1. obsèques
2. transmise
3. un bon moment
4. qu'il n'était pas gentil
5. la sensation étrange
6. revint sur ses pas, sur la pointe des pieds
7. clochardes
8. décolla
9. le fil très fin qui était scotché
10. Délicatement
11. avec d'infinies précautions
12. pour éviter de tirer brusquement sur
13. alluma
14. Déposant le paquet
15. comme un reproche

He had even gone to the Callahan funeral service[1]. The funeral service!

Suddenly he knew where to leave the cassette, where he could be sure it would be found that evening and delivered[2].

Satisfied, he walked briskly into Nedicks, ordered coffee, milk and rolls. He'd be staying a while[3] so they might as well have some food right away and some later before he left. He didn't want Sharon to think he was unkind[4].

When he left the area of the Mount Vernon track he had an odd sense[5] of being watched. His instinct was very good about that. He stopped and listened. He thought he heard something and tiptoed back[6]. But it was just one of those shopping bag ladies[7] making her way up the ramp to the terminal. She'd probably been sleeping on the platform.

With infinite care he released[8] the sliver of wire that was taped[9] to the door of the room. Gingerly[10], he took out his key and inserted it in the lock. Opening the door a hairsbreadth at a time[11] to keep from jerking[12] the wire, he slipped into the room and closed the door.

He switched on[13] the fluorescent lights and grunted in satisfaction. Sharon and the boy were just as he left them. The boy couldn't see him because of the blindfold of course, but behind him, Sharon lifted her head. Setting down the package[14], he hurried over to her and yanked the gag from her mouth.

"It wasn't very tight this time," he told her. He thought that he'd seen a kind of reproach[15] in her eyes.

"No." She was very nervous, nervous in a different way. Her eyes were very scared now. He didn't want her to be scared of him.

"Are you afraid, Sharon?" His voice was horribly gentle.

"Oh, no … not at all."

"I brought you some food."

"Oh, I'm glad, but won't you please take the gag off Neil? And please, won't you untie us, even just our hands, like before?"

His eyes narrowed.[1] There was something different about her. "Certainly, Sharon." He nuzzled[2] his nose against her face. His fingers were very strong. He could untie the knots very quickly. In a minute her hands were free and he reached for the boy.

The child shrank against[3] Sharon. "It's all right, Neil," she said, "remember what we talked about."

"What did you talk about, Sharon?"

"Just that Neil's dad would give you the money you want and that tomorrow you'd tell his dad where to find him. I said that I was going away[4] with you but that his dad would be here very soon after we left. Isn't that right[5]?"

The voice was thoughtful[6], the glittering eyes speculative[7]. "You're sure you want to go, Sharon?"

"Oh yes, very much. I … I like you[8], Foxy."

"I brought some rolls and coffee and some milk for the boy."

"That's very nice of you." She was flexing her fingers[9]. He watched as she began to rub Neil's wrists, as she smoothed his hair back from his forehead. The way she was pressing the boy's hands, like a signal, like a secret pact.

He pulled over the orange crate and deposited the bag on it. He gave Sharon a container of coffee[10].

"Thank you." She put the container down without sipping from it. "Where is Neil's milk?"

He handed it to her, watched as she put it in Neil's hands. "There it is[11]; hold onto it[12], Neil. Drink slowly." The boy's raspy breathing was irritating, worrisome[13], evoked memories[14].

1. Il plissa les yeux.
2. frotta
3. recula pour se blottir contre
4. partais
5. C'est bien cela, n'est-ce pas ?
6. La voix de l'homme était songeuse
7. interrogateurs
8. je vous aime bien
9. se dégourdissait les doigts
10. gobelet en carton rempli de café
11. Le voici
12. Tiens-le bien
13. inquiétante
14. faisait remonter des souvenirs

He brought out the rolls. He'd had them thickly buttered[1] the way he liked them. Sharon broke off[2] a piece of one of them and handed it to the boy. "Here, Neil, it's a roll." Her voice was soothing.[3] It was like she and the boy were in a conspiracy against him[4]. Sullenly[5], he watched them eat. He gulped his own coffee, barely tasting it[6]. They both ate one roll, finished the coffee and milk.

He hadn't taken his coat off. It was so cold in here and anyhow[7] he didn't want to take the chance of getting his new suit dirty[8]. He cleared off[9] the orange crate, putting the bag with the remaining rolls on the floor, sat down on the crate and stared at them.

When they were finished eating, Sharon pulled Neil over on her lap. The boy's breathing was loud and strained. The sound irritated Foxy, jangled his nerves[10]. Sharon didn't look at him at all. She just kept rubbing the boy's back, talking to him softly, telling him to try to sleep. Foxy watched as she kissed Neil's forehead, then pressed his head down on her shoulder.

She was a very young girl, Foxy thought, and probably was just trying to be nice to the boy. Maybe he should get rid of the boy right now and let her start being nice like that to him. The expression in his eyes changed, a little smile played on his lips as he began thinking about the ways Sharon could be nice to him[11]. Anticipation flooded his body with warmth. He realized that Sharon was staring at him now and he watched as her arms tightened around[12] the boy. He wanted to have those arms around *him*.

He started to get up to go over to the cot. His foot struck[13] the recorder. The recorder! The cassette Peterson had demanded[14]. It was too soon to get rid of the boy. Disappointed and angry, he sat

1. les avait fait largement beurrer
2. rompit
3. Sa voix était apaisante.
4. comme si, avec le garçon, ils complotaient contre lui
5. D'un air maussade
6. sans vraiment l'apprécier
7. de toute façon,
8. salir son costume neuf
9. débarrassa
10. lui mettait les nerfs en pelote
11. se montrer gentille à son égard
12. vit qu'elle resserrait son étreinte autour
13. heurta
14. réclamée

down again[1]. "You're going to make a recording for Peterson now," he told Sharon.

"A recording[2]?" Sharon's voice was quick and nervous. A second ago[3] she'd have sworn[4] that he was planning to do something to them; there was something about the way he was looking at them, the expression on his face. She tried to think. Was there a chance, was there any way?[5] Ever since[6] Neil had told her that this man murdered his mother, she'd been even more frantic to find a way to get out of here. Tomorrow might be too late for Ronald Thompson as well as for Neil. She didn't know what time Foxy was planning to come for her[7]. *If* he came for her. He was cunning[8]. He'd surely realize that sooner or later[9] she'd be recognized. The memory of her quest[10] to save Ronald tortured and mocked her[11]. His mother had been right. By insisting on his guilt[12], she had helped[13] condemn him. Nothing mattered except[14] to save Neil's life, to save Ronald's life. Whatever happened to her, she deserved[15]. And she had been the one to tell Steve *he* was trying to play God.

Foxy had a gun. It was in the pocket of his coat. If she could get him[16] to put his arms around her, she could reach for it.

If she had a chance[17], could she[18] kill him?

She looked down at Neil, thought of the condemned boy in the prison cell. Yes, she could kill this man.

She watched as he expertly handled the recorder, inserted the cassette. It was a TWX cassette, the most common kind[19]. They'd never be able to trace it. He pulled the crate over to the cot.

"Here, Sharon, you read this." He had a message written down. "Steve, pay the ransom if you want us back[20]. The money must be in tens, twenties and fifties. Eighty-two thousand dollars. Don't fail

1. se rassit
2. enregistrement
3. Un instant auparavant,
4. juré
5. Restait-il une chance, y avait-il un moyen ?
6. Depuis que
7. de venir la chercher
8. rusé
9. tôt ou tard
10. souvenir de sa bataille
11. la narguait
12. culpabilité
13. contribué
14. Plus rien ne comptait si ce n'est
15. le méritait
16. Si elle pouvait l'amener
17. Si l'occasion se présentait
18. serait-elle capable de
19. la marque la plus courante
20. tu veux nous revoir

to have it[1]; don't let it be marked[2]. Go to the phone-booth at Fifty-ninth and Lexington at two A.M. in your car. Be alone. Don't call the police."

She looked up at him. "Can I add[3] anything? I mean, we had a quarrel[4]. We broke off[5]. Maybe, maybe he wouldn't pay money for me, if I don't apologize[6]. You see, he's very stubborn[7]. Maybe he'll only pay half the money, for Neil, because he knows I don't love him. But we'll need all the money, won't we[8]?"

"What do you want to say, Sharon?" Was he toying[9] with her? Did he believe her?

"Just an apology, that's all." She tried to smile. She slid Neil off her lap[10], reached over and stroked[11] Foxy's hand.

"No tricks[12], Sharon."

"Why would I trick you? What do you want Neil to say?"

"Just that he wants to come home. Nothing else." His finger was poised over[13] the "record" button. "When I push this down[14], start talking. The mike is built in.[15]"

She swallowed, waited until the cassette began to wind[16]. "Steve …" she read the message slowly, trying to buy time[17], trying to phrase[18] what she would say next. She finished reading the message "… don't call the police." She paused.

He was looking at her intently[19].

"Steve," she had to begin, "Steve, Neil is going to talk to you now. But first, I was wrong[20], I hope you'll forgive me …" The recorder clicked off. She was about to say, "I made a terrible mistake …"

"That's enough[21], Sharon. That's enough apology." He pointed at Neil. She put her arm around the child.

"All right, Neil, now talk to your dad."

The wheezing was accentuated by his effort to speak. "Dad, I'm all right[22]. Sharon is taking care of me. But Mommy wouldn't want me to be here, Dad."

1. Je compte sur toi pour réunir cette somme
2. assure-toi que les billets ne soient pas marqués
3. ajouter
4. En fait, on s'est disputés
5. a rompu
6. je ne m'excuse pas
7. têtu
8. n'est-ce pas ?
9. Jouait-il
10. fit descendre Neil de ses genoux
11. caressa
12. Ne me jouez pas un sale tour
13. en position sur
14. appuierai sur cette touche
15. Le micro est intégré.
16. à se dérouler
17. de gagner du temps
18. de formuler dans sa tête
19. attentivement
20. j'ai eu tort
21. Ça suffit
22. je vais bien

The recorder stopped. *Neil had tried to give Steve a message*, had tried to connect their kidnapping to his mother's death.

The man rewound[1] the cassette, played it back[2]. He smiled at Sharon. "Very nice.[3] I'd pay to get you two back[4] if I was Peterson."

"That's good. I'm glad if you're satisfied." Was he deliberately baiting her[5]?

"Sharon." Neil groped for her sleeve, tugged it. "I have to[6] ..."

"You want to go to the john[7], kid[8]?" Foxy's voice was matter of fact[9]. "Guess you have to by now.[10]" He went over to Neil, picked him up and walked into the toilet with him, closing the door. Sharon froze[11], waiting, but almost immediately he was back, carrying Neil under his arm. She noticed that he had Neil's face turned away from him[12], almost as though he were afraid that Neil could see through the blindfold. He dropped Neil on the cot. The boy was trembling. "Sharon."

"I'm here." She moved her hand against his back.

"Sharon, you want to[13]?" The captor nodded his head toward the toilet.

"Yes."

He took her by the arm and half-carried her into[14] the musty cubbyhole. The cords bit through her legs and ankles making her wince with pain[15]. "There's a bolt up there[16], Sharon," he said. "I'll even let you put it on, if you want while you're here, 'cause otherwise the door don't stay shut. But you better come right out[17]." His hand caressed her cheek. "Because if you don't[18] and I get mad[19], the boy gets it now[20]." He stepped out, pulling the door closed behind him.

Quickly she slid the bolt and looked around. In the darkness inside the small compartment, she ran her hands down the walls[21], along the tank[22]. May-

1. rembobina
2. la repassa
3. Très émouvant.
4. pour vous faire revenir tous les deux
5. Était-il en train de l'appâter délibérément ?
6. J'ai envie
7. aller aux cabinets
8. petit
9. impassible
10. J'imagine que tu dois avoir envie depuis le temps.
11. se figea
12. qu'il détournait de lui le visage de Neil
13. vous avez besoin
14. la fit entrer en la soutenant dans
15. grimacer de douleur
16. verrou en hauteur
17. feriez mieux de vous dépêcher
18. si vous ne sortez pas rapidement
19. me mette en colère
20. va y passer maintenant
21. fit courir ses mains sur les murs
22. réservoir

1. un tuyau
2. Elle sentit la poignée branler
3. la faire tourner complètement
4. la détacher
5. ne parvint pas à l'arracher
6. Sortez d'ici !
7. nerveuse
8. sortir en clopinant
9. se rattrapa au chambranle métallique
10. Réprimant son dégoût
11. L'homme resserra son étreinte.
12. son cœur s'emballer brusquement
13. Du bout des doigts, elle lui caressait doucement le cou.
14. l'acier
15. la repoussa
16. heurta
17. jambes solidement attachées
18. se dérobant sous elle
19. Vous êtes comme les autres
20. qui lui donnaient envie de vomir ce qu'elle venait d'avaler
21. désincarné
22. fentes noires
23. déversant leur rage
24. Sale garce
25. La relevant brutalement

be there was something here, some piece of piping[1], something sharp. She felt along the floor.

"Hurry up, Sharon."

"All right."

When she started to open the door, the handle felt loose[2] in her hand. Instantly she tried to twist it completely around[3]. Maybe if she could get it off[4], she could slip it in the deep pocket of her skirt. It might have a sharp edge. But she couldn't wrest it free[5].

"Come out of there![6]" His voice was edgy[7] now. Quickly she opened the door, tried to hobble out[8], stumbled, grabbed the metal frame of the doorway[9]. He came over to her. Deliberately she put her arms around his neck. Forcing back revulsion[10], she kissed his cheek, his lips. His arms tightened.[11] She felt the sudden racing of his heart[12]. Oh, God, please …

She slid her arms down around his shoulders, his back. Her fingers made soft, petting motions on his neck.[13] Her right hand moved forward, slipped into his coat pocket, felt steel[14].

He shoved her backward[15]. She slammed onto[16] the concrete floor, her tightly bound legs[17] buckling under her[18]. Blinding, shocking pain shot through her right ankle.

"You're like the rest[19], Sharon," he screamed. He was standing over her. From the floor, through the waves of pain that were causing the food she'd just eaten to gag her[20], she could see him. His face seemed disembodied[21] as he leaned over her. The pulse under his eye was throbbing. Red spots accentuated the sharp lines of his cheeks. His eyes were black narrow pits[22] spewing over with rage[23]. "You bitch[24]," he said, "you bitch."

Yanking her up[25], he threw her on the cot and slapped her arms behind her. Pain made great foggy blackness close over her. "My ankle[1]." Was that her voice?

"Sharon, Sharon, what happened?" Neil's voice was terrified.

With a tremendous effort, she bit back a moan[2]. "I fell."

"Like all the others ... pretending[3] ... but worse ... trying to trick me. I could tell you were fooling[4], lying, I could tell ..." She felt hands close on her throat. Oh God! Powerful fingers were pressing into her neck ... God ... help ...

"No." The pressure vanished[5]. Her neck fell backward[6].

"Sharon, Sharon," Neil was crying, his voice agitated choking.

Gulping in air[7], she moved her face to his. Her eyelids[8] felt so heavy. She forced them open. Foxy was at the rusty sink, splashing water in his face. The water must be freezing. Fearfully, she watched. He was trying to calm himself. He'd been about to kill her. What stopped him? Maybe he was afraid he'd still need her.

She bit her lip against the pain[9]. There was no way out[10], no way. Tomorrow when he got the money he'd kill her and Neil. And Ronald Thompson would die for a crime he didn't commit. She and Neil were the only ones who could prove his innocence. Her ankle was swelling, pressing out against[11] the leather boot. The cords were biting into it[12]. Oh, God, please. Pain made her shiver even while it brought perspiration to her face[13].

She watched as he dried his face with a handkerchief[14]. He came over and methodically retied Neil's hands, put tight gags on both of them. He adjusted the wire from the suitcase to the door. "I'm leaving, Sharon," he said. "I'll be back tomorrow. I'll be back just once more[15] ..."

1. cheville
2. ravala un gémissement
3. à faire semblant
4. vouliez tromper ma confiance
5. disparut
6. retomba en arrière
7. Tout en aspirant des goulées d'air
8. paupières
9. pour ne pas crier de douleur
10. d'échappatoire
11. appuyant contre
12. pénétraient dans sa chair
13. alors même que son visage était couvert de sueur
14. s'essuyait le visage avec un mouchoir
15. pour la dernière fois

1. si tôt
2. exiger
3. Un bruit de pas.
4. scruta autour de lui
5. inspecta les alentours
6. arpenta la zone
7. examina avec curiosité les tuyaux et les soupapes
8. repartit lentement
9. des sueurs froides le long de
10. tournait
11. grincement de freins
12. se glissa entre les gaines de ventilation et les pompes d'égouts
13. jusqu'à
14. soulagé de se mêler
15. Traversant la 42e Rue en direction de l'ouest
16. leva les yeux par hasard
17. caché derrière son journal

He hadn't planned to leave this early[1] but he knew if he stayed any longer, he'd kill her. And he might need her again. They might demand[2] more proof that she and the boy were alive. He had to have the money. He couldn't take the chance of killing her yet.

There was a train coming in from Mount Vernon at eleven o'clock. He'd just have to wait a few minutes before it arrived. He stayed near the entrance to the tunnel. It was dark there.

Footsteps.[3] He shrank against the wall, peered out[4] cautiously. A guard! The man looked around carefully[5], walked up and down the area[6], stared curiously at the pipes and valves[7], glanced up at the stairs leading to the room, and then walked slowly back[8] onto the Mount Vernon platform.

He felt the freezing sweat drip all over[9] his body. His luck was running out[10]. He could feel it. He had to finish all this and get away. There was a rumbling sound, the squealing of brakes[11]. Carefully he slipped around the ventilating shafts, the sewer pumps[12], to[13] the ramp, gratefully melting in[14] with the disembarking passengers.

It was just eleven o'clock. He didn't want to sit in the hotel room. He was too restless. Walking west across Forty-second Street[15], he went into a movie. For four and a half hours he stared fascinated as three porno films titillated his senses, satisfied his needs. At 4:05 he was on the train to Carley.

He did not see Steve Peterson until he was already seated on the train. He happened to look up[16] as Peterson was passing. Fortunately, he already was buried behind the papers[17], a precaution against being recognized and having someone he knew sit beside him.

Steve was carrying a heavy suitcase.

It was the money! He knew it! And tonight he'd have it. The sensation of impending disaster[1] left him. It was with high confidence and good humor[2] that he left the Carley station after he was sure Steve had driven away. He walked briskly through the snow the eight blocks to his place, a shabby garage on a dead-end street[3]. The sign said "A. R. Taggert—Auto Repairs[4]."

Unlocking the door, he went inside quickly. There were no messages shoved[5] under the door. Good. Nobody had come looking for him. But even if someone had, it wouldn't be unusual not to find him. He often fixed[6] people's cars right in their own driveways.

The garage looked cold and dirty, not much better than the place in Grand Central. He'd certainly always worked in stinking[7] holes.

His car was there, ready to go. He'd filled it with gas[8] from the pump in the corner. Installing that pump had been the best idea he'd ever had. Handy[9] for the customers; they loved that touch of having their cars all gassed up[10]. Handy for him too. Easy to go around cruising the highways at night. "You're out of gas, ma'am[11]? Why, I've got some right in my trunk[12]. Cars are my business[13] ..."

The car was already equipped with an old set of license plates[14] he'd changed for a customer a couple of years ago; just in case any prying eyes[15] jotted down a number[16] tonight.

He'd unhooked[17] the C.B. radio and it was crated[18] on the front seat.

He'd gotten rid of all the other license plates he'd accumulated over the last six years and the extra sets[19] of car keys he'd made. They'd been tossed in a dump[20] near Poughkeepsie.

There were some odd tools and parts[21] on the shelves, some tires stacked[22] in the corner. Let old

1. catastrophe imminente
2. plein d'assurance et de bonne humeur
3. impasse
4. Réparations automobiles
5. glissés
6. réparait
7. puants
8. fait le plein d'essence
9. Pratique
10. ce petit plus, le fait de récupérer leur voiture avec le plein d'essence
11. en panne d'essence, m'dame
12. J'en ai justement un bidon, là, dans mon coffre
13. mon gagne-pain
14. d'anciennes plaques d'immatriculation
15. un curieux
16. relèverait son numéro
17. décroché
18. était rangée dans une caisse
19. doubles
20. jetés dans une décharge
21. divers outils et pièces détachées
22. empilés

man Montgomery worry about[1] getting rid of them. He was going to tear down[2] this place anyhow. He'd have plenty of crap to haul away[3].

This was his last time here ever. Just as well. He hadn't been able to work much the past couple of months. He'd gotten too nervous. Lucky he'd had that big job[4] on the Vogler car. Just tided him over.[5]

That's that.[6]

He went into the small shabby room in the rear[7], took a battered[8] suitcase out from under the single bed[9]. From an unsteady[10] old maple dresser[11] he extracted his meager collection of underwear and socks[12] and placed them in the suitcase.

A badly cut fraying red sports jacket and plaid pants were lifted off a hook on the back of[13] the door and folded[14] into the suitcase. His overalls[15], thick with grease, he tossed onto the bed. He'd leave them here. With all the money he wouldn't need them again.

He took his recorder from his coat pocket and listened again to the cassette he had made with Sharon and Neil. His other recorder, the Sony, was on top of the dresser. He put it on the bed, rummaged through[16] his cassettes, selected one, and put it on. He just needed the beginning part.

That was it[17].

Again he played the cassette with Sharon and Neil, letting it run just past the trailing off of Neil's voice[18]. Then he pressed the "record" button. On the other machine, the Sony, he deflected the "play" button.

It only took a minute. When he was finished, he re-ran[19] the revised cassette he was sending to Peterson. Perfect. Perfect.[20] He wrapped it in a piece of brown paper, fastened it with Scotch tape. With a red magic marker[21], he wrote a message across the front of the package.

1. Le vieux Montgomery n'avait qu'à se charger de
2. raser
3. des tas de saletés à débarrasser
4. ce gros boulot
5. Tout juste de quoi le dépanner.
6. Et voilà tout.
7. du fond
8. cabossée
9. lit à une place
10. branlante
11. commode en érable
12. sous-vêtements et chaussettes
13. Il décrocha une veste de sport rouge, mal coupée et élimée, et un pantalon à carreaux, de derrière
14. les rangea
15. bleu de travail
16. fouilla parmi
17. C'était ça.
18. juste après que la voix de Neil s'arrête
19. se repassa
20. Parfait. C'était parfait.
21. marqueur

The other cassettes and the two recording machines were placed in the suitcase between his folded clothes. The suitcase was closed, locked, and carried to the car. He'd have enough to manage[1] the suitcase with the money in the cabin of the plane. This one and his C.B. could go in the baggage compartment[2].

He opened the garage door, got into the car and turned on the engine[3]. As it idled[4], he smiled, amusing, secret smile. "Now for[5] a visit to church and a beer[6]," he said.

1. Il aurait déjà fort à faire pour prendre avec lui
2. dans la soute
3. mit le moteur en marche
4. tournait au ralenti
5. Et maintenant je vais faire
6. et prendre une bière

29

"I don't believe it," Steve told Hugh flatly, "and you are endangering[7] the lives of Neil and Sharon if you treat this as a hoax[8]."

Just back from[9] New York, he was pacing[10] the living room, his hands thrust in his pockets. Hugh watched him with a mixture of compassion and irritation. The poor guy had himself in such iron control[11] but he'd aged ten years in as many hours[12]. Even since morning, Hugh could see new lines of anguish around Steve's eyes and mouth.

"Mr. Peterson," he said crisply[13], "I assure you we are presuming this is a bona fide kidnapping. However, we are beginning to believe that Sharon and Neil's ... disappearance is going to be directly tied

7. mettez en danger
8. considérez cette affaire comme un canular
9. Tout juste rentré de
10. arpentait
11. avait une telle maîtrise de soi
12. en 10 heures
13. d'un ton cassant

1. tentative de négociation visant à obtenir la clémence
2. que ce n'est pas le cas
3. J'ai bien peur que non.
4. Vous devriez
5. filer
6. Je n'en sais pas plus que vous.
7. micro
8. parce qu'on ne sait jamais,
9. dans les bâtiments alentour
10. suivre vos déplacements
11. ne vous perdront pas de vue
12. donneront par radio l'ordre aux autres voitures
13. nous n'aurons pas l'air
14. dans un rayon de quelques rues
15. passa la tête dans
16. aimait la bouteille

into an attempt to bargain for clemency[1] for Ronald Thompson."

"And I say it won't[2]! There's been no word from Glenda?"

"I'm afraid not.[3]"

"And no sign of a tape or cassette from Foxy?"

"I'm sorry."

"Then we can only wait."

"Yes. You'd better[4] plan to leave for New York by midnight."

"The phonecall isn't till two."

"The road conditions, Mr. Peterson, are pretty grim."

"Do you think that Foxy might be afraid to meet me, afraid of not being able to make a getaway[5]?"

Hugh shook his head. "Your guess is as good as mine.[6] We've put a tap on the phone at Fifty-ninth Street, of course. But I suspect that he'll direct you immediately to another phonebooth just as he did before. We can't risk putting a mike[7] in your car because for all we know[8] he might plan to get in your car with you. We'll have agents in surrounding buildings[9] who will be able to follow your progress[10]. We'll have the area covered with cars which will keep you in sight[11] and then radio other cars[12] to pick you up. Don't worry, we won't give the appearance[13] of following you. The beeper in the suitcase will let us track you within a few blocks[14]."

Dora put her head into[15] the living room. "Excuse me." Her voice was different. Something in Hugh's steely manner intimidated her. She didn't like the way he kept studying her and Bill. Just because Bill liked his liquor[16] didn't mean he wasn't a good man. The strain of the past twenty-four hours was too much for her. Mr. Peterson would get Neil and Sharon back safely. She had to believe that; he was too good a man[1] to suffer any more than he had these two years.

Then she and Bill were going to leave. It was time to go to Florida. She was getting too old, too tired to take care of a child and this house. Neil needed someone young, someone he could talk to. She knew she fussed over him too much[2]. It doesn't do a child good[3] to be jumping[4] every time he sniffles[5].

Oh, Neil. He used to be such a happy little boy when his mother was alive. He never had asthma then and hardly ever a cold and those big brown eyes were always twinkling[6], not lost and sad the way they looked now.

Mr. Peterson should get married again soon; if not to Sharon, to someone who would make this a real home[7].

Dora realized that Steve was looking at her questioningly[8], that she'd spoken to him. It was just that she couldn't function[9] with this kind of worry; she hadn't closed her eyes all night. What did she want to say to him? Oh, yes, "I know you don't want much," she said, "but couldn't I just fix[10] a club steak for you and Mr. Taylor?"

"Not for me, thank you, Dora. Maybe, Mr. Taylor ..."

"Put on steaks for both of us if you don't mind[11], Mrs. Lufts." Hugh put his hand on Steve's arm. "Look, you haven't eaten anything since yesterday. You'll be up[12] all night. You need to be alert and able to drive and follow directions[13]."

"I guess you're right.[14]"

They were barely at the dining-room table when the bell rang. Hugh jumped up[15]. "I'll get it.[16]"

Steve wadded the napkin[17] he'd been about to put on his lap. Was it the proof he had demanded? Would he hear Neil's voice, Sharon's voice?

1. un homme trop bon
2. lui prodiguait trop d'attentions
3. Ce n'est pas bon pour un enfant
4. qu'on panique
5. renifle
6. pétillants
7. transformerait cette maison en un véritable foyer
8. d'un air interrogateur
9. perdait ses moyens
10. préparer
11. si ça ne vous ennuie pas
12. debout
13. suivre les instructions
14. Vous avez probablement raison.
15. se leva d'un bond
16. J'y vais.
17. roula en boule la serviette de table

1. Son visage lui était familier
2. avocat
3. débraillé
4. froissé
5. impénétrable
6. regard que lui lança Hugh pour lui signaler de se taire
7. J'ai été nul.
8. la graisse qui grésillait
9. se figer
10. le repoussa
11. jurés
12. casier de jeune délinquant
13. seul faux pas
14. a tenté de l'étrangler
15. participait à un concours du meilleur buveur de bière
16. à un moment ou à un autre
17. ivre
18. lui a donné
19. qui a eu la fichue malchance

Hugh was coming back, followed by a young, dark-haired man. He was familiar[1]—of course, it was Ronald Thompson's defense attorney[2]. Kurner. That was his name, Robert Kurner. He looked agitated, somehow unkempt[3]. His coat was open, his suit was rumpled[4] as though he'd slept in it. Hugh's face was inscrutable[5].

Bob did not apologize for interrupting their dinner. "Mr. Peterson," he said, "I've got to talk about your son."

"My son?" Steve felt the warning glance Hugh shot at him[6]. Under the table he clenched his hands into fists. "What about my son?"

"Mr. Peterson, I defended Ron Thompson. I did a lousy job.[7]"

"It isn't your fault Ronald Thompson was convicted," Steve said. He did not look at the young man. Instead he stared down at the steak, watching the bubbling strip of fat[8] at the edge begin to congeal[9]. He pushed it away[10]. Was Hugh right? Was the kidnapping a hoax after all?

"Mr. Peterson, Ron did not kill your wife. He was convicted because most of those jurors[11], consciously or unconsciously, thought he also killed the Carfolli girl and Mrs. Weiss."

"He had a record ..."

"A *juvenile* record[12], a single occurrence[13]."

"He attacked a girl before, was choking her[14] ..."

"Mr. Peterson, he was a fifteen-year-old kid at a party. He got into a beer drinking contest[15]. What kid doesn't do that at some point[16] in high school? When he was absolutely out of it[17], somebody slipped him[18] cocaine. He didn't know what he was doing. He had absolutely no memory of putting his hands on that girl. We all know what a combination of drugs and alcohol can do to the mind. Ron was a kid with the lousy, hard luck[19] to get in serious trouble[1] the first and only time he ever got drunk[2]. He never even had a beer for the next two years. And he had the incredibly bad luck[3] to come into your house right after your wife was murdered."

Bob's voice was trembling now, his words rushing out[4]. "Mr. Peterson, I've been studying the trial transcript[5]. Then yesterday I had Ron repeat over and over again every single thing he said or did[6] between the time he spoke to Mrs. Peterson in Timberly's Market and when he found her body. And I realized a mistake I made.

"Mr. Peterson, your son, Neil, told about coming downstairs when he heard your wife gasping, seeing a man strangle her and then seeing the man's face ..."

"Ron Thompson's face."

"No! No! Don't you see[7]. Here, look at the transcript." Bob slammed his briefcase[8] on the table, pulled out a thick sheaf of legal-sized papers[9], raced through them[10] until he came to a page near the center. "Here it is. The prosecutor asked Neil why he was so sure it was Ron. And Neil said, '*It got light*[11] *so I'm sure.*'

"I missed that.[12] I missed it. Because when Ron was going over and over his testimony[13] yesterday, he said that he rang the front doorbell. Then he waited a couple of minutes and rang it again. Neil didn't say one word about hearing chimes, not one word."

"That proves nothing," Hugh interrupted. "Neil was upstairs playing with his trains. He was probably quite absorbed and the trains were noisy[14]."

"No, no. Because he said, '*It got light.*' Mr. Peterson, this is my point[15]. Ron rang the front doorbell. He waited, rang it again, walked around the house. He gave the killer time to escape[16]. That's why the back door was open.

1. s'attirer de gros ennuis
2. s'est enivré
3. malchance
4. se bousculaient
5. procès-verbaux d'audience
6. tout ce qu'il avait pu dire ou faire
7. Vous ne comprenez pas
8. serviette
9. épaisse liasse de documents grand format
10. les parcourut rapidement
11. Il y a eu de la lumière
12. Ce détail m'avait échappé.
13. répétait encore et encore son témoignage
14. bruyants
15. voilà où je veux en venir
16. s'échapper

"Ron turned on the kitchen light. Don't you see? The reason Neil saw Ron's face clearly was because the light was coming in from the kitchen. Mr. Peterson, a little boy comes running downstairs and sees his mother being strangled. The living room was dark[1]. Remember that.[2] Only the foyer light was on[3]. Isn't it possible that[4] he went into some kind of shock[5], that he maybe even passed out[6]? Adults have been known to do that. Then when he comes to[7], he sees. *Sees*, because now the light is coming from the kitchen through to the living room[8]. Neil sees someone bending over his mother, someone tugging at her throat[9]. Ron was trying to get the scarf off[10]. But it was impossible. It was knotted so tightly[11]. And he realized she was dead and how it would look for him[12]. So he panicked and ran.

"If he were a killer would he have left an eyewitness[13] like Neil? Would he have left Mrs. Perry alive knowing she probably recognized him? She shops[14] in Timberly's. A killer doesn't leave witnesses, Mr. Peterson."

Hugh shook his head. "It doesn't wash.[15] It's all conjecture.[16] There isn't a scrap of proof[17] in this."

"But Neil can give us the proof," Bob begged[18]. "Mr. Peterson, would you consent to his being[19] hypnotized? I've spoken today to several doctors. They say if he's suppressing[20] something it might very well be revealed through hypnosis."

"That's impossible!" Steve bit his lip. He'd been about to blurt out[21] that you can't hypnotize a kidnapped child. "Get out," he said, "just get out of here[22]."

"No, I won't get out!" Bob hesitated, then reached into his briefcase again. "I'm sorry to show these to you, Mr. Peterson. I didn't want to. I've been studying them. They're the pictures taken of this house after the murder."

1. dans l'obscurité
2. Gardez ça à l'esprit.
3. allumée
4. N'est-il pas envisageable qu'
5. se soit retrouvé dans une sorte d'état de choc
6. peut-être même qu'il se soit évanoui
7. revient à lui
8. la lumière venant de la cuisine éclaire le salon
9. tirant sur son cou
10. de dénouer l'écharpe
11. si serrée
12. les conséquences que cela aurait pour lui
13. témoin oculaire
14. fait ses courses
15. Je n'y crois pas.
16. Tout ceci n'est que pure conjecture.
17. Il n'y a pas l'ombre d'une preuve
18. implora
19. accepteriez-vous qu'il soit
20. que s'il refoule
21. laisser échapper
22. fichez le camp d'ici

"Are you nuts?[1]" Hugh grabbed for the photos. "Where the hell[2] did you get them? They're state's evidence[3]."

"Never mind where[4] I got them. Look at this one. See? The kitchen. The globe isn't on the ceiling fixture.[5] That means the light might have been unusually strong."

Bob thrust open[6] the kitchen door almost knocking down Dora and Bill Lufts who were standing right behind it. Ignoring them, he dragged[7] a chair over to the light fixture, jumped on it, quickly unscrewed[8] the globe. The room brightened measurably[9]. He ran back[10] into the dining room, snapped off the light. He hurried into the foyer and turned that light on. Finally he switched off the living room lamps.

"Look, look into the living room. Now it's perfectly possible to see into it. Now wait." He rushed back into the kitchen and turned off the light. Steve and Hugh sat mesmerized at the table watching him[11]. Under Steve's hand was the photograph of Nina's body.

"Look," Bob pleaded[12]. "With the kitchen light out[13], the living room is almost dark. Suppose you're a child coming down the stairs. Please, stand in the foyer on the landing[14]. Look into the living room. What could Neil have seen? Not much more than a silhouette.[15] Someone is attacking his mother. He passes out. He never heard the bell. Remember that, *he never heard the bell*. The killer escapes. By the time[16] Ron had rung the bell, and waited and rung it again and walked around the house[17], the killer is gone. And Ron probably saved your child's life by coming here that day."

Is it possible? Steve wondered. Is it possible that boy is innocent? He stood in the foyer, staring into

1. Êtes-vous cinglé ?
2. Où diable
3. des pièces à conviction
4. Peu importe où
5. Il n'y a pas de plafonnier.
6. ouvrit brusquement
7. traîna
8. dévissa
9. s'illumina sensiblement
10. revint en toute hâte
11. le regardaient, interdits, assis à table
12. implora
13. éteinte
14. sur le palier
15. Guère plus qu'une silhouette.
16. Le temps que
17. fasse le tour de la maison

the living room. How much had Neil seen?[1] Could he have blacked out[2] for a few moments?

Hugh strode past him into[3] the living room, snapped on[4] a lamp. "It's not good enough[5]," he said flatly. "It's conjecture, pure and simple conjecture. There's not a shred of evidence[6] to back it up[7]."

"Neil is the one who could give us the evidence. He's our only hope. Mr. Peterson, I beg you to let him be questioned[8]. I've been on the phone with Dr. Michael Lane. He's willing[9] to come up tonight to question Neil. He's on the staff of[10] Mount Sinai[11]. Mr. Peterson, please, give Ron that chance."

Steve looked at Hugh, saw the faint[12], negative movement of his head. If he admitted Neil had been kidnapped, this lawyer would grasp at the excuse[13] to suggest that it was tied into[14] Nina's death. It would mean publicity; it might mean the end of any hope of getting Neil and Sharon back safely.

"My son is away[15]," he said. "There have been threats against me, because of my stand on capital punishment[16]. I will not divulge his whereabouts[17] to anyone."

"*You will not divulge his whereabouts!* Mr. Peterson, an innocent nineteen-year-old kid is going to die tomorrow morning for something he didn't do!"

"I can't help you." Steve's calm snapped.[18] "Get out of here. Get out and take those cursed[19] pictures with you!"

Bob knew it was hopeless[20]. Striding into the dining room, he jammed[21] the trial transcript into his briefcase and scooped up[22] the pictures. He started to close the bag, then reached in and yanked out[23] the copies of the statements Ron had made the day before. He slammed them[24] on the table.

"Read these, Mr. Peterson," he said. "Read them and see if you can find a killer talking[25]. Ron was sentenced to the electric chair because Fairfield

1. Qu'avait vraiment vu Neil ?
2. s'évanouir
3. passa devant lui à grandes enjambées et entra dans
4. alluma
5. Cela n'est pas suffisant
6. une once de preuve
7. pour corroborer cette hypothèse
8. de nous autoriser à l'interroger
9. Il est prêt
10. Il fait partie du personnel médical de
11. [un des plus anciens et des plus grands hôpitaux à vocation pédagogique des États-Unis]
12. léger
13. s'emparerait du prétexte
14. lié à
15. absent
16. position sur la peine capitale
17. l'endroit où il se trouve
18. Steve perdit son calme.
19. maudites
20. sans espoir
21. fourra
22. ramassa
23. sortit d'un geste brusque
24. les posa bruyamment
25. si vous y voyez les propos d'un meurtrier

County was shocked by the Carfolli and Weiss murders as well as your wife's. There have been two more murders of women alone in their cars on lonely roads in the last few weeks. You know that. I swear to God[1] those four murders are linked and I swear that somehow your wife's murder is connected to them. They were strangled with their scarves or belts[2]. Don't forget that. The only difference is that for some reason[3], the killer chose to come into your home. But every one of those five women died the same way."

He was gone, slamming[4] the front door behind him. Steve looked at Hugh. "What about[5] your theory, that the kidnapping is tied into the execution tomorrow?" he asked accusingly.

Hugh shook his head. "We only know that Kurner isn't part of any conspiracy, but we never suspected that he was."

"Is there any chance, any chance at all, that he's right about[6] Nina's death?"

"He's grasping at straws[7]. It's all 'maybe' and conjecture. He's a lawyer trying to save his client."

"If Neil were here I would have allowed that doctor to talk with him, to hypnotize him, if necessary. Neil has had recurring nightmares[8] since that night. Just last week he started talking about it again."

"What did he say?"

"He said something about being scared and not being able to forget. I've actually[9] spoken to a psychiatrist in New York who suggested that there may be some repression there[10]. Hugh, tell me honestly, are you *convinced* Ronald Thompson killed my wife?"

Hugh shrugged. "Mr. Peterson, when the evidence is as clearcut[11] as it is in this case, it's impossible to come to any other conclusion."

"You haven't answered my question."

1. Je jure devant Dieu
2. leur ceinture
3. pour une raison que nous ignorons
4. claquant
5. Qu'en est-il de
6. ait raison sur
7. fait flèche de tout bois
8. des cauchemars récurrents
9. en fait
10. qu'il peut s'agir ici d'un cas de refoulement
11. claire et nette

"I've answered it the only way I can. Please, that steak's probably not worth eating[1] by now, but have *something*[2]."

They went into the dining room. Steve crumbled a piece of roll[3], reached for the coffee. The transcripts of Ron's statement were at his elbow[4]. He picked up the top sheet, started to read it:

I was pretty down about[5] losing the job, but I understood. Mr. Timberly needed someone who could work more hours. I knew that being on the varsity[6] would help me get into college and maybe get a scholarship[7]. So I couldn't work more. Mrs. Peterson heard Mr. Timberly. She said she was sorry and that I was always so nice about bringing her packages to the car[8]. She asked me what kind of job I'd get. I said I'd done housepainting[9] during the summer. That was when we were walking out to the car. She told me that they'd just moved and there was a lot of painting to do, inside and out, and asked me to come over and look at the house[10]. I was putting her groceries in the trunk. I said I guess this is my lucky day[11] and it's just like my mom's always saying, bad luck can turn into[12] good luck. Then we joked[13] because she said, "It's my lucky day that way too[14]. At least there's room[15] in the trunk for all these darn groceries[16]." She said she really didn't like grocery shopping, that's why she always bought so much at one time. That was at four o'clock. Then …

Steve stopped reading. Nina's lucky day. *Lucky day!* He pushed the transcript away.

The phone rang. He and Hugh both jumped. He rushed to the kitchen phone. Hugh hurried to the extension in the den. "Steve Peterson?" His voice was guarded[17]. Let it be good news[18], please.

1. immangeable
2. prenez quelque chose
3. émietta un morceau de pain
4. à côté de lui
5. assez déprimé à l'idée de
6. [aux États-Unis, équipe sportive de première catégorie représentant un établissement]
7. obtenir une bourse
8. que je l'aidais toujours si gentiment à porter ses courses à sa voiture
9. des travaux de peinture
10. passer voir la maison
11. jour de chance
12. se transformer en
13. avons plaisanté
14. aussi, d'une certaine façon
15. Au moins, il y a de la place
16. provisions de malheur
17. circonspecte
18. Pourvu que ce soit de bonnes nouvelles

"Mr. Peterson, this is Father Kennedy from St. Monica's Church. I'm afraid something quite unusual has happened."

Steve felt his throat muscles close[1]. It was an effort to speak. "What is it, Father?[2]"

"Twenty minutes ago when I went on the altar[3] to offer the evening mass[4], I found a small package propped against[5] the door of the sanctuary. Let me read exactly what it says. 'Deliver[6] to Steve Peterson at once—life or death[7].' And your phone number. Could it possibly be some sort of joke?[8]"

Steve heard the hoarseness[9] in his voice, felt the clammy sweat in[10] his hands. "No, it's not a joke. It may be important. I'll be right down for it[11], Father, and please, don't say anything about this to anyone."

"Of course, Mr. Peterson. I'll wait for you in the rectory[12]."

When Steve got back to the house half an hour later, Hugh was waiting with the recorder. Grimly they leaned over the machine as the spool[13] began to turn.

For an instant they heard just a muted, rasping sound, then Sharon's voice. Steve paled and Hugh gripped his arm. The message. She was repeating the message the kidnapper had given him. What did she mean about being wrong[14]? What was he supposed to forgive her for[15]? There was something so abrupt about the way she stopped. As though she'd been cut off. Neil. That was the rasping sound. Neil, choked with asthma. Steve listened to his son's halting voice. Sharon was caring for him[16]. Why did he mention his mother? Why now?

He gripped his fists until his knuckles were white[17], held them to his lips to push back the sobs that he felt shaking his chest[18].

"That's it[19]," Hugh said. He reached out his hand. "We'll run it through again.[20]"

1. sa gorge se nouer
2. De quoi s'agit-il, mon père ?
3. je me suis approché de l'autel
4. dire la messe du soir
5. appuyé contre
6. À remettre
7. question de vie ou de mort
8. Pourrait-il s'agir d'une blague ?
9. timbre rauque
10. moiteur de
11. viens le chercher immédiatement
12. presbytère
13. bande
14. sur le fait d'avoir eu tort
15. censé lui pardonner
16. s'occupait bien de lui
17. serra les poings jusqu'à ce que ses articulations deviennent blanches
18. refouler les sanglots qui lui secouaient la poitrine
19. C'est tout
20. On va repasser le message.

But before he could press the "stop" button it came[1]. A warm, bubbly voice[2], melodic, welcoming. "Why, how nice of you[3]," it was saying, "do come in[4]."

Steve jumped up as an anguished cry broke from his lips[5].

"What is it?[6]" Hugh shouted. "Who is that?"

"Oh Christ ... oh Christ," Steve cried, "that's my wife, that's Nina!"

1. ils l'entendirent
2. Une voix chaleureuse et chantante
3. Ça alors, comme c'est gentil à vous
4. je vous en prie, entrez
5. un cri d'angoisse lui échappait
6. Qu'y a-t-il ?

30

Hank Lamont parked his car in front of Mill Tavern on Fairfield Avenue in Carley. The snow was falling hard again[7] and sharp gusts of wind were slapping it[8] against the windshield. His large innocent-looking blue eyes narrowed as he studied the dimly lit interior[9] of the tavern. It seemed pretty empty. Probably the weather had kept people home, but that was just as well[10]. He'd get more chance to talk to the bartender. Let's hope he was the kind who liked to chew the rag[11].

He stepped out of the car. God, it was cold. Lousy, lousy night. It would be hard to keep a tail on[12] Peterson's car later on. There'd probably be so few cars[13] on the road, the ones that were there would stick out like sore thumbs[14].

7. Il neigeait beaucoup à nouveau
8. de vives rafales de vent plaquaient la neige
9. l'intérieur peu éclairé
10. c'était aussi bien
11. discuter le bout de gras
12. de filer
13. si peu de voitures
14. se verraient comme le nez au milieu de la figure

He pushed open the door and stepped inside the bar. Warm air embraced him[1] and a not unpleasant beer and food smell filled his nostrils[2]. Blinking to clear his eyes of snow, he glanced at the bar. There were only four men at it. He ambled up[3], heaved his bulk onto a stool[4], and ordered a Michelob[5].

While he sipped it, his eyes flitted[6] from side to side. Two of the patrons[7] were watching a hockey game on television. Halfway down the bar, a well-dressed glassy-eyed[8] executive-type with a fringe of white hair was sipping a martini. He caught Hank's gaze. "Do you agree with me, sir, that it's the mark of a sensible man[9] not to drive ten miles in these adverse conditions[10]; that it is far more expedient[11] to call a cab?" He considered his own premise[12]. "Especially with a snootful[13]," he added unnecessarily.

"You're right, mister," Hank said heartily. "I just drove down from Peterboro and let me tell you these roads are *bad*[14]." He swallowed a large gulp of beer.

The bartender was drying glasses. "You from[15] Peterboro? Never seen you around here, have I?"

"No. Just passing through.[16] Wanted to take a break[17] and remembered my old buddy[18], Bill Lufts, says he's usually here about this time."

"Yeah, Bill's here just about every night," the bartender agreed. "But you might be out of luck[19]. Last night he didn't make it[20] 'cause he was taking his wife out for their anniversary; going to dinner and the movies. We figured he'd drop her off home[21] and come on down for a nightcap[22], but he never did show up. Really surprising he's not here again tonight, unless she's giving him a lot of flak again[23]. And if she does, we'll hear about it, right, Arty?"

The other solitary drinker looked up from where he was hunched over a beer[24]. "In one ear and

1. Il sentit une bouffée d'air chaud
2. narines
3. avança d'un pas tranquille
4. hissa son corps massif sur un tabouret
5. [bière]
6. furetaient
7. clients
8. aux yeux vitreux
9. le propre d'un homme sensé
10. par un temps si mauvais
11. opportun
12. réfléchit à sa propre déclaration
13. verre dans le nez
14. effroyables
15. Vous êtes de
16. Juste de passage.
17. faire une pause
18. mon vieux copain
19. il semble que vous jouiez de malchance
20. n'a pas pu venir
21. la raccompagnerait à la maison
22. viendrait boire un dernier verre
23. à moins qu'il ne se soit encore pris une volée de bois vert
24. penché sur sa bière, leva le nez

out the other[1]," he said, "who wants to listen to that stuff[2]?"

Hank laughed. "Well, what's a bar for if not to get your beefs out of your system[3]?"

The men watching the hockey game switched it off[4]. "Lousy game[5]," one of them commented.

"Stinks[6]," the other agreed.

"This here's a friend of Bill Lufts." The bartender jerked his head toward Hank.

"Les Watkins," the taller man said.

"Pete Lerner," Hank lied.

"Joe Reynolds," the plump man volunteered[7]. "What's your work, Pete?"

"Plumbing supply house[8] in New Hampshire; on my way to New York to pick up some samples[9]. Say, how about everyone having a beer on me?[10]"

An hour passed. Hugh learned that Les and Joe were salesmen[11] in the Modell discount house on Route 7. Arty repaired cars. The bald-headed[12] executive, Allan Kroeger, worked in an advertising agency[13].

A number of the regulars weren't around, thanks[14] to the weather. For instance, Bill Finelli hadn't been by[15] tonight, neither had Don Brannigan. Charley Pincher usually drifted in[16], but he and his wife were active in[17] the Little Theatre group and were probably rehearsing[18] a new play.

Kroeger's cab arrived. Les was giving Joe a ride[19]. They asked for their bill[20]. Arty got up to go. The bartender waved away[21] his money. "This one's on me[22]," he said. "We'll miss you."

"That's right," Les said, "good luck, Arty. Let us know how you're doing.[23]"

"Thanks: If it don't work I'll come back and take the job at Shaw's. He's always bugging me to go with him[24]."

1. Ça rentre par une oreille et ça sort par l'autre
2. ces bêtises
3. si ce n'est pour rouspéter contre le monde entier
4. éteignirent la télévision
5. Quel match pourri
6. C'est nul
7. dit alors l'homme rondouillard
8. Dans une boîte de matériel de plomberie
9. des échantillons
10. Que diriez-vous que j'offre une tournée générale ?
11. vendeurs
12. chauve
13. agence de publicité
14. à cause
15. n'était pas passé
16. se pointait d'habitude
17. faisaient partie de
18. répétaient sans doute
19. raccompagnait Joe en voiture
20. l'addition
21. repoussa d'un geste
22. est offert par la maison
23. Donne-nous de tes nouvelles.
24. n'arrête pas de m'enquiquiner pour que je travaille avec lui

"Why wouldn't he? He knows a good mechanic[1]," Les said.

"Where'ye heading for?[2]" Hank asked.

"Rhode Island—Providence."

"Too bad[3] you didn't get a chance to say goodbye to Bill," Joe commented.

Arty laughed cynically. "Rhode Island ain't[4] Arizona," he said. "I'll be back. Well, better get some sleep[5]. Want to get an early start[6] in the morning."

Allan Kroeger wove unsteadily toward[7] the door. "Arizona," he said, "home of the painted desert[8]." The four men went out together, letting in a sharp blast of cold air.

Hank studied Arty's retreating back[9]. "That Arty, he a particular[10] friend of Bill Lufts'?"

The bartender shook his head. "Nah[11]. Anybody who can *hear*[12] is a friend of Bill's after he gets a couple of boilermakers[13]. You should know that. The way the guys have it figured, Bill's wife yaks in his ear all day[14] and he comes here at night and yaks in everyone else's ear."

"I see." Hank shoved his glass across the bar. "Have one yourself.[15]"

"Don't mind if I do.[16] Don't usually if it's busy, but you could swing a cat around here[17]. Lousy kind of night anyhow. Kind of gives you the creeps.[18] Guess everybody feels that way. That Thompson kid, you know. His mother lives two blocks from me."

Hank's eyes narrowed. "That's what happens when you go around murdering people," he suggested[19].

The bartender shook his head. "Most of us can't imagine that kid murdering anyone. 'Course he did go off the deep end once before[20], so maybe it's possible. They say some of the most vicious[21] killers are real ordinary on the surface[22]."

"That's what I hear."

1. sait reconnaître un bon mécanicien
2. Vous partez où ?
3. Dommage
4. c'est pas
5. je ferais mieux d'aller dormir
6. partir tôt
7. tituba jusqu'à
8. [région de l'Arizona aux roches érodées formant des couches de couleur]
9. observa Arty pendant qu'il sortait
10. proche
11. Nan
12. entendre
13. [cocktail à base de bière et de whisky]
14. lui rebat les oreilles à longueur de journée
15. Servez-vous un verre.
16. Ce n'est pas de refus.
17. il n'y a pas grand monde
18. À vous faire froid dans le dos.
19. lança-t-il
20. a déjà pété les plombs une fois
21. violents
22. sont des gens d'un abord très ordinaire

"You know Bill and his missus[1] live at the house of the woman who was murdered—the Peterson house."

"Yeah, I did know that."

"They took it awful hard[2]. Dora Lufts worked for the Petersons for years. Bill says the little kid is still like a ghost of himself[3], cries a lot, has nightmares."

"It's tough," Hank agreed.

"Bill and the missus really want to get down to Florida. They're hanging around[4] hoping the kid's father will get married. He's going with some writer; good-looking, Bill says. She was coming up last night."

"Was she?"

"Yeah. The little kid is pretty cool about her[5], probably scared about having his mother replaced. Kids are like that."

"Guess so.[6]"

"The father's the editor of *Events* magazine, you know, that new one, just a couple of years old. Guess he sunk a lot of dough into it[7]. Second mortgage, you name it. But it's coming along pretty well[8] now. Well, guess I'll start closing up. It's a cinch[9] nobody else is coming around here tonight. Want another?[10]"

Hank considered. He needed answers. There was no more time to waste. He set his glass down, reached for his wallet[11], flipped out his badge[12]. "FBI," he said.

An hour later he was back at the Peterson house. After conferring with[13] Hugh, he called FBI headquarters[14] in Manhattan. Making sure the den door was securely closed[15], he spoke softly[16] into the phone. "Hughie was right. Bill Lufts is a bigmouth[17]. Everyone in the Mill Tavern has known for two weeks that he and Mrs. Lufts would be out last night, that Peterson had a late meeting and that Sharon Martin was

1. bourgeoise
2. ont été terriblement affectés
3. n'est plus que l'ombre de lui-même
4. restent dans le coin
5. plutôt froid à son égard
6. J'imagine.
7. y a englouti un fric fou
8. ça commence à pas mal marcher
9. C'est sûr que
10. Un autre verre ?
11. portefeuille
12. brandit son insigne
13. s'être entretenu avec
14. le quartier général du FBI
15. bien fermée
16. à voix basse
17. ne sait pas tenir sa langue

expected up. The bartender gave me a list of ten regulars who are always talking to Bill. Some of them were there tonight. They all seemed okay. You might check on a[1] Charley Pincher though, he and his wife are in theatricals[2]; maybe one of them could mimic a voice they'd heard a couple of years ago. There's an Arty Taggert who'll be pulling out[3] tomorrow for Rhode Island. Seems harmless[4]. Two salesmen, Les Watkins and Joe Reynolds—wouldn't waste time on them[5]. Here are the rest of the names ..."

When he'd concluded the list, he added, "Another thing. Bill Lufts told the whole bar about Neil's trust fund less than a month ago; overheard Peterson talking to his accountant. So everyone in the Mill Tavern and God knows where else knows about it. Okay. I'll start down with the cassette. Have you reached[6] John Owens?"

He hung up the phone, walked thoughtfully past the living room. Hugh Taylor and Steve were talking in muted tones[7]. Steve was just putting on his coat. It was nearly midnight and time for him to leave for the rendezvous with Foxy.

1. vous renseigner sur un certain
2. font du théâtre
3. se tire
4. inoffensif
5. inutile de perdre du temps avec eux
6. pu joindre
7. à voix basse

31

Lally was so upset over the intruders that when she met Rosie in the main waiting room she blurted out the story to her[8] and immediately was sorry[9]. "It's

8. lui lâcha toute l'histoire
9. le regretta immédiatement

kind of a special place for me," she finished lamely[1]. Now what would she say if Rosie wanted to share it? She couldn't let her. She just couldn't.

She needn't have worried. "You mean you bed down[2] in Sing Sing?" Rosie asked incredulously. "You couldn't get me near there with a ten-foot pole[3]. You know how I hate cats."

Of course. She'd never thought. Rosie was frightened of cats, would walk across the street to avoid one.

"Well, you know me," Lally said. "I love them. Poor things[4] get so hungry. There's more slithering around that tunnel than ever[5]," she exaggerated. Rosie shuddered.

"So I figure the two of them are staying there," Lally concluded, "and I'll scare off[6] the girl when he's out."

Rosie was deep in thought[7]. "Suppose you make a mistake," she suggested. "Suppose he's there. You say he looks mean[8]."

"More than mean. Maybe, maybe you could help me keep an eye on him[9]."

Rosie loved intrigue. She smiled widely, revealing broken yellow teeth. "Sure."

They finished their coffee, carefully putting leftover pieces[10] of the donuts in their shopping bags, and headed for the lower level.

"Might take a long time[11]," Lally fretted[12].

"It don't matter, except Olendorf's on[13] today," Rosie said.

He was one of the strictest guards. He didn't believe in[14] letting the regulars hang around the station; he was always chasing them and watching to see they didn't panhandle[15] or litter[16].

Somewhat nervously, they took up a position[17] near the *Open Book* display windows[18]. Time passed. They waited patiently, almost motionlessly[19]. Lally

1. maladroitement
2. couches
3. pour tout l'or du monde
4. Les pauvres bêtes
5. Je n'en ai jamais vu autant que dans ce tunnel
6. ferai fuir
7. plongée dans ses pensées
8. a l'air méchant
9. à garder un œil sur lui
10. les restes
11. Ça peut prendre beaucoup de temps
12. se tracassa Lally
13. est de garde
14. n'était pas pour
15. ne faisaient pas la manche
16. qu'ils ne laissaient pas de détritus
17. prirent place
18. vitrines
19. immobiles

had a story ready[1] if Olendorf came over to them. She'd say she had a friend coming to New York and had promised to meet her right here.

But the guard ignored them. Lally's feet and legs began to throb.[2] She was about to suggest to Rosie that they give up the vigil[3] when a stream of people[4] came up the steps[5] of the Mount Vernon platform. One of them had dark hair, a stiff way of walking.

She grabbed Rosie's arm. "That's him," she cried. "See, he's going toward the stairs, brown coat green pants."

Rosie's eyes narrowed. "Oh yeah, I see him."

"Now I can go down," Lally exulted.

Rosie looked doubtful. "Not with Olendorf around[6], I wouldn't. He just looked over here."

But Lally was not to be dissuaded. She waited until she saw Olendorf leave for his lunch break[7], then slipped down to the platform. The 12:10 was starting to load[8]; she knew she wasn't too conspicuous[9]. She disappeared around to the other side of the track, hurried down the ramp as fast as her arthritic knees would allow. She really didn't feel well. This had been the hardest winter ever. The arthritis was in her back now and in the soles of her feet[10]. Her whole body was hurting a lot. She couldn't wait to lie down and have a rest on her own cot. She'd have the girl out of there in the next two minutes.

"Missy," she'd say, "the cops are wise[11]. They're on their way[12] to arrest you. Get out and warn your boyfriend."

That would do it.[13]

She shuffled past the[14] generator, around the sewer pipes. The tunnel loomed dark and still at the far end of the area.[15]

She looked up at the door of her room and smiled happily. Eight more shuffling movements and she was at the base of the steps leading to it. Shifting

1. toute prête
2. Lally commençait à avoir des élancements dans les pieds et les jambes.
3. d'abandonner leur surveillance
4. flot de personnes
5. monta l'escalier
6. dans les parages
7. pause déjeuner
8. Le train de 12h10 commençait à se remplir
9. qu'elle n'attirait pas trop l'attention
10. plante des pieds
11. au courant
12. en chemin
13. Ça marcherait.
14. passa en traînant les pieds à côté du
15. Tout au bout se profilait le tunnel, sombre et silencieux.

the handles[1] of her shopping bag over one arm, she fished her key out of her jacket[2]. With the other hand she gripped the railing and began to pull herself up the steep steps[3].

"Where do you think you're going[4], Lally?" The voice was sharp. Lally let out a frightened cry and almost tumbled over backward[5]. She regained her balance[6], and fighting for time[7], turned around[8] slowly to face the menacing form of Officer Olendorf. So he'd been keeping an eye on her, just like Rosie warned; he'd tried to trap her[9] by pretending[10] to go to lunch. She let the key slide into the shopping bag. Had he seen it?

"I asked, where are you going, Lally?"

Near her the generators throbbed. There was a rushing, squealing sound as a train entered a platform somewhere overhead. She was silent, helpless.

A sudden, sharp spitting sound[11], a snarling yowl[12] came from a shadowy[13] corner and inspiration struck[14] Lally. "The cats!" With a trembling hand she pointed to the moving skeletal forms. "They're starving[15]! I wanted to bring them something to eat. I was just getting it out." Eagerly, she yanked[16] the crumpled[17] napkin with the bits of donut from her shopping bag.

The guard examined the greasy napkin with distaste[18], but his tone was somewhat less hostile when he spoke. "I'm sorry for them too, but you've no business here[19], Lally. Throw that stuff to them[20] and clear out[21]." His glance passed her, eyed the steps[22], moved upward, lingered thoughtfully on the door of her room. Lally's heart beat wildly[23]. She picked up her bag, hobbled over to[24] the cats, tossed the meager scraps[25], watched as they fought over them.

"See how hungry they are." Her voice was placating.[26] "You got cats home, Mr. Olendorf?" She was moving out of the area, willing him to follow

1. Faisant glisser les poignées
2. fouilla dans sa veste pour en sortir sa clé
3. l'escalier raide
4. Où est-ce que vous allez comme ça
5. faillit tomber à la renverse
6. retrouva l'équilibre
7. cherchant à gagner du temps
8. se retourna
9. de la piéger
10. faisant semblant
11. Le bruit soudain et aigu d'un sifflement
12. miaulement féroce
13. sombre
14. saisit
15. sont affamés
16. Elle s'empressa de sortir
17. froissée
18. d'un air dégoûté
19. vous n'avez rien à faire ici
20. Jetez-leur tout ça
21. décampez
22. Son regard passa de Lally à l'escalier
23. battait la chamade
24. se dirigea en boitillant vers
25. secoua les quelques miettes
26. Elle prenait une voix apaisante.

her. Suppose he[1] used his passkey[2] and checked her room? If he found the girl there, they'd surely change the lock. Maybe padlock it.[3]

He hesitated, shrugged, decided to follow her. "Used to[4], but my wife isn't much for cats anymore[5], not since we lost the one she was crazy about[6]."

Safely back in the waiting room, Lally realized her heart was still beating wildly. That was that. She wouldn't go near her place again until tonight when Olendorf went home. Thanking her stars[7] that the cats had staged their fights[8], she went over to a bin and plucked out[9] a discarded copy[10] of *People* magazine and the crumpled first section of the *Village Voice*.

1. Et s'il
2. passe-partout
3. Peut-être qu'ils la cadenasseraient.
4. Avant, oui
5. n'a plus trop envie d'avoir un chat
6. qu'elle adorait
7. Remerciant sa bonne étoile
8. aient fait tout ce raffut
9. en extirpa
10. numéro abandonné

32

Neil knew Sharon was hurt. She hadn't fooled him[11] when she said she fell. The man must have pushed her down[12]. He wanted to talk to Sharon but the rag on his mouth was so tight he couldn't. It was much tighter than before. He wanted to tell Sharon how brave she was to try to fight that man. He'd been too scared to fight him when he was hurting Mommy. But even Sharon, who was almost as tall as the man, wasn't strong enough to beat him.

Sharon had told him that she was going to try to get the man's gun. She had said, "Don't be scared

11. ne l'avait pas berné
12. avait dû la faire tomber

if you hear me talking about leaving you. I won't leave you. But if I can get his gun, maybe we can make him take us out of here. We both made a mistake and we're the only ones who can save Ronald Thompson."

Her voice had been all funny and growly trying[1] to talk and his had too[2], but somehow he'd been able to tell her about it[3] … how Sandy said that he should have helped Mommy; how he kept dreaming about that day; how Sandy said the Lufts would probably take him to Florida; how the kids asked him if he wanted Ronald Thompson to fry.

Even though it was hard to talk with the gag on it was easier to breathe after he talked. He knew what Sharon meant[4]. They were going to kill Ronald Thompson for hurting Mommy and he hadn't done it. But Neil said he had. Neil hadn't meant[5] to lie. That was what he was trying to tell Daddy on the message.

Now he had to be careful to breathe very slowly through his nose and not to get scared or cry because then he wouldn't be able to breathe.

It was cold and his arms and legs hurt so much. But even so[6], something inside him had stopped hurting[7]. Sharon would figure a way[8] to get them out of here[9] away from[10] the man so they could tell about[11] Ronald. Or Daddy would come and get them. Neil was sure of that.

He could feel Sharon's breath on his cheek. His head was right under her chin. Sometimes she made a funny sound, like something was hurting her. But being squished against her[12] made him feel better. It was like when he was a little kid and sometimes woke up in the middle of the night with a bad dream and used to get into bed with[13] Mommy and Daddy. Mommy would pull him close[14] and say, "stop

1. Sa voix ressemblait à un grognement bizarre alors qu'elle essayait
2. comme la sienne
3. à lui raconter toute l'histoire
4. voulait dire
5. n'avait pas eu l'intention
6. Malgré tout
7. avait cessé de lui faire mal
8. trouverait un moyen
9. de les faire sortir d'ici,
10. loin de
11. dire la vérité au sujet de
12. serré tout contre elle
13. qu'il avait pris l'habitude d'aller dans le lit de
14. l'attirait tout près d'elle

wiggling[1]" in a sleepy voice, and he'd go back to sleep all tucked against her[2].

Sharon and Daddy would take care of him. Neil wiggled a fraction closer to[3] Sharon. He wished he could tell her not to worry about him. He'd take long, slow breaths through his nose. His arms hurt so much. Determinedly he pushed that thought away[4]. He'd think about something nice … the room on the top floor and the Lionel trains Sharon would give him.

1. de gigoter
2. blotti contre elle
3. se rapprocha, en se tortillant, encore davantage de
4. chassa cette pensée

33

"For God's sake, dear, it's nearly midnight. Give it up.[5]" Roger watched helplessly as Glenda shook her head. Alarmed, he saw that the vial[6] of nitroglycerin tablets on her night table was nearly empty. It had been full only this morning.

"No. I'll get it.[7] I know I will.[8] Roger, here[9] … let's try this[10]. I'll tell you everything I did over the past month. I've been going back day by day but I still have missed something. Maybe if I tell it to you …"

He knew it was useless to protest. Pulling up a chair close to the bed[11], he prepared to concentrate. His head was throbbing. The doctor had come back and been furious that Glenda was upsetting herself so much[12]. Of course they hadn't been able to explain why she was so agitated.

5. Laisse tomber.
6. flacon
7. Je vais y arriver.
8. Je sais que je vais y arriver.
9. tiens
10. essayons ceci
11. Approchant une chaise du lit
12. se fasse tant de souci

The doctor wanted to give her a strong shot, but Roger knew she'd never forgive him if he okayed it[1]. Now, watching her ashen pallor[2] and the telltale purplish-blue lips[3], he thought of that day when she'd had the coronary: ... we're doing everything we can, Mr. Perry ... it's touch and go[4] ... it might be wise[5] to send for[6] your sons ...

But she'd pulled out of it[7]. Oh God, if she knows anything let her remember, Roger prayed. Let me help her remember. If Neil and Sharon died and afterward Glenda felt she could have saved them, it would kill her too.

What was Steve feeling right now? It would soon be time for him to leave for New York with the ransom money.

Where was Ronald Thompson's mother now? What was she thinking? Did she know this same futile anguish? Of course she did.[8]

What about Sharon and Neil? Were they terrified, had they been abused[9]? Were they still alive or was it already too late?

And Ronald Thompson. At the trial, Roger had been able to think only of how much he resembled[10] Chip and Doug at that age[11]. At nineteen, his boys had been sophomores in college; Chip at Harvard, Doug at the University of Michigan. That's where nineteen-year-olds belong[12]—in college, not in prison cells on Death Row[13].

"Roger." Glenda's voice was remarkably steady. "Maybe if you make a diagram of each day, nine o'clock, ten o'clock, that kind of thing[14], it will help to point up whatever I'm missing[15]. There's a pad in my desk."

He walked over and got it. "All right," she said, "I'm sure of yesterday and Sunday, so we won't waste time on them. Let's start with last Saturday ..."

1. donnait son accord
2. son teint livide
3. le bleu violacé éloquent de ses lèvres
4. elle est entre la vie et la mort
5. sage
6. de faire venir
7. s'en était sortie
8. Très certainement.
9. les avait-on maltraités
10. n'avait réussi qu'à penser à sa grande ressemblance avec
11. au même âge
12. C'est là que devaient se trouver les jeunes de 19 ans
13. dans le couloir de la mort
14. ce genre de choses
15. mettre en évidence ce que j'ai raté

34

"No questions, Mr. Peterson? You're sure you've got it straight[1]?" Hugh and Steve were in the foyer. Steve had the heavy suitcase containing the ransom money gripped in his hand.

"I think so.[2]" Steve's voice was even, almost a monotone[3]. Somewhere in the past hours[4], the fatigue had retreated[5]; overwhelming numbness[6] had anesthetized pain and worry. He could think clearly, almost abstractly. He was standing on a high hill overlooking a drama[7]. He was viewer[8] as well as participant.

"All right. Run it down[9] for me." Hugh recognized the symptoms in the other man. Peterson was coming to the end of his emotional tether[10]. Already he was in some kind of shock, of course. That business of imitating[11] his wife's voice had been the limit[12]. And the poor guy kept insisting it was her. What a cheap, clumsy way[13] to try to link the abduction[14] to Nina Peterson's death. There were a couple of other things[15] Hugh had noticed; Sharon's request for Steve to forgive her. Neil saying, "Sharon is taking care of me." Wasn't that the tip-off[16] that this was a fraud[17]?

Was it?[18]

1. d'avoir tout bien compris
2. Je crois.
3. presque monocorde
4. Au cours des dernières heures
5. s'était envolée
6. une torpeur irrésistible
7. en haut d'une colline d'où il assistait au drame
8. spectateur
9. Récapitulez
10. était au bout du rouleau et émotionnellement vidé
11. Cette histoire d'imitation de
12. l'avait poussé à bout
13. Quelle façon minable et maladroite
14. enlèvement
15. une ou deux autres choses que
16. Cela ne révélait-il pas
17. imposture
18. Était-ce bien une imposture ?

Maybe John Owens could help them. They'd located him and he was meeting Hugh at headquarters in New York.

Steve said, "I go directly to the Fifty-ninth Street phonebooth. If I'm early[1], I sit and wait in the car until just before two A.M., then get out of the car and stand at the phone. I'll probably be directed to another phone. I go there. Then hopefully I make direct contact and turn the suitcase over to the abductor[2]. After I leave him, I drive to FBI headquarters on Sixty-ninth Street and Third Avenue. You'll be waiting to take the cameras out of the car and develop the film."

"That's it. We'll be trailing you from a distance.[3] The beeper in your car will keep us informed of your movements. One of our men is waiting to follow you down the parkway now to make sure you don't get stuck or delayed[4]. Mr. Peterson ..." Hugh reached out his hand, "good luck."

"Luck?" Steve said the word with wonderment[5] as though he were hearing it for the first time. "I haven't been thinking of luck so much as I have of an old Wexford curse[6]. Do you know it by any chance[7]?"

"I don't think so."

"I can't remember all of it, but it's something like this[8]: 'May the fox build his nest[9] on your hearthstone[10]. May the light fade from your eyes[11] so you never see what you love. May the sweetest drink you take be the bitterest cup of sorrow[12] ...' There's more[13], but that pretty much sums it up[14]. Rather appropriate[15], isn't it?"

Without waiting for an answer, Steve left. Hugh watched the Mercury pull out of the driveway, turn left toward the parkway. *May the fox build his nest on your hearthstone.* God help that guy Peterson. Shaking his head to try to relieve[16] the persistent

1. en avance
2. j'établis un contact direct avec le ravisseur et lui remets la valise
3. On vous filera à distance.
4. que vous ne serez ni coincé ni retardé sur la route
5. étonnement
6. malédiction
7. par hasard
8. elle dit à peu près ceci
9. son terrier
10. ton foyer
11. disparaisse de tes yeux
12. calice de chagrin le plus amer
13. Les paroles ne s'arrêtent pas là
14. elles résument assez bien l'idée générale
15. C'est plutôt de circonstance
16. de dissiper

sense of impending doom[1], Hugh grabbed his own coat. None of the FBI cars were in the driveway. He and the other agents were slipping out[2] the back door, across the two acres of vacant woods[3] next to Steve's place. Their cars were parked on the narrow road that had been made in the woods when sewer lines were laid[4]. There they were invisible from the street.

Maybe John Owens could make something[5] of the cassette the kidnapper had sent. A retired agent[6] who'd gone blind from glaucoma twenty years before, John had developed his hearing so keenly[7] that he could interpret background sounds[8] on recordings with remarkable accuracy[9]. They brought him in whenever this kind of evidence came into a case[10]. Later on of course, they'd run the cassette through regular lab tests, but that would take days.

Without explaining his reason, Hugh had asked Steve about Nina's background[11]: Philadelphia Main Line family[12], fourth generation. Nina had attended a Swiss boarding school[13], Bryn Mawr College[14]. Her parents spent most of their time now in their home in Monte Carlo. Hugh remembered meeting them at Nina's funeral. They'd flown in[15] for the service and internment[16]; hardly spoken to Steve, a pair of cold potatoes[17] if ever he saw them[18].

But the information would be enough for Owens to give a pretty accurate opinion whether that voice actually[19] was Nina's or an impersonation[20]. Hugh had little doubt about the outcome[21].

The Merritt Parkway had been sanded[22] and even though fresh snow was still falling, the driving was better than Steve had expected. He'd been fearful that the abductor might call off[23] meeting him if the roads were hazardous[24]. Now he was sure they'd somehow make contact.

1. le sentiment de catastrophe imminente qui ne le quittait pas
2. sortaient discrètement par
3. et traversaient l'hectare de forêt
4. ils avaient installé le tout-à-l'égout
5. tirer quelque chose
6. Agent à la retraite
7. développé une ouïe si fine
8. les bruits de fond
9. une précision remarquable
10. se présentait dans une affaire
11. le milieu où avait grandi Nina
12. grande famille de Philadelphie
13. avait fait sa scolarité dans un pensionnat en Suisse
14. puis était allée à Bryn Mawr College
15. venus en avion
16. pour les obsèques
17. deux vrais glaçons
18. s'il en est
19. véritablement
20. imitation
21. résultat
22. sablée
23. n'annule
24. dangereuses

He wondered why Hugh had queried him[1] about Nina's background. He'd only wanted a few basic facts. "What college did your wife go to, Mr. Peterson? Where was she raised[2]?"

"She went to Bryn Mawr." They'd met when they were both seniors[3]. He was at Princeton. It was love at first sight[4]. Corny[5] but true.

"Her family is fourth generation Philadelphia Main Line." They were outraged[6] about him. They wanted Nina to "marry her own kind[7]," as they put it[8]. Someone with good family and money and a preppie background[9]. Not an impoverished[10] student who waited table[11] at the Nassau Inn to stretch his scholarship[12], who'd graduated from Christopher Columbus High School in the Bronx.

God, they'd been formidable[13] when he and Nina were going around together[14]. He'd said to Nina, "How did you ever get to be *their* daughter?" She was so funny, so bright, so unpretentious[15]. They'd been married right after graduation[16]. Then he'd gone into service[17], been commissioned[18] and sent to Vietnam. They didn't see each other for two years. Finally he'd gotten an R and R[19] and she'd met him in Hawaii. She'd been so beautiful, running down the steps of the plane, tumbling into his arms.

After he was discharged[20], he'd gone to Columbia for a Master's in Journalism. Then he got the job at *Time* and they moved up to Connecticut and she became pregnant with[21] Neil.

He'd bought her the Karman Ghia when Neil was born, and you'd have thought it was a Rolls. Which, of course, was what her father had.

He'd sold Nina's car the week after the funeral. It was impossible to see it parked next to his Mercury in the garage. That night when he'd come home to find her dead, he'd walked out to it, hoping against hope[22]. "Your carelessness will get you killed!" But

1. l'avait interrogé
2. a-t-elle grandi
3. en licence
4. le coup de foudre
5. Une histoire à l'eau de rose
6. indignés
7. épouse une personne de son milieu
8. pour reprendre leur expression
9. BCBG
10. sans le sou
11. travaillait comme serveur
12. compléter sa bourse
13. redoutables
14. sortaient ensemble
15. modeste
16. tout de suite après l'obtention de leur diplôme
17. était parti au service militaire
18. promu
19. obtenu une permission
20. démobilisé
21. était tombée enceinte de
22. gardant espoir malgré tout

the new radial[1] was back on the front wheel; the balding spare was in the trunk. If she hadn't bothered[2] to have it changed that day, it would have meant that she didn't take his annoyance too seriously[3].

Nina, Nina, I'm sorry.

Sharon. She'd made him come alive again[4]. Because of her the numbness and pain had dissolved like ice gradually melting in a spring thaw[5]. These six months had been so good. He'd started to believe that he'd been given a second chance at happiness[6].

You didn't fall in love the first time you met someone. He was thirty-four now, not twenty-two.

Or didn't you?[7]

That first meeting on the *Today* show. After it was over they walked out of the studio together and stood talking in front of the building. He hadn't been even vaguely interested in any woman after Nina died, but that morning he'd found himself reluctant[8] to let Sharon go. He was due at an early meeting[9] and couldn't suggest having breakfast with her. Finally he'd blurted out[10], "Look, I have to run[11] now but how about dinner tonight[12]?"

Sharon said yes[13], quickly, almost as though she'd been hoping he'd ask. The whole day had seemed interminably long before he was finally at her apartment ringing her doorbell. At that time their debate[14] over capital punishment was more ideological than personal. It was only when Sharon began to feel that she couldn't save Ronald Thompson that she started to turn on him[15].

He was on the Cross County Parkway. His hands were working independently, selecting the roads without his conscious awareness[16].

Sharon. It was so good to talk to someone again, over dinner, over a nightcap at her place. She understood the problems of launching a new magazine,

1. pneu
2. ne s'était pas donné la peine
3. n'attachait pas vraiment d'importance à son irritation
4. lui avait redonné le goût de vivre
5. fondant peu à peu lors du dégel printanier
6. qu'on lui avait donné une seconde chance d'être heureux
7. À moins que... ?
8. était peu disposé
9. attendu à une réunion en tout début de matinée
10. avait laissé échapper
11. filer
12. que diriez-vous de dîner ensemble ce soir
13. avait accepté
14. discussion
15. à le prendre à partie
16. sans en avoir vraiment conscience

1. annonceurs publicitaires
2. fidéliser un nombre important de lecteurs
3. On n'est pas loin des confidences sur l'oreiller
4. véritable coup de poker
5. gagnait beaucoup d'argent
6. ténor du journalisme
7. prouver sa valeur au
8. lui ferait ravaler ses paroles
9. le tenait responsable de
10. une maison bien gardée, dotée d'un personnel qualifié
11. Tel père, tel fils.
12. grandi
13. en ressentant cruellement l'absence d'une mère
14. enseignante suppléante
15. dessiner des cartes pour la Fête des Mères
16. cartable
17. l'avait déchirée
18. se vantant à la ronde
19. ne s'était pas réveillé
20. ne s'était pas présenté au travail
21. au cours des dernières années
22. avait pris cette position

the struggle to get advertisers[1], to get readership[2]. The nearest thing to pillowtalk[3], he'd joked.

He'd left his job at *Time* to go with *Events* a few months before Nina died. It had been a real gamble[4]. He was making important money[5] at *Time*. Part of it had been pride. He was going to help create the best magazine in the country. He was going to be a rich, hotshot editor[6] and show[7] Nina's father. He'd make him eat his words[8].

Nina's parents blamed him for[9] her death. "If she'd been in a properly staffed, properly secured house[10], this never would have happened," they said. They'd wanted to take Neil back with them to Europe. Neil, with those two!

Neil. The poor little kid. Like father, like son.[11] Steve's mother had died when he was three. He didn't remember her at all. His father had never remarried. That was a mistake. Steve had grown up[12] wanting a mother[13]. He remembered when he was seven, there'd been a substitute teacher[14] in his class and she'd had them draw Mother's Day cards[15].

At the end of the day she noticed that he didn't put his in his schoolbag[16]. "You're not going to leave that here, are you?" she'd asked. "Your mother will be so pleased to have it Sunday."

He'd torn it up[17] and run out of the room.

He didn't want that for Neil. He wanted Neil to grow up in a happy home, a home with brothers and sisters. He didn't want to live the way his father had, alone, making Steve his whole life, bragging to everybody[18] in the post office about his son in Princeton. A lonely man in a lonely apartment. One morning he hadn't awakened[19]. When he didn't show up for work[20], they'd investigated. And Steve had been called out of class.

Maybe that was why over the past years[21] he'd taken the stand[22] on capital punishment. Because he knew how elderly, poor people[1] lived, how little they had[2]. Because it sickened him[3] to think of any of them being brutally murdered by thugs[4].

The suitcase was on the front seat next to him. Hugh had assured him the electronic device wouldn't be detected. Now he was glad that he'd let them put it in.

At 1:30 Steve pulled off the Fifty-seventh Street exit of the West Side Highway. At twenty of two, he was parked in front of the payphone outside Bloomingdale's. At ten of two he got out of the car and, unmindful of the[5] wet, icy wind, stood in the booth.

At precisely 2:00 A.M.[6] the phone rang. The same muffled, whispering voice instructed him to go immediately to a phone on[7] Ninety-sixth Street and Lexington Avenue.

At 2:15 that phone rang. Steve was told[8] to drive over[9] the Triborough Bridge, take the Grand Central Parkway to the Brooklyn Queens Expressway exit[10]. He was to drive on the BQE to Roosevelt Avenue, turn left to the end of the first block, and park immediately. He was to turn out his headlights[11] and wait. "Be sure to have the money. Be alone."

Frantically, Steve scribbled[12], repeated the instructions. The abductor hung up.

At 2:35 he turned off[13] the BQE onto Roosevelt Avenue. A large sedan was parked halfway down the block[14] on the other side of the street. As he passed it[15] he twisted the wheel a fraction[16], hoping the hidden cameras might be able to pick up the make and license number; then he pulled over to the curb and waited.

It was a dark street. The doors and windows of the shabby old stores were protected with chains and bars; the elevated tracks[17] helped cut off[18] the street lights; the snow blocked remaining visibility.

1. comment les personnes âgées et pauvres
2. combien ils avaient peu de moyens financiers
3. cela le rendait malade
4. des voyous
5. indifférent au
6. 2 heures
7. à l'angle de
8. reçut l'ordre
9. franchir
10. la sortie de la voie express de Brooklyn Queens
11. devait éteindre ses phares
12. griffonna
13. sortit de
14. au milieu du pâté de maisons
15. la dépassa
16. tourna très légèrement le volant
17. voie ferrée aérienne
18. contribuait à masquer

1. suivre son parcours grâce à l'émetteur
2. On cogna brutalement
3. tourna brusquement la tête
4. devenir sèche
5. lui faisait signe
6. mit la clé de contact
7. aperçu
8. une tête recouverte d'un bas
9. sensation de malaise
10. au creux de l'estomac

Were the FBI agents able to trace his course through the beeper[1]? Suppose it stopped working. He hadn't noticed any cars following him. But they'd said they wouldn't get too close.

There was a thump[2] at the driver's door. Steven spun his head around[3], felt his mouth go dry[4]. A gloved hand was gesturing for him[5] to pull the window down. He switched the ignition key on[6], deflected the window button.

"Don't look at me, Peterson."

But he'd already glimpsed[7] a brownish coat, a stocking mask[8]. Something was dropped on his lap, some large canvas bag—a duffel bag. He felt a sick feeling[9] in the pit of his stomach[10]. This man was not going to take the suitcase with the tracer. He knew it.

"Open that suitcase and put the money in the bag. Hurry up."

11. de gagner du temps
12. relâcherez indemnes mon fils et Sharon
13. une note aiguë
14. En tâtonnant
15. extirpa

He tried to stall for time[11]. "How do I know that you'll return my son and Sharon unharmed[12]?"

"*Fill that bag!*" He could hear the high-pitched undercurrent[13] in the voice. The man was violently nervous. If he panicked and ran off without the money, he might kill Sharon and Neil. With fumbling hands[14], Steve wrenched[15] the neat packets of money from the suitcase, jammed them into the duffel bag.

"Close it!"

He drew the strings tightly together, knotted them.

16. Passez-le moi.
17. droit devant lui
18. les regarder attentivement
19. Rigides

"Hand it over.[16] Don't look at me."

He stared straight ahead[17]. "What about my son and Sharon?"

Gloved hands reached in through the window, yanked the bag away from him. The gloves. He tried to notice them[18]. Stiff-looking[19], cheap imitation leather, dark gray or brown, large. The sleeve of the coat was frayed[1]; broken pieces of thread spidered out from it[2].

"You're being watched, Peterson." The abductor's voice was hurried, almost trembling. "Don't leave here for[3] fifteen minutes; remember that, *fifteen minutes.* If I'm not followed and the money is all here, you'll be told where to pick up your son and Sharon at eleven-thirty this morning."

Eleven-thirty. The exact minute of Ronald Thompson's execution. "Did you have anything to do with my wife's death?" Steve burst out.

There was no answer. He waited, then cautiously turned his head. The abductor had slipped away[4]. Across the street, a car started[5].

His watch said[6] 2:38. The entire meeting had taken place in less than three minutes. Was he being watched? Was there an observer on the roof of one of those buildings ready to report if he moved? The FBI wouldn't get any signal of location change from the suitcase. Did he dare start sooner?[7]

No.

At 2:53 Steve made a U turn[8] and headed back toward[9] Manhattan. At 3:10 he was at the FBI headquarters on Sixty-ninth Street and Third Avenue. Grim-faced agents rushed to his car and began unscrewing[10] the headlights. A somber-looking Hugh listened to his explanation as they rode up[11] to the twelfth floor. There he was introduced to a man with snow-white hair and a patient, intelligent expression that was not concealed by dark glasses[12].

"John has been listening to the cassette," Hugh explained. "From[13] the quality of their voices and a certain echo, he concludes that Sharon and Neil are being kept[14] in a nearly empty, cold room, about eleven by twenty-three feet in size[15]. They may be in the basement of a freightyard[16]; there's a continu-

1. effilochée
2. des fils en pendaient
3. Ne partez pas d'ici avant
4. avait filé
5. démarra
6. affichait
7. Oserait-il partir avant ?
8. fit demi-tour
9. prit la direction de
10. à dévisser
11. montaient
12. que ses lunettes noires ne cachaient pas
13. D'après
14. sont détenus
15. d'environ trois mètres sur sept
16. sous-sol d'une gare de marchandises

ing faint sound of trains pulling in and leaving from somewhere nearby."

Steve stared.

"I'll be able to be considerably more specific[1] later," the blind agent said. "There's no magic to this.[2] It's simply a case of[3] listening with the same degree of intensity with which you'd study a specimen under a microscope."

A cold room, nearly empty. A freightyard. Steve looked accusingly at Hugh. "What does this do to your theory that Sharon may have planned this?"

"I don't know," Hugh replied simply.

"Mr. Peterson, about the last voice on the cassette," John Owens' manner was hesitant, "by any chance was your late wife's first tongue[4] French rather than English?"

"No, not at all. She was raised in Philadelphia till she went to boarding school at ten. Why?"

"There's an intonation in that voice that to an expert definitely suggests that English was not the first language[5]."

"Wait a minute! Nina did tell me that she'd had a French nurse[6], that as a young child she actually[7] thought in French rather than English."

"That's exactly what I'm talking about.[8] Then that was no imposter or mimic. You are correct[9] in identifying your wife's voice."

"All right. I was wrong about that[10]," Hugh said. "But John says that last voice was definitely[11] added to the cassette after Neil and Sharon were recorded. Think, Mr. Peterson. Somebody who knows a great deal about[12] your personal life has planned this. Were you ever at a party, maybe, where people were doing home movies[13], where someone might have recorded a voice track of your wife and excerpted those few words from it[14]?"

1. précis
2. Il n'y a rien de surnaturel à cela.
3. Il s'agit tout simplement d'
4. est-ce que par hasard la langue maternelle de votre défunte épouse était
5. langue maternelle
6. nourrice
7. effectivement
8. C'est exactement là où je veux en venir.
9. avez raison
10. J'avais tort sur ce point
11. sans aucun doute
12. en sait long sur
13. des films d'amateur
14. en extraire ces quelques mots

It was so hard to think[1] … Steve frowned. "The country club. When it was renovated and redecorated four years ago, they made a film for some charity[2]. Nina was the narrator, going from room to room, explaining what had been done."

"Now we're getting somewhere[3]," Hugh said. "Might she have used those words within the framework[4] of that film?"

"Possibly."

The phone rang. Hugh grabbed it, identified himself[5], listened intently. "Good. Get right on it![6]" He slammed the receiver down; he had the look of a hunter[7] on a fresh scent[8]. "Things are beginning to break[9], Mr. Peterson," he said. "You got a clear picture[10] of the car and license plate. We're tracing it now."

The first faint hope[11] he'd been offered! Then why was the knot in his throat still choking him? It's too easy, something was saying[12]; it's not going to work out.

John Owens stretched out his hand in the direction of Steve's voice. "Mr. Peterson, just one question. My impression is that, if that actually is your wife on the cassette, she spoke while she was in the process of opening a door[13]. Are you aware by any chance of a particular door with a faint squealing sound[14] when it opens, something like this—'eerkkk'?" He gave a startling[15] imitation of a rusty hinge[16] moving.

Hugh and Steve stared at each other. It is a mockery[17], Steve thought dully[18]. It is a farce; it is already too late for everybody.

Hugh answered for him. "Yes, John," he said.

"That's exactly the way Mr. Peterson's kitchen door sounds as it's being opened."

1. Il avait tant de mal à réfléchir
2. œuvre de bienfaisance
3. Nous avons enfin quelque chose
4. dans le cadre
5. déclina son identité
6. Occupez-vous de ça immédiatement !
7. chasseur
8. piste nouvelle
9. Les choses commencent à se décanter
10. photo nette
11. La première lueur d'espoir
12. lui disait une petite voix
13. tout en ouvrant une porte
14. qui grince légèrement
15. saisissante
16. gond rouillé
17. plaisanterie
18. pensa Steve, accablé

35

Arty drove away[1] from the Mill Tavern, a nagging worry[2] sending out alarm signals through his body, dissolving the euphoric sense of infallibility he'd been enjoying[3].

He'd really counted on Bill Lufts being in the bar, it would have been helpful to pump[4] Bill. Oh, the boy's away? Where is he? How's Mr. Peterson? Has he had any company?

He'd figured[5] that Peterson wouldn't admit to the Lufts[6] that Neil and Sharon were missing. He'd figured Peterson knew that the Lufts shot their mouths off about everything[7].

So if Bill wasn't there, it was because Peterson had called the cops—no, not the cops, the FBI.

That guy who called himself Pete Lerner, who asked so many questions. He was an FBI agent. Arty knew it.

He steered the dark-green Beetle onto[8] the Merritt Parkway south. Anxiety made perspiration ooze from[9] his forehead and armpits[10] and hands.

Twelve years slipped away.[11] He was being grilled[12] in FBI headquarters in Manhattan. "Come on, Arty, the news vendor[13] saw you leave with that kid. Where'd you take her?"

1. s'éloigna en voiture
2. inquiétude tenace
3. qu'il avait jusqu'alors ressenti
4. tirer les vers du nez à
5. avait supposé
6. ne révèlerait pas aux Lufts
7. ne savaient pas tenir leur langue
8. À bord de la Coccinelle vert foncé, il s'engagea sur
9. faisait couler la sueur sur
10. sous ses aisselles
11. Il se revit 12 ans en arrière.
12. On le mettait sur le grill
13. marchand de journaux

"I put her in a cab. She said she was meeting some guy."

"What guy?"

"How do I know? I carried her bag out, that's all."

They couldn't prove anything. But they tried. God, they tried.

"How about[1] the other girls, Arty. Take a look at these pictures. You're always hanging around[2] the Port Authority[3]. How many of them did you carry bags for?"

"I don't know what you mean."

They were coming too close[4]. It was too dangerous. That was when he left New York, drifted up to[5] Connecticut, got a job pumping gas[6]. Six years ago he'd taken over the repair shop[7] in Carley.

Arizona. That had been a bad mistake[8]. Why did he say, "Rhode Island ain't Arizona?" Probably that guy who called himself Pete Lerner hadn't noticed, but even so it had been a mistake.

They had nothing on him unless they started checking way back[9], unless they came up with the time[10] they questioned him about the kid from Texas. "Come on down to my place[11] in the Village," he'd told her. "I have a lot of artist friends who can use[12] a good-looking model."

But they didn't have proof then and they didn't have it now. Nothing. There hadn't been any slip-ups[13]. He was sure of it.

"*Is this your place*[14]," she'd asked, "*this dump*[15]*?*"

The Merritt faded into the Hutchinson River Parkway. He followed the signs leading to the Throgs Neck Bridge. His plan was ingenious. Stealing a car was dangerous. There was always the chance that the owner might come back in ten minutes; that the cops would have an alert before it had gone five miles[16]. You shouldn't steal a car unless you're sure

1. Et
2. traînes toujours autour
3. [Principal terminal de bus de Manhattan]
4. étaient trop près de la vérité
5. poussa jusqu'au
6. en tant que pompiste
7. avait repris le garage
8. grossière erreur
9. fouiller dans son passé
10. remontent à l'époque où
11. Passez chez moi
12. recherchent
13. faux pas
14. C'est là que vous habitez
15. ce taudis
16. vous n'ayez parcouru huit kilomètres

the owner is out of the way[1]—like sitting, watching a thirty-year-old movie, or taking off on a plane[2].

The Throgs Neck Bridge had caution signs flashing. Ice. Wind. But that was all right. He was a good driver and tonight the chicken drivers[3] would be staying home. That would make it easy for him to move around[4] later.

At 11:20 he drove into LaGuardia Airport into parking lot five[5], the one with special rates for long-term parkers[6].

He took a ticket from the machine; the gate[7] lifted and he drove slowly through the lot, taking care to get well away from the view of the cashier[8] in the exit line next to the automatic check-in[9]. He pulled into an empty space in section nine, between a Chrysler and a Cadillac, behind an Oldsmobile wagon[10]. In the midst of them the Beetle was diminished and hidden[11].

He leaned back[12] in the seat and waited. Forty minutes passed[13]. Two cars came into the lot, one a flashy red, the other a yellow station wagon. Both too easy to spot[14]. He was glad when they ignored the empty spaces near him and drove further down[15] into the far-left section.

Another car drove slowly by. A dark-blue Pontiac that pulled into a spot[16] three rows[17] ahead. The lights went off. He watched as the driver got out walked around to the trunk and extracted[18] a large suitcase. This guy would be away for a while[19].

Slumped[20] in the Volks[21], only the top of his head above the level of the windshield, he watched as the man slammed the trunk down[22], picked up the suitcase and made his way to[23] the nearest bus shelter[24] from which the courtesy airport bus[25] would take him to the departure terminal.

1. n'est pas dans le coin
2. qu'il prend l'avion
3. automobilistes froussards
4. se déplacer
5. pénétra au volant de son véhicule dans le parking numéro 5 de l'aéroport de LaGuardia
6. les tarifs spéciaux pour les stationnements de longue durée
7. barrière
8. de se tenir hors de vue du caissier
9. caisse automatique
10. break
11. paraissait plus petite et était cachée
12. s'adossa
13. s'écoulèrent
14. à repérer
15. poursuivaient leur route
16. trouva une place
17. rangées
18. en sortit
19. pour un certain temps
20. Affalé
21. [Volkswagen]
22. l'homme fermer violemment le coffre
23. se diriger vers
24. Abribus
25. navette gratuite de l'aéroport

The bus came in a few minutes[1]. Foxy observed the silhouetted figure get on[2] the vehicle. The bus pulled away[3].

Slowly, quietly, he got out of the Beetle and looked around. There were no headlights approaching. In quick strides[4] he was at the side of the Pontiac. The second key he tried opened the door. He was in the car.

It was still comfortably warm. He put the key he was holding in the ignition[5]. The engine turned over almost noiselessly; the tank[6] was three-quarters full.

Perfect.

He'd have to wait. The guard would be suspicious if he collected on[7] a ticket with less than a couple of hours' parking in this lot. But he had plenty of time and he wanted to think. He leaned back, closed his eyes, and Nina's image floated across his mind, the way she'd looked that first night …

He'd been cruising around, knowing he shouldn't be out, knowing it was too soon after Jean Carfolli and Mrs. Weiss, but not able to stay in[8]. And he'd seen her. The Karmann Ghia pulled over[9] on Route 7 in that quiet, lonely spot. The slender, small body caught up in his headlights[10]. The dark hair. The little hands that were struggling with the jack[11]. The enormous brown eyes that looked startled[12] when he slowed down and pulled over[13]. Probably hearing in her head all the talk about the highwayman murders.

"Can I help you, miss? That's rough work[14] for you, but it's my job. I'm a mechanic."

The worried look disappeared. "Oh, great," she said. "I don't mind telling you[15] that I'm a bit nervous … of all the crazy places to get a flat[16]."

He never glanced at her; just at the tire, like she didn't exist, like she was nine hundred years old. "You've picked up some glass[17], no big deal[18]."

1. quelques minutes plus tard
2. la silhouette de l'homme alors qu'il montait dans
3. démarra
4. enjambées
5. mit la clé de contact et démarra
6. réservoir
7. encaissait
8. rester chez lui
9. arrêtée sur le côté
10. pris dans la lumière de ses phares
11. cric
12. effrayés
13. s'arrêta
14. Ce n'est pas une tâche de tout repos
15. Je ne vous cacherai pas
16. quelle poisse de crever dans un endroit pareil
17. vous avez roulé sur du verre
18. rien de bien méchant

Quickly, effortlessly, he changed it. Less than three minutes. No cars coming in either direction. He stood up.

"How much do I owe you?" Her purse[1] open, her neck bent[2]. Her breast rising and falling under the suede[3] coat. Class.[4] Something about her that showed it.[5] Not a scared kid like Jean Carfolli, not an outraged old bitch[6] like Weiss, just a beautiful young woman who was very grateful to him[7]. He reached out his hand to touch her breast.

The light began on the tree[8] across the road, swung around[9], illuminated the two of them. A cop car. He could see the dome[10]. "It's three dollars to change the tire," he said briskly, "and I can fix your flat[11] if you want." He had his hand in his pocket now. "I'm Arty Taggert, I have a repair shop in Carley on Monroe Street, about half a mile[12] from Mill Tavern."

The police car was coming up, pulling toward them. The trooper[13] got out. "You all right, ma'am?" His look at Arty was very funny, very suspicious.

"Oh, fine, officer[14], I certainly was in luck[15]. Mr. Taggert is from my town and he came along[16] just as I got the flat."

She made it sound like she knew him. What a break![17] The policeman's expression changed. "You're lucky, ma'am, to be helped by a friend. It's not safe for women to be alone in disabled cars[18] these days."

The cop got back in the patrol car but stayed there watching. "Will you fix the tire for me?" she asked. "I'm Nina Peterson. We live on Driftwood Lane."

"Sure.[19] Be glad to.[20]" He got back in his car, very indifferent, very casual[21], like this was just another cheap repair job, never showing that he *had* to see her again. He could tell the way she looked at him that she was sorry the cop had come along too. But

1. porte-monnaie
2. son cou penché
3. en daim
4. De la classe.
5. Quelque chose qui émanait d'elle.
6. vieille garce indignée
7. lui était très reconnaissante
8. éclaira d'abord l'arbre
9. oscilla
10. gyrophare
11. réparer votre pneu crevé
12. à environ 800 mètres
13. policier
14. très bien, monsieur l'agent
15. J'ai vraiment de la chance
16. passait par là
17. Quelle veine !
18. une voiture en panne
19. Bien sûr.
20. Avec plaisir.
21. d'un air très naturel

it was important to get away before the cop started thinking about Jean Carfolli and Mrs. Weiss; before the cop asked, "You in the habit[1] of stopping to help out ladies who are alone, mister?"

So he'd driven away and the next morning just when he was thinking about calling her, she called him. "My husband just gave me what-for[2] about driving on the spare[3]," she said, and her voice was very warm and intimate and amused like they had a private joke[4]. "When can I pick up my tire?"

He thought fast. Driftwood Lane was in a quiet area; the houses weren't close together. If she came to his place, there'd be no way[5] of getting friendly with her[6]. That would be too dangerous.

"I have to go out on a job right now," he lied, "I'll bring it by late this afternoon[7], maybe about five." It got dark by five.

"Wonderful," she said, "just as long as the darn thing[8] is back on the car before I go to pick up my husband at half-past six."

He was so excited that day that he could hardly think. He went out for a haircut[9] and bought a new checkered sportshirt[10]. When he got back he didn't bother at all with work[11]. He just showered[12] and dressed and while he waited he listened to some of his cassettes. Then he put a fresh new cassette[13] in the recorder and labeled it "Nina." He made sure his camera was loaded[14] and reflected on the[15] pleasure of developing pictures, watching the images forming on the prints[16] …

At ten after five he left for Driftwood Lane. He cruised her street[17] before deciding to park in the woods next to her house. Just in case[18] …

He walked through the woods near the shore[19]. He remembered how the water was lapping on the beach[20], a friendly sound that thrilled and warmed him[21] even on the cold night.

1. C'est dans vos habitudes
2. vient de me passer un savon
3. parce que je roule avec la roue de secours
4. comme si c'était une plaisanterie entre eux
5. il n'y aurait aucun moyen
6. se montrer amical à son égard
7. en fin d'après-midi
8. cette fichue roue
9. se fit couper les cheveux
10. polo à carreaux
11. ne s'embêta même pas à travailler
12. prit une douche
13. cassette vierge
14. chargé
15. pensa au
16. épreuves
17. roula dans sa rue
18. Au cas où
19. près du rivage
20. du clapotis de l'eau sur la plage
21. qui l'électrisait et le réchauffait

Her car was in the driveway behind the house; her keys were in the ignition. He could see Nina through the kitchen window; moving around[1], unpacking[2] groceries. The globe was off the fixture so the room was very bright. And she was so beautiful with that pale blue sweater over her slacks and that scarf knotted at her throat. He changed the tire very fast, keeping an eye out for any signs of other people in the house[3]. He knew he'd make love to her and that secretly she wanted him to. Just the way she hinted[4] that her husband had been angry at her showed[5] she needed a sympathetic[6] man. He turned on the recorder and began to whisper into it his plans for making Nina happy when he told her his feelings about her.

He went up to the kitchen door and knocked on it softly. She ran over, looked startled[7], but he held up[8] her keys, smiling at her through the glass. Right away[9] she began to smile and opened the door, all warm and friendly, her voice like arms around him, inviting him in, telling him how nice he was.

Then she asked him what she owed him[10]. He reached his hand up, he had his gloves on, of course, and switched off the kitchen light. He put his hands on her face and kissed her. "Pay me like this," he whispered.

She slapped him[11], a stunning slap[12], impossibly hard[13] from that small hand. "Get out of here," she said, spilling the words out like he was dirt[14], like he hadn't gotten all dressed up[15] for her, like he hadn't done her a favor.

He went wild[16]. Like the other times. Rejection did that to him.[17] She should have known better than[18] to lead him on[19] like that. He stretched out his hands, wanting to hurt her, to squeeze that nastiness out of her[20]. He reached for[21] her scarf. But somehow she slipped away from him[22] and ran into

1. se déplaçant
2. déballant
3. gardant un œil sur la maison pour s'assurer qu'elle y était seule
4. La façon dont elle avait laissé entendre
5. fâché contre elle montrait
6. compréhensif
7. étonnée
8. lui montra
9. Aussitôt
10. ce qu'elle lui devait
11. le gifla
12. une gifle stupéfiante
13. d'une force inimaginable
14. aboyant après lui comme s'il était un moins que rien
15. ne s'était pas mis sur son trente-et-un
16. fut pris de rage
17. Ça lui faisait ça quand on le rejetait.
18. Elle aurait mieux fait de ne pas
19. le faire marcher
20. extirper cette méchanceté de son être
21. voulut attraper
22. lui échappa

the living room. She never uttered a sound[1], never screamed for help[2]. Afterward he understood why. She didn't want him to know the child was in the house. But she tried to pick up a poker[3] from the fireplace.

He just laughed. He talked to her very low telling her what he would do. He held both her hands in one of his and put the poker back. Then he grabbed her scarf and twisted it around her neck, twisted while she gurgled[4] and gagged, and her hands like a doll[5]'s hands waved[6] and dropped[7] and went limp[8], while her great brown eyes widened and glazed and accused[9], while her face turned blue[10].

The gurgling stopped. He was holding her with one hand, snapping the picture[11], wishing her eyes would close, when somewhere behind him the gurgling, choking sound began again.

He swung around[12]. The boy was standing in the foyer, staring at him with huge[13] brown eyes that burned through him[14]. The boy was gasping just like she'd been gasping.

It was like he hadn't killed her at all; like she'd moved into the boy's body and was going to punish him, was taunting him[15], promising revenge.

He started across the room[16] for the boy. He'd make him stop that noise, he'd close those eyes. He cupped his hands[17], bent over the boy …

The bell rang.

He had to run. He raced through the foyer into the kitchen[18], slipped out the back door[19] while he heard the bell ring again. He was out through the woods, in his car, back in his shop in a few minutes. Calm. Be calm. He went to the Mill for a hamburger and beer, was there[20] when the news of the murder on Driftwood Lane swept through the town[21].

But he was scared. Suppose that trooper recognized Nina's picture in the paper, said at

1. ne proféra aucun son
2. ne cria jamais à l'aide
3. tisonnier
4. émettait des gargouillis
5. poupée
6. s'agitaient
7. tombaient
8. devenaient molles
9. devenaient vitreux et accusateurs
10. bleuissait
11. prenant la photo
12. fit volte-face
13. immenses
14. le fixaient au point de le transpercer
15. comme si elle le narguait
16. s'élança à travers la piece
17. mit ses mains en coupe
18. traversa en toute hâte le vestibule puis entra dans la cuisine
19. se glissa dehors par la porte de derrière
20. et y était encore
21. se répandit dans toute la ville

1. au poste
2. C'est bizarre
3. quitter la ville
4. faisait ses bagages
5. un garçon du coin de 17 ans
6. enfouit
7. buisson
8. à s'en prendre au gosse
9. s'était approché
10. un jour
11. hantait
12. tout au long de ses nuits agitées
13. à travers
14. se lia d'amitié avec
15. ressente le besoin impérieux de déterrer

headquarters[1], "Funny thing[2], last night I saw her on the road, some guy named Taggert was fixing her car ..."

He decided to get out of town[3]. But when he was packing[4] he heard on the news that an eyewitness, a neighbor, had been knocked down by someone running out of the Peterson house, that she had positively identified him as Ronald Thompson, a local seventeen-year-old[5], and that Thompson had been seen talking to Mrs. Peterson a few hours before the crime.

Arty put his camera and recorder and prints and film and cassettes inside a metal box and buried[6] it under a bush[7] behind his shop. Something told him to wait.

Then Thompson was caught at that motel in Virginia, and the kid identified him, too.

The luck. The incredible luck. The living room had been dark. The boy might not have seen his face clearly and then Thompson had gone into the house.

But he'd started to go for the kid[8]; he'd gotten close[9] to him. Neil must have been in shock. But suppose he remembered some day[10].

The thought haunted[11] Arty's dreams. The eyes followed him all through his restive nights[12]. Sometimes he woke up in the middle of the night, sweating, trembling, thinking the eyes were looking in[13] his bedroom window, or the wind would be making that same gurgling sound.

He never went looking for girls after that. Never. He just went to the Mill Tavern most nights and got friendly with[14] the guys there and especially with Bill Lufts. Bill talked a lot about Neil.

Until last month; until he knew he had to dig out[15] his cassettes from where he'd buried them and listen to them again.

That night on his C.B. he heard the Callahan girl saying she had a blowout, and he went looking for her. Two weeks later he went out when Mrs. Ambrose got on the C.B.[1] looking for directions[2], saying she was almost out of gas[3].

Now Fairfield County was in an uproar again[4], looking for a guy they called the C.B. killer[5]. You didn't leave any trace, he told himself.

But after these last two, the dreams of Nina came every single night[6]. Accusing. Then a couple of weeks ago, Bill Lufts drove up to his place with the boy Neil beside him in the wagon. Neil stared at Arty.

That was when he knew he had to kill Neil before he left Carley. And when Lufts bragged about the[7] trust fund in Neil's name—his wife had seen the bank statement[8] on Peterson's desk—he'd known how to get the money he needed.

Whenever he[9] thought about Nina, he hated Steve Peterson more. Peterson had been able to touch her without getting slapped; Peterson was a big-shot editor[10]; Peterson had people to wait on him[11]; Peterson had a good-looking new girlfriend. He'd show him.[12]

The room in Grand Central had always been there in his consciousness. A place to hide if ever he needed it, or a place to take a girl where no one would find her.

He used to think all the time about blowing up[13] Grand Central Station when he was working in that room. He'd think about how scared and shocked the people would be when a bomb went off, when they felt the floor give way[14] under them and the ceilings fall in[15]; all those people who ignored him when he was trying to be friendly, who never smiled at him, who rushed past him, who looked through him[16], who ate off the dishes[17] he had to wash and left

1. se brancha sur la CB
2. pour demander son chemin
3. n'avait presque plus d'essence
4. à nouveau en ébullition
5. le tueur à la CB
6. toutes les nuits
7. se fit mousser en parlant du
8. relevé de compte
9. Chaque fois qu'il
10. ténor du journalisme
11. à son service
12. Ça lui apprendrait
13. faire sauter
14. céder
15. s'effondrer
16. l'ignoraient
17. mangeaient dans les assiettes

1. grasses, pleines de coquilles
2. de vinaigrette
3. de traces de beurre
4. tout se mit en place
5. méritait
6. s'être interposé
7. gravats
8. ce que ça fait d'être pris au piège
9. tout serait terminé
10. que beaucoup de temps s'était écoulé
11. caisse
12. L'homme au guichet
13. endormi
14. commençait à avoir faim
15. [aux États-Unis, petit snack ouvert toute la nuit]
16. dirigea laconiquement

them greasy with shells[1] and salad dressing[2] and smears of butter[3].

Then everything came together[4]. The plan. The August *Rommel* Taggert plan. A fox's plan.

If only Sharon didn't have to die; if only she'd loved him. But in Arizona many girls would be friendly. He'd have so much money.

It was a good idea to have Sharon and Neil die just at the minute the Thompson kid was executed. Because he was executing them, too, and Thompson deserved[5] to die for having interfered[6] that night.

And all those people in Grand Central—tons of rubble[7] falling on them! They'd know how it felt to be trapped[8].

And he'd be free.

Soon. Soon it would be over[9].

Arty narrowed his eyes realizing that much time had passed[10]. It was always like that when he began to think of Nina. It was time to go.

He turned the ignition key in the Pontiac. At quarter of two he drove to the tollbooth[11] and handed over the ticket he'd taken at the automatic gate for his Volks. The collector[12] looked sleepy[13]. "Two hours and twenty-five minutes—that'll be two bucks, mister."

He drove out of the airport to a phone on Queens Boulevard. Promptly at two, he called the payphone outside Bloomingdale's. As soon as Peterson answered, he directed him to the public phone at Ninety-sixth Street.

He was getting hungry[14] and he had fifteen minutes.

In an all-night diner[15], he gulped down coffee and some toast as he watched the clock.

At 2:15, he dialed the Ninety-sixth Street public phone and tersely directed[16] Steve to the meeting place he'd selected.

Now for[1] the really dangerous part.

At 2:25 he began driving toward Roosevelt Avenue. The streets were nearly deserted. There was no sign of unmarked[2] cop cars. He'd be able to pick them out[3]; he was the master of cruising around on roads[4] without looking suspicious[5].

Last week he'd selected Roosevelt Avenue for the meeting place. He'd timed how long it would take[6] to get back to LaGuardia Airport from there. Exactly six minutes. Just in case the cops came along with Peterson, he'd have a good chance of getting away from them[7].

Because of the elevated train[8], Roosevelt was filled with pillars[9] that obstructed[10] the view, that made it hard to see[11] what was happening across the street[12] or down the block[13]. It was the best place to make contact[14].

At exactly 2:35 he parked on Roosevelt Avenue, facing the Brooklyn Queens Expressway, less than half a block to the access road[15].

At 2:36, he saw the lights of a car coming off the BQE from the opposite direction. Instantly he slipped the stocking mask[16] over his face.

It was Peterson's Mercury. For a second[17] he thought Peterson was going to pull up to him[18], the car swerved right at him[19]. Or was he trying to take a picture of the Pontiac? A lot of good that would do.[20]

Peterson's car stopped almost directly across the street. He swallowed nervously. But there were no other headlights coming off the expressway. He had to move fast[21]. He reached for the duffel bag. In his electronics magazine he'd read that in payments of ransom, suitcases were usually bugged[22]. He wasn't taking any chances.

The feel of the duffel bag, light, empty, ready to be filled, was reassuring. He opened the car door and

1. C'était à présent
2. banalisées
3. les repérer
4. passé maître dans l'art de rôder
5. avoir l'air suspect
6. chronométré le temps qu'il lui faudrait
7. leur échapper
8. voie ferrée aérienne
9. il y avait des piliers tout le long de l'avenue Roosevelt
10. bouchaient
11. faisaient qu'on distinguait difficilement
12. de l'autre côté de la rue
13. au bout du pâté de maisons
14. prendre contact
15. bretelle d'accès
16. enfila le bas qui lui servait de masque
17. Un instant
18. s'arrêter à sa hauteur
19. fit une embardée dans sa direction
20. Ça lui ferait une belle jambe.
21. agir vite
22. dotées d'un émetteur

crossed the street noiselessly. He needed just sixty seconds and then he'd be safe. He tapped on the window of Peterson's car, motioned him[1] to open it. As the window slid down he looked quickly into the car. Peterson was alone. He shoved in the duffel bag.

The dim street lights threw shadows of the pillars against[2] the car. In the soft, whispery voice he'd practiced[3], he told Peterson not to look at him, to put the money in the duffel bag.

Peterson didn't argue[4]. Behind the stocking mask, Foxy's eyes roamed[5] the area. His ears strained.[6] But there was no sound of anyone coming. The cops had to be tailing[7] Peterson, but probably wanted to be sure he made contact.

He watched Peterson drop the last packet of bills[8] in the duffel bag and told him to close it and hand it over. Greedily, he felt its weight.[9] Remembering to speak very low, he warned Peterson to wait fifteen minutes and told him that Sharon and Neil could be picked up at 11:30.

"Did you have anything to do[10] with my wife's death?"

The question startled[11] Foxy. How much were they beginning to suspect?[12] He had to get away. He was sweating now, heavy beads[13] of perspiration that soaked[14] his suit under the brown coat, that warmed the soles of his feet even while the sharp wind bit at his ankles[15].

He crossed the street, got back in the Pontiac. Would Peterson dare to follow him?

No. He was still parked in the dark, silent car.

Foxy floored the accelerator[16] of the Pontiac, shot onto[17] the access road to the Brooklyn Queens Expressway, drove on that two minutes to the Grand Central Parkway, slipped into the light eastbound traffic[18] and three minutes later exited at LaGuardia Airport.

1. lui fit signe
2. À la faible lueur des réverbères, les piliers projetaient leur ombre sur
3. s'était entraîné à prendre
4. ne discuta pas
5. balayaient
6. Il tendait l'oreille.
7. suivaient certainement
8. liasse de billets
9. Avidement, il le soupesa.
10. Avez-vous quelque chose à voir
11. ébranla
12. Jusqu'à quel point commençaient-ils à le soupçonner ?
13. de grosses gouttes
14. trempait
15. malgré la morsure du vent glacé sur ses chevilles
16. appuya sur l'accélérateur
17. déboucha en trombe sur
18. se mêla à la circulation fluide en direction de l'est

At 2:46 he was reaching for a parking ticket at the automatic entry to parking lot five.

Ninety seconds later, the Pontiac was parked exactly where he'd found it, the only perceptible difference a fraction less gas[1] and six more miles[2] registered on the odometer[3].

He got out of the Pontiac, carefully locked it, and carried the duffel bag to the dark-green Beetle. His first easy breath[4] came when he was inside the Volks and clawing at[5] the cord of the duffel bag.

Finally he had it loose.[6] He switched the beam of his flashlight[7] inside the bag. A smile, humorless as a jack-o'-lantern[8]'s, played on his lips[9]. He reached for the first packet of money and began to count.

It was all there. Eighty-two thousand dollars. He reached for the empty suitcase in the back seat and neatly began to pile the packets inside it. This bag he'd carry on[10] the plane.

At 7:00 A.M. he pulled out of the parking lot, blended with the early morning commuter traffic into[11] Manhattan, parked the car in the Biltmore garage, and hurried upstairs to his room for a shave[12] and shower and room service.

1. étant un tout petit peu moins d'essence
2. une dizaine de kilomètres de plus
3. compteur
4. soupir de soulagement
5. essayant de défaire
6. Il finit par le desserrer.
7. dirigea sa lampe de poche vers
8. [personnage d'Halloween incarné par une citrouille au visage grimaçant]
9. s'esquissa sur ses lèvres
10. C'est ce bagage qu'il prendrait avec lui dans
11. se fondit dans la circulation matinale des banlieusards qui entraient dans
12. pour se raser

36

By 4:00 A.M. it was clear that the one lead[1] they had, the license number of the car the abductor had used, was going sour[2].

The first blow[3] was to find that the car was registered to[4] Henry A. White, a vice-president of the International Food Company of White Plains.

Agents rushed to White's home in Scarsdale and put it under surveillance. But the Pontiac was not in the garage and the house had a closed-up look[5]. Not one[6] window in the sprawling[7] house was open even a fraction[8] and the single light shining through the drawn drapes[9] was probably on a timer[10].

The security guard at International Food was contacted. He called the head of the personnel department[11]. In turn a product manager[12] from White's department was reached[13]. In a sleepy voice, he told investigators[14] that White had just returned[15] from a three-week stay[16] at their world headquarters[17] in Switzerland; that he'd had dinner with two of his staff[18] in Pastor's Restaurant in White Plains and was leaving directly from there to join his wife for a brief skiing vacation[19]. She was staying either in Aspen or Sun Valley with friends.

1. piste
2. tournait court
3. coup dur
4. au nom de
5. semblait complètement fermée
6. Pas une
7. immense
8. n'était, ne serait-ce qu'entrouverte
9. qui brillait au travers des rideaux tirés
10. sur minuterie
11. chef du personnel
12. chef de produit
13. fut joint
14. aux enquêteurs
15. venait de rentrer
16. séjour
17. siège social
18. membres de son personnel
19. un court séjour aux sports d'hiver

At five o'clock, Hugh and Steve started for[1] Carley. Hugh drove. Steve watched the road thread through[2] Westchester, approach Connecticut. There were so few cars out[3]. Most people were in bed, able to reach for their wives, able to make sure their children were covered, that open windows weren't too drafty[4]. Were Neil and Sharon in a drafty, cold place now?

Why am I thinking that? he wondered. Vaguely he remembered reading that when people couldn't control overwhelming events[5], they became concerned[6] about small problems. Were Sharon and Neil still alive? That's what he should be worrying about. Spare, oh Lord in mercy[7], spare them[8] ...

"What do you make of[9] the Pontiac?" he asked Hugh.

"It'll probably turn out[10] that White's car was stolen from wherever[11] he left it," Hugh replied.

"What do we do next?"

"We wait."

"For what?"

"He may release them. He did promise[12]. He has the money."

"He's covered his tracks[13] so carefully. He's thought of everything. You don't really expect him to release two people who could identify him, do you[14]?"

"No," Hugh admitted.

"Is there nothing else we can do?"

"If he doesn't keep his word[15] and let them go, we have to consider blowing this open[16], releasing it to the media[17]. Maybe somebody saw or heard something."

"What about Ronald Thompson?"

"What about him?"

"Suppose he's been telling the truth. Suppose we find that out after eleven-thirty?"

"What is your point?[18]"

1. partirent pour
2. passer par
3. si peu de voitures dehors
4. ne laissaient pas trop passer les courants d'air
5. des événements qui les dépassaient
6. s'attachaient
7. Seigneur miséricordieux
8. épargnez-les
9. Que pensez-vous de
10. On s'apercevra probablement
11. volée à l'endroit où
12. a effectivement promis
13. dissimulé ses traces
14. franchement
15. ne tient pas parole
16. envisager de faire éclater l'affaire au grand jour
17. en la divulguant aux médias
18. Où voulez-vous en venir ?

"My point is, do we have the right not to admit that Neil and Sharon have been kidnapped?"

"I doubt that it would affect the Governor's decision about Thompson. There's absolutely no proof that this is a hostage situation[1] but if she thinks it is[2], it might only make her anxious to get the execution over with[3]. She's already been criticized for granting Thompson two stays. Those kids in Georgia had the switch pulled on them[4] right on the dot[5]. And there still may be a simple explanation of how Foxy managed to get a tape or cassette with your wife's voice on it ... an explanation that has nothing to do with her death."

Steve stared ahead[6]. They were passing[7] Greenwich. He and Sharon had been at a party in Brad Robertson's house in Greenwich during the holidays. Sharon wore a black velvet skirt[8], a brocaded jacket[9]. She looked lovely[10]. Brad said to him, "Steve, if you have any sense[11], you'll latch onto[12] that girl."

"Could publicity panic the kidnapper?" He knew the answer. Even so he had to ask.

"I would say so.[13]" Hugh's inflection was different, crisper[14]. "What's on your mind[15], Mr. Peterson?"

The question. Flat.[16] Direct. Steve felt his mouth go dry. It's only a hunch, he told himself. It's probably irrelevant[17]. If I begin this, I can't stop it. It may cost Neil and Sharon their lives.

Bleakly, miserably[18], he waited, poised like a diver for a leap that would throw him[19] into an uncontrollable current. He thought of Ronald Thompson at the trial, the young face, scared but adamant[20]. "I didn't do it. She was dead when I got there. Ask the kid ..."

"How would you feel if it were your only child? How would you feel ..."

It is my only child, Mrs. Thompson, he thought.

1. qu'il s'agisse d'une prise d'otages
2. si elle pense que c'est le cas
3. désireuse d'en finir avec cette exécution
4. sont passés sur la chaise électrique
5. exactement à l'heure prévue
6. regardait fixement droit devant lui
7. dépassaient
8. jupe en velours noir
9. veste de brocard
10. était ravissante
11. si vous avez une once de bon sens
12. ne laissez pas filer
13. Je dirais que oui.
14. plus tranchée
15. À quoi pensez-vous
16. Nette.
17. sans rapport
18. L'air sombre et pitoyable
19. tel un plongeur sur le point de se jeter
20. catégorique

He began to speak. "Hugh, do you remember what Bob Kurner said, that he thought the murders of those four women and Nina's murder were tied together[1]?"

"I heard him and I told you what I think. He's grasping at straws."

"Suppose I told you that Kurner may be right, that there may be a link between Nina's death and the others."

"What are you talking about?[2]"

"Remember Kurner said that the only thing he couldn't understand is that the others had car trouble[3] and Nina didn't; that she'd been strangled at home, not somewhere on the road?"

"Go on.[4]"

"The night before she was murdered, Nina got a flat. I was at a late meeting[5] in New York and didn't get home till well after midnight. She was asleep. But the next morning when she drove me to the train, I noticed the spare was on her car ..."

"Go on."

"Remember that transcript Kurner left? The Thompson boy said something about joking with[6] Nina about bad luck turning into good luck and she said something about the groceries all fitting in the trunk[7]."

"What are you saying?"

"Her trunk was small. If she had extra room in it[8], it can only mean that the spare tire hadn't been put back. That was after four o'clock and she must have gone directly home. Dora was at the house cleaning that day and she said Nina drove her home shortly before five[9]."

"Then she and Neil went straight back[10] to your house?"

"Yes, and he went up to play with his trains. Nina unloaded the car. Remember all those bundles[11]

1. liés

2. Qu'est-ce que vous racontez ?

3. un problème avec leur voiture

4. Continuez.

5. réunion tardive

6. Le jeune Thompson a mentionné avoir plaisanté avec

7. qui tenaient toutes dans le coffre

8. S'il y avait plus de place

9. l'a raccompagnée chez elle en voiture peu avant 17 heures

10. sont rentrés directement

11. paquets

were on the table? We know she died in the next few minutes[1]. I looked at her car that night. The spare tire was in the trunk. The new radial was back on her front wheel."

"You're saying that someone brought the tire back, changed it, then killed her?"

"When else[2] could the tire have been changed except right at that time[3]? And if that happened, that Thompson boy may be innocent. He may even have frightened off the killer[4] by ringing the bell. For God's sake, find out[5] if he remembers whether the spare was in the trunk when he loaded those groceries. I should have realized[6] that tire might be important when I checked it that night[7]. But I hated remembering that I'd blown up at[8] Nina the very last minute I was with her."

Hugh pressed his foot on the accelerator. The speedometer[9] climbed from sixty to seventy to eighty[10]. The car screeched[11] into the driveway as the first hint of dawn cut across[12] the somber sky. Hugh rushed to the phone. Before he took off[13] his coat, he dialed[14] the prison at Somers and demanded to speak to the warden[15]. "… no, I'll hold on[16]." He turned to Steve. "The warden's been in his office all night, just in case the Governor decided to call. They're shaving the kid now."

"Good God."

"Even if he claims[17] that the trunk was empty, it's not proof. Everything is still supposition. Somebody could have dropped off[18] that tire, changed it for her, been gone[19]. It still doesn't let Thompson off the hook.[20]"

"We both believe Thompson is innocent," Steve said. Dully[21] he thought, I have always believed it. Dear God, in my heart I have always believed it and never faced it[22].

1. dans les minutes qui ont suivi
2. À quel autre moment
3. si ce n'est à cet instant précis
4. fait fuir le tueur
5. tâchez de savoir
6. J'aurais dû comprendre
7. je l'ai vérifié ce soir-là
8. je m'étais emporté contre
9. compteur
10. de 100 à 110, puis 130
11. crissa
12. les premières lueurs de l'aube apparaissaient dans
13. Avant même d'avoir enlevé
14. composa le numéro de
15. directeur
16. je reste en ligne
17. prétend
18. apporter
19. et repartir
20. Thompson n'est pas tiré d'affaire pour autant.
21. Abattu,
22. je n'ai jamais voulu l'admettre

"Yes, I'm here ..." Hugh listened. "Thank you very much." He slammed down the phone. "Thompson swears[1] the spare was missing when he loaded the groceries."

"Call the Governor," Steve pleaded. "Tell her, beg her, to at least delay the execution. Put me on[2] if it will help[3]."

Hugh was dialing the State House[4]. "It's not evidence," he said. "It's a string of coincidences[5]. I doubt she'll postpone it on this[6]. When she hears that Sharon and Neil are missing—and you have to tell her that now—she may be convinced this is some kind of last-ditch trick[7]."

The Governor absolutely could not be reached. She had referred all requests[8] for further postponements of the execution[9] to the Attorney General[10] to appraise[11]. He would be in his office at eight o'clock. No, his private phone number would not be given out.

There was nothing to do except wait. Steve and Hugh sat silently in the den as faint, watery[12] light began to filter through the window. Steven tried to pray, could only think Dear God, they are so young, all three so young, please ...

At six o'clock Dora came down the stairs, her footsteps heavy and unsteady. Looking aged and infinitely weary[13], she silently began to make coffee.

At six-thirty Hugh spoke to FBI headquarters in New York. There were no new leads. Henry White had taken a 1:00 A.M. flight to Sun Valley. They'd been too late to catch him at the airport there. He'd been driven away[14] in a private car. They were checking motel registrations[15] and condominium rentals[16]. The APB[17] for the Pontiac hadn't produced any results. They were still checking the regulars from the Mill Tavern.

1. jure que
2. Passez-la-moi
3. si besoin est
4. [siège de la législature de l'État]
5. enchaînement de coïncidences
6. qu'elle l'ajourne pour cela
7. d'ultime stratagème
8. soumis toutes les demandes
9. d'autres sursis à l'exécution
10. [aux États-Unis, équivalent du garde des Sceaux]
11. pour qu'il prenne la décision
12. délavée
13. lasse
14. On était venu le chercher
15. les réservations dans les motels
16. les locations d'appartement
17. alerte à toutes les patrouilles

1. déboucha en trombe sur
2. s'engagea dans
3. passa en trombe devant
4. exigea

At seven-thirty-five Bob Kurner's car plummeted down[1] the road and pulled into[2] the driveway. He rang the bell furiously, stalked past[3] Dora and demanded[4] to know why Ronald had been asked about the spare tire.

Hugh glanced at Steve. Steve nodded. Tersely Hugh explained.

5. l'avez caché

Bob paled. "Do you mean to say that your son and Sharon Martin were kidnapped, Mr. Peterson, and you've been covering it up[5]?" he demanded. "When the Governor knows this, she'll have to postpone the execution. She has no choice."

6. N'y comptez pas trop

"Don't count on it[6]," Hugh warned.

"Mr. Peterson, I'm sorry for you, but you had no right not to tell me about this last night," Bob said bitterly. "My God, can't we reach the Attorney General before eight?"

"That's only twenty minutes."

"Twenty minutes is a lot when you've got only three hours and fifty minutes left to live, Mr. Taylor."

7. d'une voix énergique, affirmative, implorante

At exactly eight o'clock Hugh reached the Attorney General. He spoke for thirty-five minutes, his voice forceful, arguing, pleading[7]. "Yes sir, I realize the Governor has already granted two stays. ... I understand that the Connecticut Supreme Court unanimously confirmed the verdict. ... No sir, we don't have *proof.* ... It's more than *speculation* though ... the cassette. ... Yes sir, I'd appreciate if you'll call the Governor. ... May I put Mr. Peterson on ... ? All right, I'll hold."

8. couvrit le combiné avec sa main
9. se prononcer en faveur d'

Hugh cupped his hand over the phone[8]. "He's going to call her but let me tell you, he's not going to recommend[9] a stay."

Three minutes passed slowly. Steve and Bob did not look at each other. Then Hugh said, "Yes, I'm here ... but ..."

He was still protesting when Steve heard the unmistakable sound[1] of the dial tone[2]. Hugh let the phone drop. "The execution's on[3]," he told them flatly.

1. bruit reconnaissable
2. tonalité
3. est maintenue

37

The pain. It was so hard to think with the pain shooting up through her body[4]. If she could only unzip[5] her boot. Her ankle was a mass of burning concrete[6], swelling against[7] the boot, against the biting twine[8].

She should have taken a chance and screamed when they were going through the terminal. Better to have risked it then. What time was it? Time didn't exist[9]. Monday night. Tuesday. Was it still Tuesday? Was it Wednesday yet?

How could they get out of here?

Neil. She could hear the rasping breath close to hers. He was trying to breathe slowly, trying to obey her[10]. Sharon heard the moans coming from her lips, tried to bite them back[11].

She felt Neil sliding closer to her, trying to comfort her. Neil would be so like Steve when he grew up[12]. *If* he grew up …

Steve. What would it be like[13] to live with Steve, to make a life[14] with him and Neil? Steve who had known so much pain.

4. irradiant dans tout son corps
5. baisser la fermeture Éclair de
6. sa cheville, dure comme du bois, la brûlait
7. elle enflait contre
8. la corde coupante
9. n'existait plus
10. lui obéir
11. les ravaler
12. il deviendrait adulte
13. À quoi cela ressemblerait-il
14. faire sa vie

Everything had always been so easy for her. Her father saying, "Sharon was born in Rome, Pat in Egypt, Tina in Hong Kong." Her mother, "We have friends all over the world." Even when they found out that she was dead, they'd have each other[1]. When Steve lost Neil, he'd have no one.

Steve asking, "How come you're still single[2]?" Because she hadn't wanted the responsibility of loving someone else.

Neil. So afraid that the Lufts would take him with them. So afraid that she'd take Steve away from him[3]. She had to get him out of here.

Again she tried rubbing[4] her wrists against the cinderblock wall[5]. But the cords were too tight, biting into[6] her wrists. She couldn't get them in contact with[7] the wall.

She tried to think. Her only hope was to get Neil free[8], to get him out of this room. If he opened the door from the inside, would the bomb explode?

The knob[9] in the bathroom. If Foxy came back, if he let her go into the bathroom[10] again, maybe she could pull the knob, break it off.

What would he do with them when he got the money? She was drifting off[11]. Time … how much time … time passing … was it day or night? … muted train sounds … come for us, Steve … I blame you[12], Miss Martin … it is the issue, Miss Martin … none so blind as those who will not see[13] … I love you, Sharon, I've missed you terribly … big, gentle hands on her face …

Big gentle hands on her face. Sharon opened her eyes. Foxy was bending over her. With horrible gentleness his hands were running over her face, her neck. He slipped the gag from her mouth and kissed her. His lips were pokerhot[14], his mouth mushy[15]. She tried to turn her head. It was such an effort.

1. seraient là l'un pour l'autre
2. célibataire
3. lui enlève Steve
4. de frotter
5. le mur en parpaing
6. s'enfonçant dans
7. leur faire toucher
8. libérer Neil
9. poignée
10. aller aux toilettes
11. se sentait partir
12. C'est votre faute
13. il n'est pire aveugle que celui qui ne veut pas voir
14. brûlantes comme la braise
15. pâteuse

He whispered, "It's all finished, Sharon. I have the money. I have to go now."

She tried to focus her eyes[1]. His features emerged from the blur[2], glittering eyes and a throbbing pulse and narrow lips.

"What are you going to do to us?" It was so hard to talk.

"I'm going to leave you right here. I'll tell Peterson where to pick you up."

He was lying[3]. It was like before, when he'd been leading her on, toying with her. No, she'd tried to trick him[4] and then he'd pushed her down[5].

"You're going to kill us."

"That's right, Sharon."

"You killed Neil's mother."

"That's right, Sharon. Oh, I almost forgot[6]." He was moving away from her, reaching down, unfolding something. "I'll put this picture up[7] with the others." Something was floating over her head. Neil's eyes were staring down at her, eyes that were part of a sprawled body[8], a body with a scarf around its neck. A shriek tore her throat[9], pushing back pain and dizziness[10]. Suddenly she was completely rational[11], focusing[12], looking at the picture, at the glittering, mad eyes of the man holding it.

He was hanging it next to the others on the wall over the cot, hanging it carefully, ritualistic in his exactness[13].

Fearfully, she watched him. Would he kill them now, strangle them as he'd strangled those women?

"I'm going to set the clock[14] for you now," he told her.

"The clock?"

"Yes. It will make the bomb go off[15] at eleven-thirty. You won't feel anything, Sharon. You'll just be gone[16], and Neil will be gone, and Ronald Thompson will be gone."

1. fixer son regard
2. Ses traits devinrent moins flous
3. mentait
4. de lui jouer un tour
5. l'avait fait tomber
6. j'ai failli oublier
7. vais accrocher cette photo
8. qui appartenaient à un corps affalé
9. Un hurlement lui déchira la gorge
10. effaçant en un instant sa douleur et son vertige
11. lucide
12. concentrée
13. avec une précision presque rituelle
14. régler le réveil
15. Il déclenchera la bombe
16. Vous partirez, tout simplement

1. vérifiait l'heure à sa montre
2. réglait

Carefully, delicately, he was opening the suitcase. She watched as he took a clock out, as he consulted his wristwatch[1] and set[2] the clock to 8:30. It was 8:30 Wednesday morning. The alarm—he was setting the alarm to 11:30. Now he was attaching wires to the clock.

Three hours.

3. cadran du réveil
4. juste en face d'elle, de l'autre côté de la pièce
5. Les aiguilles et les chiffres luisaient.

Carefully, he lifted the suitcase, put it on top of the deep sinks near the door. The face of the clock[3] was directly opposite her across the room[4]. The hands and numerals glowed.[5]

"Do you want to have anything before I go, Sharon, a glass of water? Would you like me to kiss you goodbye?"

6. Bien sûr
7. se dérobèrent sous elle
8. s'évanouir

"Could I ... would you let me go into the bathroom?"

"Sure[6], Sharon." He came over, untied her hands, picked her up. Her legs crumbled under her[7]. Pain made her shiver. Black curtains closed over her eyes. No ... no ... no ... she could not faint[8].

9. agrippée à
10. pour qu'on n'entende pas le bruit
11. craquement
12. céda

He left her inside the dark cubbyhole, holding onto[9] the doorknob. She twisted it around, around, around, praying the sound wasn't carrying[10]. A faint cracking sound[11]. The handle broke off[12].

13. fit courir ses doigts sur
14. bord déchiqueté
15. en la ramenant

Sharon ran her fingers over[13] the separated end, felt the jagged edge[14] of the broken metal. She slipped the handle in the deep pocket of her skirt. When she opened the door she had one hand in her pocket. If he felt anything when he carried her back[15] to the cot, he'd think it was her fist.

It worked. He was hurrying now, anxious to be out of there. He tossed her back down; retied her hands quickly. She was able to keep them a little separated, those cords were not as tight as the others. The gag was yanked over her mouth.

He was bending over her. "I could have loved you very much, Sharon, as I think you could have loved me."

With a quick movement he pulled off[1] Neil's blindfold. Neil blinked, his eyes swollen[2], his pupils enormous.

The man looked directly into the eyes; his gaze slid to the picture on the wall then back to[3] Neil's face.

Abruptly he dropped the child's head, turned and clicked off the lights as for the last time he slipped out of the room.

Sharon stared at the glowing face of the clock. It was 8:36.

1. retira
2. gonflés
3. revint se poser sur

38

Glenda's bed was strewn with[4] pages, pages crumpled, begun again[5]. "No ... on the fourteenth I didn't go straight[6] to the doctor. I stopped at the library[7] ... put that in[8], Roger, I spoke to a couple of people[9] there ..."

"I'll start a new sheet. This one's too cluttered[10]. Who did you talk to in the waiting room at the doctor's?"

Minutely[11], they reviewed[12] every detail of the past month. Nothing triggered awareness[13] in Glenda of the man who called himself Foxy. At 4:00 A.M. at her persuasion, Roger called[14] FBI headquarters and asked to speak to Hugh. Hugh told him about the contact.

4. jonché de
5. froissées, réécrites
6. directement
7. bibliothèque
8. note ce détail
9. deux personnes
10. remplie
11. Avec minutie
12. passèrent en revue
13. n'éveilla le souvenir chez
14. elle persuada Roger d'appeler

"He says that the kidnapper has promised that Sharon and Neil can be picked up at eleven-thirty," Roger told her.

"They don't trust him, do they?"

"No, I don't think they do."

"If it is someone familiar to me[1], it might be someone Neil knows from this area. He couldn't let Neil go."

"Glenda, we're both so tired we're incapable of thinking. Let's try to sleep for a few hours. Then maybe something will come to you[2]. Your subconscious works when you're sleeping. You know that."

"All right." Wearily, she started to stack[3] the sheets of paper in chronological order.

He set the alarm for seven. For three hours they slept—exhausted, troubled sleep[4].

At seven Roger went down to make tea. Glenda slipped a nitroglycerin tablet under her tongue, went into the bathroom, washed her face, got back into bed and picked up her pad.

At nine Marian arrived. At 9:15 she came up to see Glenda. "I'm sorry you're not feeling well, Mrs. Perry."

"Thank you."

"I'll stay out of your way.[5] If it's all right[6], I'll concentrate on one room at a time downstairs."

"That would be fine.[7]"

"That way by the end[8] of the week, downstairs[9] will be shipshape[10]. I can tell you like a house kept nice[11]."

"Yes, I do. Thank you."

"I'm just glad to be here, that I didn't have to disappoint you with the trouble[12] we had over our car ..."

"My husband mentioned something[13]." Deliberately, Glenda raised her pen, held it poised[14].

1. une personne que je connais
2. te reviendra
3. à classer
4. ils dormirent, épuisés, d'un sommeil troublé
5. Je ne vous dérangerai pas.
6. Si cela vous convient
7. Ce serait parfait.
8. d'ici la fin
9. le rez-de-chaussée
10. impeccable
11. qu'une maison soit bien tenue
12. ennuis
13. y a fait allusion
14. prête à noter

"Really awful.[1] After just spending four hundred dollars to get it fixed[2]. Normally we wouldn't spend that much on an old car, but Arty's such a good mechanic that my husband said it was worth it[3]. Well, I see you're busy. I shouldn't be gabbing[4]. Would you like a little breakfast?"

"No thank you, Mrs. Vogler."

The door closed behind her. A few minutes later Roger came back in. "I spoke to a couple of people at the office. Said I had a touch of flu[5]."

"Roger ... wait a minute." Glenda depressed the button on the recorder. The now familiar sentence filled their ears: *Be at the Exxon service station.* ... Glenda snapped the machine off. "Roger, when did we get my car serviced[6]?"

"A little over a month ago[7], I think. Bill Lufts took it over to that place he recommended."

"Yes, and you dropped me off on your way to work[8] when it was ready. *Arty*, that was the name, wasn't it?"

"I believe so. Why?"

"Because the car was ready but he was just about to fill it with gas[9]. I was talking to him, standing next to it. I noticed his sign said[10] 'A. R. Taggert' and asked if the 'A' stood for[11] Arthur, because I'd heard Bill call him Arty.

"Roger." Glenda's voice became high-pitched. She sat up and grabbed his hand. "Roger, he told me that people around here[12] started to call him Arty because of the sign 'A. R. Taggert,' but that his name really was August Rommel Taggert.

"And I said, 'Rommel—wasn't he the famous[13] German General?'

"And he said, 'Yes, Rommel was the Desert Fox.' The way he said *fox* ... and the way he said *foxy* on the phone the other night. Roger, I swear to you,

1. C'était l'horreur.
2. pour la faire réparer
3. que ça en valait la peine
4. papoter
5. que j'étais légèrement grippé
6. a-t-on fait réviser ma voiture
7. Il y a un peu plus d'un mois
8. m'as déposée en te rendant au travail
9. il lui restait juste à faire le plein d'essence
10. que sur son enseigne était écrit
11. la lettre A voulait dire
12. du coin
13. célèbre

that mechanic is Foxy and he's the one who kidnapped Neil and Sharon!"

It was 9:31 A.M.

39

She was going to her room. Olendorf was off[1] today and the other guard would never bother her[2]. Lally hadn't slept all night. She was getting sick[3]. The arthritis was murder[4], but it was more than that. There was something inside her winding down[5]. She could feel it. She just wanted to get into her room and lie down on the cot and close her eyes.

She *had* to.

She drifted down with[6] the 8:40 Mount Vernon passengers and slipped around to the ramp. She had extra newspapers in her shopping bag to cover herself, but she didn't stop for coffee. She wasn't hungry for anything, just[7] her room.

It didn't even matter if the man was there. She'd take her chances[8]. The comforting noise of the generators and vents greeted her. It was gloomy here like always, and that was good with her[9]. Her heavy sneakers[10] were silent as she padded across[11] to the staircase.

And then she heard it.

1. de repos
2. ne l'embêterait pas
3. était en train de tomber malade
4. un calvaire
5. qui se dégradait
6. se laissa porter par le flot des
7. n'avait envie de rien, si ce n'est de
8. prendrait le risque
9. cela lui convenait
10. baskets
11. avançait à pas feutrés

The muffled sound of a door opening slowly. Her door. Lally shrank behind[1] the generator into the shadows[2].

Soft, low footsteps. He was coming down the metal steps, the same man. She melted back[3], pressed her bulk[4] against the wall. Should she confront him[5]? No … no. Every instinct warned her to hide. She watched him stand[6], listen intently, then move swiftly[7] toward the ramp. In a minute he'd be gone and she'd be in her room. If the girl was still there, she'd scare her off.

Her arthritic fingers started to pull the key from her pocket, fumbled. It fell with a ping at her feet.[8]

She held her breath[9]. Had he heard? She didn't dare to look out[10]. But the footsteps were completely gone. There was no sound of anyone coming back. She waited ten minutes, ten long minutes, trying to calm the pounding[11] of her heart. Then slowly, painfully, she bent down[12], felt on the ground for her key[13]. It was so dark here; her eyes were so bad now. She felt the outline of the key and sighed with relief[14].

Lally was just beginning to straighten up[15] when something grazed against her back[16], something shivery cold[17]. She gasped[18] as it touched her skin, touched and slipped in[19], so sharp, so quickly that she barely felt the blinding[20] pain, the warm gushing of her blood[21] as she clumsily sank to her knees[22] and slumped forward[23]. Her forehead took the impact of the fall[24]; her left arm arced out[25]. As she slipped[26] into unconsciousness, her right fist closed around[27] the key to her room.

1. se recroquevilla derrière
2. se fondant dans l'ombre
3. se fit toute petite
4. s'appuyant de tout son poids
5. lui faire face
6. s'arrêter
7. rapidement
8. Elle tomba à ses pieds, dans un bruit métallique.
9. retint sa respiration
10. regarder autour d'elle
11. les palpitations
12. se baissa
13. chercha à tâtons sa clé par terre
14. poussa un soupir de soulagement
15. se redresser
16. effleura son dos
17. de glacial
18. eut le souffle coupé
19. s'enfonça
20. fulgurante
21. le sang chaud qui jaillissait
22. tombait maladroitement à genoux
23. s'affaissait en avant
24. Dans sa chute, son front heurta le sol
25. s'ouvrit en arc de cercle
26. sombrait
27. se referma sur

40

At 9:30 an agent from FBI headquarters phoned Hugh Taylor at Steve's home. "We think we have something, Hughie."

"What is it?"

"That Arty—the mechanic, Arty Taggert."

"Yeah.[1]"

"There used to be[2] a guy known as Gus Taggert who got picked up[3] for hanging around the Port Authority about twelve years ago. Suspect in disappearance of some sixteen-year-old runaway[4]. We couldn't pin anything on him[5], but a lot of guys[6] thought he did something to her. He was questioned about disappearances of other young girls, too. His description matches[7] the one you gave us."

"Good work. What else have you got on him?"

"We're trying to check out where he used to live[8]. He had a bunch of jobs[9] in New York, pumping gas[10] on the west side, busboy[11] in an Eighth Avenue joint[12], dishwasher[13] in the Oyster Bar …"

"Concentrate on where he lived; find out if he has any family."

Hugh hung up the phone. "Mr. Peterson," he said carefully, "there's a chance we have a new lead. A mechanic who hangs around Mill Tavern seems to

1. Ouais.
2. Il y avait
3. s'était fait pincer
4. fugueuse
5. On n'a rien pu retenir contre lui
6. beaucoup de nos gars
7. correspond à
8. de se renseigner sur l'endroit où il habitait
9. un tas de boulots
10. pompiste
11. serveur
12. boui-boui
13. plongeur

have been a suspect in several cases of young girls disappearing about twelve years ago. Name of[1] Arty Taggert."

"A mechanic." Steve's voice rose[2]. "A *mechanic*."

"Exactly. I know what you're thinking. It's a slim chance[3], but if someone fixed your wife's tire that day, is it possible she'd have written a check in payment[4]? Do you have your canceled checks[5] or stubs[6] from January two years ago?"

"Yes, I'll look."

"Remember, we're only examining any lead we can. We have no proof at all of anything about this Arty except that he was questioned once years ago."

"I see." Steve walked over to his desk.

The phone rang. It was Roger Perry shouting the news that Glenda was positive a mechanic called A. R. Taggert was Foxy.

Hugh slammed the phone down, was about to pick it up to dial New York when it rang again. Impatiently he barked[7] "Yes." His expression changed, became inscrutable[8]. "What? Hold it, start again[9]."

Steve watched as Hugh's eyes hardened[10] into slits of concentration[11]. When Hugh whipped out[12] a pen, he held the memo pad for him. Ignoring the other man's attempt to screen[13] what he was writing, Steve stared at the pad, digesting[14] the words as they went down[15].

> Thank you for the money. It is all there.[16] You have kept your promise[17]. Now I will keep mine. Neil and Sharon are alive. At 11:30 they will be executed during an explosion in New York State[18]. In the rubble from that explosion[19] you can dig for their bodies[20].
>
> Foxy

1. Un dénommé
2. monta d'un ton
3. Il y a sans doute peu de chances
4. l'ait réglé par chèque
5. chèques annulés
6. vos talons
7. aboya
8. impénétrable
9. Attendez, redites-moi ça
10. regardait Hugh dont le regard se durcit,
11. ses yeux mi-clos, sous l'effet de la concentration
12. sortit vivement
13. pour cacher
14. assimilant
15. à mesure que Hugh les écrivait
16. Tout est là.
17. tenu votre promesse
18. l'État de New York
19. Dans les décombres laissés par cette explosion
20. creuser pour trouver leurs corps

Hugh said, "Repeat that again so I'm sure I have it straight[1]." A moment later he said, "Thank you. We'll be in touch with you shortly.[2]" He hung up the phone.

"Who took the call?" Steve asked. Merciful numbness[3] was paralyzing his capacity to think, to fear.

Hugh waited a long minute before answering. When he did his voice was infinitely weary. "The mortician[4] in Carley who handled your wife's funeral arrangements[5]," he said.

It was 9:35 A.M.

1. d'avoir tout bien compris
2. On vous recontactera sous peu.
3. C'était une bénédiction que cette torpeur qui
4. entrepreneur des pompes funèbres
5. s'est occupé de l'enterrement de votre femme

41

If that old hag[6] hadn't made that noise! Arty was drenched in perspiration[7]. His new green suit smelled really bad[8] now, just the way it always did after ...

Suppose he hadn't heard her? She must be the one who'd been staying in[9] the room, who dragged that cot in. That meant she must have a key. If he hadn't heard her, she'd have gone in, found them. They'd have time to get experts to deactivate the bomb.

He walked rapidly through[10] the terminal to the arcade[11] that led to the Biltmore and picked up the car from the Biltmore garage. The suitcase and radio were already packed in it[12]. He drove swiftly up the East Side Drive to the Triborough Bridge. It was

6. vieille sorcière
7. trempé de sueur
8. sentait vraiment mauvais
9. occupait
10. traversa rapidement
11. galerie marchande
12. s'y trouvaient déjà

the quickest way to LaGuardia. He was frantic[1] now to get out of New York. The plane to Phoenix left at 10:30.

He returned to the parking lot he'd left only hours before. The thought of how successful his plan had been to pick up the ransom soothed him[2]. This time he parked the Volks far away from the tollgate in the area where people parked for the Eastern Shuttle. That section was always crowded[3]. He'd filed the engine number off[4] the Volks and the license plate could never be traced to him[5]. He'd taken it off a junked car[6] five years ago. Anyhow, it might be a month before someone noticed that the Volks had been here a long time.

He pulled his two suitcases, the light one with the clothes and cassettes and the heavy one with his money, and the crated C.B. radio out of the trunk. Now there was absolutely nothing to link him with[7] the car.

He walked swiftly over to the bus stop. The courtesy airport bus came along and he got on it. The other passengers glanced at him indifferently. He could feel their dismissal[8]. Just because he wasn't all dressed up[9]. He sat next to a girl about nineteen years old, a very attractive girl. He didn't miss the wrinkle of distaste[10], the way the girl turned away from him[11]. Bitch. Little did she know[12] that he was a clever, wealthy man.

The bus stopped at the domestic terminal[13]. He walked two hundred feet[14] to the American Airlines special entrance. An attendant was checking in luggage[15]. He wouldn't have to drag all this stuff around[16]. He yanked out his ticket. The name on the ticket was Renard. That meant fox in French. It was the name he planned to use in Arizona.

"Check all three pieces[17], sir?"

1. extrêmement pressé
2. l'apaisa
3. bondée
4. avait effacé le numéro du moteur de
5. ne permettrait jamais de remonter jusqu'à lui
6. l'avait récupérée sur une voiture mise à la casse
7. il n'y avait absolument plus rien qui permette d'établir un lien entre lui et
8. dédain
9. bien habillé
10. remarqua le rictus de dégoût
11. se détourna de lui
12. Elle était loin de se douter
13. aérogare des lignes intérieures
14. une soixantaine de mètres
15. Un employé enregistrait les bagages
16. à transbahuter tous ces trucs
17. bagages

"No! Not that one." He yanked the suitcase with the money out of the reach of the attendant.

"Sorry, sir. I'm not sure you can carry one that big[1] on board."

"I must!" Deliberately, he tried to curb the intensity[2] in his voice. "I have papers I have to work on."

The attendant shrugged. "All right, sir. I guess the stewardess[3] can always put it in the cabin closet[4] if necessary."

It was 9:28 and he was hungry again. But first he had the call to make. He selected a phonebooth in a far corner[5] of the terminal and wrote down what he wanted to say so there'd be no mistake. He pictured[6] what Steve Peterson would think when he got the message.

The funeral home phone[7] was picked up promptly. His voice low, Foxy said, "You will be needed to pick up remains[8]."

"Of course, sir. Who is calling?[9]" The other voice was subdued[10].

"Are you ready to write this down[11]?"

"Certainly."

Foxy's voice changed, became harsh. "Write it down, then read it right back to me and make sure you have it straight." He began to dictate, enjoying the shocked gasp he heard on the other end of the phone[12]. "Now read it back," he demanded. A trembling voice obeyed then said, "My God, please ..."

Smiling, Foxy hung up.

He went into a cafeteria in the terminal and selected bacon, rolls, orange juice and coffee. He ate slowly, watching the people hurrying past.

Now he was beginning to relax[13]. The thought of the phone call to the funeral home made him chuckle deep in the pit of his stomach[14]. At first he was going to warn them[15] of an explosion in New York *City*[16]. At the very last minute he'd changed it to

1. garder un bagage aussi volumineux
2. maîtriser l'intensité
3. l'hôtesse
4. placard de la cabine
5. dans un coin reculé
6. imagina
7. Le téléphone de l'entreprise de pompes funèbres
8. On va avoir besoin de vous pour une levée de corps
9. Qui est à l'appareil ?
10. feutrée
11. à noter
12. se réjouissant du hoquet de surprise qu'il perçut à l'autre bout de la ligne
13. se détendre
14. le fit se tordre de rire
15. Au début, il avait pensé les avertir
16. la ville

New York *State*[1]. He could just imagine the cops going nuts[2] now. A lot of good it would do them.[3]

Arizona, land of the painted desert.

Looking into the boy's eyes[4] had been necessary. He wouldn't have to run away from them ever again[5]. He imagined what it would be like[6] at 11:30 in Grand Central. The explosion would go upward. The whole ceiling would come crashing down on[7] Neil and Sharon, tons and tons and tons of cement.

It was easy to make a bomb just like it was easy to fix an engine. All you did was[8] read everything about it[9]. Now the whole world would want to know who Foxy was. They'd probably write about him the way they did about Rommel.

He finished his coffee, wiped the back of his hand over his mouth[10]. From the window he watched as people carrying bags hurried across the terminal to departure gates[11]. He remembered the bombing[12] of LaGuardia at Christmastime a couple of years before. That had caused panic, closed the airport. He's seen it on television.

He was already looking forward to being[13] in a bar tonight in Phoenix watching the news reports[14] of the explosion in Grand Central. It would be on television all over the world. But it would be even better if the cops had some place to start looking[15]. The people who put those bombs in the office buildings did it that way[16]. They called up and gave a big list[17] of where they'd put bombs and the cops didn't know where to go first. They'd had to make people leave[18] every building they talked about.

He could still do something like that. What should he tell them? He stared out[19]. This was a busy airport. People running back and forth all over the place[20] and it wasn't even as big as Kennedy.

Just like Grand Central. Or the bus terminal. Everybody rushing. Paying no attention to anybody.

1. l'État
2. en train de devenir dingues
3. Ils seraient bien avancés.
4. Regarder le garçon droit dans les yeux
5. n'aurait plus jamais à les fuir
6. s'imagina la scène
7. s'effondrerait sur
8. Il suffisait de
9. toutes les informations existantes sur le sujet
10. s'essuya la bouche du revers de la main
11. portes d'embarquement
12. l'attentat à la bombe
13. se réjouissait déjà de se retrouver
14. reportages
15. avaient une idée de l'endroit où ils devaient commencer à chercher
16. procédaient de la sorte
17. longue liste
18. devaient faire évacuer
19. regarda autour de lui
20. courant partout dans tous les sens

Just wanted to get where they were going. Didn't notice anybody. Didn't smile back.[1]

An idea slowly took shape. Suppose he warned the cops. Suppose he told them that Sharon and Neil and the bomb were in a transportation center[2] in New York City. That would mean they'd have to clear out[3] both airports and the two bus terminals[4] and Penn Station[5] as well as Grand Central. They'd start searching under seats in the waiting rooms and opening lockers[6]. They wouldn't know where to start. And all these people, these lousy people would be made to get out of all those places[7], to miss their trains and planes and buses.

They'd never find Sharon and Neil. Never. The only one who knew about that room was the old hag and he'd taken care of her[8]. All by himself[9] he could keep people in or out of the biggest city in the world with one more phone call. Peterson thought he was a big shot with his magazine and his trust fund and his girlfriend. Foxy laughed aloud. The couple sitting at the next table looked at him curiously.

He *would* call[10], just before he got on the plane. Who would he call?

The funeral home again? No.

Who else would be sure the call wasn't a fake[11]?

He knew! Smiling, anticipating the reaction he'd get, he went for[12] another coffee. At twelve minutes past ten he left the cafeteria, the suitcase gripped in his hand. He deliberately waited that long so that when they were x-raying the carry-on luggage[13] they'd be hurrying[14]. No one would be curious about his suitcase. Airlines loved to keep to their schedules[15].

At 10:15 he slipped into a phonebooth near departure gate 9, pulled out quarters and dimes[16] and dialed a number. When the receiver at the other end was picked up, he whispered a message. He replaced

1. Ne rendant jamais un sourire.
2. centre de transport
3. évacuer
4. les deux gares routières
5. [autre grande gare ferroviaire située à Manhattan]
6. les consignes
7. ces minables seraient obligés de quitter tous ces endroits
8. lui avait réglé son compte
9. À lui tout seul
10. Il allait le passer, ce coup de fil
11. canular
12. alla chercher
13. passeraient aux rayons X les bagages à main
14. seraient pressés
15. respecter leurs horaires
16. de la petite monnaie

the receiver gently, walked to the check-in desk[1] and went through the inspection without a hitch[2].

The "boarding[3]" sign was flashing[4] as he walked across the waiting area to the covered ramp leading to the plane.

It was 10:16 A.M.

1. comptoir d'enregistrement
2. passa le contrôle sans anicroches
3. embarquement immédiat
4. clignotait

42

Her clothes felt wet and warm and sticky[5]. Blood. She was bleeding to death[6].

Death. She was going to die. Lally knew it. Through the dim fading light in her mind, she sensed it. Someone had killed her … the man who had taken her room had taken her life.

The room. Her room. She wanted to die in it. She wanted to be there. He'd never come back. He'd be afraid. Maybe no one would find her. Entombed.[7] She'd be entombed in the only home she'd ever had. She'd be here sleeping forever with the comforting roar of her trains. Her mind was clearing[8] … but she didn't have long[9]. She knew it. She had to get to her room.

Aware of the key in her right fist, Lally tried to drag herself up[10]. Something was pulling …. the knife … the knife was still plunged into her[11]. She couldn't reach it. She began to crawl[12] …

5. poisseux
6. se vidait de son sang
7. Ensevelie.
8. Elle avait les idées plus claires
9. elle n'en avait plus pour longtemps
10. essaya péniblement de se relever
11. le couteau était encore enfoncé dans son dos
12. à ramper

She had to arc around[1]. She'd been lying facing away from where the room was[2]. The effort of turning her body … too much, too much[3]. Slowly, inch by inch[4], she crawled until she was in the direction of her room. Twenty feet[5] at least to the staircase. And then the stairs. Could she?[6] Lally shook her head trying to clear away the darkness[7]. She could feel blood running from[8] her mouth. She tried to clear it from her throat[9].

Right hand … keep gripping the key … left hand forward … right knee, drag it forward … left knee … right hand … She would do it[10]. Somehow she would manage to get up those stairs.

She kept in her mind the vision of opening the door, closing it … crawling inside … pulling herself up[11] on the cot … lying there … closing her eyes … waiting.

In her room death would come as a friend, a friend with cool and gentle hands …

1. faire demi-tour en s'aidant des bras
2. tournant le dos à la pièce
3. c'était trop dur
4. centimètre par centimètre
5. Il restait 6 mètres
6. En serait-elle capable ?
7. dissiper l'obscurité qui l'envahissait
8. couler de
9. l'évacuer de sa gorge
10. y parviendrait
11. se hissant

43

They are dead, Steve thought. When you are condemned you are already dead. This afternoon Ronald Thompson's mother would claim[12] her son's body. This afternoon the Sheridan Funeral Home would go to the site of an explosion and wait for Sharon's and Neil's bodies.

12. réclamerait

Somewhere in New York State, digging in[1] the rubble … He was standing by the window. A knot of reporters[2] and television cameras was grouped outside. "The word goes fast[3]," he said. "We vultures of the media[4] love a good story."

Bradley had just phoned. "Steve, what can I do?"

"Nothing. Nothing. Just let me know if you happen to see a Volks beetle, dark green, with a guy about thirty-eight years old in it. He probably had the license plates changed so that won't help[5]. We have an hour and twenty minutes—an hour and twenty minutes."

"What have you done about the bomb threat[6]?" he had asked Hugh.

"Alerted every major city[7] in the state to stand by for an emergency[8]. There's nothing more we can do. An explosion in New York State, *New York State*. Do you know how many thousands of square miles[9] that covers? Mr. Peterson, there's still a chance this is a hoax. I mean, the threat of the explosion, the call to the funeral parlor[10]."

"No, no, it's too late for them, too late." Steve thought, Bill and Dora Lufts moved in because of Nina's death. They were staying here to do him a favor[11], to take care of Neil for him. But Bill Lufts discussing his affairs may have caused Neil and Sharon's kidnapping—their death. Circle of death. No, please let them live, help us to find them …

Restlessly, he turned from[12] the window. Hank Lamont had just come in with Bill. They were going over his story again[13]. Steve knew it by heart.

"Mr. Lufts, you've talked to this Arty a lot. Please try to remember. Has he ever mentioned wanting to go some particular place? Has he ever talked about some place a lot, like Mexico … or Alaska?"

Bill shook his head. All this was too much for him. He knew that they thought Arty had kidnapped Neil

1. fouillant
2. Un petit groupe de journalistes
3. Les nouvelles vont vite
4. Nous autres, vautours des médias
5. cela ne nous sera pas d'un grand secours
6. pour l'alerte à la bombe
7. toutes les grandes villes
8. de se tenir prêtes pour une urgence
9. kilomètres carrés
10. pompes funèbres
11. pour lui rendre service
12. se détourna de
13. reprenaient tout le déroulement de son histoire

and Sharon. Arty, a quiet fellow[1], a good mechanic. Just a couple of weeks ago he'd driven over to his place. Neil rode with him[2]. He could remember the day exactly because Neil had a bad asthma attack[3] that night. Desperately, he tried[4] to remember what Arty talked about, but it seemed as though he never said much, just seemed real interested in Bill's stories.

Hank was furious at himself. He'd been sitting in the Mill Tavern buying that guy beers. He'd even told the office not to bother much about checking him[5]. Lufts *had* to remember something. Like Hughie said, everything a man does leaves traces. He could see that guy walking out of the Mill—and he, Hank, not suspecting[6]. Hank frowned. There had been some kind of crack[7] Arty made when he said goobye. What was it?

Bill was saying, … and a nice quiet fellow, like I tell you. Minds his business.[8] Maybe he did ask questions, just seemed friendly and interested like …"

"Hold on.[9]" Hank interrupted.

"What is it?" Hugh turned quietly to the younger agent. "You've got something?"

"Maybe. When Arty left with the others … and they said something about not having the chance to see Bill before he left for Rhode Island …"

"Yeah. And in a pig's eye[10] Arty's heading for Rhode Island."

"That's what I mean. He said something else … and that advertising guy[11] Allan Kroeger made a crack on top of it. A crack about … about the painted desert. That's it!"

"What?" Hugh demanded.

"When they said, 'too bad[12] Bill Lufts isn't around[13] to say goodbye,' Arty said, 'Rhode Island's not Arizona.' Could that have been a slip[14]?"

1. gars tranquille
2. l'avait accompagné
3. crise d'asthme aiguë
4. Il essayait de toutes ses forces
5. de se renseigner sur lui
6. ne soupçonnant rien
7. Il y avait bien eu cette plaisanterie
8. Il s'occupe seulement de ses affaires.
9. Attendez.
10. il n'y a aucune chance que
11. gars de la publicité
12. dommage que
13. ne soit pas là
14. lapsus

"We'll find out soon.[1]" Hugh ran for the phone.

Roger came in, put his hand on Steve's shoulder and listened with him as Hugh barked orders[2] into the phone, putting the awesome power[3] of the Federal Bureau of Investigation into tracking down the new lead[4].

Finally Hugh put the phone down. "If he's heading for Arizona, we'll get him, Mr. Peterson. I can promise you that."

"When?"

Roger's face was the color of the bleak morning. "Steve, get out of here," he said. "Glenda wants you to come over[5]. Please."

Steve shook his head.

"We'll both go[6]," Hugh said briskly. "Hank, take over[7] here."

Steve considered. "All right." He started toward the front door.

"No, let's go out the back way[8] and through[9] the woods. You'll be able to avoid[10] the reporters."

A ghost of a smile touched[11] Steve's lips. "But that's just it.[12] I don't intend[13] to avoid them."

He opened the door. The cluster of reporters[14] broke past the agents[15] stationed on the walk[16] and raced to him. Microphones were shoved[17] in front of his face. Television cameras angled[18] to catch his drawn, tired face[19].

"Mr. Peterson, has there been any further word[20]?"

"No."

"Do you think the kidnapper will carry out his threat[21] to execute your son and Sharon Martin?"

"We have every reason to believe he's capable of this kind of violence."

"Do you think it's more than coincidence[22] that the threatened explosion will occur[23] at the exact minute Ronald Thompson is executed?"

1. On va le savoir sous peu.
2. hurlait ses instructions
3. mettant les moyens impressionnants
4. pour suivre la nouvelle piste
5. voudrait que vous passiez à la maison
6. Nous venons tous les deux
7. prenez la relève
8. sortons par derrière
9. et prenons par
10. Ça vous permettra d'éviter
11. L'ombre d'un sourire effleura
12. Au contraire.
13. n'ai pas l'intention
14. essaim de journalistes
15. brisa le cordon de policiers
16. trottoir
17. se bousculaient
18. cherchaient le meilleur angle
19. son visage aux traits tirés, épuisés
20. d'autres nouvelles
21. mettra sa menace à exécution
22. que ce soit plus qu'une simple coïncidence
23. l'explosion soit prévue

"I do not think it is coincidence. I think the kidnapper Foxy may very well have been involved in my wife's death. I have tried to get that word[1] to the Governor, who refuses to speak with me. I now publicly implore her to delay the Thompson execution. That boy may very well be innocent—I think he is."

"Mr. Peterson, has your position on capital punishment changed in view of your terrible worry over your son and Miss Martin? When this kidnapper is apprehended[2] would you want to see him executed?"

Steve reached down and pushed the microphones back from his face. "I want to answer your questions. Please give me the opportunity.[3]" The reporters became quiet[4]. Steve looked directly into[5] the camera. "Yes. I have changed my mind.[6] I say this knowing that it is very unlikely[7] that my son and Sharon will be found alive. But even if their kidnapper is apprehended too late to save them, I have learned something in these past two days. I have learned that no man has the right to determine the time of death[8] of one of his fellow human beings[9]. I believe that power rests only with Almighty God[10] and ..." his voice broke, "I only ask you to pray to God that Neil and Sharon and Ronald will be spared[11] this morning."

Tears streamed down his cheeks[12]. "Let me pass."

Quietly the reporters separated[13]. Roger and Hugh ran behind him as he darted across the street[14].

Glenda was watching at[15] the door. She opened it for them, put her arms around Steve. "Let it out[16], dear," she said quietly. "Go ahead[17]."

"I can't let them go," he cried brokenly[18]. "I can't lose them ..."

She let him cry, hugging him[19] as the broad shoulders heaved[20]. If I had only remembered sooner, she agonized[21]. Oh God, I've been too late to help him[22]. She felt the shuddering of his body[23] as he tried to stifle his sobs[24].

1. d'en toucher un mot
2. arrêté
3. Laissez-moi l'occasion de le faire.
4. firent silence
5. regarda droit dans
6. J'ai changé d'avis.
7. tout en sachant qu'il est fort peu probable
8. fixer l'heure de la mort
9. de l'un de ses semblables
10. n'appartient qu'à Dieu tout-puissant
11. épargnés
12. ruisselaient sur ses joues
13. se poussèrent pour le laisser passer
14. traversait la rue comme une flèche
15. depuis
16. Ne retenez pas vos larmes
17. Allez-y
18. dit-il en sanglotant
19. le serrant dans ses bras
20. alors que ses larges épaules étaient secouées de sanglots
21. se tourmenta-t-elle
22. je n'ai pas réussi à l'aider à temps
23. son corps trembler
24. réprimer ses sanglots

"Sorry, Glenda, you've had enough[1] ... you're not well."

"I'm all right[2]," she said. "Steve, like it or not[3], you're going to have a cup of tea and some toast. You haven't eaten or slept in two days."

Somberly[4], they went into the dining room.

"Mr. Peterson," Hugh said carefully, "remember that pictures of Sharon and Neil are coming out[5] on special editions of morning newspapers; they're being shown on every television station[6]. Someone may have seen them, seen something."

"Do you think whoever has them[7] paraded them[8] in public?" Steve asked bitterly.

"Someone may have seen unusual activity; someone may have heard one of those phone calls being made; may have heard people talking in a bar ..."

Marian poured[9] water from the kettle into the teapot[10]. The door between the kitchen and dining room was open and she could overhear the conversation. That poor, poor Mr. Peterson. No wonder[11] he'd seemed so rude[12] when she spoke to him. He'd been all choked up about[13] the little boy being kidnapped and she'd only upset him[14] by talking about Neil. Shows you should never[15] judge people. You don't know what kind of grief they're carrying around inside them[16].

Maybe if he'd just have some tea.

She brought in the teapot. Steve's face was buried in his hands.[17]

"Mr. Peterson," she said gently, "let me fix you[18] a nice hot cup of tea."

She picked up his cup. With the other hand she began to pour.

Slowly Steve lowered his hands[19] from his face. The next instant[20] the teapot was flying across[21] the table; spilling down[22] into the sugar bowl[23], running

1. vous en avez suffisamment supporté
2. Je vais très bien
3. que cela vous plaise ou non
4. L'air sombre
5. vont paraître
6. on va les montrer sur toutes les chaînes de télévision
7. que celui qui les détient
8. les a exhibés
9. versa
10. théière
11. Ce n'était pas étonnant
12. impoli
13. était accablé par
14. en plus, elle l'avait bouleversé
15. Comme quoi, il ne faut jamais
16. quel chagrin est enfoui au plus profond d'eux-mêmes
17. Steve avait le visage enfoui dans ses mains.
18. vous servir
19. retira ses mains
20. L'instant d'après,
21. volait à travers
22. se déversant
23. sucrier

1. le thé dégoulinant sur
2. sets de table à fleurs
3. tel un flot bouillonnant et ambré
4. agrippait les bras de Marian, terrifiée

across[1] the flowered placemats[2], a bubbling, tawny stream[3].

Glenda, Roger and Hugh jumped up. Shocked, they stared at Steve, who was gripping a terrified Marian's arms[4]. "Where did you get that ring?" he shouted. "Where did you get that ring?"

44

5. fixait d'un regard absent
6. l'endroit rasé sur son crâne, semblable à la tonsure d'un moine
7. fentes
8. ne pleura pas
9. Sois courageux
10. Je le serai.
11. qu'il veillerait sur toi
12. balayée par le vent
13. s'arrêta à sa hauteur
14. vous déposer quelque part
15. messes

At Somers State Prison, Kate Thompson kissed her son goodbye. She stared unseeingly at[5] the shaven spot like a monk's tonsure on his head[6], the slits[7] in the side of his trousers.

She was dry-eyed[8] as she felt his strong young arms around her. She pulled his face down. "Be brave[9], dear."

"I will.[10] Bob said he'd look out for you[11], Mama."

She left him. Bob was going to stay until the end. She knew it was easier if she went now … easier for him.

She walked out of the prison, along the cold, windswept[12] road to town. A police car came by[13]. "Let me drop you[14], ma'am."

"Thank you." With dignity, she got in the car.

"You're staying at the motel, Mrs. Thompson?"

"No. Take me to St. Bernard's, please."

The morning masses[15] were over; the church was empty. She knelt at the statue of the Virgin. "Be with him at the end. Take the bitterness from my heart. You who gave up your innocent Son, help me if I must give up mine. ..."

45

A trembling Marian tried to speak. But she couldn't talk over the dryness in her mouth, the knot in her throat[1]. Her tongue was so heavy. The tea had burned her hand. Her finger hurt where Mr. Peterson had wrenched the ring from it[2].

They were all looking at her as though they hated her. Mr. Peterson's grip on her wrist tightened.[3] "Where did you get that ring?" he shouted again.

"I ... I ... I found it." Her voice quivered[4], broke[5].

"You *found* it!" Hugh shoved Steve away from[6] Marian. His voice dripped with scorn[7]. "You *found* it."

"Yes."

"Where?"

"In my car."

Hugh snorted[8] and looked directly at Steve. "Are you positive[9] this is the ring you gave Sharon Martin?"

"Absolutely. I bought it in a village in Mexico. It's one of a kind.[10] Look!" He tossed it[11] at Hugh. "Feel for a ridge[12] on the left side of the band[13]."

1. car elle avait la bouche sèche et un nœud dans la gorge
2. à l'endroit où M. Peterson lui avait arraché la bague
3. M. Peterson resserra son étreinte sur son poignet
4. trembla
5. se brisa
6. éloigna sans ménagement Steve de
7. trahissait son mépris
8. grommela
9. certain
10. Elle est unique en son genre.
11. la lança
12. Il y a une arête
13. anneau

Hugh ran his finger over the ring. His expression hardened[1]. "Where's your coat, Mrs. Vogler? You're coming in for questioning.[2]" Rapidly he spat out[3] the Miranda warning[4]. "You are not obliged to answer questions. Anything you say may be used against you. You have the right to call a lawyer. Let's go."

Steve shouted, "Damn you! Don't tell her she doesn't have to answer questions! Are you crazy? She's *got* to[5] answer questions!"

Glenda's face was stony[6]. She stared at Marian with angry disgust. "You talked about Arty this morning," she accused. "You talked about him fixing[7] your car. How *could* you?[8] How could you, a woman with children of her own[9], be part of this?"

Hugh spun around[10]. "She talked about Arty?"

"Yes."

"Where is he?" Steve demanded. "Where has he got them? My God, the first minute I met you, you talked about Neil."

"Steve, Steve, calm down." Roger gripped his arm[11].

Marian knew she was going to faint[12]. She had kept the ring and it wasn't hers[13]. Now they thought she had something to do with the kidnapping. How could she make them believe her? Waves of dizziness made her vision cloudy.[14] She'd make them call[15] Jim. They had to call Jim. He'd help her. He'd come here and tell them about the car being stolen and that she'd found the ring in it. He'd *make* them believe her. The room started spinning[16]. She clutched at[17] the table.

Steve jumped forward[18] to catch her before she fell. Through blurring eyes, she looked into his eyes, saw the agony[19] in them. Pity for him[20] calmed her. She grabbed him for support[21], forced herself to push back the dizziness[22]. "Mr. Peterson." She could speak now. She had to speak. "I couldn't

1. se durcit
2. Nous vous emmenons pour vous interroger.
3. Il débita à toute vitesse
4. [lecture au prévenu de ses droits]
5. doit absolument
6. impassible
7. Vous avez dit qu'il avait réparé
8. Comment avez-vous pu faire une chose pareille ?
9. qui a des enfants
10. pivota sur ses talons
11. lui saisit le bras
12. s'évanouir
13. elle ne lui appartenait pas
14. Les vertiges qui l'assaillaient par vagues lui troublaient la vue.
15. Elle insisterait pour qu'ils appellent
16. à tourner
17. se raccrocha à
18. bondit vers elle
19. souffrance atroce
20. La pitié qu'elle ressentit à son égard
21. s'agrippa à lui pour ne pas tomber
22. à combattre la sensation de vertige

harm anybody.[1] I want to help you. I *did* find the ring. In our car. Our car was stolen Monday night. Arty had just fixed it for us."

Steve looked down into the frightened, earnest face, the truth-filled eyes. Then the impact of what he had just heard sank into him. "Stolen![2] Your car was stolen Monday night?" Oh God, he thought, is there still a chance to find them?

Hugh snapped. "Let me handle this[3], Mr. Peterson." He pulled over a chair[4], helped Marian into it[5]. "Mrs. Vogler, if you are telling the truth, you must help us. How well do you know[6] Arty?"

"Not well. He's a good mechanic[7]. I picked the car up from him on Sunday. Then on Monday I went to the four o'clock movie at the Carley Square. I parked it in the movie lot[8]. It was gone when I got out just before seven-thirty."

"So he knew the condition[9] of the car," Hugh said. "Did he know you'd be going to the movie?"

"He might have.[10]" Marian frowned. "Yes, we were talking about it at his place[11]. And then he filled up the car with gas[12]. He said it was a bonus because it was such an expensive job."

Glenda murmured, "Remember I said that it was a dark car, a wide one."

"Mrs. Vogler," Hugh said, "this is very important. Where was your car recovered?[13]"

"In New York City. The police towed it. It was illegally parked."

"*Where?* By any chance do you know where they found it?"

Marian tried to think. "By a hotel, by some hotel."

"Mrs. Vogler, try to remember. Which hotel? You can save us[14] so much time."

Marian shook her head. "I can't."

"Would your husband remember?"

1. Je ne pourrais pas faire de mal à qui que ce soit.

2. Volée !

3. Laissez-moi faire

4. avança une chaise

5. à s'asseoir

6. Connaissez-vous bien

7. mécanicien

8. parking du cinéma

9. état

10. Cela se pourrait bien.

11. chez lui

12. a fait le plein d'essence

13. Où votre voiture a-t-elle été retrouvée ?

14. nous faire gagner

"Yes, but he's on an outside job[1] today. You'll have to phone the plant[2] and see if they can reach him[3]."

"What is the license number[4] of your car, Mrs. Vogler?"

Quickly Marian gave it to him. What hotel? Jim had said something about the street it was on? Why? It would take them so long to reach Jim … to check the towing records[5]… She had to remember. It was something about an[6] old car on easy street[7]. That's what Jim said. No, he said the *block* was named after a family that's always been on easy street[8]. "Vanderbilt Avenue," she cried, "that's it. My husband told me the car was parked on Vanderbilt Avenue in front of some hotel … the … the *Biltmore* Hotel."

Hugh grabbed the phone[9] and dialed FBI headquarters[10] in New York. He issued rapidfire orders[11]. "Get back to me fast.[12]" He hung up the phone.

"An agent is rushing over to the Biltmore with an old mug shot[13] we have of Taggert," he said. "Let's hope it still looks like him and let's hope they can tell us something."

Tensely[14] they waited.

"Please," Steve prayed. "Dear God, please!" The phone rang.

Hugh yanked the receiver off the hook[15]. "What have you got?" He listened, then yelled, "Sweet Jesus. I'll take the copter down.[16]" He dropped the phone, looked at Steve. "The room clerk positively identified[17] the picture as an[18] A. R. Renard who checked in on Sunday night. He had a dark green Beetle in the Biltmore garage. He checked out[19] this morning."

"*Renard.* That's French for fox!" Glenda cried.

"Exactly," Hugh said.

"Was he?" Steve gripped the table.

1. en déplacement à l'extérieur
2. usine
3. le joindre
4. numéro d'immatriculation
5. le registre des enlèvements de véhicules
6. Il était question d'une
7. qui se la coulait douce
8. qui se l'était toujours coulé douce
9. saisit le combiné
10. composa le numéro du quartier général du FBI
11. donna des ordres en rafale
12. Rappelez-moi au plus vite.
13. photo d'identité judiciaire
14. Dans un état de grande tension nerveuse
15. décrocha le combiné d'un coup sec
16. Je vais prendre l'hélico.
17. a formellement identifié
18. comme étant celle d'un certain
19. a quitté l'hôtel

"He was alone. But the clerk remembers that he's been going in and out of the hotel at odd hours[1]. Sometimes he's only been gone a short time[2], which could mean that he's been keeping Neil and Sharon somewhere in midtown[3]. Remember that John Owens picked up[4] a lot of train noises in the background of[5] the cassette."

"We've got no time, no time." Steve's voice was bitter. "What good will knowing this do?[6]"

"I'm taking the copter down to the Pan Am building. They'll clear us for an emergency landing there.[7] If we can get Taggert in time, we'll make him talk. If we don't[8] our best bet is still to concentrate our search[9] in the area of the Biltmore. Do you want to come?"

Steve didn't bother to[10] answer. He ran to the front door.

Glenda looked at the clock. "It is half past ten," she said tonelessly[11].

1. à des heures bizarres
2. il ne s'absentait que peu de temps
3. quelque part dans le centre-ville
4. a perçu
5. en arrière-plan sur
6. À quoi sert de savoir tout ça ?
7. Ils vont nous autoriser à atterrir en urgence là-bas.
8. Dans le cas contraire
9. le plus sûr est de continuer à concentrer nos recherches
10. ne prit pas la peine de
11. d'une voix blanche

46

1. Le père
2. le presbytère de St. Monica
3. bulletins d'informations
4. visage déchiré par l'angoisse
5. était venu chercher le paquet
6. Ce n'était pas étonnant qu'il ait été si bouleversé.
7. à temps
8. se produirait cette explosion
9. D'un geste las
10. d'avoir remis
11. autel
12. prêtre
13. sa gorge se serrer
14. Inutile de poser des questions.
15. indice
16. explosera
17. dans un important centre de transports
18. fouiller
19. La ligne fut coupée.

Father[1] Kennedy sat at his desk in St. Monica's rectory[2] listening to the news bulletins[3]. He shook his head thinking of the agonized face[4] of Steven Peterson when he picked up the package[5] at the rectory last night. No wonder he'd been so upset.[6]

Could they possibly find that child and young woman in time[7]? Where would that explosion occur[8]? How many others would be killed?

The phone rang. Wearily[9], he picked it up. "Father Kennedy."

"Thanks for delivering[10] the package I left on your altar[11] last night, Father. This is Foxy."

The priest[12] felt his throat constrict[13]. The press had been told only that the cassette was found in the church. "What ..."

"Never mind any questions.[14] You just call Steve Peterson for me and give him another hint[15]. Tell him I said the bomb will go off[16] at a major transportation center[17] in New York City. He can do his digging[18] there."

The phone went dead.[19]

47

Foxy moved slowly across the waiting area of gate[1] 9 toward the enclosed ramp that led to the plane. A presentiment of danger as definite as a tripped alarm[2] was jangling nerves through his entire system[3]. His eyes moved restlessly around[4] the area. His fellow passengers[5] were ignoring him, intent on juggling on-board luggage with pocketbooks[6] or attaché cases while preparing to present boarding passes[7].

He glanced down at his own boarding pass neatly protruding from the ticket envelope he'd presented at the desk. In his other hand he was firmly gripping the old black suitcase.

Sound! That was it. The sound of running feet. Police! He dropped the ticket, vaulted[8] the low divider[9] between the boarding area and corridor. Two men were running swiftly down the corridor toward him. Desperately, he glanced around and noticed an emergency exit door some fifty feet away[10]. It had to lead to the field[11].

The suitcase. He couldn't run with the suitcase. With only the briefest hesitation, he threw it backward. It thumped against the stone floor, slid a few

1. traversa lentement la salle d'attente située à la porte
2. le déclenchement d'une alarme
3. lui mettait les nerfs à vif
4. Son regard balayait sans cesse
5. Les autres passagers
6. occupés à jongler avec leurs bagages à main et leurs sacs à main
7. cartes d'embarquement
8. sauta d'un bond par-dessus
9. muret de séparation
10. à une quinzaine de mètres de là
11. l'aire de trafic

inches and burst open. Money scattered over[1] the corridor.

"Stop or we'll shoot[2]!" a commanding voice shouted.

Foxy threw open[3] the emergency door, setting off a loud pealing sound[4]. He yanked it closed behind him and wove across the field. The Phoenix-bound plane[5] was in his path[6]. He ran around it. A small service van, its engine running, was near the left wing of the plane. The driver was just getting back in. Foxy grabbed him from behind, punched him viciously[7] in the neck. The man grunted and collapsed[8]. Foxy shoved him aside and jumped into the van. Pressing his foot down on the accelerator, he zigzagged around the plane. They wouldn't dare shoot with that plane in the way[9].

The cops would be following him in a car any second[10]. Or they'd send cars from other areas to head him off[11]. It was risky to get out of this car, more risky to stay in it. The runways[12] were fenced off[13] or ended at the Sound[14]. If he drove down one of them, he'd be trapped[15].

They were looking for a man driving a service van on the field. They'd never look for him in the terminal. He spotted an identical van parked near a hangar, swung next to it[16] and stopped. On the seat beside him a looseleaf book[17] was open. He glanced at it swiftly. Something about requisitions[18], supplies[19]. He grabbed it and got out of the van. A door marked "authorized personnel only[20]" was opening. Bending his head over the book, he reached for it, prevented it from closing. A brisk-looking young woman in an airline uniform came out, glanced at the book in his hand, and sped past him[21].

Now his walk became authoritative, swift. He strode through[22] the small corridor with the individual offices and an instant later was in the departure

1. se répandit dans
2. on tire
3. ouvrit brutalement
4. déclenchant une sonnerie stridente
5. L'avion à destination de Phoenix
6. se trouvait sur son passage
7. le frappa violemment
8. émit un grognement et s'écroula
9. dans leur ligne de mire
10. d'une seconde à l'autre
11. pour lui barrer le passage
12. pistes
13. entourées de clôtures
14. au détroit de Long Island
15. il se ferait piéger
16. vira brusquement pour se garer à côté de lui
17. registre à feuillets mobiles
18. Cela concernait des commandes
19. des livraisons
20. « Réservé au personnel autorisé »
21. passa à vive allure devant lui
22. parcourut à grandes enjambées

area. Airport police were running past him toward the field. Ignoring them, he walked through the terminal, out to the curb and[1] hailed a cab.

"Where to?[2]" the driver asked.

"Grand Central Station." He pulled out a twenty-dollar bill, the last of his money. "How fast can you get there?[3] My plane's been canceled and I gotta make a train[4] before eleven-thirty."

The driver was a kid, not more than twenty-two. "Mister, that's calling it a little close[5], but I'll do it[6]. The roads are pretty good now and the traffic is real light[7]." He pressed his foot on the gas pedal[8]. "Hang on.[9]"

Foxy leaned back. Icy perspiration chilled his body. They knew who he was now. Suppose they'd looked up his old record. Suppose someone said, "He used to work in the Oyster Bar. He was a dishwasher[10]." Suppose they thought about the room and went to look in it.

The bomb was attached[11] to the clock now. That meant that if anyone went into the room, they'd have time to get Sharon and Neil out; maybe time to deactivate the bomb. No, it would probably go off if anyone touched it; it was that sensitive[12]. But what good[13] if Sharon and Neil got out[14]?

He shouldn't have made that last phonecall. It was Sharon's fault. He should have strangled her[15] yesterday. He remembered the feeling of his hands squeezing[16] her neck, reaching for the soft pulse in her throat. He hadn't touched any of the others with his hands; he'd just knotted[17] and twisted their scarves or belts. But her! His hands burned with the need to surround that throat. She had ruined it for him[18]. She had tricked him[19], pretending to be in love with him. The way she'd looked at him, even from the television, acting like she wanted him, wanted him to take her away[20]. Then yester-

1. et, une fois à l'extérieur
2. Où voulez-vous aller ?
3. Combien de temps vous faut-il pour y aller ?
4. dois attraper un train
5. ça risque d'être un peu juste
6. je vais y arriver
7. vraiment fluide
8. appuya sur l'accélérateur
9. Accrochez-vous.
10. plongeur
11. reliée
12. tellement sensible
13. à quoi cela servirait-il
14. parvenaient à sortir
15. aurait dû l'étrangler
16. serrant
17. noué
18. gâché toutes ses chances
19. l'avait roulé
20. comme si elle voulait qu'il l'emmène

day she'd put her arms around him and tried to get his gun. She was no good[1]. She was the worst of all of them, all the women in the foster homes[2], the matrons[3] in the detention homes[4], all of them, pushing him away[5] when he tried to kiss them. "Stop that! Don't do that!"

He shouldn't have taken Sharon to the room. If he'd just taken the boy, this wouldn't have happened. She'd made him take her, and now the money was gone[6] and they knew who he was and he'd have to hide somewhere.

But he'd kill her first. By now[7] they were probably just starting to evacuate the terminals and airports. They probably wouldn't think of the room this fast[8]. The bomb was too good for her. She had to look up and see him and feel his hands on her throat. He had to look down at her and see her die. He had to talk to her and tell her what he was going to do and listen to her beg him not to, and then he'd squeeze.

He closed his eyes and swallowed over the dryness in his mouth, the shiver of ecstasy that made the perspiration tingle.

He only needed four or five minutes inside the terminal. If he got into[9] the room by 11:27, he'd have enough time. He'd get away through[10] the Park Avenue tunnel.

And even though he didn't have his recorder, he'd remember how Sharon sounded[11]. He wanted to remember. He'd fall asleep remembering how she sounded when she died.

The boy. He'd just leave him there. Let the bomb take care of him, him and all the stinking[12] cops and all the people who wouldn't get out in time. Didn't even know what was going to happen to them.

They were entering the midtown tunnel. This kid was a good driver. It was only ten minutes of eleven. Another ten or fifteen minutes and he'd be on

1. une bonne à rien
2. familles d'accueil
3. surveillantes
4. centres de détention
5. le repoussant
6. avait disparu
7. À cette heure-ci,
8. aussi rapidement
9. entrait dans
10. Il s'enfuirait par
11. de la voix de Sharon
12. infects

Forty-second Street. He'd have plenty of time. Plenty of time for Sharon.

The cab came to an abrupt halt[1] halfway through the tunnel. Foxy looked up from his meditation. "What's the matter[2]?"

The cabby shrugged. "Sorry, mister. There's a disabled truck[3] up there[4]. Looks like he lost[5] some of his cargo[6] too. Both lanes[7] are blocked. But it shouldn't take long. Don't worry, I'll get you there for your train[8]."

Frantic with impatience to get to Sharon, Foxy waited. His hands were burning so much now, like they were on fire[9]. He thought about getting out and walking the rest of the way but rejected the idea. The cops would stop him sure.

It was seventeen minutes past eleven when they inched out of the[10] tunnel and turned north. The traffic began to back up[11] at Fortieth Street. The driver whistled[12]. "This is some mess.[13] I'll try cutting west[14] here."

At Third Avenue they came to a complete stop[15]. Motionless cars[16] blocked the intersections[17]. Horns tooted angrily.[18] Tense-looking pedestrians[19], scurrying east, tried to make their way around[20] the cars. "Mister, there must be something wrong. Looks like some streets are closed off[21] up there. Wait. I'll turn on[22] the radio. Maybe it's another bomb threat[23]."

They were probably clearing out[24] the terminal. Foxy tossed the twenty-dollar bill at the driver, opened the door and slid out into[25] the traffic.

At Forty-second Street he saw them. Cops. Cops all over the place[26]. Forty-second Street closed off. He pushed and shoved his way through[27]. Bomb. Bomb. He stopped. People were talking about a bomb in the station. Had they found Sharon and the boy? The thought sent black fury

1. s'arrêta brusquement
2. Que se passe-t-il ?
3. camion immobilisé
4. un peu plus haut
5. Il semblerait qu'il ait perdu
6. une partie de son chargement
7. files
8. vous arriverez à temps pour votre train
9. en feu
10. sortirent lentement du
11. Des bouchons se formaient
12. siffla
13. C'est un vrai bazar.
14. de couper vers l'ouest
15. s'arrêtèrent complètement
16. Des voitures à l'arrêt
17. carrefours
18. Des coups de Klaxon furieux se faisaient entendre.
19. Des piétons à l'air préoccupé
20. contourner
21. barrées
22. Je vais allumer
23. alerte à la bombe
24. évacuaient probablement
25. se glissa dans
26. partout
27. se fraya un passage

gushing through him[1]. He shouldered people aside[2], forced his way through the crowd.

"Stand back, buddy[3]. You can't go any further[4]." A burly, young policeman tapped his shoulder as he tried to cross Third Avenue.

"What's the matter?" He had to know.

"Nothing, we hope, sir. But there's been a bomb threat phoned in[5]. We have to take precautions."

Phoned in. His phonecall to that priest. *Threat!* That meant they hadn't found the bomb. It was all right. Exultation leaped through him.[6] His fingers and palms tingled the way they always did when he started to go to a girl and knew nothing could stop him. His voice was smooth, his expression concerned when he spoke to the cop. "I'm a surgeon. I'm joining the emergency medical squad[7] in case it's needed[8]."

"Oh, sorry, Doctor. Go right through.[9]"

Foxy ran up[10] Forty-second Street, taking care to keep close to the buildings. The next cop who stopped him might be smart enough to ask for identification. People were streaming out[11] of office buildings and shops, prodded by the urgency[12] of the bullhorns the police were using[13]. "Move quickly but do not panic. Walk to Third or Fifth Avenue. Your cooperation may save your life."

It was exactly 11:26 when Foxy, pushing his way through the confused and frightened crowds[14], reached the main entrance to the terminal. The doors had been wedged open[15] to speed the exodus[16]. A veteran policeman was standing guard[17] at the far left door. Foxy tried to duck past him[18]. His arm was grabbed. "Hey, you can't go in there!"

"Terminal engineer," Foxy said crisply. "I've been sent for.[19]"

"You're too late. The searchers will be clearing out[20] in a minute."

1. À cette pensée, il sentit monter en lui une bouffée de fureur
2. écarta les gens d'un coup d'épaule
3. Reculez, mon pote
4. ne pouvez pas aller plus loin
5. on a reçu une alerte à la bombe par téléphone
6. Il exulta.
7. équipe médicale d'urgence
8. au cas où on aurait besoin de moi
9. Allez-y.
10. remonta au pas de course
11. Des flots de personnes sortaient
12. poussés par le sentiment d'urgence
13. communiqué par les mégaphones des policiers
14. foule désorientée et effrayée
15. étaient maintenues ouvertes à l'aide d'une cale
16. pour permettre à la foule de sortir plus rapidement
17. posté
18. passer subrepticement devant lui
19. On m'a appelé.
20. Les équipes de recherche vont quitter les lieux

"I've been sent for," Foxy repeated.

"Suit yourself.[1]" The cop dropped his arm.

The deserted newsstand beyond the doors was piled with morning papers. Foxy saw the huge black headline. *Kidnap.* It was about him, what he'd done—the fox.

He ran past the stand and looked down into the main terminal. Grim-faced policemen[2] with construction hats[3] were searching behind counters and booths. There were probably dozens more all over the station. But he'd outsmarted them[4]! All of them!

A small group of people was clustered[5] near the information desk. The taller one, a broad-shouldered, sandy-haired[6] man, hands shoved in his pockets, was shaking his head. Steve Peterson! It was Steve Peterson! Sucking in his breath[7], Foxy raced down to the main floor and dashed for the staircase to the lower level.

Now he only needed two more minutes. His fingers throbbed and burned. He curled and uncurled them[8] as he rushed down the stairs[9]. Only his thumbs were rigid as he ran, unchallenged[10], across the lower terminal and disappeared down the steps[11] leading to the Mount Vernon platform and the room beyond it.

1. Faites comme vous voulez.
2. Des policiers au visage grave
3. portant des casques de chantier
4. il s'était montré plus malin qu'eux
5. se trouvait
6. aux cheveux blond roux
7. Prenant une profonde inspiration
8. les pliait et les dépliait
9. tout en descendant l'escalier à toute allure
10. sans rencontrer d'opposition
11. disparaissait dans l'escalier

1. parvint à
2. aboya au téléphone
3. Bon Dieu
4. gares routières
5. l'air totalement abattu
6. tout en croisant et décroisant nerveusement les mains
7. occupait tout un pâté de maisons
8. impossible
9. Ne pouvez-vous pas faire voler cet engin plus rapidement ?
10. La vitesse du vent
11. il ne manquait plus que ça
12. marmonna
13. Inutile de se raconter des histoires.
14. La situation n'est pas brillante.
15. partir du principe qu'il a mis à exécution sa menace
16. de poser cette bombe

48

The news of Foxy's phonecall reached[1] Hugh and Steve as the helicopter passed over the Triborough Bridge.

"*Major transportation center, New York City,*" Hugh snapped into the phone[2]. "Christ[3], that includes both airports, both bus terminals[4], Penn Station, and Grand Central. Have you started evacuating them?"

Steve listened, his shoulders slumped forward[5], his hands restlessly clasping and unclasping[6]. Kennedy Airport! LaGuardia Airport! The Port Authority bus terminal took up a square block[7]; the one at the bridge was probably bigger. Sharon ... Neil ... oh God, it was hopeless[8] ... may the fox build his nest on your hearthstone. ...

Hugh hung up the phone. "Can't you push this thing any faster?[9]" he urged the pilot.

"That wind is getting awful strong," the pilot replied, "I'll try going lower."

"Wind velocity[10], just what we need[11] if there's a fire when that thing goes off," Hugh muttered[12]. He looked over at Steve. "There's no use kidding.[13] It's bad.[14] We have to assume he's carried out his threat[15] to set that bomb[16]."

"With Sharon and Neil somewhere near it?" Steve's voice was ragged[1]. "Where do you start looking?"

"We're gambling[2]," Hugh said tersely[3]. "The main search will be in Grand Central. Remember, he parked the car on Vanderbilt and stayed at the Biltmore. He knows the terminal like a book[4]. And John Owens says the train sounds he heard on the cassette are more consistent with commuter trains[5] than subways[6]."

"What about the Thompson boy?"

"If we don't catch Foxy and get a confession out of him, he's finished[7]."

At 11:05 the helicopter landed on the Pan Am building. Hugh threw open the door. A thin-faced[8] agent ran over to them[9] as they jumped to the ground. White with anger[10], lips tightly compressed[11], he briefed them on Foxy's escape[12].

"What do you mean, *escaped*?" Hugh exploded. "How the hell[13] did that happen? How sure are you that it was Foxy?"

"Absolutely sure. He dropped the ransom. They're searching the field and terminal for him now. But the whole airport is being evacuated so it's a mess out there."

"The ransom doesn't tell us where he set that bomb and it can't help the Thompson kid," Hugh snapped. "*We've got to find Foxy and make him talk.*"

Foxy escaped. With numb disbelief[14], Steve absorbed the words[15]. Sharon. Neil. "Steve, I was wrong, forgive me." "Mommy wouldn't want me to be here." Was that bizarre cassette to be his last contact with them?

The cassette. Nina's voice ...

He grabbed Hugh's arm. "That cassette he sent. He must have dubbed Nina's voice on it[16]. You said he'd cleared everything out of[17] the garage. Did he have any luggage? He may have been carrying a suitcase,

1. éteinte
2. C'est un coup de poker
3. sèchement
4. comme sa poche
5. ressemblent davantage à ceux des trains de banlieue
6. qu'à ceux des métros
7. fichu
8. au visage mince
9. se précipita vers eux
10. Pâle de colère
11. les lèvres serrées
12. leur expliqua brièvement que Foxy avait pris la fuite
13. Comment diable
14. Muet de stupeur
15. s'imprégna des paroles
16. a dû y ajouter l'enregistrement de la voix de Nina
17. qu'il avait vidé

something with him. Maybe he still has the other cassette with Nina's voice, maybe he has something that would show where Sharon and Neil are."

Hugh spun around to[1] the other agent. "What about any luggage?"

"There are two stubs clipped onto the[2] ticket he dropped. But the plane took off[3] about twenty-seven minutes ago. No one thought to stop it. We'll get those bags in Phoenix."

"That's not good enough," Hugh shouted. "Sweet Christ[4], that's not good enough. Get that goddamn plane back.[5] Have every baggage handler[6] in LaGuardia ready to unload it[7]. Tell the control tower to clear a runway[8]. Don't let any dumb ass[9] stand in your way[10]. Where's a phone?"

"Inside."

Hugh pulled out his notebook as he ran. Rapidly he dialed Somers prison and got the Warden's office[11]. "We're still trying to locate evidence[12] to prove Thompson's innocence. Have a phone manned to the last split second.[13]"

He called the Governor's office, got through to her private secretary. "Make damn sure[14] the Governor's available[15] and that you have a phone open to our guys in LaGuardia and another to the prison. Or else, the Nutmeg State[16] may go down in history[17] for frying an innocent kid." He dropped the phone. "Let's go," he told Steve.

Nineteen minutes, Steve thought as they plummeted down in the elevator[18]. Nineteen minutes.

The lobby[19] of the Pan American building was jammed with people streaming from the terminal[20]. Bomb threat … bomb threat … The words were on everyone's lips.

Steve and Hugh shoved their way through the surging bodies[21]. How can anyone know where to search? Steve agonized[22]. He'd been here only yes-

1. se retourna vivement vers
2. coupons agrafés au
3. a décollé
4. Doux Jésus
5. Faites revenir ce fichu avion.
6. tous les bagagistes
7. à le décharger
8. de dégager une piste
9. un abruti quelconque
10. se mettre en travers de votre chemin
11. bureau du directeur
12. rassembler des éléments
13. Arrangez-vous pour qu'on puisse vous joindre au téléphone jusqu'à la dernière fraction de seconde.
14. Assurez-vous bien
15. disponible
16. [surnom donné au Connecticut]
17. pourrait rester dans l'histoire
18. l'ascenseur descendait à vive allure
19. hall d'entrée
20. était bondé de gens qui quittaient la gare en un flot ininterrompu
21. flot de personnes
22. se tourmentait Steve

terday. Sitting in the Oyster Bar, waiting for his train. Had Sharon and Neil been here all along[1], helpless[2]? Over the loudspeaker[3] an urgent voice[4] kept repeating, "Leave the building immediately. Walk to the nearest exit. Do not panic. Do not congregate at exits.[5] Leave the area ... leave the area ...."

The Information Booth on the upper level of the terminal, its red emergency lights flashing ominously[6], was the command desk for the investigators. Engineers were poring over charts and diagrams[7], issuing rapidfire orders to searching parties[8].

"We're concentrating on the area between the floor of this level and the ceiling of the lower level now," a supervisor told Hugh. "It's accessible from all the platforms and a good hiding place[9]. We've done a fast check on the platforms and we're hitting[10] all the lockers[11]. We figure that[12] even if we find the bomb, it's probably too risky to try to dismantle it[13]. The bomb squad[14] brought over[15] all the bomb blankets[16] they could lay their hands on[17]. They're distributed among the searching parties. We can count on one of them being ninety percent effective in containing an explosion."

Steve's eyes swept the terminal. The loudspeaker was off now and the vast area was becoming quiet, a hushed, mocking silence. The clock. His eyes searched out[18] the clock over the information desk. Relentlessly the hands[19] kept moving: 11:12 ... 11:17 ... 11:24 ... He wanted to hold those hands back. He wanted to run into every platform, every waiting room, every cubicle[20]. He wanted to shout their names, Sharon! Neil!

Frantically, he turned his head. He had to *do* something, search for them himself. His gaze fell[21] on a tall, bony[22] man who rushed in from the Forty-second Street entrance[23], ran down the stairs and disappeared down the second staircase that led to the

1. pendant tout ce temps
2. sans défense
3. Du haut-parleur
4. voix pressante
5. Ne vous rassemblez pas près des sorties.
6. qui clignotaient de façon inquiétante
7. étudiaient de près des graphiques et des schémas
8. équipes de recherche
9. cachette
10. nous fouillons actuellement
11. consignes
12. pensons que
13. la désamorcer
14. l'équipe de déminage
15. a apporté
16. protections anti-bombe
17. qu'ils ont pu se procurer
18. Il cherchait du regard
19. aiguilles
20. tous les recoins
21. Son regard tomba
22. anguleux
23. entrait précipitamment par la porte d'accès située dans la 42e Rue

lower level. There was something vaguely familiar about him[1]—one of the agents maybe? What good could he do now?

The loudspeaker went on. "It is eleven-twenty-seven. All searchers immediately proceed to[2] the nearest exit. Leave the terminal immediately. Repeat. Leave the terminal immediately."

"No!" Steve clutched Hugh's shoulders, spun him around[3]. "No!"

"Mr. Peterson, make sense[4]. If that bomb goes off, we may all be killed. Even if Sharon and Neil are here, we can't help them that way."

"I'm not leaving," Steve said.

Hugh grabbed his arm. Another agent took the other one. "Mr. Peterson, be reasonable. It may only be a precaution."

Steve wrenched himself free[5]. "Let go of me[6], damn you[7]," he shouted. "Let go of me."

1. chez lui
2. doivent immédiatement gagner
3. le fit pivoter
4. faites preuve de bon sens
5. se dégagea d'un mouvement violent
6. Lâchez-moi
7. bordel

49

It was no use[8], no use, no use. Her eyes magnetized to[9] the clock, Sharon frantically tried to jab[10] the broken edge of the handle[11] into the cords of her wrists. It was so hard to hold the handle in one fist, to try to push at the cords of the other.

More times than not[12], she missed the cords completely, and the metal cut into her hand[13]. She could

8. Ça ne servait à rien
9. vissés sur
10. de planter
11. bord tranchant de la poignée cassée
12. La plupart du temps
13. lui entaillait la main

feel the warm, soft, sticky blood, running, crusting[1]. She was beyond pain.[2] But what if she jabbed[3] an artery and passed out[4]?

The blood was making the cord softer, more resilient[5]. The metal jabbed at it[6], not in it[7]. She'd been trying for over an hour[8] now … it was twenty-five of eleven.

Twenty of eleven.

Ten of … five of … five after …

She worked on[9], her face clammy with perspiration, her hands sticky with blood, not feeling pain anymore. She felt Neil's eyes watching her. Pray, Neil.

At ten after eleven, she felt the cord weakening, giving[10]. Summoning up a last reserve of energy[11], Sharon pulled her hands apart[12]. They were free; the cords were dangling from them[13].

She held them up, shook them, tried to get feeling back into them[14]. Fifteen minutes.

Leaning on her left elbow[15], Sharon dragged herself up[16]. She swung just enough to support[17] her back against the wall and managed to squirm to a sitting position[18]. Her legs fell over the side of the cot. Raw pain screeched through[19] her ankle.

Fourteen minutes.

Her fingers trembled with weakness as she tugged at the gag. The gauze was so tightly knotted[20]. She couldn't get it loose[21]. Tugging frantically, she managed to pull the gag down. Great gulping breaths of air helped to clear her head[22].

Thirteen minutes.

She couldn't walk. Even if she could drag herself over to[23] the bomb she might jar it[24], trying to pull up on the sink[25], to reach it[26]. Or she might set it off just by touching it. She remembered the infinite care Foxy had shown when he touched the wires.

1. former une croûte
2. Elle ne sentait plus la douleur.
3. touchait
4. perdait connaissance
5. résistante
6. s'y enfonçait
7. mais ne s'y plantait pas
8. depuis plus d'une heure
9. persévérait
10. céder
11. Rassemblant ce qui lui restait d'énergie
12. écarta ses mains
13. pendaient de ses poignets
14. ramener la circulation dans ses mains
15. Prenant appui sur son coude gauche
16. se redressa péniblement
17. appuyer
18. se tortiller pour s'asseoir
19. Une vive douleur irradia dans
20. solidement nouée
21. la relâcher
22. l'aidèrent à s'éclaircir les idées
23. se traîner jusqu'à
24. l'ébranler
25. prendre appui sur l'évier pour se mettre debout
26. l'atteindre.

There was no hope for her. She had to try to free Neil. If she could get him loose, he could get out, could warn people. She yanked his gag off[1].

"Sharon ..."

"I know. I'm going to try to untie you[2]. I can't help it if I hurt you."

"All right, Sharon."

And then she heard it. The sound. Something thudding against[3] the door. Was he coming back? Had he changed his mind? Clutching Neil to her[4], Sharon stared at the door. It was opening. The light switch clicked.

In the dusty light, she saw what seemed to be an apparition stumbling toward her[5], a woman, an old woman with a trickle of blood coming from her mouth[6] with deep sunken eyes that were out of focus[7].

Neil shrank back against her[8] as the woman came toward them, stared in horror as the woman began to fall forward, to slump downward[9] like an unsupported laundry bag[10].

The woman fell on her side[11], tried to speak. "Knife ... still in my back ... help .., please ... take it out[12] ... hurts ... want to die here ..."

The woman's head was against her foot. Her body angled grotesquely out. Sharon saw the handle of the knife between her shoulder blades[13].

She could free Neil with the knife. Shuddering[14], Sharon put both hands around the handle, pulled.

The knife held[15], then suddenly came free[16]. She was holding it, the blade wickedly sharp[17], matted with blood[18].

The woman whimpered[19].

In an instant Sharon had cut Neil's bindings[20]. "Neil ... run ... get out of here ... yell to people that there's going to be an explosion ... hurry ... down those stairs ... and there's a big ramp ... run toward

1. lui enleva son bâillon d'un coup sec
2. te détacher
3. Un bruit sourd contre
4. Tout en serrant Neil contre elle
5. avancer vers elle en titubant
6. filet de sang qui lui coulait de la bouche
7. et des yeux hagards enfoncés dans leurs orbites
8. se figea contre elle
9. s'affaisser sur le sol
10. sac rempli de linge sale
11. tomba sur le côté
12. enlevez-le
13. omoplates
14. Tout en tremblant
15. tint bon
16. céda
17. dangereusement tranchante
18. maculée de sang
19. gémit
20. les liens qui retenaient Neil

it … at the train platform, go up the stairs … you'll see people there … Daddy will come for you[1] … hurry … get out of this building … get people out of it …"

"Sharon," Neil's voice was pleading[2]. "What about you?"

"Neil … just go. Go!"

Neil slid off the cot[3]. He tried to walk, stumbled[4], righted himself[5]. "My legs …"

"Neil, hurry. Run! Run!"

With a last beseeching[6] glance at her, Neil obeyed. He ran out of the room, onto the landing[7]. Down the stairs. Sharon had said to go down the stairs. It was so quiet[8] here, so spooky[9]. He was so afraid. The bomb. Maybe if he could find someone, they'd help Sharon. He had to make someone help Sharon.

He was at the foot of the stairs. Which way should he go? There were so many pipes[10] around here[11]. A ramp. Sharon said a ramp. That must be it. Like the ramp they had in school between the classrooms and the auditorium.

He raced along it[12]. He wanted to shout for help[13]. But he had to hurry. He had to find someone. He was at the end of the ramp. He was in a station, a train station. The tracks were right there[14]. Sharon said to go upstairs. He ran around the platform where the tracks ended.

A voice started to talk. It sounded like when the principal[15] talked on the loudspeaker at school. It was telling everyone to get out. Where was the man who was talking?

He could hear footsteps coming down a staircase. Someone was coming, someone who would help Sharon. He was so relieved[16] he tried to yell and couldn't. He had no breath from running.[17] His legs hurt so much it was hard to run. He

1. viendra te chercher
2. implorante
3. se glissa hors du lit de camp
4. trébucha
5. se redressa
6. implorant
7. sortit de la pièce en courant et arriva sur le palier
8. silencieux
9. sinistre
10. tuyaux
11. par ici
12. la remonta au pas de course
13. appeler au secours
14. juste là
15. On aurait dit le proviseur lorsqu'il
16. soulagé
17. La course lui avait coupé le souffle.

stumbled toward[1] the stairs and began to climb[2]. He had to tell whoever was coming about Sharon.

Neil looked up and saw the face that had stalked his dreams[3] rushing down at[4] him.

Foxy saw Neil. His eyes narrowed. His mouth twisted. He stretched out his hands[5] …

Neil jumped to one side[6], stuck out his foot[7]. The man's flailing leg jammed against his sneaker[8]. The man sprawled down the last three steps[9]. Eluding the arms that swung out at him[10], Neil ran up the steps. He was in a big, empty place. There was no one here. Another staircase. Over there. Maybe there were people upstairs. The bad man was going to Sharon.

Sobbing[11], Neil ran up the stairs. Daddy, he tried to yell, Daddy. Daddy. He was on the last step. There were policemen all over here. They were all running away from him[12]. Some of them were pushing another man.

They were pushing Daddy.

"Daddy," Neil shouted. "Daddy!"

With a last, final burst of energy[13], he stumbled across the terminal. Steve heard him, turned, ran to him, grabbed him.

"Daddy," Neil sobbed, "that man is going to kill Sharon now … just like[14] he killed Mommy."

1. avança en titubant vers
2. monter les marches
3. hanté ses rêves
4. descendre précipitamment vers
5. tendit les bras
6. fit un bond de côté
7. tendit la jambe
8. vint heurter sa basket
9. dégringola les trois dernières marches, la tête la première
10. Esquivant les coups de poings que l'homme essayait de lui donner
11. En sanglotant
12. couraient tous dans la direction opposée
13. Dans un dernier sursaut d'énergie
14. tout comme

50

A determined Rosie was fighting the efforts to put her out[1]. Lally was down in Sing Sing. She knew it. Cops were all over the place. There was a bunch of them[2] right at the Information Desk. Rosie spotted Hugh Taylor. He was the nice FBI guy who always talked to her when he was around the station. She ran to him, tugged his arm[3]. "Mr. Taylor, Lally ..."

He glanced down at her, pulled his arm free. "Get the hell out of here[4], Rosie," he ordered.

A loudspeaker came on, ordering everyone out[5]. "No!" Rosie sobbed.

The tall man near Hugh Taylor grabbed him, turned him around[6]. She watched as Hugh and another cop wrestled[7] with him.

"Daddy! Daddy!"

Was she hearing things?[8] Rosie spun around. A little boy was weaving across[9] the terminal. Then the big guy who was shouting at Mr. Taylor ran past her to the child. She heard the boy say something about a bad man and rushed over[10]. Maybe he'd seen the guy she and Lally were watching[11].

The boy was crying. "Daddy, help Sharon. She's hurt. She's all tied up[12] and there's a sick old lady[13] ..."

1. se démenait pour qu'on ne la fasse pas sortir de la gare

2. Il y en avait tout un groupe

3. le tira par la manche

4. Fichez le camp d'ici

5. ordonnant à tout le monde de sortir

6. le fit pivoter

7. luttaient

8. Entendait-elle des voix ?

9. courait en titubant à travers

10. se précipita

11. surveillaient

12. attachée

13. vieille dame malade

"Where, Neil, where?" Steve begged.

"A sick old lady," Rosie shrieked[1]. "That's Lally. She's in her room. You know it, Mr. Taylor, in Sing Sing—the old dishwasher room[2]."

"Come on," Hugh shouted.

Steve thrust Neil at[3] a policeman. "Get my son out of here," he ordered. He ran behind Hugh. Two men struggling with a heavy metal sheet[4] followed them.

"Christ, let's get out of here!" Someone thrust an arm around Rosie's waist[5] and dragged her toward an exit. "That bomb will go off any minute!"

51

Sharon heard the padding of Neil's sneakers[6] as he ran down the steps. Please God, let him be safe[7]. Let him get away.[8]

The old woman's moans[9] stopped, resumed[10], stopped for a longer instant. When the sound began again, it was lower, softer, it had a fading quality[11].

With detached clarity, Sharon remembered what this woman said about wanting to die here. Leaning down, she[12] felt the matted hair[13], patted it gently[14]. Her fingertips smoothed the wrinkled forehead[15]. The skin felt damp[16] and cold. Lally shuddered violently. The moaning[17] stopped.

Sharon knew the woman was dead. And now she was going to die. "I love you, Steve," she said aloud.

1. cria
2. salle de plonge
3. poussa Neil vers
4. se débattant avec une lourde plaque de métal
5. prit Rosie par la taille
6. bruit feutré des baskets de Neil
7. faites qu'il s'en sorte sain et sauf
8. Faites qu'il arrive à s'échapper.
9. gémissements
10. reprenaient
11. il faiblissait
12. Elle se pencha et
13. cheveux emmêlés
14. les tapota légèrement
15. Du bout des doigts, elle lui lissa les rides du front
16. moite
17. Les gémissements

"I love you, Steve." His face filled her mind.[1] Her need for him was physical pain; primal, acute, transcending the throbbing agony of[2] her leg and ankle.

She closed her eyes. "Forgive us our trespasses as we forgive those who trespass against us[3] … Into Your Hands, I commend my spirit.[4]"

A sound.

Her eyes flew open.[5] Foxy was framed in the doorway[6]. An ear to ear smile slashed his face.[7] His fingers curved[8], his thumbs rigid, he started toward[9] her.

52

Hugh led the way down to[10] the Mount Vernon plat form, around the tracks, down the ramp into the lowest depths of the terminal. Steve raced beside him[11]. The men carrying the bomb blanket struggled to keep up with them[12].

They were on the ramp when they heard the screaming.

"No … no … no ... Steve … help me … Steve …"

Steve's track team days were twenty years in the past.[13] But once again he felt that tremendous surge of power[14], that terrible burst of energy[15] he had always summoned[16] in a race. Crazed with[17] the need to reach Sharon in time, he flew past[18] the others.

"Steeeeeevvvweeee …" The scream choked off[19].

1. Elle ne voyait plus que son visage.
2. douleur lancinante dans
3. Pardonne-nous nos péchés comme nous pardonnons à ceux qui nous ont offensés
4. Entre Tes mains, je remets mon esprit.
5. Elle ouvrit brusquement les yeux.
6. se tenait dans l'encadrement de la porte
7. Le visage fendu d'un large sourire.
8. recourbés
9. s'avança vers
10. marchait en tête vers
11. courait à toute vitesse à ses côtés
12. avaient du mal à les suivre
13. Steve n'avait pas participé à des compétitions de course à pied depuis vingt ans.
14. vague de puissance
15. réserve d'énergie
16. trouvée
17. Dévoré par
18. passa à toute vitesse devant
19. s'interrompit

Stairs. He was at the foot of a staircase. He lunged up it[1], burst through an open door[2].

His brain absorbed[3] the nightmarish quality of the scene, the body on the floor, Sharon half-lying, half-sitting, her legs tied, her hair dangling behind her, trying to pull away from the figure bent over her[4], the figure with the thick fingers that were squeezing her throat.

Steve threw himself[5] on the man, butted his head[6] into the arched[7] back. Foxy sprawled forward[8]. They both fell on Sharon. Under their weight[9], the sagging cot broke and they rolled together on the floor. The hands were still on Sharon's throat but broke loose[10] under the impact of the fall. Foxy stumbled to his feet[11], crouched[12]. Steve tried to leap up[13], tripped on[14] Lally's body. Sharon's breathing was a tortured, choking gasp[15].

Hugh raced into the room.

Cornered[16], Foxy backed away[17]. His hand found the door to the toilet cubicle. He jumped past it, slammed it shut[18]. They heard the bolt slide into place.

"Get out of there, you crazy fool[19]," Hugh shouted.

The agents carrying the bomb blanket were in the room. With infinite care, they draped[20] the black suitcase with the heavy metal sheet.

Steve reached for[21] Sharon. Her eyes were closed. Her head flopped backwards[22] as he picked her up. Ugly welts[23] were rising[24] on her throat. But she was alive; she was alive. Holding her to him[25], he turned to the door. His eyes fell on the posters, on Nina's picture. He hugged Sharon tightly.

Hugh bent over Lally. "This one's gone."

The large hand of the clock was moving to six.

"Get out of here!" Hugh shouted.

They tumbled down[26] the stairs.

"The tunnel. Head for the[27] tunnel!"

1. les monta quatre à quatre
2. entra brusquement dans une pièce
3. enregistra
4. se dégager de l'emprise de la forme penchée sur elle
5. se jeta
6. donna un coup de tête
7. courbé
8. s'affala
9. poids
10. lâchèrent prise
11. se releva en titubant
12. s'accroupit
13. se lever d'un bond
14. trébucha sur
15. halètement rauque et désespéré
16. Acculé
17. recula vers le fond de la pièce
18. la referma violemment
19. espèce de cinglé
20. enveloppèrent
21. tendit la main vers
22. partit en arrière
23. marques
24. apparaissaient
25. La serrant contre lui
26. dévalèrent
27. Allez au

They raced past the generator, past the vents, onto the tracks, through the darkness …

Foxy heard the retreating steps[1]. They were gone. They were gone. He slid the bolt[2] and opened the door. Seeing the metal blanket over the suitcase, he began to laugh, a deep, rumbling, staccato sound[3].

It was too late for him. But it was too late for them too. In the end the Fox always won.

He reached his hand to the metal blanket, tried to tug it off the suitcase[4].

A blinding flash[5], a roar[6] that shattered his eardrums[7] hurtled him into eternity[8].

11:42 A.M.

Bob Kurner burst into[9] St. Bernard's Church, raced up the aisle[10] and threw his arms around[11] the kneeling figure.

"Is it over?" Her eyes were tearless.

"*Is it over!* Mamma, come on and take your kid home. They've got absolute proof that another guy committed the murder; they've got a tape[12] of him doing it. The Governor said to get Ron out of that prison *now.* "

Kate Thompson, mother of Ronald Thompson, staunch believer[13] in the goodness and mercy of her God, fainted[14].

Roger Perry hung up the phone, turned to Glenda. "They were on time," he said.

"Sharon, Neil, both safe?" Glenda whispered.

"Yes, and the Thompson boy is going home."

Glenda raised her hand to her throat[15]. "Thank God." She saw his expression. "Roger, I'm fine. Put away those damn pills and make me a good stiff[16] old-fashioned[17]!"

Hugh had his arm around a softly weeping Rosie[18]. "Lally saved her station," he said. "And we're going

1. les pas s'éloigner
2. déverrouilla
3. un grondement sourd et saccadé
4. découvrir la valise
5. Un éclair aveuglant
6. vacarme assourdissant
7. lui creva les tympans
8. le projeta dans l'éternité
9. entra en trombe dans
10. remonta l'allée centrale en courant
11. pris dans ses bras
12. cassette
13. fervente croyante
14. s'évanouit
15. porta la main à sa gorge
16. bien tassé
17. [cocktail à base de whisky]
18. avait passé son bras autour de Rosie qui pleurait doucement

to start a petition[1] to put up a plaque for her[2]. I'll bet[3] Governor Carey himself will unveil it[4]. He's a nice guy."

"A plaque for Lally," Rosie whispered. "Oh, she'd love that!"

A face was floating[5] somewhere above her. She was going to die and never see Steve again. "No ... no ..."

"It's all right, darling. It's all right."

Steve's voice. It was Steve's face she was seeing.

"It's all over. We're on the way to the hospital. They'll fix up[6] that leg."

"Neil ..."

"I'm here, Sharon." A hand butterfly soft[7] in hers.

Steve's lips on her cheeks, her forehead, her lips.

Neil's voice in her ear. "Sharon, just like you told me, I kept thinking the whole time about the present[8] you promised me. Sharon, exactly how many Lionel trains have you got for me?"

1. lancer une pétition
2. pour faire apposer une plaque commémorative en son honneur
3. Je parie que
4. la dévoilera
5. flottait
6. soigneront
7. toute douce
8. cadeau

Imprimé en Italie par La Tipografica Varese S.p.a
Dépôt légal : mai 2014
314156-01/11026501-mai 2014